60 SECONDS OF LIGHT

ISBN 9798623913821

This book is dedicated to
Munga and George
Grandma and Grandpa

The day is long, it may never end,
Get up even when beat - don't let the rhythm bring you down,
The door is open, it may soon close,
Keep moving towards your goal - don't let the forces stop your motion,
The dawn is coming, it may wake you,
Run with joy in your heart, hope in your soul and belief in yourself.

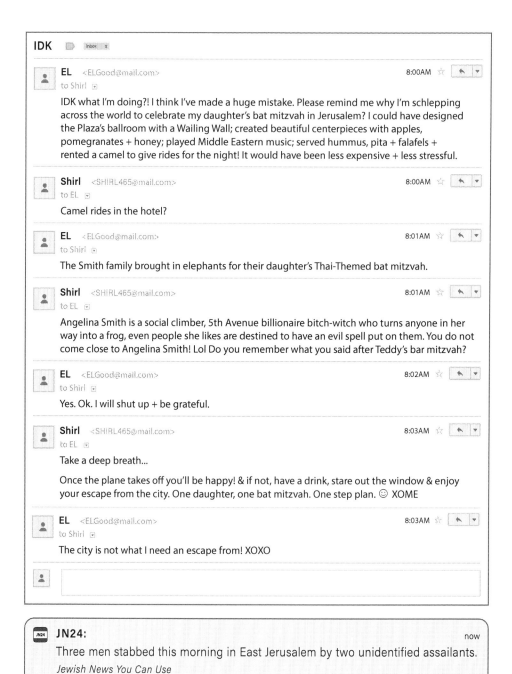

IDK Inbox x

EL <ELGood@mail.com>   8:00AM
to Shirl

IDK what I'm doing?! I think I've made a huge mistake. Please remind me why I'm schlepping across the world to celebrate my daughter's bat mitzvah in Jerusalem? I could have designed the Plaza's ballroom with a Wailing Wall; created beautiful centerpieces with apples, pomegranates + honey; played Middle Eastern music; served hummus, pita + falafels + rented a camel to give rides for the night! It would have been less expensive + less stressful.

Shirl <SHIRL465@mail.com>   8:00AM
to EL

Camel rides in the hotel?

EL <ELGood@mail.com>   8:01AM
to Shirl

The Smith family brought in elephants for their daughter's Thai-Themed bat mitzvah.

Shirl <SHIRL465@mail.com>   8:01AM
to EL

Angelina Smith is a social climber, 5th Avenue billionaire bitch-witch who turns anyone in her way into a frog, even people she likes are destined to have an evil spell put on them. You do not come close to Angelina Smith! Lol Do you remember what you said after Teddy's bar mitzvah?

EL <ELGood@mail.com>   8:02AM
to Shirl

Yes. Ok. I will shut up + be grateful.

Shirl <SHIRL465@mail.com>   8:03AM
to EL

Take a deep breath...

Once the plane takes off you'll be happy! & if not, have a drink, stare out the window & enjoy your escape from the city. One daughter, one bat mitzvah. One step plan. ☺ XOME

EL <ELGood@mail.com>   8:03AM
to Shirl

The city is not what I need an escape from! XOXO

JN24:   now

Three men stabbed this morning in East Jerusalem by two unidentified assailants.
Jewish News You Can Use

LUCACLOSELY
@LUCACLOSELY

What is always coming but never arrives?

8:06 AM – June

💬 1 ♡ 2 ↻ 0

LUCACLOSELY @LUCACLOSELY
Replying to @LUCACLOSELY

Tomorrow.

Goodman Trip 📋 inbox x

EL <ELGood@mail.com>   8:07AM ☆ ↩ ▾
to RimonTours ▾

Shalom Moshe, I just read that there was a stabbing in Jerusalem today + there are protests in the streets. Are we going to be okay? I don't want to overreact but my family is questioning our safety. Todah

Aliza Goodman's Daily Motivational Quote #1:   now

"It isn't enough to talk about peace. One must believe in it. And it isn't enough to believe it. One must work at it."
Eleanor Roosevelt

MotiQuote.com

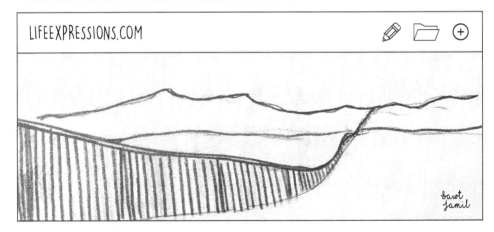

LIFEEXPRESSIONS.COM

EL <ELGood@mail.com>   8:10AM ☆ ↰ ▾

to Dahlia

I received the envelope. Thank you for sending it on time for Aliza's bat mitvah tour in Israel. This is all part of the plan to make mom's dream come true. When I was 13, mom sent me to Israel to spend the summer with my cousins on the kibbutz. That trip is still one of the highlights of my life. I flew all alone on TWA very embarrassed, forced to wear a huge unescorted minor plastic necklace holding my plane ticket. I worried that if I removed this shackle around my neck, the flight attendant would somehow tell mom + dad + they'd make me come back to New York for a hot, sweaty, boring summer. I remember the trip like yesterday: the religious man sitting next to me wore a silver colored kippah + prayed the whole time except for when he went to the back of the plane to smoke. He was fat + smelled terrible of moldy cigarettes. After what felt like forever, we landed in Israel + at the bottom of the stairs, passengers kneeled + started kissing the holy ground. I removed the necklace, shoved it in my bag + kissed the warm tarmac tasting the welcoming flavor of my new found independence.

Auntie Marcel + Uncle Doron adopted me that summer + treated me just like one of their own. Living on the kibbutz was incredible. I hung out at the pool, went to the beach + took bus tours with the other kibbutz kids around the country. I was free! Israeli adults never worried about their children's safety, the exact opposite of my immigrant parents who worried about everything I did + everywhere I went in New York City.

That summer I spoke to my mother two times. Phone calls were incredibly expensive + there was no internet or no texting. I didn't miss anything back home. I joined a pack of kibbutz teenagers + was immediately enamored by one of the group leaders, a quiet, good-looking boy with a beautiful smile. Hezzi was a year older than me, but I was a little taller than him. He spoke some English, which helped me until the middle of the summer when I could finally speak with the other kids in Hebrew. At the beginning of August, we went to camp out at the beach for a whole week with two eighteen-year-old counselors who were about to join the army; they spent the entire week smoking a hookah + drinking bottles of scotch. We built stunning bonfires on the beautiful soft sandy beach, ate fresh pita + hummus + sang a combination of Israeli + Beatle's songs.

One night Hezzi was sitting next to me as we were singing Let It Be + we started kissing under the star filled sky. I was in heaven.

The most wonderful summer of my life ended way too quickly + I was back in my parents' strict home full of rules + very little freedom. I felt like a caged animal. I lived in fear that if I complained, I wouldn't be allowed to go back to Israel the next summer so I kept my mouth shut, got good grades, practiced the piano + sang in the school choir. My immigrant parents were thrilled to have what appeared to be a successful American teenager.

JN24:   now

Israel approves millions for settlements after rabbis voice their support for funding. Tens of thousands protest in cities across the country.

Jewish News You Can Use

Family Group

EL, Teddy, Aliza, Lucas, Benj

EL
Last call for laundry.
If you have any clothes that need to be washed for our trip, please have them in the laundry room in one hour. I am writing as to avoid any confusion on this matter + last minute travel clean wardrobe complaints my dear children. Of course, you are more than welcome to wash your own clothing in the hotel sink, but I will be on strike in Israel. I won't be washing clothes.

Teddy
I thought we were staying at a hotel with laundry service?

EL
Yes, but 'We' are not paying $10 to wash a pair of underwear.

Aliza
Im already packed all good

Lucas
I need a bathing suit my old one is too small

EL
Teddy, see if you have a bathing suit for Lucas.

Teddy
I'm 17

EL
An old one.

Lucas
I don't want a hand me down I want a new bathing suit

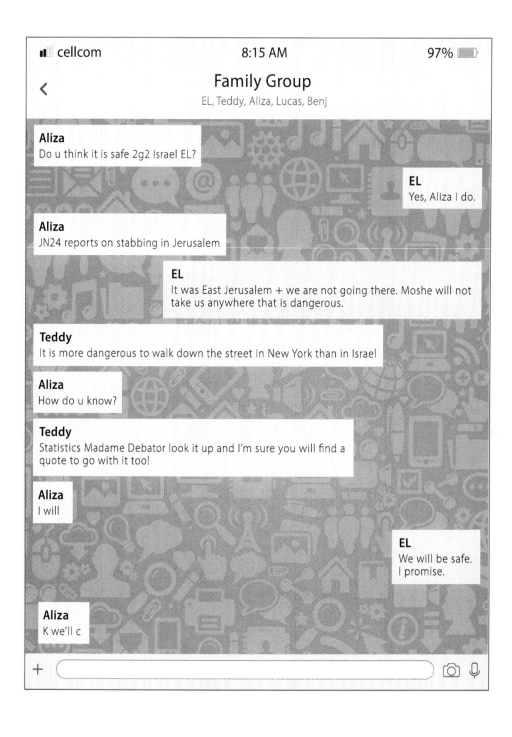

il cellcom   8:15 AM   97% ▐▊▊▊

< Family Group
EL, Teddy, Aliza, Lucas, Benj

Aliza
Do u think it is safe 2g2 Israel EL?

> **EL**
> Yes, Aliza I do.

Aliza
JN24 reports on stabbing in Jerusalem

> **EL**
> It was East Jerusalem + we are not going there. Moshe will not take us anywhere that is dangerous.

Teddy
It is more dangerous to walk down the street in New York than in Israel

Aliza
How do u know?

Teddy
Statistics Madame Debator look it up and I'm sure you will find a quote to go with it too!

Aliza
I will

> **EL**
> We will be safe.
> I promise.

Aliza
K we'll c

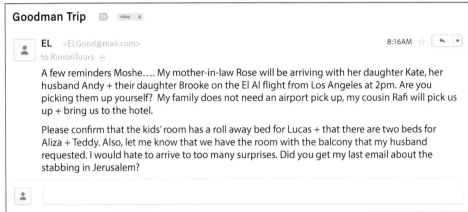

Goodman Trip 📩 inbox x

EL <ELGood@mail.com> 8:16AM
to RimonTours

A few reminders Moshe…. My mother-in-law Rose will be arriving with her daughter Kate, her husband Andy + their daughter Brooke on the El Al flight from Los Angeles at 2pm. Are you picking them up yourself? My family does not need an airport pick up, my cousin Rafi will pick us up + bring us to the hotel.

Please confirm that the kids' room has a roll away bed for Lucas + that there are two beds for Aliza + Teddy. Also, let me know that we have the room with the balcony that my husband requested. I would hate to arrive to too many surprises. Did you get my last email about the stabbing in Jerusalem?

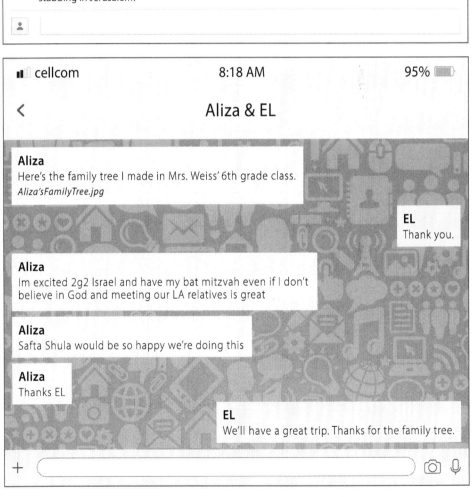

📶 cellcom 8:18 AM 95% 🔋

‹ **Aliza & EL**

Aliza
Here's the family tree I made in Mrs. Weiss' 6th grade class.
Aliza'sFamilyTree.jpg

EL
Thank you.

Aliza
Im excited 2g2 Israel and have my bat mitzvah even if I don't believe in God and meeting our LA relatives is great

Aliza
Safta Shula would be so happy we're doing this

Aliza
Thanks EL

EL
We'll have a great trip. Thanks for the family tree.

➕

Aliza's Family Tree

Mrs. Weiss' 6th Grade

Shula ⓜ Yacov		Rose ⓜ Wayne	
	(Deceased)		(Deceased)
Iraq	Poland	St. Louis	New York
Israel	Israel	Los Angeles	Los Angeles
New York	New York	Santa Barbara	

Ethan	EL ⓜ Benj		Kate ⓜ Andy
New York	New York	Los Angeles	Los Angeles	Los Angeles
?		New York	

Teddy	Aliza	Lucas	Brooke
New York	New York	New York	Los Angeles

EL <ELGood@mail.com>   8:30AM
to Dahlia

Ok. I'm back....

I went back to Israel every summer until I graduated high school. Hezzi + I always picked up where we left off the summer before + we never grew tired or bored of our time together. We knew it was so limited + we had to make the most of it. We wrote letters but they took weeks to get from NY to Israel. Hezzi came to visit me in college a couple of times, but I never told my parents. They knew I had a boyfriend in Israel but back then mom was very strict + did whatever dad wanted.

After I graduated college, I was completely lost. I worked all summer, saved my money + bought a one way ticket to Israel. I arrived at my tiny kibbutz room with a small bag + big dreams. I worked six days a week in the kibbutz' sandal factory. Hezzi was in the army in a secret location, so I settled in + patiently waited for his return.

After two months, Hezzi returned in khaki uniform with an uzzi over his shoulder. I was so excited to see him but by then, we were worlds apart. He was fixed in his covert army career + I was pathetically searching for myself + way too needy. We argued for two weeks straight + then Hezzi returned to his secret life. A few weeks later, I received a job offer back in New York, but I still waited for Hezzi on the kibbutz. After a few months when Hezzi was clearly AWOL from my life, I sadly packed up my bag + came back to New York to start a new chapter in my life.

I got a job in the village + one day at lunch, I met Benj at a falafel stand near my office. We both had little money + loved hummus. I was young + thought Benj was my ticket out of my parents' apartment + escape from the only love I had ever known. Please don't get me wrong, I went to grad school, had three kids + we had good times, but I learned early on that Benj had some real anger management issues. I think I already wrote some of this to you?

Now I am about to take this trip for Aliza's bat mitzvah with Benj + I just want everything to go well. I hope Benj will control himself. We are going with his mom + his sister - both of whom he has no relationship with, but I feel that my kids need to know their relatives + they are all we have in America. I wonder if I will see Hezzi? I have told you so much in the last month of emails + welcome any advice you can give me. From what mom told me, you might relate + share your thoughts. I have become quite uncertain of what I am doing deep down, but continue to present a happy + strong front. It is kind of killing me.

Maybe when I am back, we can meet in the city or I will come to you. Mom would like this I am sure.

I miss mom like crazy.

Aliza Goodman's Daily Motivational Quote #2:   now

"If everyone demanded peace instead of another television set, then there'd be peace."
John Lennon

MotiQuote.com

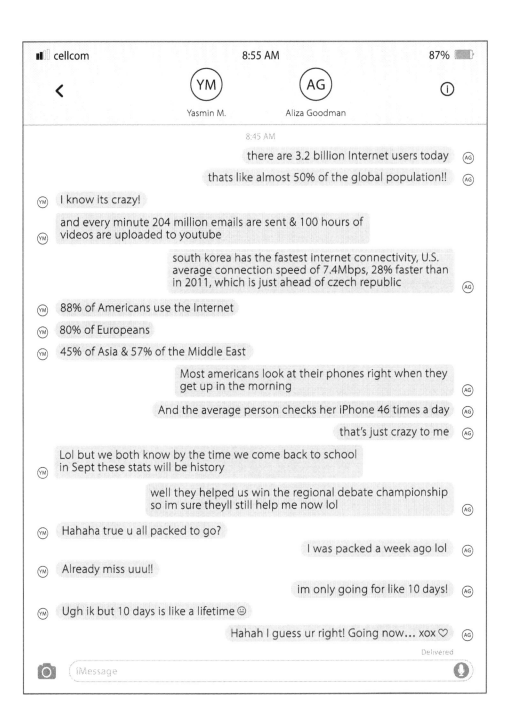

YM Yasmin M.   **AG** Aliza Goodman

8:45 AM

there are 3.2 billion Internet users today (AG)

thats like almost 50% of the global population!! (AG)

(YM) I know its crazy!

(YM) and every minute 204 million emails are sent & 100 hours of videos are uploaded to youtube

south korea has the fastest internet connectivity, U.S. average connection speed of 7.4Mbps, 28% faster than in 2011, which is just ahead of czech republic (AG)

(YM) 88% of Americans use the Internet

(YM) 80% of Europeans

(YM) 45% of Asia & 57% of the Middle East

Most americans look at their phones right when they get up in the morning (AG)

And the average person checks her iPhone 46 times a day (AG)

that's just crazy to me (AG)

(YM) Lol but we both know by the time we come back to school in Sept these stats will be history

well they helped us win the regional debate championship so im sure theyll still help me now lol (AG)

(YM) Hahaha true u all packed to go?

I was packed a week ago lol (AG)

(YM) Already miss uuu!!

im only going for like 10 days! (AG)

(YM) Ugh ik but 10 days is like a lifetime ☺

Hahah I guess ur right! Going now… xox ♡ (AG)

Delivered

iMessage

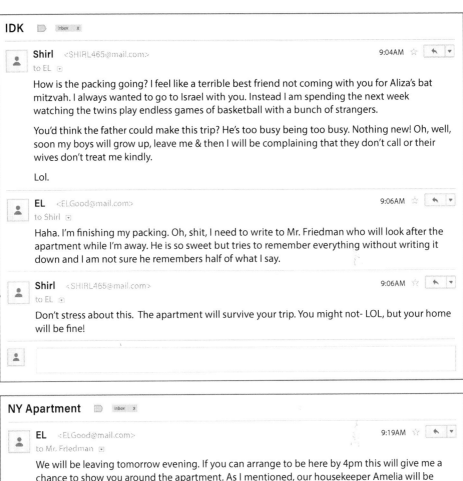

IDK Inbox x

Shirl <SHIRL465@mail.com>   9:04AM
to EL

How is the packing going? I feel like a terrible best friend not coming with you for Aliza's bat mitzvah. I always wanted to go to Israel with you. Instead I am spending the next week watching the twins play endless games of basketball with a bunch of strangers.

You'd think the father could make this trip? He's too busy being too busy. Nothing new! Oh, well, soon my boys will grow up, leave me & then I will be complaining that they don't call or their wives don't treat me kindly.

Lol.

EL <ELGood@mail.com>   9:06AM
to Shirl

Haha. I'm finishing my packing. Oh, shit, I need to write to Mr. Friedman who will look after the apartment while I'm away. He is so sweet but tries to remember everything without writing it down and I am not sure he remembers half of what I say.

Shirl <SHIRL465@mail.com>   9:06AM
to EL

Don't stress about this. The apartment will survive your trip. You might not- LOL, but your home will be fine!

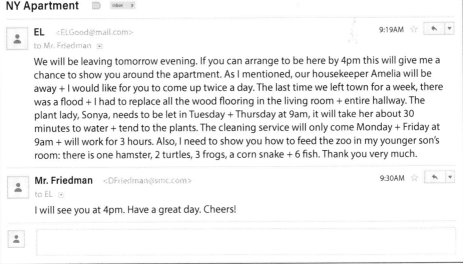

NY Apartment Inbox x

EL <ELGood@mail.com>   9:19AM
to Mr. Friedman

We will be leaving tomorrow evening. If you can arrange to be here by 4pm this will give me a chance to show you around the apartment. As I mentioned, our housekeeper Amelia will be away + I would like for you to come up twice a day. The last time we left town for a week, there was a flood + I had to replace all the wood flooring in the living room + entire hallway. The plant lady, Sonya, needs to be let in Tuesday + Thursday at 9am, it will take her about 30 minutes to water + tend to the plants. The cleaning service will only come Monday + Friday at 9am + will work for 3 hours. Also, I need to show you how to feed the zoo in my younger son's room: there is one hamster, 2 turtles, 3 frogs, a corn snake + 6 fish. Thank you very much.

Mr. Friedman <DFriedman@smc.com>   9:30AM
to EL

I will see you at 4pm. Have a great day. Cheers!

My Life 📁 Inbox ✕

👤 **Aliza** <AlizaGood@mail.com>   9:45AM ☆ ↩ ▾
   to RoamingRoman ▾

It's crazy how little I know about u & how little u know about me. I've been warned by my mother & my teachers not to talk to strangers on the Internet, so it's a little creepy that U are asking me to share my story w u in an email. But here I go -

Yesterday, I finished 8th grade & I can proudly say that I survived middle school. I survived the Plastics w sour faces; I survived pot-smoking cool boys w attitudes; I survived teachers who knew my name, but not me; I survived endless hours of homework, but I'm not sure what I really learned; & I survived gossip, Facebook & Instagram 'Liking' & 'Unliking'. In many ways, Im a typical teenage girl: I love Beyonce, I love hip-hop & my parents buy me lots of iEverything. Unlike many teenagers, I don't have FOMO (Fear of Missing Out) because I'd rather do my own thing & don't really care about what the rest of my peers are doing.

While I'm predictable, I do have an adventurous YOLO (You Only Live Once) side of my personality where I do crazy, irrational things when I'm inspired. I love to write & use quotes & metaphors even to the point of driving my teachers crazy. I have no idea what I want to do exactly when I grow up, but I have a burning desire to bring amazing changes to the world. My favorite foods are sushi, pizza, chocolate chip cookies & if I could have lunch w anyone famous in the world, I would pick either Beyonce or Hillary Clinton.

When I was a little girl, my grandmother read me a story about a family of bears who set very high goals to bring change to what was wrong w their home forest. All the other animals laughed at them, but this didn't deter the bear family. They kept doing what they believed was morally correct & by the end of the book, they had achieved their goals & the other animals thanked them for making their animal world a better place to live. I know it's simple & cliché, but this story stuck w me & I think it's a metaphor for how I see myself. I guess I'm like these bears in the world I live in!

👤

Goodman Trip 📁 Inbox ✕

👤 **Moshe** <Moshe@RimonTours.com>   10:10AM ☆ ↩ ▾
   to EL ▾

All room requests have been confirmed. I will pick up your famly at 2pm. Don't worry about Jerusalem. We will stay in safe areas. Everything will be fine. Shalom

👤

📱 **JN24:**   now
Ten Palestinians and five Israeli policemen wounded in West Bank clashes.
Jewish News You Can Use

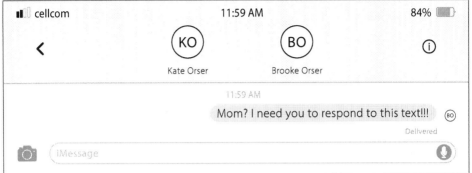

11:59 AM

Mom? I need you to respond to this text!!!   (BO)

Delivered

iMessage

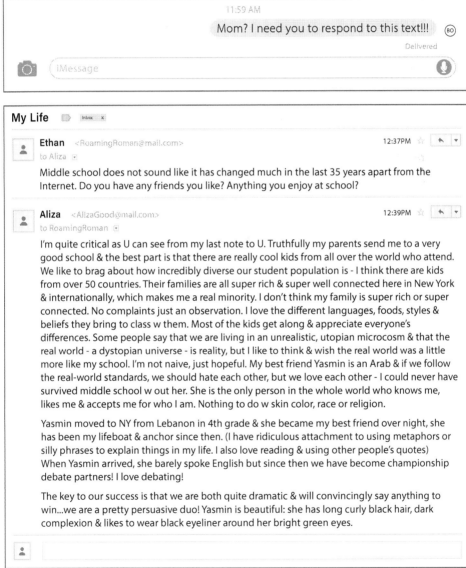

My Life   Inbox x

Ethan <RoamingRoman@mail.com>   12:37PM
to Aliza ⊡

Middle school does not sound like it has changed much in the last 35 years apart from the Internet. Do you have any friends you like? Anything you enjoy at school?

Aliza <AlizaGood@mail.com>   12:39PM
to RoamingRoman ⊡

I'm quite critical as U can see from my last note to U. Truthfully my parents send me to a very good school & the best part is that there are really cool kids from all over the world who attend. We like to brag about how incredibly diverse our student population is - I think there are kids from over 50 countries. Their families are all super rich & super well connected here in New York & internationally, which makes me a real minority. I don't think my family is super rich or super connected. No complaints just an observation. I love the different languages, foods, styles & beliefs they bring to class w them. Most of the kids get along & appreciate everyone's differences. Some people say that we are living in an unrealistic, utopian microcosm & that the real world - a dystopian universe - is reality, but I like to think & wish the real world was a little more like my school. I'm not naive, just hopeful. My best friend Yasmin is an Arab & if we follow the real-world standards, we should hate each other, but we love each other - I could never have survived middle school w out her. She is the only person in the whole world who knows me, likes me & accepts me for who I am. Nothing to do w skin color, race or religion.

Yasmin moved to NY from Lebanon in 4th grade & she became my best friend over night, she has been my lifeboat & anchor since then. (I have ridiculous attachment to using metaphors or silly phrases to explain things in my life. I also love reading & using other people's quotes) When Yasmin arrived, she barely spoke English but since then we have become championship debate partners! I love debating!

The key to our success is that we are both quite dramatic & will convincingly say anything to win...we are a pretty persuasive duo! Yasmin is beautiful: she has long curly black hair, dark complexion & likes to wear black eyeliner around her bright green eyes.

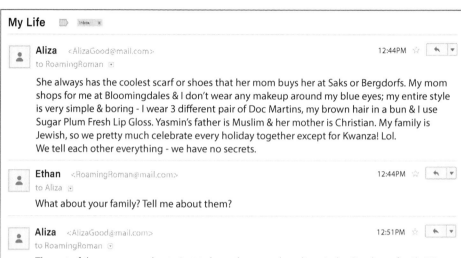

Aliza <AlizaGood@mail.com>
to RoamingRoman

12:44PM

She always has the coolest scarf or shoes that her mom buys her at Saks or Bergdorfs. My mom shops for me at Bloomingdales & I don't wear any makeup around my blue eyes; my entire style is very simple & boring - I wear 3 different pair of Doc Martins, my brown hair in a bun & I use Sugar Plum Fresh Lip Gloss. Yasmin's father is Muslim & her mother is Christian. My family is Jewish, so we pretty much celebrate every holiday together except for Kwanza! Lol.
We tell each other everything - we have no secrets.

Ethan <RoamingRoman@mail.com>
to Aliza

12:44PM

What about your family? Tell me about them?

Aliza <AlizaGood@mail.com>
to RoamingRoman

12:51PM

The rest of the crew on my boat - just to keep the metaphor alive - is the Goodman family. We are a perfectly dysfunctional 21st Century collection of individuals cohabiting: we eat dinner together every night like clockwork, because my mother, the captain, read that families who eat together have less drug & alcohol problems. So far it's working - no one has fallen overboard! (Can't help myself!) Half the time my father Benj doesn't make it home for dinner & when he does, his mind is usually on his latest business transaction. He used to bring his Blackberry to the dinner table but after one very important email too many, EL threw his Blackberry in the garbage disposal & flipped the switch. Both the Blackberry & the garbage disposal were destroyed. This resulted in a massive cold war that lasted about a week in our house. I like my mom most of the time; she can get a little crazy, but I know she means well. She doesn't have it that easy w Dad or Teddy.

Teddy is like a 17-year-old cave-boy who other than for school comes out of his man-cave for his dutiful 15 minutes each night to indulge us w his presence at dinner; usually he grunts a few answers & just stares at his plate while he devours a lot of food; & then returns to his man-cave.

Lucas, my 10-year-old brother, is an intense little character: whatever his passion of the month is, he is fully obsessed.

He currently tweets weird things & makes short funny videos w his iPhone. U need to be careful cuz he will take videos of our most embarrassing moments: these days the focus of his videos is Amelia, our housekeeper. He posts them on Vine - Amelia has become quite a local celebrity. Lucas is also obsessessed with astronomy. He is a member of a young astronauts group – they get dressed in space suits + sleep out on hills eating astronaut food from small packages + staring into the sky. Mostly Lucas brings humor to our family & he is undoubtedly the star of our family (Can't help myself!) & I being the middle child, play my role as the contradictory & dramatic teenage girl. It all kind of works & even though we push the limits of what I believe to be normal in so many ways, we have not capsized.

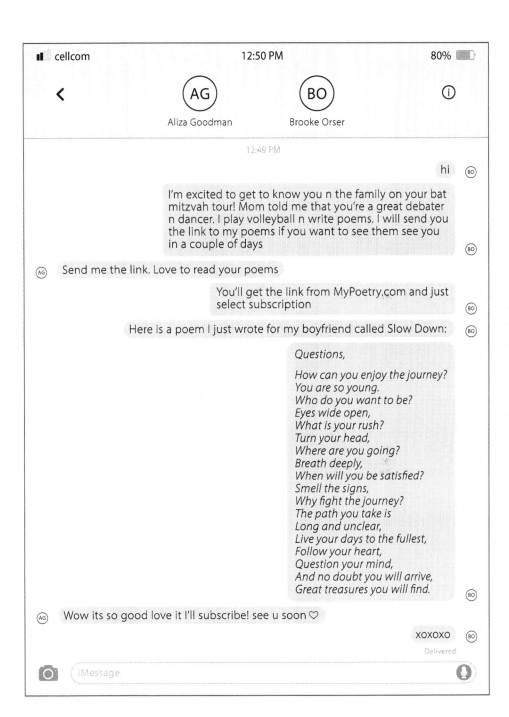

12:49 PM

hi

I'm excited to get to know you n the family on your bat mitzvah tour! Mom told me that you're a great debater n dancer. I play volleyball n write poems. I will send you the link to my poems if you want to see them see you in a couple of days

Send me the link. Love to read your poems

You'll get the link from MyPoetry.com and just select subscription

Here is a poem I just wrote for my boyfriend called Slow Down:

Questions,

How can you enjoy the journey?
You are so young.
Who do you want to be?
Eyes wide open,
What is your rush?
Turn your head,
Where are you going?
Breath deeply,
When will you be satisfied?
Smell the signs,
Why fight the journey?
The path you take is
Long and unclear,
Live your days to the fullest,
Follow your heart,
Question your mind,
And no doubt you will arrive,
Great treasures you will find.

Wow its so good love it I'll subscribe! see u soon ♡

XOXOXO

Delivered

iMessage

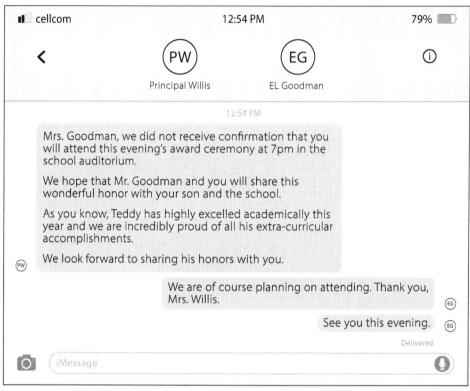

cellcom   12:54 PM   79%

<   (PW)   (EG)   ⓘ

Principal Willis   EL Goodman

12:54 PM

Mrs. Goodman, we did not receive confirmation that you will attend this evening's award ceremony at 7pm in the school auditorium.

We hope that Mr. Goodman and you will share this wonderful honor with your son and the school.

As you know, Teddy has highly excelled academically this year and we are incredibly proud of all his extra-curricular accomplishments.

We look forward to sharing his honors with you.

We are of course planning on attending. Thank you, Mrs. Willis.

See you this evening.

Delivered

iMessage

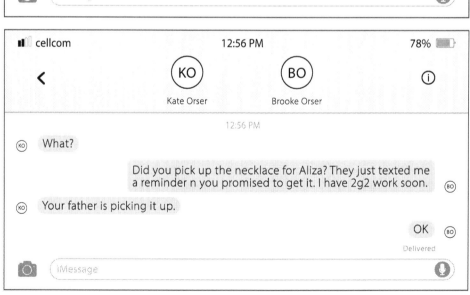

cellcom   12:56 PM   78%

<   (KO)   (BO)   ⓘ

Kate Orser   Brooke Orser

12:56 PM

What?

Did you pick up the necklace for Aliza? They just texted me a reminder n you promised to get it. I have 2g2 work soon.

Your father is picking it up.

OK

Delivered

iMessage

AO
Andy Orser

BO
Brooke Orser

12:59 PM

Dad did you pick up the necklace for Aliza?

No, was I supposed to?

Mom said she asked you to get it.

Ugh!

I have 2g2 work can you please go to Anne's n pick it up?

Its engraved n ready

Yes.

Don't worry.

If I didn't worry we would arrive in Israel w out the gift

Good point.

Now stop worrying.

Love YOU!

Love you toooo

Delivered

iMessage

JN24:   now

Police Report: No imminent threat of Tel Aviv terror attack.

Jewish News You Can Use

Aliza Goodman's Daily Motivational Quote #3:   now

"For every minute you remain angry, you give up sixty seconds of peace of mind."
Ralph Waldo Emerson

MotiQuote.com

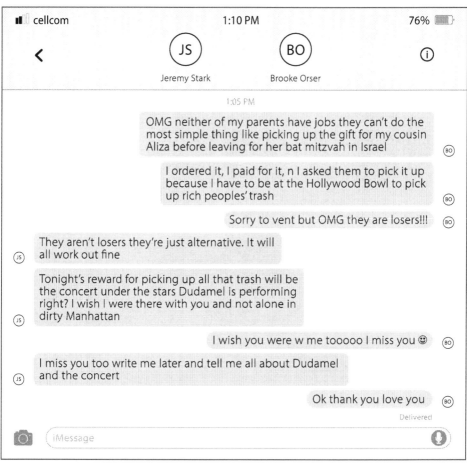

JS
Jeremy Stark

BO
Brooke Orser

1:05 PM

OMG neither of my parents have jobs they can't do the most simple thing like picking up the gift for my cousin Aliza before leaving for her bat mitzvah in Israel (BO)

I ordered it, I paid for it, n I asked them to pick it up because I have to be at the Hollywood Bowl to pick up rich peoples' trash (BO)

Sorry to vent but OMG they are losers!!! (BO)

They aren't losers they're just alternative. It will all work out fine (JS)

Tonight's reward for picking up all that trash will be the concert under the stars Dudamel is performing right? I wish I were there with you and not alone in dirty Manhattan (JS)

I wish you were w me tooooo I miss you ☺ (BO)

I miss you too write me later and tell me all about Dudamel and the concert (JS)

Ok thank you love you (BO)

Delivered

iMessage

Happy?   Inbox x

Ethan   <RoamingRoman@mail.com>   1:12PM
to GoodTeddy

What about your mom? What's she like? Is she happy?

Teddy   <GoodTeddy@mail.com>   1:13PM
to RoamingRoman

My mother EL does it all right - being a mom & all - but I cannot tell if she is really 'happy'. You asked me if we were a 'happy' family. I'm not sure what a 'happy' family is? Do they exist?

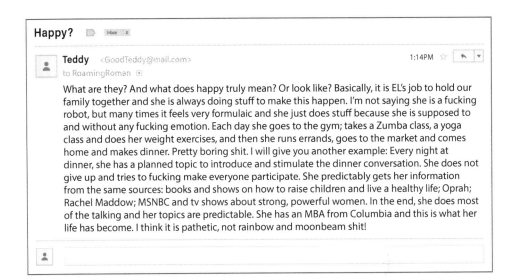

Happy? Inbox x

Teddy <GoodTeddy@mail.com>   1:14PM

to RoamingRoman

What are they? And what does happy truly mean? Or look like? Basically, it is EL's job to hold our family together and she is always doing stuff to make this happen. I'm not saying she is a fucking robot, but many times it feels very formulaic and she just does stuff because she is supposed to and without any fucking emotion. Each day she goes to the gym; takes a Zumba class, a yoga class and does her weight exercises, and then she runs errands, goes to the market and comes home and makes dinner. Pretty boring shit. I will give you another example: Every night at dinner, she has a planned topic to introduce and stimulate the dinner conversation. She does not give up and tries to fucking make everyone participate. She predictably gets her information from the same sources: books and shows on how to raise children and live a healthy life; Oprah; Rachel Maddow; MSNBC and tv shows about strong, powerful women. In the end, she does most of the talking and her topics are predictable. She has an MBA from Columbia and this is what her life has become. I think it is pathetic, not rainbow and moonbeam shit!

Dear Lucas Goodman, Astronaut in Training –

@JUNIORNASAUSA

| Crew | About | Photos |

TODAY ON THE INTERNATIONAL SPACE STATION:

Looking down on Earth day and night from the International Space Station (@ISS) there is an abundance of spectacular views we enjoy. Tonight, we are passing over the incredible Nile River in Egypt. As we look to the East, the glowing lights of Tel Aviv, Israel and Amman, Jordan illuminate the clear sky. Tonight, we also see clearly the Gulf of Suez and the Gulf of Aqaba as the western and eastern coastlines of the Sinai Peninsula are outlined with lights. Cloudless nights provide incredible photo opportunities of this rich region.

The International Space Station is the largest manmade body in orbit, 357 ft in length and spanning close to the size of an American football field. The International Space Station is a microgravity laboratory where the international space crew lives and works while traveling at a speed of 17,500 mph, 250 miles above the earth circling the globe every 90 minutes. See Posted Photos #NASA @ISS #ISS #spacestation #earth #NileRiver #Egypt #Israel #Jordan #GulfofSuez #GulfofAqaba #space

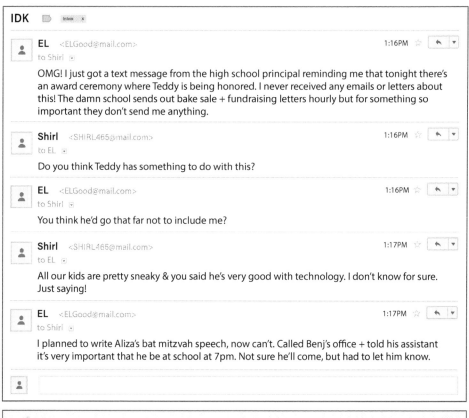

IDK 🏷 Inbox ×

👤 **EL** <ELGood@mail.com> 1:16PM ☆ ↰ ▾
   to Shirl ▾

OMG! I just got a text message from the high school principal reminding me that tonight there's an award ceremony where Teddy is being honored. I never received any emails or letters about this! The damn school sends out bake sale + fundraising letters hourly but for something so important they don't send me anything.

👤 **Shirl** <SHIRL465@mail.com> 1:16PM ☆ ↰ ▾
   to EL ▾

Do you think Teddy has something to do with this?

👤 **EL** <ELGood@mail.com> 1:16PM ☆ ↰ ▾
   to Shirl ▾

You think he'd go that far not to include me?

👤 **Shirl** <SHIRL465@mail.com> 1:17PM ☆ ↰ ▾
   to EL ▾

All our kids are pretty sneaky & you said he's very good with technology. I don't know for sure. Just saying!

👤 **EL** <ELGood@mail.com> 1:17PM ☆ ↰ ▾
   to Shirl ▾

I planned to write Aliza's bat mitzvah speech, now can't. Called Benj's office + told his assistant it's very important that he be at school at 7pm. Not sure he'll come, but had to let him know.

👤

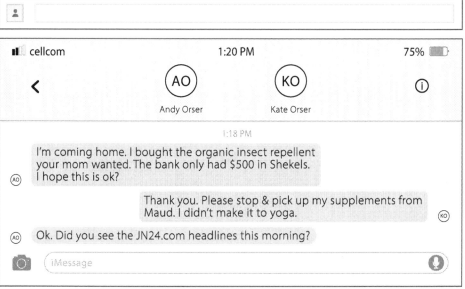

📶 cellcom 1:20 PM 75% 🔋

‹ (AO) Andy Orser (KO) Kate Orser ⓘ

1:18 PM

(AO) I'm coming home. I bought the organic insect repellent your mom wanted. The bank only had $500 in Shekels. I hope this is ok?

Thank you. Please stop & pick up my supplements from Maud. I didn't make it to yoga. (KO)

(AO) Ok. Did you see the JN24.com headlines this morning?

📷 iMessage 🎤

20

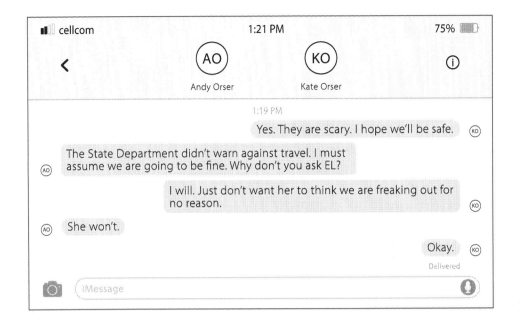

Unknown

Brooke G.O.

I'm young with an old soul
People ask where I am going
It's nobody's business

★ ★ ★

Not a clue from my young lips
Can't trust people's tips
I answer with a blank stare
Already know life's unfair

★ ★ ★

Constantly questioning
Answers keeping score
Learning who I am
At my deepest core

♡ 100   141 ◎

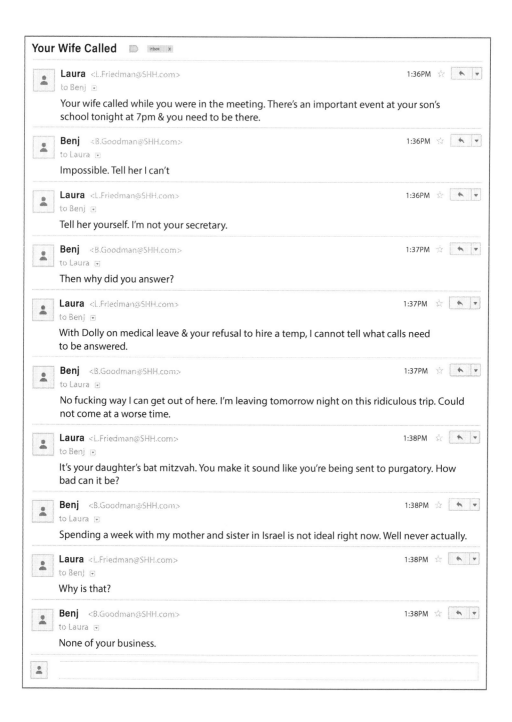

Your Wife Called 📩 inbox x

Laura <L.Friedman@SHH.com> 1:36PM ☆ ← ▼
to Benj ▼

Your wife called while you were in the meeting. There's an important event at your son's school tonight at 7pm & you need to be there.

Benj <B.Goodman@SHH.com> 1:36PM ☆ ← ▼
to Laura ▼

Impossible. Tell her I can't

Laura <L.Friedman@SHH.com> 1:36PM ☆ ← ▼
to Benj ▼

Tell her yourself. I'm not your secretary.

Benj <B.Goodman@SHH.com> 1:37PM ☆ ← ▼
to Laura ▼

Then why did you answer?

Laura <L.Friedman@SHH.com> 1:37PM ☆ ← ▼
to Benj ▼

With Dolly on medical leave & your refusal to hire a temp, I cannot tell what calls need to be answered.

Benj <B.Goodman@SHH.com> 1:37PM ☆ ← ▼
to Laura ▼

No fucking way I can get out of here. I'm leaving tomorrow night on this ridiculous trip. Could not come at a worse time.

Laura <L.Friedman@SHH.com> 1:38PM ☆ ← ▼
to Benj ▼

It's your daughter's bat mitzvah. You make it sound like you're being sent to purgatory. How bad can it be?

Benj <B.Goodman@SHH.com> 1:38PM ☆ ← ▼
to Laura ▼

Spending a week with my mother and sister in Israel is not ideal right now. Well never actually.

Laura <L.Friedman@SHH.com> 1:38PM ☆ ← ▼
to Benj ▼

Why is that?

Benj <B.Goodman@SHH.com> 1:38PM ☆ ← ▼
to Laura ▼

None of your business.

YM
Yasmin M.

AG
Aliza Goodman

1:39 PM

Omg its WW3 over here

EL and Teddy are screaming fuck you & slamming doors and EL is livid

She just found out that tonight Teddy will receive the Leonardo da Vinci Award at his school

Whats it for

Being the most accomplished & well-rounded high school student

Oh thats sick! he never said anything to anyone?

Nope!

ur favorite caveman never mentioned anything to anyone in our house

EL only learned about the award when the principal texted her. I went to the school's site and found out that Teddy spent the year building a working 3D printer in his STEAM class, made lunches for the homeless, took a private online studies program in Hebrew & passed the SAT 2 w a perfect score

his classmates even voted him most likely to succeed! Not sure what he will succeed at tho...he's a real creep lol

I also don't get how EL missed the school's emails

shes normally so on top of these things

Maybe he blocked the emails from getting to her?

Stfu no way he would do that if he did he's really an asshole!!

You said he knows things that he shouldnt... maybe he's monitoring ur server at home

Wtf that's too creepy

Just saying...

iMessage

23

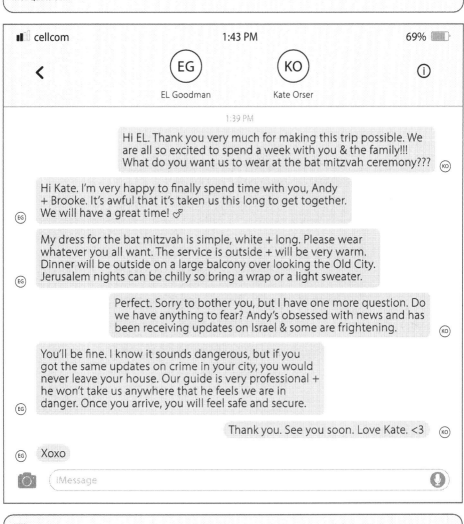

EG   KO

EL Goodman   Kate Orser

1:39 PM

KO: Hi EL. Thank you very much for making this trip possible. We are all so excited to spend a week with you & the family!!! What do you want us to wear at the bat mitzvah ceremony???

EG: Hi Kate. I'm very happy to finally spend time with you, Andy + Brooke. It's awful that it's taken us this long to get together. We will have a great time! ☺

EG: My dress for the bat mitzvah is simple, white + long. Please wear whatever you all want. The service is outside + will be very warm. Dinner will be outside on a large balcony over looking the Old City. Jerusalem nights can be chilly so bring a wrap or a light sweater.

KO: Perfect. Sorry to bother you, but I have one more question. Do we have anything to fear? Andy's obsessed with news and has been receiving updates on Israel & some are frightening.

EG: You'll be fine. I know it sounds dangerous, but if you got the same updates on crime in your city, you would never leave your house. Our guide is very professional + he won't take us anywhere that he feels we are in danger. Once you arrive, you will feel safe and secure.

KO: Thank you. See you soon. Love Kate. <3

EG: Xoxo

iMessage

<   **Kate & Rose**

Kate
Hi mom. EL sounds so nice. I'm not sure how she is married to your son.

Rose
He is also your brother. Be nice. We are going on a peace mission - no further destruction of our little family is necessary.

Kate
I will behave if he does!

Rose
You will behave either way Katlin Violet Goodman.

Rose
You are too old and have come too far to ruin this trip.

Kate
I know Mom! I'm just venting.

Rose
Do you have bug spray and sunscreen for me?

Kate
Yes, the organic ones. See you at the airport. Love You!

Rose
Love you sweetie.

Kate
Say hi to Theo.

Rose
I will. Thank you.

\+ (　　　　　　　　　　　　　) 📷 🎤

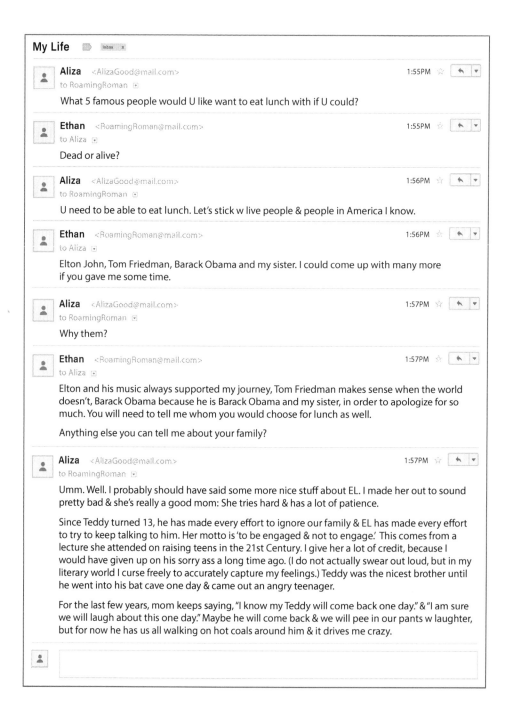

My Life 〉 Inbox x

Aliza ‹AlizaGood@mail.com›   1:55PM
to RoamingRoman

What 5 famous people would U like want to eat lunch with if U could?

Ethan ‹RoamingRoman@mail.com›   1:55PM
to Aliza

Dead or alive?

Aliza ‹AlizaGood@mail.com›   1:56PM
to RoamingRoman

U need to be able to eat lunch. Let's stick w live people & people in America I know.

Ethan ‹RoamingRoman@mail.com›   1:56PM
to Aliza

Elton John, Tom Friedman, Barack Obama and my sister. I could come up with many more if you gave me some time.

Aliza ‹AlizaGood@mail.com›   1:57PM
to RoamingRoman

Why them?

Ethan ‹RoamingRoman@mail.com›   1:57PM
to Aliza

Elton and his music always supported my journey, Tom Friedman makes sense when the world doesn't, Barack Obama because he is Barack Obama and my sister, in order to apologize for so much. You will need to tell me whom you would choose for lunch as well.

Anything else you can tell me about your family?

Aliza ‹AlizaGood@mail.com›   1:57PM
to RoamingRoman

Umm. Well. I probably should have said some more nice stuff about EL. I made her out to sound pretty bad & she's really a good mom: She tries hard & has a lot of patience.

Since Teddy turned 13, he has made every effort to ignore our family & EL has made every effort to try to keep talking to him. Her motto is 'to be engaged & not to engage.' This comes from a lecture she attended on raising teens in the 21st Century. I give her a lot of credit, because I would have given up on his sorry ass a long time ago. (I do not actually swear out loud, but in my literary world I curse freely to accurately capture my feelings.) Teddy was the nicest brother until he went into his bat cave one day & came out an angry teenager.

For the last few years, mom keeps saying, "I know my Teddy will come back one day." & "I am sure we will laugh about this one day." Maybe he will come back & we will pee in our pants w laughter, but for now he has us all walking on hot coals around him & it drives me crazy.

My Conductor

Brooke G.O.

I exist in your essence
Pride in your presence
Notes vibrate from our core
Escape from every pore

★ ★ ★

Frantic curls dance passionate
Magical fingers, a dynamic fit
Potential fills empty lives
Spirit to succeed now drives

★ ★ ★

Crescent moon appears to spy
Stars fill the dark night sky
Alone embraced by you
A love you never knew

♡ 136   235 ◉

∎∎ cellcom   2:01 PM   65% ▭

‹   (YM)   (AG)   ⓘ
              Yasmin M.   Aliza Goodman

1:57 PM

(YM) Just talked w everyone & theyre all ready for uuuu
we'll wait for ur direction. Timing could be an issue

Got it thanks (AG)

(YM) Btw there are almost 7.5 billion people in the world population
350,000 babies born today, this is 2 per second OMG

More than 50% of the world's population is under 30 1.9 billion
kids in the world gtg now I'll text u again before I go (AG)

Delivered

📷 (iMessage   ) 🎤

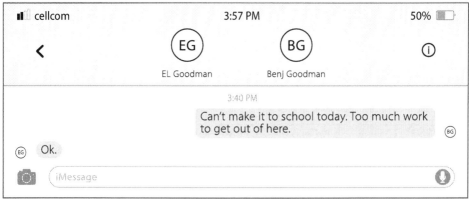

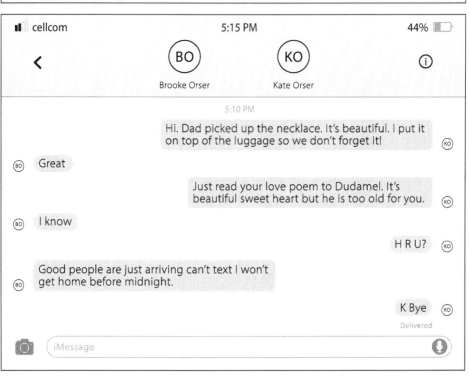

JN24:   now

Rabbi blesses Miami operating room where two-year-old Jewish Siamese twins will undergo a sixteen-hour separation surgery.

Jewish News You Can Use

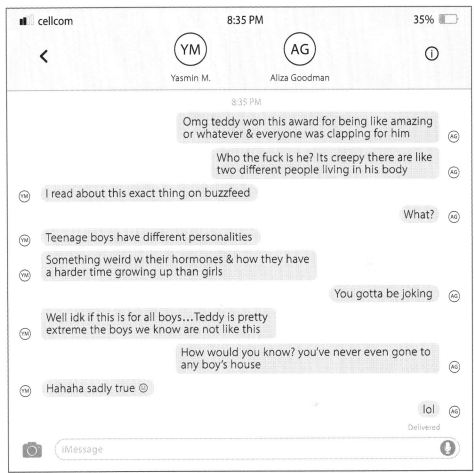

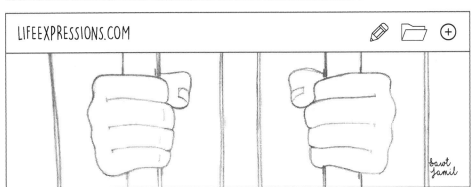

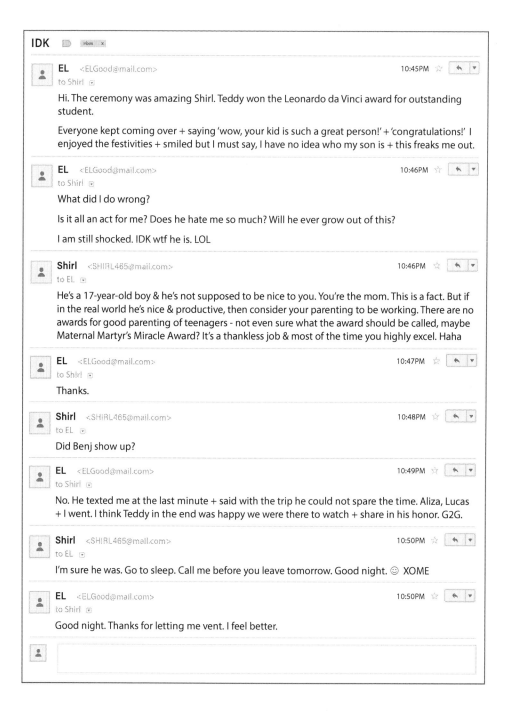

IDK 📨 ~~inbox~~ x

EL <ELGood@mail.com>
to Shirl ▾   10:45PM ☆ ↰ ▾

Hi. The ceremony was amazing Shirl. Teddy won the Leonardo da Vinci award for outstanding student.

Everyone kept coming over + saying 'wow, your kid is such a great person!' + 'congratulations!' I enjoyed the festivities + smiled but I must say, I have no idea who my son is + this freaks me out.

EL <ELGood@mail.com>
to Shirl ▾   10:46PM ☆ ↰ ▾

What did I do wrong?

Is it all an act for me? Does he hate me so much? Will he ever grow out of this?

I am still shocked. IDK wtf he is. LOL

Shirl <SHIRL465@mail.com>
to EL ▾   10:46PM ☆ ↰ ▾

He's a 17-year-old boy & he's not supposed to be nice to you. You're the mom. This is a fact. But if in the real world he's nice & productive, then consider your parenting to be working. There are no awards for good parenting of teenagers - not even sure what the award should be called, maybe Maternal Martyr's Miracle Award? It's a thankless job & most of the time you highly excel. Haha

---

EL <ELGood@mail.com>
to Shirl ▾   10:47PM ☆ ↰ ▾

Thanks.

Shirl <SHIRL465@mail.com>
to EL ▾   10:48PM ☆ ↰ ▾

Did Benj show up?

EL <ELGood@mail.com>
to Shirl ▾   10:49PM ☆ ↰ ▾

No. He texted me at the last minute + said with the trip he could not spare the time. Aliza, Lucas + I went. I think Teddy in the end was happy we were there to watch + share in his honor. G2G.

Shirl <SHIRL465@mail.com>
to EL ▾   10:50PM ☆ ↰ ▾

I'm sure he was. Go to sleep. Call me before you leave tomorrow. Good night. ☺ XOME

EL <ELGood@mail.com>
to Shirl ▾   10:50PM ☆ ↰ ▾

Good night. Thanks for letting me vent. I feel better.

👤

Happy? 📁 Inbox ×

Ethan <RoamingRoman@mail.com>   11:20PM ⭐ ↩ ▾
to GoodTeddy ▾

You haven't mentioned your sister or brother. I will refrain from asking if they are 'happy' but can you tell me interesting things about them?

Teddy <GoodTeddy@mail.com>   11:20PM ⭐ ↩ ▾
to RoamingRoman ▾

Aliza is the type of daughter that parents fucking dream to have. She is quite dramatic, but overall she does what is asked of her without too much complaining and she is a very good student, debater and dancer. We do not spend a lot of time together now, but when we were little we were shipped off to our grandparents' apartment every weekend and on holidays - just the two of us. We had a lot of fun - we were kind of like the dynamic duo. Safta Shula and Saba Jacob took us everywhere in the city: parks, museums, movies, and shows; they let us stay up late watching tv feasting on oreos and milk in their bed: Safta Shula let us take long bubble baths and then scrubbed us clean like we were two filthy beggar children arriving at her castle and she told us stories about her childhood that were magical.

Safta Shula made growing up in fucking Basra, Iraq feel like a real enchanting fairytale. She remembered incredible details about the sounds, scents and sights of her family and her life, the street vendors, the animals, the sea by her house, her school, the food and all the holidays and celebrations. She remembered her uncle's rough fingers squeezing her cheek when he arrived for a visit and her grandmothers' giant smiles when she and her sister sang and danced for them. She had a picture-perfect memory of her life all in her head; no fucking iPhone full of selfies to memorialize any of her youth.

Ethan <RoamingRoman@mail.com>   11:24PM ⭐ ↩ ▾
to GoodTeddy ▾

What about Saba Jacob?

Did he tell you about growing up?

Teddy <GoodTeddy@mail.com>   11:25PM ⭐ ↩ ▾
to RoamingRoman ▾

Not as much as Safta. I know he took care of his brothers, Teodore (who I am named after) and Leo (who Lucas is named after) because his mother was busy with the baby sister Anne who was always sick. He took his brothers to school every day and played with them until dinner. When we were with them, Saba Jacob pretty much fucking did what Safta Shula told him to do; they spoke in Hebrew when they did not want us to understand them and they spoiled us rotten! Going to their apartment was always best part of my week. Saba always talked to me about how important it was to work hard and his favorite expression was, "There's no such thing as a free lunch." He always quoted Thomas Edison, "There is no substitute for hard work." He never talked about the war, I know he survived the concentration camp and all his family was killed. Safta told me about this part of his life but mostly after he died.

👤

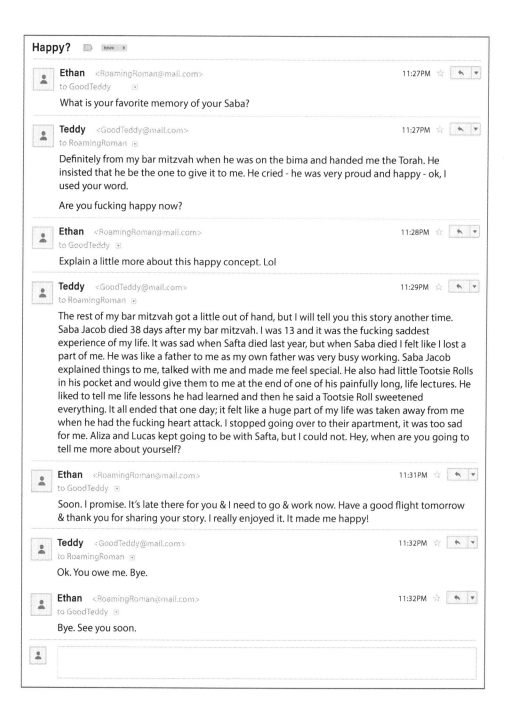

Happy? Inbox

Ethan <RoamingRoman@mail.com>   11:27PM
to GoodTeddy

What is your favorite memory of your Saba?

Teddy <GoodTeddy@mail.com>   11:27PM
to RoamingRoman

Definitely from my bar mitzvah when he was on the bima and handed me the Torah. He insisted that he be the one to give it to me. He cried - he was very proud and happy - ok, I used your word.

Are you fucking happy now?

Ethan <RoamingRoman@mail.com>   11:28PM
to GoodTeddy

Explain a little more about this happy concept. Lol

Teddy <GoodTeddy@mail.com>   11:29PM
to RoamingRoman

The rest of my bar mitzvah got a little out of hand, but I will tell you this story another time. Saba Jacob died 38 days after my bar mitzvah. I was 13 and it was the fucking saddest experience of my life. It was sad when Safta died last year, but when Saba died I felt like I lost a part of me. He was like a father to me as my own father was very busy working. Saba Jacob explained things to me, talked with me and made me feel special. He also had little Tootsie Rolls in his pocket and would give them to me at the end of one of his painfully long, life lectures. He liked to tell me life lessons he had learned and then he said a Tootsie Roll sweetened everything. It all ended that one day; it felt like a huge part of my life was taken away from me when he had the fucking heart attack. I stopped going over to their apartment, it was too sad for me. Aliza and Lucas kept going to be with Safta, but I could not. Hey, when are you going to tell me more about yourself?

Ethan <RoamingRoman@mail.com>   11:31PM
to GoodTeddy

Soon. I promise. It's late there for you & I need to go & work now. Have a good flight tomorrow & thank you for sharing your story. I really enjoyed it. It made me happy!

Teddy <GoodTeddy@mail.com>   11:32PM
to RoamingRoman

Ok. You owe me. Bye.

Ethan <RoamingRoman@mail.com>   11:32PM
to GoodTeddy

Bye. See you soon.

JN24: now

Flotilla headed from Ankara, Turkey to Gaza is blocked and brought to Ashdod port. No violence reported.

Jewish News You Can Use

Aliza Goodman's Daily Motivational Quote #5: now

"Peace is not merely a distant goal that we seek, but a means by which we arrive at that goal."
Martin Luther King, Jr.

MotiQuote.com

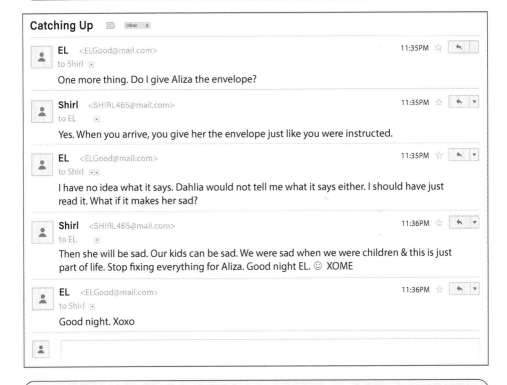

Catching Up inbox x

EL <ELGood@mail.com> to Shirl	11:35PM ☆

One more thing. Do I give Aliza the envelope?

Shirl <SHIRL465@mail.com> to EL	11:35PM ☆

Yes. When you arrive, you give her the envelope just like you were instructed.

EL <ELGood@mail.com> to Shirl	11:35PM ☆

I have no idea what it says. Dahlia would not tell me what it says either. I should have just read it. What if it makes her sad?

Shirl <SHIRL465@mail.com> to EL	11:36PM ☆

Then she will be sad. Our kids can be sad. We were sad when we were children & this is just part of life. Stop fixing everything for Aliza. Good night EL. ☺ XOME

EL <ELGood@mail.com> to Shirl	11:36PM ☆

Good night. Xoxo

 JN24: now

One rocket explodes over Ashkelon, damaging a school; second and third rockets intercepted by Iron Dome.

Jewish News You Can Use

The Fucked-Up Son
Teddy Goodman

My refusal to include my family from my school reality would have been successful if it were not for the stupid award ceremony this evening. The principal managed to reach EL and like clockwork, she was in the audience with my two siblings. I am not sure why I did not want them to attend or be a part of my life, and have diligently attempted to rationalize these feelings with little success. I just know that they continue to bother me. High school is bad enough and to have to deal with parents who are always arguing and siblings who are needy is not fun. EL was furious I had not shared any of my accomplishments with her, but they are mine and not hers.

So why does she give a fuck?

I hate it when parents try and live vicariously through their children like they fucking missed something when they were young and are trying to pathetically relive their lost childhoods through their kids. Maybe this is why I don't tell them things? I know the times I have told her about what I was doing, I felt angry. So, little by little it just felt better to hide and not say much.

Tonight, EL did show up and was proud as hell and was confused by all the attention I received. I was a little surprised too. Our school is known for its egalitarian philosophy and an awards ceremony is a bit off putting, but what the hell, I received the Leonardo Da Vinci Award for overall achievement and everyone saw this except my father Benj who was too busy to attend. This was not surprising just once again highly noticeable, as every other fucking father seemed to be in the audience even for their loser children.

I attend a highly selective school where all the students are raised to think they are the very fucking best and brightest, they know it all and they are the second coming of Christ. I must admit, it felt great to be the best of the best and for two reasons. First, I worked really hard and excelled in areas that I enjoyed. Second, I did these things for me and not for the stupid colleges that encourage students' accomplishments as a prerequisite for attendance.

I am not even sure I want to go to college or what I will do in a year when I graduate?

Dahlia <FreeDahlia@mail.com>   11:45PM ☆ ↰ ▾

to EL ▾

Sweetheart, your mama's dream was to be at Aliza's mitzvah in Israel. Bless her heart, she almost made it. She was very happy y'all planned to carry out her dream. You were a wonderful, lovin' daughter n her spirit will be with y'all. I guarantee it.

Heavens to Betsy your husband sounds like he could start an argument in an empty house. He n my ex are like two peas in a pod. They fly off the handle to their hearts content n we catch all the pieces n put it all back together again. My divorce after 40 years of marriage took place 5 years ago after one too many conniption fits when I went batshit crazy n kicked his sorry ass out of our house.

Tonight, I celebrate back at home with my bottle of red Italian passion, my full bowl of popcorn n the salty seabreeze enterin' my windows as the fresh Atlantic waves crash. I write about what I learned in my journey n took so long to achieve: My Freedom.

I met Rick at a party senior year of college. He was visitin' a friend from California dressed in jeans n a Berkley hoodie while a New Jersey snowstorm swallowed our cozy campus in a sea of white. I looked at this inadequately dressed stranger who appeared clueless to the frozen deluge outside while drinkin' a beer and makin' himself at home with a room full of warm strangers. He thought he was the best thing since sliced bread. Later in the evenin' he tapped me on the shoulder n introduced himself. He had heard that after college I was dreamin' to join the Peace Corp n he was interested in pursuin' a similar path. We spent the rest of the night n well into the early morning entangled in a small cushioned bay window sharin' our passions and dreams to make the world a better place. Good lord, the joys of youth! I was a southern belle in New Jersey & for cryin' out loud had no idea what I was doin'. In retrospect, our beginnin' was naïve n simplistic; we were both youthful dreamers who fueled each other's excitement about the unknown possibilities that lay waitin' for us.

We joined the Peace Corp n went to live in Sierra Leone for two years; I was a schoolteacher for youngins n trained local young women to be teachers as well. Rick helped the local villagers build their infrastructure to make their lives easier. After work each day Rick n I walked through the rice fields n banana plants hand in hand, we sat along the banks of the Scarcies River dreamin', talkin', talkin' n dreamin'. These were two of the most powerful years in my life.

Back in New York n married, I continued teachin' n Rick started workin' for an investment company that supported 3rd world communities. Soon we had little ones n our Peace Corp dreams melted into our dedicated partnership in raisin' a family n growin' a business of our own. I found myself bouncin' a baby, feedin' two toddlers, payin' our bills n reviewin' business contracts at the same time. I was so exhausted each night n usually fainted on the couch while Rick shared his day with me n woke at 2am to get into my real bed. Rick worked around the clock, but left all kid related activities to me. He loved our family but I soon realized, he had no idea what to do with a heard of small children. They didnt want to discuss business or listen to Peace Corp stories n they needed their diapers changed. I, on the other hand, could do all the mommy n housework & still find time n energy to help with buildin' the business. I was not resentful. I didn't know better; I was raised a good Southern Belle thinkin' barefoot n pearls go...

Freedom 📨 Inbox ✕

👤 **Dahlia** <FreeDahlia@mail.com>   11:45PM ☆ ↩ ▾
to EL ▾

...with everythin'. We lived modestly for a long time; our money payin' for food n shelter for a family of 5. Rick traveled for weeks at a time leavin' me with the kids, the house n all the bookkeeping n managerial work. I smiled n thought; I'll put my big girl panties on n deal with it. I have three healthy n happy kids, a devoted husband n a warm n beautiful home. Our children grew up as our business developed.

Years flew by.

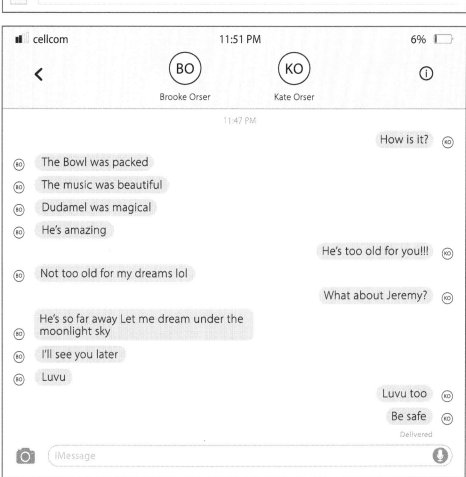

📶 cellcom   11:51 PM   6% 🔋

‹   (BO)   (KO)   ⓘ
         Brooke Orser   Kate Orser

                         11:47 PM

                                              How is it? (KO)

(BO) The Bowl was packed

(BO) The music was beautiful

(BO) Dudamel was magical

(BO) He's amazing

                                     He's too old for you!!! (KO)

(BO) Not too old for my dreams lol

                                     What about Jeremy? (KO)

(BO) He's so far away Let me dream under the
      moonlight sky

(BO) I'll see you later

(BO) Luvu

                                              Luvu too (KO)

                                              Be safe (KO)
                                              Delivered

📷 (iMessage   🎤

Growing Out

Brooke G.O.

I am alone
I seek my bearing

Parent's love
Never a question
Always a challenge
Steeped in history
Engraved for the future
I bask in its warmth

Freedom fleeting
Independence frail
Impulse to escape
Surround and enclose
Grace on the rocks
I dig down deep

I pledge allegiance to myself
And stand strong questioning
the god I am told to believe in
with light in my heart and hope for
the good of all I love

You will find me writing in my dreams
Answers far from my curious fingers
Words racing so fast I can hardly catch
Plans for it all to come together at some juncture

My heart is packed
My soul is ticketed
My thoughts high in the clouds
The journey begins

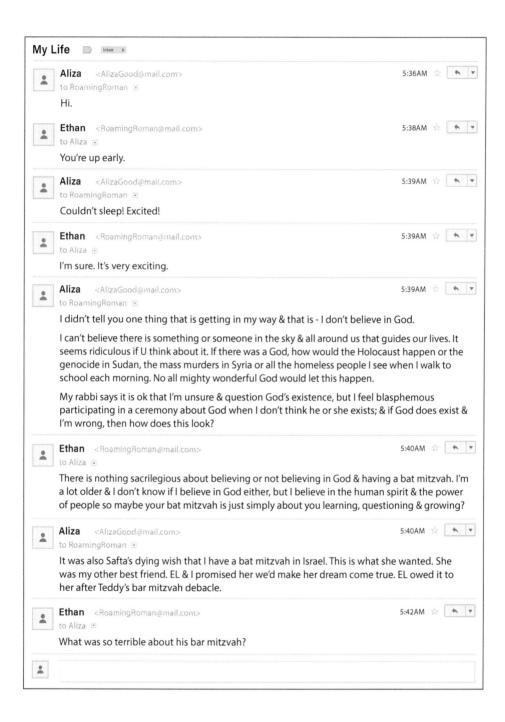

My Life 📥 Inbox ✕

👤 **Aliza** <AlizaGood@mail.com>   5:36AM ☆ ↩ ▾
to RoamingRoman ▾

Hi.

👤 **Ethan** <RoamingRoman@mail.com>   5:38AM ☆ ↩ ▾
to Aliza ▾

You're up early.

👤 **Aliza** <AlizaGood@mail.com>   5:39AM ☆ ↩ ▾
to RoamingRoman ▾

Couldn't sleep! Excited!

👤 **Ethan** <RoamingRoman@mail.com>   5:39AM ☆ ↩ ▾
to Aliza ▾

I'm sure. It's very exciting.

👤 **Aliza** <AlizaGood@mail.com>   5:39AM ☆ ↩ ▾
to RoamingRoman ▾

I didn't tell you one thing that is getting in my way & that is - I don't believe in God.

I can't believe there is something or someone in the sky & all around us that guides our lives. It seems ridiculous if U think about it. If there was a God, how would the Holocaust happen or the genocide in Sudan, the mass murders in Syria or all the homeless people I see when I walk to school each morning. No all mighty wonderful God would let this happen.

My rabbi says it is ok that I'm unsure & question God's existence, but I feel blasphemous participating in a ceremony about God when I don't think he or she exists; & if God does exist & I'm wrong, then how does this look?

👤 **Ethan** <RoamingRoman@mail.com>   5:40AM ☆ ↩ ▾
to Aliza ▾

There is nothing sacrilegious about believing or not believing in God & having a bat mitzvah. I'm a lot older & I don't know if I believe in God either, but I believe in the human spirit & the power of people so maybe your bat mitzvah is just simply about you learning, questioning & growing?

👤 **Aliza** <AlizaGood@mail.com>   5:40AM ☆ ↩ ▾
to RoamingRoman ▾

It was also Safta's dying wish that I have a bat mitzvah in Israel. This is what she wanted. She was my other best friend. EL & I promised her we'd make her dream come true. EL owed it to her after Teddy's bar mitzvah debacle.

👤 **Ethan** <RoamingRoman@mail.com>   5:42AM ☆ ↩ ▾
to Aliza ▾

What was so terrible about his bar mitzvah?

👤

My Life 📥 Inbox ✕

👤 **Aliza** <AlizaGood@mail.com>   5:42AM ☆ ↩ ▾
  to RoamingRoman ▾

After the mega disco 80s themed bar mitzvah party that EL threw for Teddy, Safta was convinced that my bat mitzvah should be just the family in Israel. The party was crazy like when the Titanic crashed into the iceberg: I'm not exaggerating when I say that there were 500 drunk strangers, half naked dancing girls, food flying & wild kids w shiny tattoos & rainbow hats running around the hotel ballroom & lobby. Ironically, most of the partiers were not at the temple that morning, when Teddy chanted & described his Torah portion, which was all about humility & thoughtfulness. Safta was very 'disappointed' by the entire spectacle & vowed not to let it happen again for me. I can still see her shaking her head from side to side & raising her eyebrows.

On Safta's deathbed, she said her only regret was not making good on the promise to take me to the Jewish Homeland for my bat mitzvah. Since Safta died, EL has made it her life's mission to organize my bat mitzvah trip in a manner that would make Safta proud & for the last six months she has dedicated herself to making this trip happen. She also invited Benj's family from Los Angeles to join us. She keeps saying, "There is nothing like family" & Benj keeps rolling his eyes when she says this. EL & Benj rarely agree on anything. Truthfully Benj has no relationship w his sister or his mother & we have barely spent time together. One good thing that has come out of this is that I will finally get to know my only family. BTW - did U have a bar mitzvah?

👤

Aliza Goodman's Daily Motivational Quote #1:   now

"Be kind whenever possible. It is always possible."
Dalai Lama

MotiQuote.com

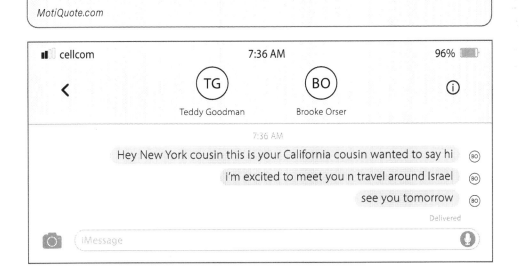

📶 cellcom   7:36 AM   96% 🔋

‹   (TG)   (BO)   ⓘ
    Teddy Goodman   Brooke Orser

                    7:36 AM

Hey New York cousin this is your California cousin wanted to say hi (BO)

i'm excited to meet you n travel around Israel (BO)

see you tomorrow (BO)

                    Delivered

📷 (iMessage   🎤)

My Life 📩 Inbox ×

👤 **Ethan** <RoamingRoman@mail.com> 8:20AM ☆ ↩ ▾
to Aliza ▾

I did. Nothing fancy. We went to temple in the morning & after we went to a Chinese restaurant called The Golden Dragon & we had lunch with Uncle Sam & some family friends. No party or anything fancy, but I remember it was a very good day. We were all happy & my parents were very proud of me. I did feel like a man when I stepped off the bima. Uncle Sam gave me a $50 bill & I thought I was rich. Then my fortune cookie at lunch said, "The world is your oyster & you will travel to meet your riches." I remember swelling with pride & believing I was off to a great start in my manhood. I did travel, but still have not made a fortune - Haha! Listen, I should work now. Have a great trip & please write to me when you get to Israel. I want to know what you think!

👤 **Aliza** <AlizaGood@mail.com> 8:22AM ☆ ↩ ▾
to RoamingRoman ▾

Ok. Bye.

👤

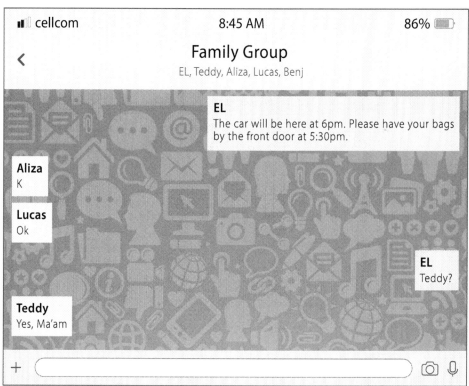

📶 cellcom 8:45 AM 86% 🔋

‹ **Family Group**
EL, Teddy, Aliza, Lucas, Benj

EL
The car will be here at 6pm. Please have your bags by the front door at 5:30pm.

Aliza
K

Lucas
Ok

EL
Teddy?

Teddy
Yes, Ma'am

+ 📷 🎤

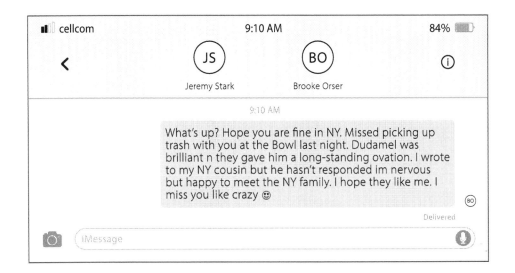

JS

Jeremy Stark

BO

Brooke Orser

9:10 AM

What's up? Hope you are fine in NY. Missed picking up trash with you at the Bowl last night. Dudamel was brilliant n they gave him a long-standing ovation. I wrote to my NY cousin but he hasn't responded im nervous but happy to meet the NY family. I hope they like me. I miss you like crazy 😊

Delivered

iMessage

MYPOETRY.COM

Not Ready

Brooke G.O.

I am alone without you
Please take me back
I am not ready for freedom
So much I still lack

★ ★ ★

I see your face
I hear your voice
I miss your touch
I need your love

♡ 200   315 👁

Aliza Goodman's Daily Motivational Quote #2:   now

"To resolve conflict, excessive ambitions and one's own fears and aspirations must be sacrificed."
Zbigniew Brzezinski

MotiQuote.com

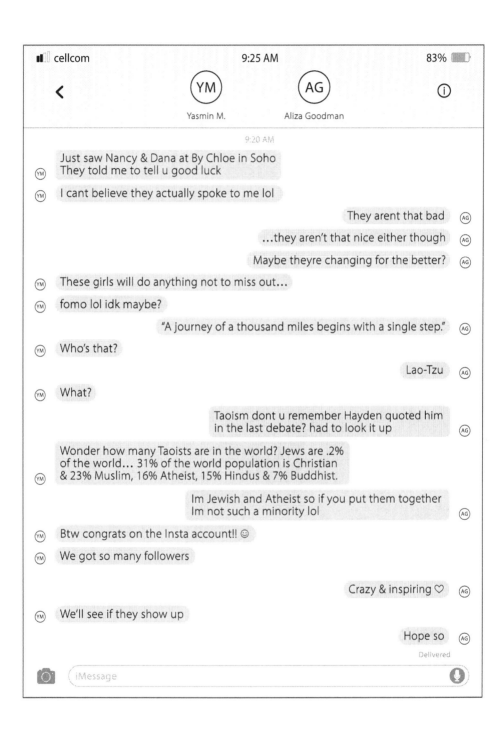

9:20 AM

YM: Just saw Nancy & Dana at By Chloe in Soho
They told me to tell u good luck

YM: I cant believe they actually spoke to me lol

AG: They arent that bad

AG: ...they aren't that nice either though

AG: Maybe theyre changing for the better?

YM: These girls will do anything not to miss out...

YM: fomo lol idk maybe?

AG: "A journey of a thousand miles begins with a single step."

YM: Who's that?

AG: Lao-Tzu

YM: What?

AG: Taoism dont u remember Hayden quoted him in the last debate? had to look it up

YM: Wonder how many Taoists are in the world? Jews are .2% of the world... 31% of the world population is Christian & 23% Muslim, 16% Atheist, 15% Hindus & 7% Buddhist.

AG: Im Jewish and Atheist so if you put them together Im not such a minority lol

YM: Btw congrats on the Insta account!! ☺

YM: We got so many followers

AG: Crazy & inspiring ♡

YM: We'll see if they show up

AG: Hope so

Delivered

iMessage

LUCACLOSELY
@LUCACLOSELY

Who makes it, has no need of it.
Who buys it, has no use for it.
Who uses it can neither see nor feel it,
What is it?

10:41 AM – June

💬 1   ♡ 4   ↻ 0

LUCACLOSELY @LUCACLOSELY
Replying to @LUCACLOSELY

A Coffin

Dear Lucas Goodman, Astronaut in Training –

@JUNIORNASAUSA

| Crew | About | Photos |

TODAY ON THE INTERNATIONAL SPACE STATION:

Looking down on Earth from the International Space Station (@ISS) is incredible. Astronauts complete 15½ orbits each day, which means that we see a sunrise and a sunset every 92 minutes. Today we are passing over the beautiful 6-million-year-old and 277-mile long Grand Canyon in Arizona. On a clear day, no matter how many times we pass, the canyon's jagged paths, distinct ridges and dramatic colors are mesmerizing and the blue Colorado river featured snaking its way between the pink and gray colored canyon surfaces is a highlight. Beyond the canyon, we are also treated to clear views of Lake Meade, the Colorado Plateau and the city of Las Vegas, which at night is the brightest city on Earth, followed by Tokyo. The majority of the light emanating to the universe comes from big cities' street lights.

 JN24:   now

Eitan Dankner of Berlin broke the world record for matza ball eating in one sitting last night. He ate 39 matza balls.

Jewish News You Can Use

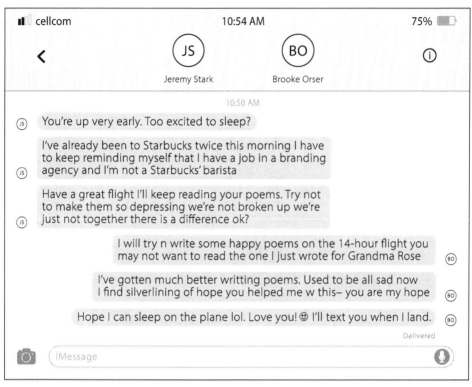

cellcom   10:54 AM   75% ▭

(JS) Jeremy Stark   (BO) Brooke Orser

10:50 AM

You're up very early. Too excited to sleep?

I've already been to Starbucks twice this morning I have to keep reminding myself that I have a job in a branding agency and I'm not a Starbucks' barista

Have a great flight I'll keep reading your poems. Try not to make them so depressing we're not broken up we're just not together there is a difference ok?

I will try n write some happy poems on the 14-hour flight you may not want to read the one I just wrote for Grandma Rose

I've gotten much better writting poems. Used to be all sad now I find silverlining of hope you helped me w this– you are my hope

Hope I can sleep on the plane lol. Love you! ☺ I'll text you when I land.

Delivered

iMessage

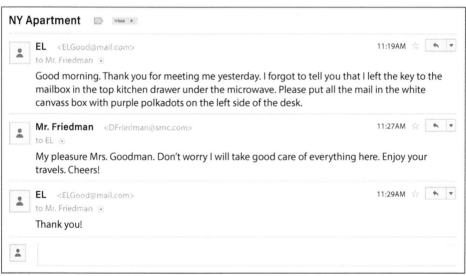

NY Apartment   Inbox ×

EL <ELGood@mail.com>   11:19AM
to Mr. Friedman

Good morning. Thank you for meeting me yesterday. I forgot to tell you that I left the key to the mailbox in the top kitchen drawer under the microwave. Please put all the mail in the white canvass box with purple polkadots on the left side of the desk.

Mr. Friedman <DFriedman@smc.com>   11:27AM
to EL

My pleasure Mrs. Goodman. Don't worry I will take good care of everything here. Enjoy your travels. Cheers!

EL <ELGood@mail.com>   11:29AM
to Mr. Friedman

Thank you!

Googled Relatives
Teddy Goodman

Tomorrow I will arrive in Israel for my younger sister Aliza's marathon bat mitzvah experience. I am excited to go to Israel, I am not excited to spend the week with my family and to make matters worse, I am forced to spend it with estranged relatives. They are referred to as "the California relatives."

Grandma Rose, my father's mother, I have met a few times here in NY, but I don't know her. Benj does not like her or his sister Kate, who is also coming with her husband Andy and their daughter, Brooke. My cousin, Brooke, is my age and we have met I think two times. I stalked them all online to get some additional information.

Aunt Kate is a former child television star who made Barbie and Corn Flake commercials when she was little and then was the spoiled, entitled, and beautiful teenage daughter on a popular TV series for 5 years. One article said that "Kate grew up before America's eyes" and another said, "Kate was all of America's most beautiful and troubled teens." She was a very pretty girl with a gorgeous smile; there were endless photos of her until she was about 18. Then she reappears as a woman in her 40s with a cooking and restaurant blog called, Food Affair with Kate; there are hundreds of photos of herself, once again, smiling with Chefs and lots of food. Strangely there are twenty years missing and two very different characters with the same name. I wonder what she did for all those years? She is married to Andy who seems like a pretty cool documentary filmmaker. He has filmed South American Indigenous People battling to keep their lands, he followed the lives of mothers in South Central LA whose sons are gang members, and he recently finished a film on transgender Americans' battle for respect, equality and public bathroom freedom. Their daughter Brooke looks like a typical California beach girl with blonde hair, blue eyes, and a sunny smile. She writes for the school newspaper, plays volleyball, and from the photos appears to have a black boyfriend named Jeremy. The Californians live in a small contemporary house with floor to ceiling windows looking out to trees and mountains, and the article says they are a ten-minute walk from Santa Monica beach.

I hope they will bring some California sunshine to our New York dim and overcast family.

We all could use some fresh light.

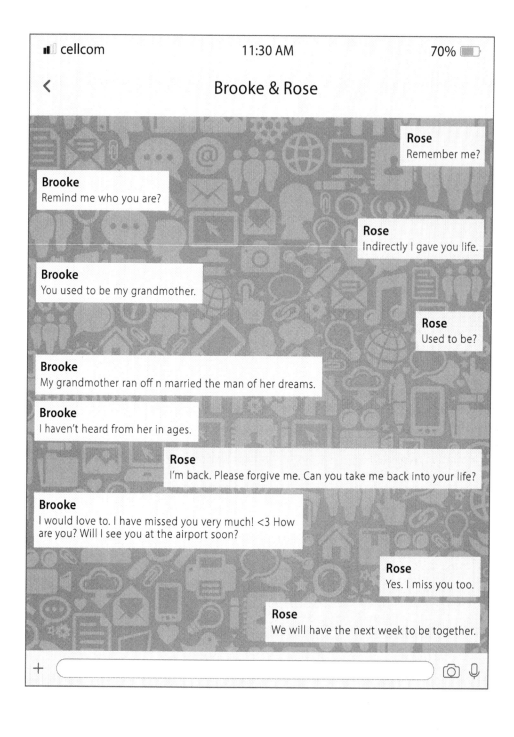

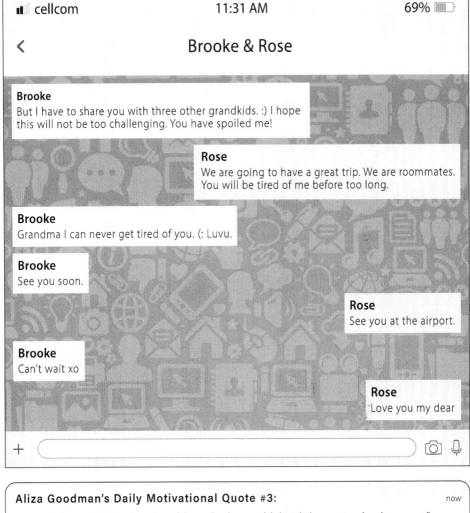

‹   Brooke & Rose

Brooke
But I have to share you with three other grandkids. :) I hope this will not be too challenging. You have spoiled me!

Rose
We are going to have a great trip. We are roommates. You will be tired of me before too long.

Brooke
Grandma I can never get tired of you. (: Luvu.

Brooke
See you soon.

Rose
See you at the airport.

Brooke
Can't wait xo

Rose
Love you my dear

Aliza Goodman's Daily Motivational Quote #3:   now

"Hate, it has caused a lot of problems in the world, but it has not solved one yet."
Maya Angelou

MotiQuote.com

 JN24:   now

Initial reports of stabbing attack against IDF soldier near Ramallah.
Jewish News You Can Use

FOOD AFFAIR WITH KATE

Inquiring Minds Want to Know

★ ★ ★ ☆ ☆

Shayne wrote from Berkeley to ask me what my food journey has been like as she struggles with her decision to follow a vegan diet. While I am not a professional nutritionist or doctor, I wanted to share with all of you my dietary development over the years and how I arrived at deciding to eat what I want and not be limited by certain diet categories. I hope you will find this interesting or helpful.

When I was a small child, I ate everything that was put on my plate as my mother constantly reminded me that there were poor children starving in the world. I did not question this rationale and like clock work at 6pm each night, I was served a dinner consisting of a green salad swimming in thick Italian dressing, a meat cooked in the broiler (lamb chops and pork chops), a carbohydrate baked or boiled (mostly potatoes), and a green frozen vegetable (a lot of peas!) heated on the stove. Food was prepared with lots of butter and Crisco (hydrogenated vegetable oil), and a little pepper, and a lot of salt (I even had a friend growing up whose name was Pepper Salter!). Every night for dessert, mom bought freshly baked goods from Weby's, our local bakery – my favorites were the jumbo soft chocolate chip cookies and the chocolate cupcakes with chocolate frosting topped by candy sprinkles and a plastic treat. They were terribly fattening but mom's rationale was that they were not processed like Hostess cupcakes and therefore healthy desserts for her family.

During my troubling teen years, mom served us a version of the Pritikin diet as my stepfather had high cholesterol, high blood sugar and heart disease. We ate lots of fresh fruits and vegetables, whole grains, lean meats with little oil, sugar, salt, or processed white carbohydrates. Weby's Bakery became a weekend and holiday treat and fresh fruit salads became the dessert norm. Food became completely boring. The only soft drink we had at home was ginger ale for guests and upset stomachs. Oh, how I loved the forbidden, bittersweet refreshing taste of ginger ale!

As a rebellious young adult living on my own, I stopped eating all meat and became a pescatarian and slowly worked my way to becoming a dedicated vegetarian. I ate a lot of green salads, vegetable, tofu stir-fries, egg white omelettes, and artichokes with Dijon mustard. I was terribly lost in this period of my life and food was one place I exercised control over my surroundings myself. I ate very healthy, boring food and physically

FOOD AFFAIR WITH KATE

looked great, but I did not feel very good about myself.

Then in my 30s I became a devout vegan - never satisfied by food but thrilled by the clean diet. It was trendy and cool to be a vegan. I have many friends who are still vegan and I respect their diets, but for me it never felt right.

My 40s have served as a transitional period in my life and this is reflected in my food choices: I am now a flex-a-tarian who juggles the food paradigm. I realize that it is time to fully enjoy my experiences and eat what is pleasing to me. My father dropped dead from a heart attack at forty-five years old. I check my heart annually, but if I go tomorrow like my father, I don't want to regret that I did not try everything that I wanted to eat. Tomorrow please join me as I travel across the world to begin a whole new food adventure in the Middle East.

See the photos below and check out Food Affair with Kate on Instagram and Facebook. #FoodaffairwithKate #culinaryadventures #yummyfood #foodies #holymeals

---

MYPOETRY.COM

My Rose

Brooke G.O.

I climbed to the highest peak
Over the ice and thick terrain
Dense fog obscured my view
Rebelled against the pain

I dodged the frozen deluge
Made a deal with my destiny of trust
Focused on the storm's eye
Thrown by the violent gust

I tumbled to the valley floor
Sun burned through the haze of gray
A bright yellow rose stopped my breath
Inviting me out to play

♡ 212   400 ◎

‹ Theo & Rose

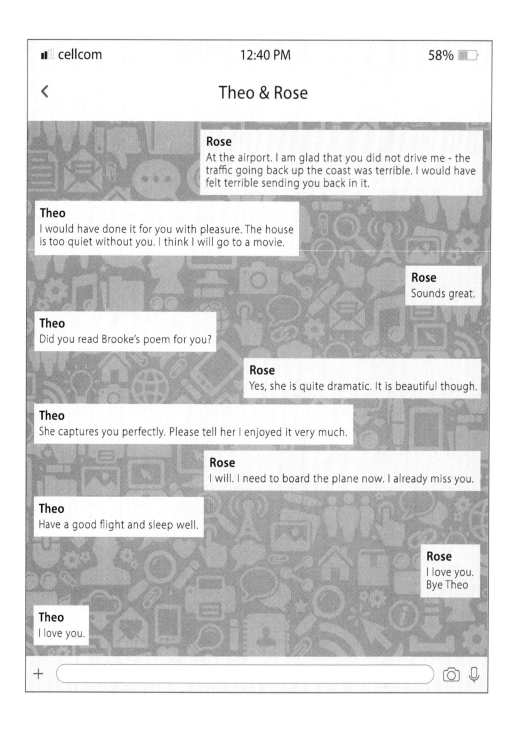

Rose
At the airport. I am glad that you did not drive me - the traffic going back up the coast was terrible. I would have felt terrible sending you back in it.

Theo
I would have done it for you with pleasure. The house is too quiet without you. I think I will go to a movie.

Rose
Sounds great.

Theo
Did you read Brooke's poem for you?

Rose
Yes, she is quite dramatic. It is beautiful though.

Theo
She captures you perfectly. Please tell her I enjoyed it very much.

Rose
I will. I need to board the plane now. I already miss you.

Theo
Have a good flight and sleep well.

Rose
I love you.
Bye Theo

Theo
I love you.

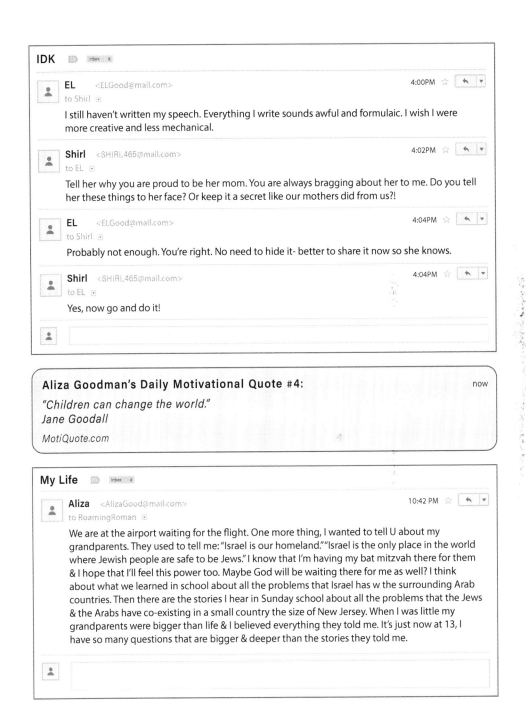

IDK   Inbox x

EL   <ELGood@mail.com>   4:00PM
to Shirl

I still haven't written my speech. Everything I write sounds awful and formulaic. I wish I were more creative and less mechanical.

Shirl   <SHIRL465@mail.com>   4:02PM
to EL

Tell her why you are proud to be her mom. You are always bragging about her to me. Do you tell her these things to her face? Or keep it a secret like our mothers did from us?!

EL   <ELGood@mail.com>   4:04PM
to Shirl

Probably not enough. You're right. No need to hide it- better to share it now so she knows.

Shirl   <SHIRL465@mail.com>   4:04PM
to EL

Yes, now go and do it!

Aliza Goodman's Daily Motivational Quote #4:   now

"Children can change the world."
Jane Goodall

MotiQuote.com

My Life   Inbox x

Aliza   <AlizaGood@mail.com>   10:42 PM
to RoamingRoman

We are at the airport waiting for the flight. One more thing, I wanted to tell U about my grandparents. They used to tell me: "Israel is our homeland." "Israel is the only place in the world where Jewish people are safe to be Jews." I know that I'm having my bat mitzvah there for them & I hope that I'll feel this power too. Maybe God will be waiting there for me as well? I think about what we learned in school about all the problems that Israel has w the surrounding Arab countries. Then there are the stories I hear in Sunday school about all the problems that the Jews & the Arabs have co-existing in a small country the size of New Jersey. When I was little my grandparents were bigger than life & I believed everything they told me. It's just now at 13, I have so many questions that are bigger & deeper than the stories they told me.

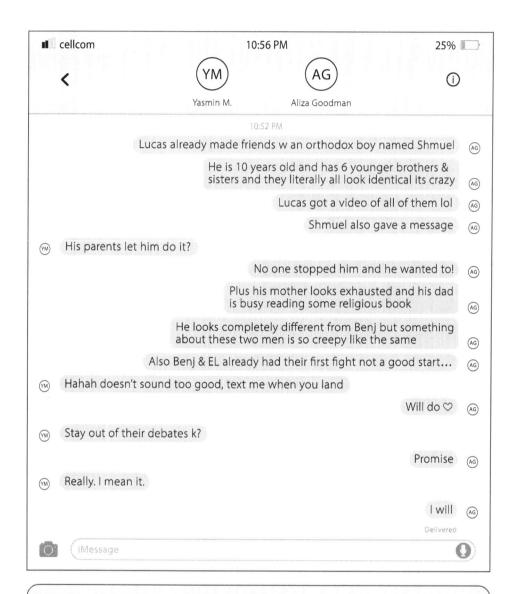

YM
Yasmin M.

AG
Aliza Goodman

10:52 PM

Lucas already made friends w an orthodox boy named Shmuel

He is 10 years old and has 6 younger brothers & sisters and they literally all look identical its crazy

Lucas got a video of all of them lol

Shmuel also gave a message

His parents let him do it?

No one stopped him and he wanted to!

Plus his mother looks exhausted and his dad is busy reading some religious book

He looks completely different from Benj but something about these two men is so creepy like the same

Also Benj & EL already had their first fight not a good start…

Hahah doesn't sound too good, text me when you land

Will do ♡

Stay out of their debates k?

Promise

Really. I mean it.

I will

Delivered

iMessage

Aliza Goodman's Daily Motivational Quote #5:　　　now

"The right way is not always the popular and easy way. Standing for right when it is unpopular is a true test of moral character."
Margaret Chase Smith

MotiQuote.com

Words of Encouragement Inbox x

Dahlia <FreeDahlia@mail.com>   11:29PM ⭐
to EL

Sugah, please forgive the break.

Smack dab in the middle of writin', I fainted from a little too much Chianti. Just woke up to a fresh breeze n the sound of waves breakin', embracin' my laptop as a symbol of my commitment to ya. Two of the sweetest little birds were nibblin' on leftover popcorn in the bowl.

I reckon my last sentence should have been, I woke up many years later in a loveless marriage, wonderin' how I arrived at this low n very sad moment but aware that I had a whole life still ahead to celebrate myself n live a full life.

Here is what I learned Sugah... Victims of abuse do not see the partner's mistreatment as abusive. Y'not alone. I lived this way. We're survivors n we develop copin' mechanisms like convincin' ourselves that we're responsible for the behavior, apologizin' for things we did not do, keepin' our opinions n thoughts to ourselves n numbin' with drugs n alcohol. Underneath this, we are depressed n anxious like soldiers comin' home from battle with post-traumatic stress disorder. On the surface, we are well versed in proper wife etiquette, "Pearls go with everythin' n always smilin". I'm sure y' have your pearls too.

Y'already know you're a victim. The way your husband speaks with y' n treats y' is disgraceful. Sugah, y' may have enabled him to get to this place, but this does not exonerate him from bein' an abuser. For cryin' out loud, I was sure it was my fault as Rick told me it was time after time. Emotional abusers are blamers. It's never their fault, but this took time for me to learn n accept. They present a different image to everyone else that they're good, kind n supportive.

I don't care that your husband's father died when he was a teenager. This aint no reason to treat his wife badly. Rick's mother was an alcoholic n narcissist, a combination that was deadly to grow up he explained to me early on. She was very hard on him n he admitted he could never please her. I realized one day, n pretty late in the game he wouldn't quit bein' a bully.

Sweetheart, I feel terrible dumpin' this on y' as y' begin the bat mitzvah trip. Y' not alone Sugah. Let me know how I can help y'? I feel close enough to help y' maybe even better than your mama. She certainly would chuckle knowin' we were united on this front! I miss her sweet smile like crazy!

I hope Israel is a wonderful adventure. If Benj tries to ruin it, stick his goddamn Blackbery where the sun doesn't shine.

Y' deserve to enjoy - it is a once in a lifetime opportunity for Aliza n y'all.

Goodnight Sugah.

JN24:   now

Katusha rockets fall in empty fields by Sderot in Southern Israel.

Jewish News You Can Use

Leap of Faith

Brooke G.O.

The anchor lifts
Don't look back
The sails fill
Keep moving forward
The hull glides
Follow the current
The horizon plays with my thought
Take a chance on all I sought

♡ 105

162 ◎

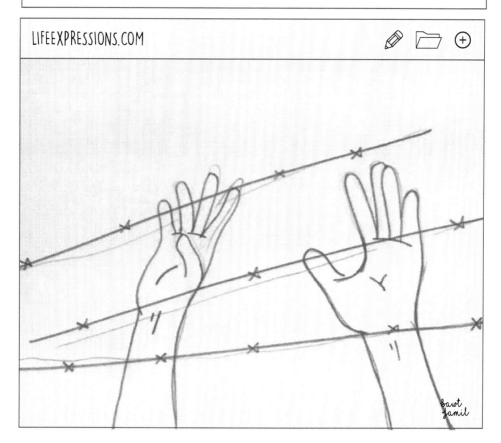

BOKER TOV

Goodman Family!

The Holy Land

Welcome to the Holy Land!

We have an incredible week planned touring our beautiful country in honor of Aliza's Bat Mitzvah.

Israel, the democratic Jewish State founded on May 14, 1948, is a small nation of 8 million inhabitants bordered by Lebanon, Syria, Jordan, Egypt and the Mediterranean Sea. We will stay in Jerusalem, the nation's capital. Our goal each day is to provide you with an enjoyable and life changing holiday full of tradition and culture spanning modern and ancient days; you will visit sites rich in religion, revolution, and renewal; you will meet diverse Sabras and experience the many compelling facets of Israeli society.

Tonight, we will attend a reception in the Chagall State Hall at the Knesset. This very special venue features Chagall's art work in the form of tapestry and mosaic and it will be a wonderful experience. Please bring your passports as security is very strict and all who enter need their picture identification.

We are here to make your stay in the Holy Land comfortable, exciting and challenging. We are sure that this will be a trip of a lifetime.

Please ask many questions and keep your eyes wide open.

Shabbat Shalom!

Moshe

Rimon Tours

The Arrival

Teddy Goodman

The airport passport control agent was a skinny freckle faced kid named Avi, practically my age and in charge of Israel's security. In New York, the best job I could get is taking orders at McDonalds. Avi seriously asked us a lot of the same questions and stared intently at each one of us. We are not the most dangerous looking family, but he was trained to drill us and not give any visitor the benefit of the doubt. He was annoying, but I must believe he has meaning in his life; he is doing something that matters. He is not flipping fucking hamburgers at McDonalds.

My mother's cousin, Uncle Raffi, picked us up and drove us to Jerusalem in his old and dented, burgundy minivan. I remember him a little from when he came to my bar mitzvah. Raffi seems like a nice enough guy and speaks English with a thick accent.

Tomorrow we are going for lunch with his family on the kibbutz where he grew up; his mom and sister still live there. Every summer when EL was young, her parents shipped her off to this same kibbutz. EL always tells us what a paradise the kibbutz was for a young American city girl with overprotective immigrant parents.

Tonight, at the hotel, we are having dinner with our estranged Californian family: Grandma Rose, Aunt Kate, Uncle Andy, and Cousin Brooke. Grandma Rose has come to visit in NY over the years but we never talked so I don't know her like I did Safta Shula. They all came to my bar mitzvah, but I did not pay attention to them. I was too busy having my first drink and partying with the other fucked-up, ridiculous 13-year-olds.

Meeting these relatives may help me learn more about my fucked-up parents who don't reveal a lot (not that I have been very open to them in the last few years). I think this will help me figure myself out a little better.

I fucking hate that I don't know who I am or what I want in life.

 JN24:   now

Jewish philanthropist arrives in Israel and declares his intent to invest $250 million in West Bank high tech industry.

Jewish News You Can Use

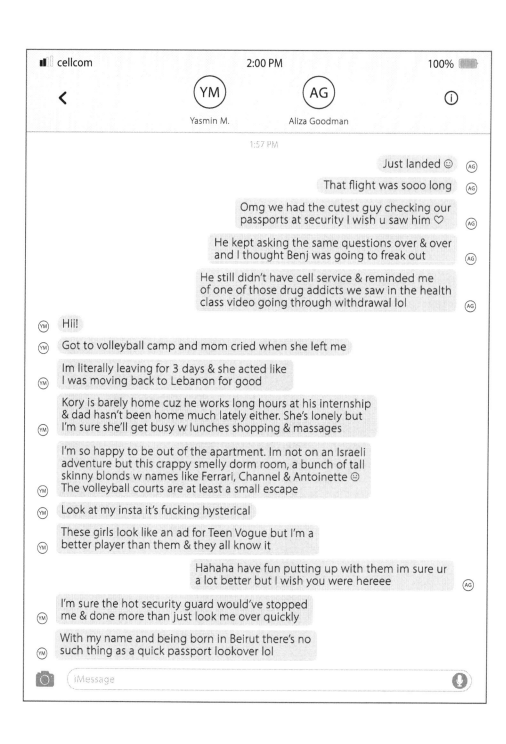

YM
Yasmin M.

AG
Aliza Goodman

1:57 PM

Just landed ☺

That flight was sooo long

Omg we had the cutest guy checking our passports at security I wish u saw him ♡

He kept asking the same questions over & over and I thought Benj was going to freak out

He still didn't have cell service & reminded me of one of those drug addicts we saw in the health class video going through withdrawal lol

Hii!

Got to volleyball camp and mom cried when she left me

Im literally leaving for 3 days & she acted like I was moving back to Lebanon for good

Kory is barely home cuz he works long hours at his internship & dad hasn't been home much lately either. She's lonely but I'm sure she'll get busy w lunches shopping & massages

I'm so happy to be out of the apartment. Im not on an Israeli adventure but this crappy smelly dorm room, a bunch of tall skinny blonds w names like Ferrari, Channel & Antoinette ☺ The volleyball courts are at least a small escape

Look at my insta it's fucking hysterical

These girls look like an ad for Teen Vogue but I'm a better player than them & they all know it

Hahaha have fun putting up with them im sure ur a lot better but I wish you were hereee

I'm sure the hot security guard would've stopped me & done more than just look me over quickly

With my name and being born in Beirut there's no such thing as a quick passport lookover lol

iMessage

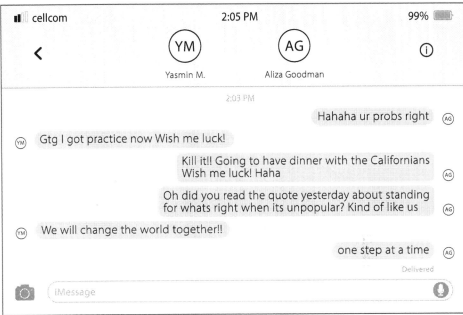

YM — Yasmin M.   **AG** — Aliza Goodman

2:03 PM

Hahaha ur probs right (AG)

(YM) Gtg I got practice now Wish me luck!

Kill it!! Going to have dinner with the Californians Wish me luck! Haha (AG)

Oh did you read the quote yesterday about standing for whats right when its unpopular? Kind of like us (AG)

(YM) We will change the world together!!

one step at a time (AG)

Delivered

iMessage

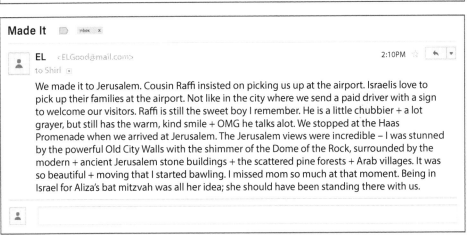

Made It   Inbox   x

EL < ELGood@mail.com>   2:10PM
to Shirl

We made it to Jerusalem. Cousin Raffi insisted on picking us up at the airport. Israelis love to pick up their families at the airport. Not like in the city where we send a paid driver with a sign to welcome our visitors. Raffi is still the sweet boy I remember. He is a little chubbier + a lot grayer, but still has the warm, kind smile + OMG he talks alot. We stopped at the Haas Promenade when we arrived at Jerusalem. The Jerusalem views were incredible – I was stunned by the powerful Old City Walls with the shimmer of the Dome of the Rock, surrounded by the modern + ancient Jerusalem stone buildings + the scattered pine forests + Arab villages. It was so beautiful + moving that I started bawling. I missed mom so much at that moment. Being in Israel for Aliza's bat mitzvah was all her idea; she should have been standing there with us.

Aliza Goodman's Daily Motivational Quote #1:   now

"I can promise you that women working together - linked, informed and educated - can bring peace and prosperity to the forsaken planet."
Isabel Allende

MotiQuote.com

63

JS — Jeremy Stark

BO — Brooke Orser

3:01 PM

☺ Hi!!!

We just got to Israel

I was going crazy cramped in a small seat for so long

we're now in Jerusalem I haven't seen much but the drive from the airport was beautiful the hotel is really nice there's a glass wall btwn the bathroom n bedroom that blacks out with a switch. Very cool!

I'm sharing a room with Grandma Rose, which is perfect she is like a teenager texting Theo back home. I'm not sure what she is writing but she is smiling. It's amazing to see her so happy n finally in love!!!

Delivered

iMessage

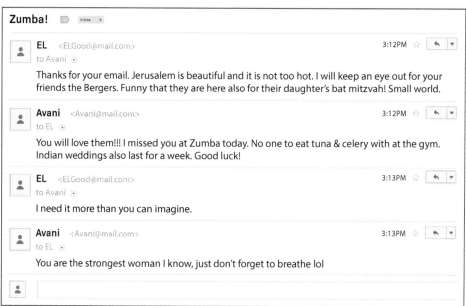

Zumba!   Inbox x

EL <ELGood@mail.com>   3:12PM
to Avani

Thanks for your email. Jerusalem is beautiful and it is not too hot. I will keep an eye out for your friends the Bergers. Funny that they are here also for their daughter's bat mitzvah! Small world.

Avani <Avani@mail.com>   3:12PM
to EL

You will love them!!! I missed you at Zumba today. No one to eat tuna & celery with at the gym. Indian weddings also last for a week. Good luck!

EL <ELGood@mail.com>   3:13PM
to Avani

I need it more than you can imagine.

Avani <Avani@mail.com>   3:13PM
to EL

You are the strongest woman I know, just don't forget to breathe lol

Andy Orser
Now · Israel

•••

GOY IN THE HOLY LAND

Just arrived in Jerusalem for my niece's bat mitzvah. This is a remarkable holy city for Jews, Muslims, and Christians. I have read extensively about and seen this powerful, religious city in countless movies; and now the human drama plays out live in front of my curious eyes. I am ready to discover the wonderous Jewish homeland, where the Jewish people have lived and shared their biblical lands since 1312 B.C.E.

Driving through the stunning city, I am awed by the juxtaposition of the white, ancient coarse Jerusalem limestone building facades and the bright lively colors of the stores, the brave people, and the defiant, beating daily life of the city. Everyone has a story that I want to hear, each street carries a piece of history I'm passionate to learn.

Only here for a few short hours and already the dynamism of this old, battled city mixed with young celebrating energy passionately pulses through my foreign cells and beckons me, the total jubilant goy, to learn and discover as much as I can in my short, heart warming visit.

Dear Friends, I am embarking on an amazing adventure that I feel will be life altering. Only a few hours here and I am a slowly becoming a different man. #Israel #Knesset #ChagallHall #Holyland

 Like   Comment   Share

LUCACLOSELY
@LUCACLOSELY

⌄

What creature walks on four legs in the morning, two legs in the afternoon, and three legs in the evening?

3:17 PM · June

💬 1   ♡ 2   ⟲ 2

LUCACLOSELY @LUCACLOSELY
Replying to @LUCACLOSELY

Man. He crawls on all fours as a baby. Then he walks on two feet as an adult. And then walks with a cane as an old man.

 JN24:   now

Initial report of attempted stabbing attack at West Bank Gush Etzion Junction.
Jewish News You Can Use

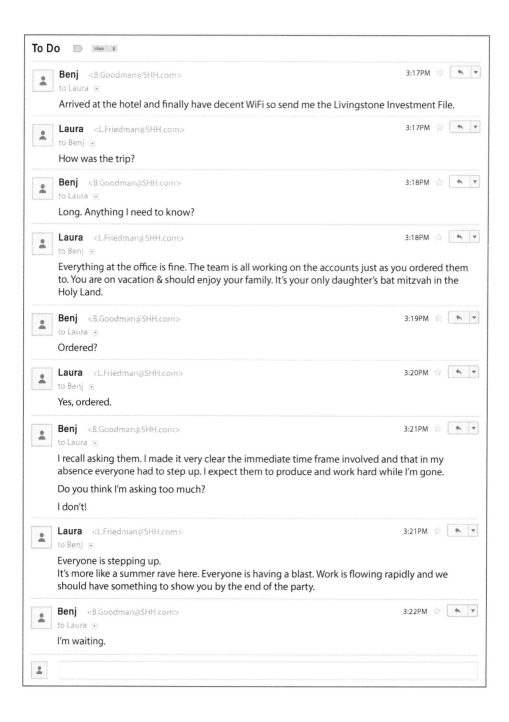

To Do 📋 inbox x

👤	**Benj** <B.Goodman@SHH.com>	3:17PM ☆
	to Laura ▾	

Arrived at the hotel and finally have decent WiFi so send me the Livingstone Investment File.

👤	**Laura** <L.Friedman@SHH.com>	3:17PM ☆
	to Benj ▾	

How was the trip?

👤	**Benj** <B.Goodman@SHH.com>	3:18PM ☆
	to Laura ▾	

Long. Anything I need to know?

👤	**Laura** <L.Friedman@SHH.com>	3:18PM ☆
	to Benj ▾	

Everything at the office is fine. The team is all working on the accounts just as you ordered them to. You are on vacation & should enjoy your family. It's your only daughter's bat mitzvah in the Holy Land.

👤	**Benj** <B.Goodman@SHH.com>	3:19PM ☆
	to Laura ▾	

Ordered?

👤	**Laura** <L.Friedman@SHH.com>	3:20PM ☆
	to Benj ▾	

Yes, ordered.

👤	**Benj** <B.Goodman@SHH.com>	3:21PM ☆
	to Laura ▾	

I recall asking them. I made it very clear the immediate time frame involved and that in my absence everyone had to step up. I expect them to produce and work hard while I'm gone.

Do you think I'm asking too much?

I don't!

👤	**Laura** <L.Friedman@SHH.com>	3:21PM ☆
	to Benj ▾	

Everyone is stepping up.
It's more like a summer rave here. Everyone is having a blast. Work is flowing rapidly and we should have something to show you by the end of the party.

👤	**Benj** <B.Goodman@SHH.com>	3:22PM ☆
	to Laura ▾	

I'm waiting.

👤	

MYPOETRY.COM

Ideal

Brooke G.O.

Fireworks on the 4th of July,
Flying to the moon for a space walk,
Hitting the winning ball to win state championship,
Reading my poem on the steps of the capital,
Eating the perfect hamburger and fries,
Holding hands as we walk along the beach,
Breakfast poetry with Beyonce,
Traveling across the world for a mysterious journey,
Escaping into the vibrant concerto,
Running the New York marathon,
Drinking the perfect Matcha tea,
Dreaming I find another missing piece of who I am.
Feeling safe when I'm alone,
Hearing voices that encourage me,
Looking in the mirror and feeling love,
Running fast, keeping my heart beat slow,
Dreaming I find another missing piece of who I am

♡ 350   395 ◎

Aliza Goodman's Daily Motivational Quote #2:   now

"Imagine all the people living life in peace. You may say I'm a dreamer, but I'm not the only one. I hope someday you'll join us, and the world will be as one."
John Lennon

MotiQuote.com

Chagall Hall
Teddy Goodman

One of my favorite escapes is the Metropolitan Art Museum, a few blocks from where we live in the city. It is a safe place to dream and think; I never run into anyone I know there. I enjoy the classic art, which is probably strange for an almost 18-year-old boy to reveal, but it is true.

My grandparents took me there when I was little and it was always a magical experience. They told me stories about the art that I am sure were a mix of fact and fiction but nevertheless; I was thrilled to be there with them and I was a true believer. After the museum, we would go into Central Park and they would buy me a forbidden hot dog — EL never let me eat hot dogs, as they were processed and full of chemicals — my immigrant grandparents believed hot dogs were the true symbol of a real American food for their real American grandson and the sign said they were kosher. Somehow with each bite, I validated their life in their adopted country. I would play with other small children and my grandparents would wait patiently for me on a nearby bench. I still remember these days so vividly.

Museums remain magical settings for me. I know this is an odd statement from a 17-year-old boy but it is true.

Today, after our arrival in Jerusalem, we went to the Chagall Hall in the Knesset. Standing in front of the floor to ceiling Chagall Tapestries there was a giant triptych. Telling the story of the Jews throughout history, I felt my grandparents' presence like when I was little holding both of their hands admiring incredible art in the Met. I missed them terribly at that very moment knowing they would have loved to share this awesome experience with me telling me stories of how they arrived in Israel as Jewish refugees from hostile lands.

For a few minutes, I closed my eyes and felt their warm presence beckon me. I realized at that moment, my grandfather arrived in Israel practically at my age and under completely different circumstances as a World War 2 Jewish refugee and orphan. All these years later with a simple passport, I arrived in Israel and now visited the Knesset building with ease and opportunity.

It seems unfair. Grandpa Yacov always said, "Life isn't fair." He knew this first hand. He was right.

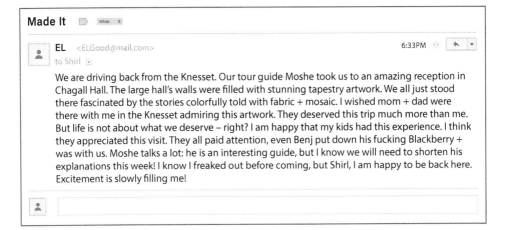

Made It 📭 Inbox ✕

EL <ELGood@mail.com> 6:33PM ☆
to Shirl

We are driving back from the Knesset. Our tour guide Moshe took us to an amazing reception in Chagall Hall. The large hall's walls were filled with stunning tapestry artwork. We all just stood there fascinated by the stories colorfully told with fabric + mosaic. I wished mom + dad were there with me in the Knesset admiring this artwork. They deserved this trip much more than me. But life is not about what we deserve – right? I am happy that my kids had this experience. I think they appreciated this visit. They all paid attention, even Benj put down his fucking Blackberry + was with us. Moshe talks a lot: he is an interesting guide, but I know we will need to shorten his explanations this week! I know I freaked out before coming, but Shirl, I am happy to be back here. Excitement is slowly filling me!

MYPOETRY.COM

Step Carefully, Hands Welcome

Brooke G.O.

Birds, Life + Joy,
Calf, Youth + Innocence,
Step Carefully, Hands Welcome,
Candlestick, Light + Life,
Horn, Fish + Tradition,
Step Carefully, Hands Welcome,
Fruit, Fertility + Health,
Star of David, Guidance + Hope,
Step Carefully, Hands Welcome,
Rooster, Flowers + Love,
Art, Politics + Government,
Step Carefully, Hands Welcome.

♡ 192 240 👁

Made It 📭 Inbox ✕

Shirl <SHIRL465@mail.com> 9:00PM ☆
to EL

You deserve happiness EL!

69

The Californians

Teddy Goodman

Benj does not like his mother or his sister, so even though they are our only living relatives in America, we have no fucking relationship with them. But after one meal, they seem nice and we all talked a lot.

Grandma Rose lives in Santa Barbara and is married to her fourth husband. She told us some funny stories at dinner; she learned to shoot a bb gun when she was 7. Her dad taught her so she could kill the wild rabbits that were eating his vegetable garden on their property. Now she hates all guns. Last year she joined a protest march against the NRA and picketed the two gun shops near her house. She is cool for an old lady.

Cousin Brooke is different from the girls I go to school with - for starters she does not act spoiled and she talks about things other than herself. She did not once mention a designer's name, a famous person, and she did not take selfies or photos of the food on our table for her Instagram account. Her boyfriend Jeremy is black and moved to NY to attend Columbia. She writes poetry and plays volleyball. I think she is actually the adult in her family.

Her parents, Aunt Kate and Uncle Andy, are nice enough, but they are the stereotypical Southern Californian self-absorbed crazies: everything they eat, say, or do requires a lengthy description, explanation and conversation. I have read about these types in the New Yorker and, at this point, their juvenile craziness is a welcome break from my parents constant arguing. Aunt Kate and Uncle Andy spent about 10 minutes ordering their version of what was on the menu. Brooke on the other hand ordered a hamburger and fries at dinner and laughed at her parents' stupid comments.

I am still not sure why my dad, his sister, and mother fucking hate each other so much, but I can see after one meal that other than shared DNA, as they all look amazingly alike, they have nothing in common. Their familial cold war has lasted for almost as long as the disputing Jews and Arabs over the State of Israel.

A few hours earlier, we had to avoid stepping on the Chagall Mosaics on the Knesset hall floor; a precursor to the week ahead where we will need to avoid stepping on the invisible land mines the older generation has planted.

I am reminded of the old Chinese Proverb, "May you live in interesting times."

NY Apartment Inbox x

EL <ELGood@mail.com>   9:33PM
to Mr. Friedman

How's it going at the apartment?

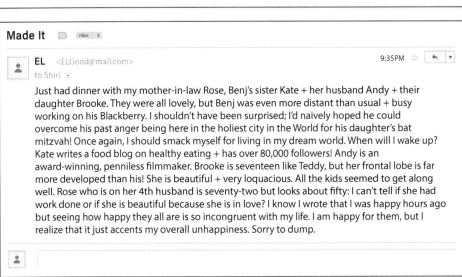

Made It Inbox x

EL <ELGood@mail.com>   9:35PM
to Shirl

Just had dinner with my mother-in-law Rose, Benj's sister Kate + her husband Andy + their daughter Brooke. They were all lovely, but Benj was even more distant than usual + busy working on his Blackberry. I shouldn't have been surprised; I'd naively hoped he could overcome his past anger being here in the holiest city in the World for his daughter's bat mitzvah! Once again, I should smack myself for living in my dream world. When will I wake up? Kate writes a food blog on healthy eating + has over 80,000 followers! Andy is an award-winning, penniless filmmaker. Brooke is seventeen like Teddy, but her frontal lobe is far more developed than his! She is beautiful + very loquacious. All the kids seemed to get along well. Rose who is on her 4th husband is seventy-two but looks about fifty: I can't tell if she had work done or if she is beautiful because she is in love? I know I wrote that I was happy hours ago but seeing how happy they all are is so incongruent with my life. I am happy for them, but I realize that it just accents my overall unhappiness. Sorry to dump.

LIFEEXPRESSIONS.COM

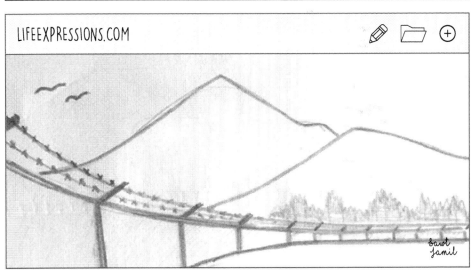

Andy Orser
Now · Israel

GOY IN THE HOLY LAND PART 1

I am a kid in a candy shop and don't know where to start?! I want it all! I am exhausted from the 14-hour flight but enthralled by everything I experience. Our guide Moshe took us to see the Chagall Hall at the Knesset this afternoon; there is no rest for the weary. We are in Israel for 8 packed days of touring and bat mitzvah celebrations. I will write as best I can to share this incredible adventure with you. The Israeli Knesset sits on a large land parcel in Jerusalem. We had to go through very tight security at two different locations before arriving at Chagall Hall – a large room with a wonderous Chagall triptych tapestry, incredible Chagall mosaics on the floor and a large Chagall mosaic on a wall with a large angel of redemption with arms stretched out that I feel welcomes me to Israel. At this very moment, I have arrived home and I am not even Jewish. I cannot wait for what tomorrow will bring.

Dear Friends, I never thought I would feel so at home in a foreign country. I am beyond excited to be here. #Israel #Knesset #ChagallHall #Holyland

    👍 Like   💬 Comment   ↪ Share

Aliza Goodman's Daily Motivational Quote #3:   now

"You cannot find what you do not seek. You cannot grasp when you do not reach. Your dreams won't come up to your front door. You have got to take a leap if you want to soar."   Senator Cory Booker

MotiQuote.com

LIFEEXPRESSIONS.COM

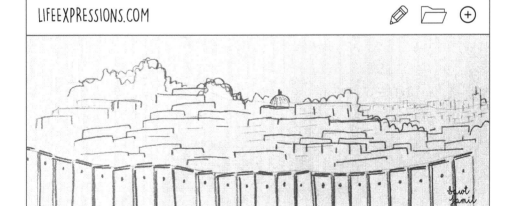

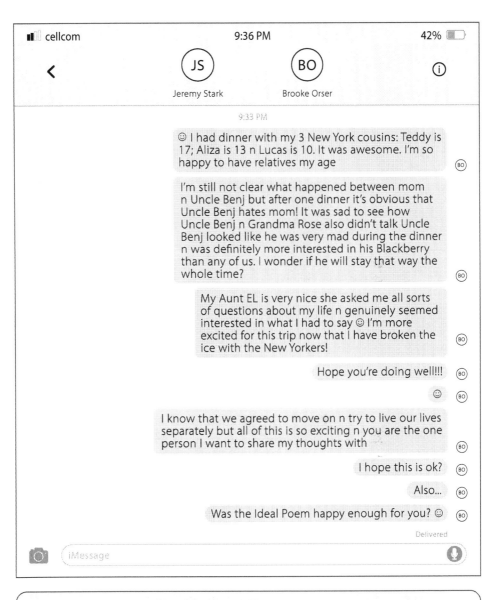

JS — Jeremy Stark

BO — Brooke Orser

9:33 PM

☺ I had dinner with my 3 New York cousins: Teddy is 17; Aliza is 13 n Lucas is 10. It was awesome. I'm so happy to have relatives my age

I'm still not clear what happened between mom n Uncle Benj but after one dinner it's obvious that Uncle Benj hates mom! It was sad to see how Uncle Benj n Grandma Rose also didn't talk Uncle Benj looked like he was very mad during the dinner n was definitely more interested in his Blackberry than any of us. I wonder if he will stay that way the whole time?

My Aunt EL is very nice she asked me all sorts of questions about my life n genuinely seemed interested in what I had to say ☺ I'm more excited for this trip now that I have broken the ice with the New Yorkers!

Hope you're doing well!!!

☺

I know that we agreed to move on n try to live our lives separately but all of this is so exciting n you are the one person I want to share my thoughts with

I hope this is ok?

Also...

Was the Ideal Poem happy enough for you? ☺

Delivered

iMessage

Aliza Goodman's Daily Motivational Quote #4:   now

"Peace cannot be kept by force; it can only be achieved by understanding."
Albert Einstein

MotiQuote.com

FOOD AFFAIR WITH KATE

DIVINE, DELICIOUS, AND DELIGHTFUL   ABOUT   RECIPES   CONTACT

The Eagle Has Landed...

★ ★ ★ ★ ★

I am thrilled to be writing to you from Israel where over the next week I will share the tantalizing treasures of Middle Eastern cuisine dating back thousands of years created by the confluence of Asian, Mediterranean, Middle Eastern, and North African influences. I am enthusiastic to travel this country and enjoy the Israeli cuisine alive beyond the obvious olives, pickled vegetables, olive oil, garbanzo beans, honey, dates, sumac, mint, parsley, and sesame seed: and how a vast array of people from deserts, mountains, and seas influence a nation's and region's diet. I look forward to sharing my delight in discovering new and tasty foods.

At the same time, I hope to begin learning how Jews, Christians, and Muslims are commonly bonded with the divine joy of sharing mouth-watering cuisine in this region. I am enamored and excited by the culinary dynamics of individuals and cultures and hope to meet the chefs who bring these magical tastes alive. I am eager to dig in and eat everything I can for the next week and share with you, my devout and delicious readers. Stay tuned for Blog Posting, Instagram, and Facebook highlights of my Israeli culinary adventures. See the photos below and check out Food Affair with Kate on Instagram and Facebook.

Made It 📭 Inbox ✕

Shirl ‹SHIRL465@mail.com›   9:37PM ☆ ↰ ▾
to EL ▾

You don't have to be happy for them. You can be resentful that they have good relationships & you don't - you just can't show it. Haha. I know you will find some happiness so don't throw a pity party for yourself. Ok? Did you give Aliza the envelope?

EL ‹ELGood@mail.com›   9:37PM ☆ ↰ ▾
to Shirl ▾

Yes. I gave it to her at dinner tonight. She was very surprised that her grandmother had secretly prepared this before she died. No pity party – I promise!

Shirl ‹SHIRL465@mail.com›   9:38PM ☆ ↰ ▾
to EL ▾

Surprises are good! It keeps your mom alive & on the trip with you all. I wish I could've come with you. Little Rock, Arkansas is no Jerusalem. Haha. Today, we went out with all the kids & their parents to a teenage version of Chuck E Cheese. I'm the only single mom & felt so alien like my sliding door opened in the wrong place & I took the wrong path. All the other parents appear on the surface to be happy couples, but I'm not fully convinced! The women are utterly boring: they laugh about their friends' Botox mishaps, drunken teenagers & cheating couples & the men sit separately, guzzle beer & practically tell fart jokes. Not sure what I'm missing but part of me here feels like a loser. Like I failed at the one thing I was supposed to be good at - staying married. I haven't felt like this for a long time. The first game tomorrow is at 7am & between both boys, I have 5 games to watch during the day. Promise not to be too jealous - haha & keep writing so I don't go crazy - :-) XOME

👤

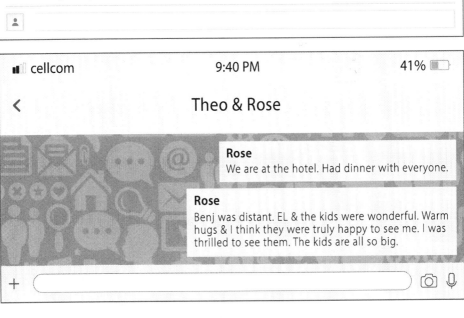

◂ᜒ cellcom   9:40 PM   41% ▭

‹   **Theo & Rose**

Rose
We are at the hotel. Had dinner with everyone.

Rose
Benj was distant. EL & the kids were wonderful. Warm hugs & I think they were truly happy to see me. I was thrilled to see them. The kids are all so big.

+ (   ) ⟨◎⟩ ⎘

Theo & Rose

Rose
I have missed so much. Hope this trip will allow me to catch up.

Theo
If they have not already, they will shortly discover what a spectacular grandmother they have.

Rose
You are biased.

Theo
I am, and truthful. Tell me about them.

Rose
Teddy is 17. He is tall & good-looking like my first husband, Wayne. But he is still a little awkward & slouches, he has a sweet smile & is very smart. He just won an award at school for building a 3D printer - not sure how it works, but sounds very impressive. He learned to speak Hebrew this year on his own & he is a straight A student.

Theo
And what about Aliza, the bat mitzvah girl?

Rose
She is beautiful but she does not know it. She is petite with large blue eyes and olive skin. She talks with her hands and is very animated. She looks a lot like EL's mom Shula. We talked about her life back in New York. She told me all about her best friend and that she loves to dance Hip Hop. Not quite sure which one Hip Hop is exactly, but she said she would show me.

Rose
Little Lucas cannot sit still.

< Theo & Rose

Rose
He has curly light brown hair and is always bouncing. He loves basketball and dreams to play for the New York Knicks and after this he plans to be an astronaut. During dinner, he took videos on his iPhone and said he was sending them somewhere on the Internet for his friends to watch. He is 10 and he knows more about the iPhone than me. The kids are great - their stone-cold father is the only obstacle I have.

Theo
Give Benj time. He may thaw to your surprise.

Rose
Do you think it is possible? He still blames me for his father's death. He knows I did not kill him, but I am the one he holds responsible for this loss. I told you that the night before Wayne died they had a huge argument about his grades. I still remember going to both & begging them to apologize. Maybe it was a sixth sense, but I just felt it was the right thing to do. They were so similar & so stubborn that my pleading was met with deaf ears. There was no reconciliation & then Wayne died the next day.

Theo
Not sure what he thinks now, but when his dad died, he was a young boy and thought it was his fault. It was easier for him to blame you than himself. Enough years have passed and I hope he can resolve this with you. It will take some time

Rose
The Jews & the Arabs have a better chance to reconcile than we do.

Theo
Trust me.

<   **Theo & Rose**

Rose
I will.

Theo
I miss you very much.

Rose
I miss you too. I wish you were here. I feel alone without you.

Rose
You have spoiled me with your love & care.

Theo
You have spoiled me with your beauty and your heart.

Rose
You are in my heart. I just wish you were physically beside me. Holding my hand. Touching me. Keeping me warm.

Theo
Nothing would make me happier than to be touching all of you.

Rose
I will be back soon. Hold that thought.

Theo
I will. Sleep well my love.

Rose
I will dream of you.
I love you.

Theo
I love you Rosie.

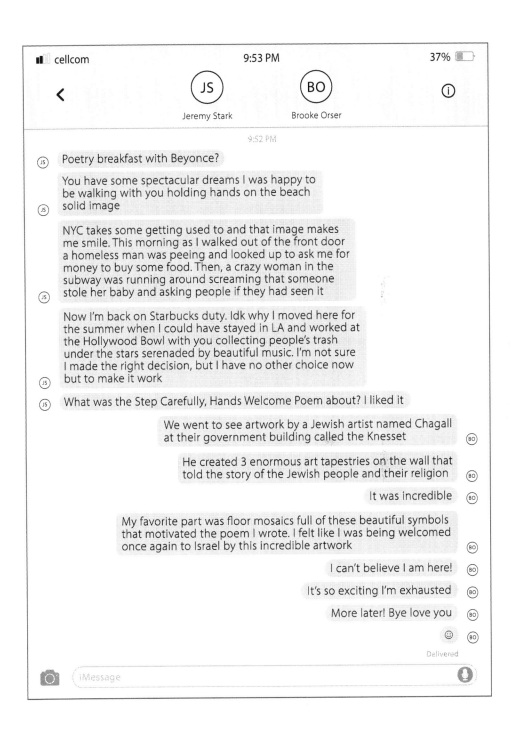

JS
Jeremy Stark

BO
Brooke Orser

9:52 PM

JS Poetry breakfast with Beyonce?

JS You have some spectacular dreams I was happy to be walking with you holding hands on the beach solid image

JS NYC takes some getting used to and that image makes me smile. This morning as I walked out of the front door a homeless man was peeing and looked up to ask me for money to buy some food. Then, a crazy woman in the subway was running around screaming that someone stole her baby and asking people if they had seen it

JS Now I'm back on Starbucks duty. Idk why I moved here for the summer when I could have stayed in LA and worked at the Hollywood Bowl with you collecting people's trash under the stars serenaded by beautiful music. I'm not sure I made the right decision, but I have no other choice now but to make it work

JS What was the Step Carefully, Hands Welcome Poem about? I liked it

We went to see artwork by a Jewish artist named Chagall at their government building called the Knesset BO

He created 3 enormous art tapestries on the wall that told the story of the Jewish people and their religion BO

It was incredible BO

My favorite part was floor mosaics full of these beautiful symbols that motivated the poem I wrote. I felt like I was being welcomed once again to Israel by this incredible artwork BO

I can't believe I am here! BO

It's so exciting I'm exhausted BO

More later! Bye love you BO

☺ BO

Delivered

iMessage

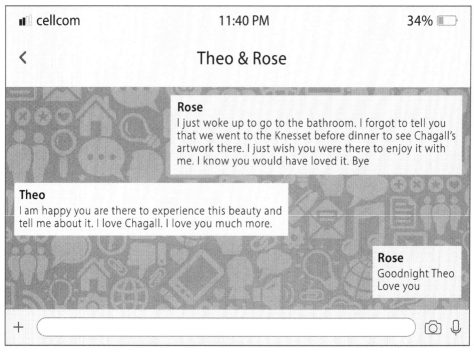

Rose
I just woke up to go to the bathroom. I forgot to tell you that we went to the Knesset before dinner to see Chagall's artwork there. I just wish you were there to enjoy it with me. I know you would have loved it. Bye

Theo
I am happy you are there to experience this beauty and tell me about it. I love Chagall. I love you much more.

Rose
Goodnight Theo
Love you

NY Apartment Inbox x

Mr. Friedman <DFriedman@smc.com>   11:45PM
to EL

The Marshalls were robbed today. They were at their summer home in the Hamptons and the housekeeper was on vacation. The temporary doorman, a young fellow, was supposedly busy texting and did not pay good attention. They have the robbers on the cameras but not their faces. They believe it was an inside job and these scoundrels had done work for the Marshalls. They took jewelry + silver as well as a few awards he received for the music he wrote over the years. Your apartment is fine and that doorman was let go after he admitted he did not keep an eye out. Cheers.

JN24:   now
Jewish - Arab school in Jerusalem burned down in afternoon fire that started in the trash behind classroom building. Two men in black hats and jackets were seen running from the scene.
Jewish News You Can Use

YM
Yasmin M.

AG
Aliza Goodman

12:30 AM

Hows volleyball camp going?

Cute boys? Good food? I miss U I wanna be updated!

Pls be awake it's the middle of night here and i literally have been trying to fall asleep for a year

Ugly boys terrible food hard work no new friends I miss u so much ☺ What time is it there?

12:30 in the fucking morning

Jet lag sucks I need it to wear off soon

But it rly is beautiful here - something special that I can't rly explain

When we got to Jerusalem my uncle Raffi drove us to this view of the walled Old City & all the surrounding land it was so sick

Hills full of Arab villages & Jewish houses w the Old City in the middle it was all there in front of me, not in a textbook or on the news

the Golden Dome is soo pretty

There was a slight breeze & I stood there w my eyes closed & said, "Todah Safta"

at that moment I knew exactly why she was so desperate for me to have my bat mitzvah here still no sign of God, but 'll keep looking for her lol

Still stuck as a hostage in a hotel room w Dopey & Grumpy

cant wait to get out & start my adventure! ☺

Im not sure youll find God but ik u are gonna have a great time

Youll def start changing the world rly soon ☺

Hahah hopefully just wish I could get some sleep kinda running out of what to do in a dark room other than like stare at the ceiling

Delivered

iMessage

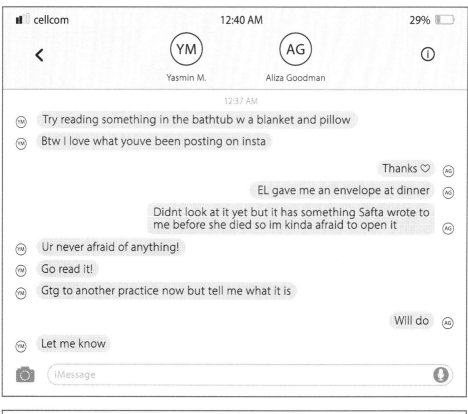

YM   **AG**

Yasmin M.   Aliza Goodman

12:37 AM

(YM) Try reading something in the bathtub w a blanket and pillow

(YM) Btw I love what youve been posting on insta

Thanks ♡ (AG)

EL gave me an envelope at dinner (AG)

Didnt look at it yet but it has something Safta wrote to me before she died so im kinda afraid to open it (AG)

(YM) Ur never afraid of anything!

(YM) Go read it!

(YM) Gtg to another practice now but tell me what it is

Will do (AG)

(YM) Let me know

iMessage

Freedom   inbox x

EL <ELGood@mail.com>   3:30AM
to Dahlia

If I'm not alone, why do I feel so lonely?

I'm stuck at a dead end + do not see any way out. I am not sure I can do anything. I have so many unanswered questions. How did you know it was over for you? And how did you find the courage to go forward. What is Freedom as an adult like? How does it feel? Taste? The last time I felt Freedom, I was 18 spending a final summer on the kibbutz with my boyfriend. Freedom now sounds ideal but it feels intangible.

Help!

I need some good old-fashioned Southern advice. Mom would be smiling, you are right. You knew her very well! I will always be grateful for how well you took care of her in the last few months. You gave her so much. I could never thank you enough.

Dearest Aliza,

You are reading my words and I regret that I am not there to recite them to you in person. I hope my words - many you have heard and others you may be surprised to read — will enrich and inspire you. I remember perfectly the first moment I held you in my arms just minutes after you were born. I looked into your wise eyes and they told me that you, my precious granddaughter, had been in my world before. I whispered into your ear "We are going to have lots of fun together" and you smiled. My only granddaughter and somehow I felt like we were sisters in another life. Your mom may freak out when she reads this but I am not a crazy, loony old grandmother. I do believe this. We share a special bond and I see no other explanation.

I am sorry that I am not in Israel for your bat mitzvah. I am overjoyed you will become a woman in the Holy Land with God as your witness. You are a blessing my sweet and special granddaughter. I am sharing a piece of me with you — the only gift I can give at this time. You have been one of the greatest joys of my life. Priceless gifts of love and respect we shared and will always bind us. I love you. I am proud of you. I know you will have a wonderful life. I will be watching from up above, smiling and feeling a piece of me is always carried in your heart and soul.

Enjoy and indulge in my stories. Mazel Tov Motek.

Love Safta Shula

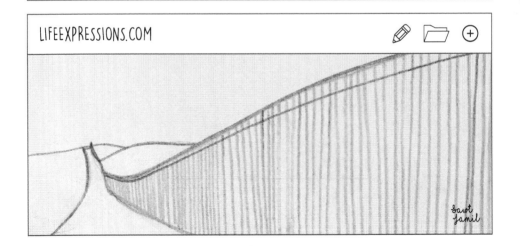

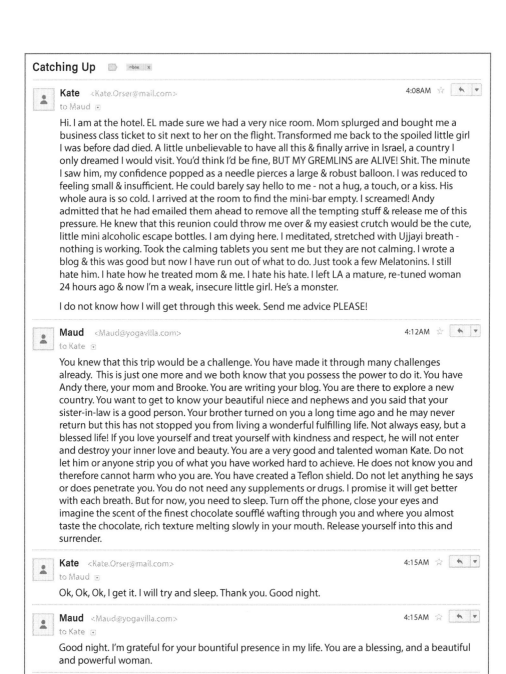

Catching Up

Kate <Kate.Orser@mail.com>
to Maud

4:08AM

Hi. I am at the hotel. EL made sure we had a very nice room. Mom splurged and bought me a business class ticket to sit next to her on the flight. Transformed me back to the spoiled little girl I was before dad died. A little unbelievable to have all this & finally arrive in Israel, a country I only dreamed I would visit. You'd think I'd be fine, BUT MY GREMLINS are ALIVE! Shit. The minute I saw him, my confidence popped as a needle pierces a large & robust balloon. I was reduced to feeling small & insufficient. He could barely say hello to me - not a hug, a touch, or a kiss. His whole aura is so cold. I arrived at the room to find the mini-bar empty. I screamed! Andy admitted that he had emailed them ahead to remove all the tempting stuff & release me of this pressure. He knew that this reunion could throw me over & my easiest crutch would be the cute, little mini alcoholic escape bottles. I am dying here. I meditated, stretched with Ujjayi breath - nothing is working. Took the calming tablets you sent me but they are not calming. I wrote a blog & this was good but now I have run out of what to do. Just took a few Melatonins. I still hate him. I hate how he treated mom & me. I hate his hate. I left LA a mature, re-tuned woman 24 hours ago & now I'm a weak, insecure little girl. He's a monster.

I do not know how I will get through this week. Send me advice PLEASE!

Maud <Maud@yogavilla.com>
to Kate

4:12AM

You knew that this trip would be a challenge. You have made it through many challenges already. This is just one more and we both know that you possess the power to do it. You have Andy there, your mom and Brooke. You are writing your blog. You are there to explore a new country. You want to get to know your beautiful niece and nephews and you said that your sister-in-law is a good person. Your brother turned on you a long time ago and he may never return but this has not stopped you from living a wonderful fulfilling life. Not always easy, but a blessed life! If you love yourself and treat yourself with kindness and respect, he will not enter and destroy your inner love and beauty. You are a very good and talented woman Kate. Do not let him or anyone strip you of what you have worked hard to achieve. He does not know you and therefore cannot harm who you are. You have created a Teflon shield. Do not let anything he says or does penetrate you. You do not need any supplements or drugs. I promise it will get better with each breath. But for now, you need to sleep. Turn off the phone, close your eyes and imagine the scent of the finest chocolate soufflé wafting through you and where you almost taste the chocolate, rich texture melting slowly in your mouth. Release yourself into this and surrender.

Kate <Kate.Orser@mail.com>
to Maud

4:15AM

Ok, Ok, Ok, I get it. I will try and sleep. Thank you. Good night.

Maud <Maud@yogavilla.com>
to Kate

4:15AM

Good night. I'm grateful for your bountiful presence in my life. You are a blessing, and a beautiful and powerful woman.

Dear Aliza,

Safta Shula's BELIEF.

1939, I was born in Basra, the second largest Iraqi city in the country located on the Shatt al-Arab River where the Tigris and Euphrates river shores meet in the southern part of Iraq. We had very hot summers and found some comfort in swimming in the cool river.

My sweet mother stayed home with the four children and took care of the house. My loving father was a successful merchant and we lived a nice life. My twin sister Marcel and I attended a good school. We were happy. Many Jews were also doing well in Iraq, that is, until the military regime took over in 1948 and then there was violence against the Jews. Each day, we listened to our parents speak about whose stores were ransacked or who was arrested— all Jews!

One day, I heard that my father's friend Shafiq was arrested. He was the richest Jew we knew. His Arab partners and he sold spare parts from the scrap metal left by the British to Italy. The Iraqi government that was at war against Israel since announcing independence in May 1948 accused only Shafik of selling arms to the Zionist enemy and using Italy as a front for the sales. Shafik was brought to court; he was not allowed to defend himself and there were no witnesses. After a short trial, Shafik was found guilty and executed by hanging in front of his house. Many thousands of Iraqis came to see the hanging of this falsely accused traitor. My parents prohibited us from seeing this barbaric act, but I was a very curious young girl and snuck out of my house. I do not regret this decision but it forever changed my life and I cried at night alone for years. My father's friend hanging in the air with crowds of our Muslim neighbors celebrating his death as though he were a terrible criminal. His Arab business partners were neither called to his defense nor found guilty of the same crime of working with the Zionist enemy. He was killed not for a crime, but simply because he was Jewish.

I never told my parents that I saw Shafik's lifeless body hanging there, but I knew at that moment the world I lived in was not all full of kind people like my parents. There were people who hated others for being different. After the execution, my parent's nightly talks between themselves or with friends were done at a whisper. They would not speak in front of us about the problems. Marcel and I understood our parents were trying to figure out how to leave Iraq. Many Jews from Baghdad escaped from Iraq through Basra as they could quickly get into Iran and from there travel to Israel. Little by little I saw things in our home disappear. I said nothing to my parents. One evening, my parents called us to the living room and told us that our older brothers Reuben and Nissim had left for Israel. We never even said goodbye to them. I cried for days following their departure.

A couple of weeks later in the middle of May 1950 we were told to gather what we could carry and a few hours later we simply left our home. Once again I cried, this time leaving my treasured books and memories behind. My parents could not openly sell the house and reveal that they were leaving the country. They were very worried that my father would be arrested and put in jail or maybe even executed like Shafik. I had been expecting this day to come and already had identified what was most important to me - some photos, my diary, a small collection of glass animals and three books I loved. We left in the dark and I never saw my home again.

The hate, injustice and pain people experienced struck me at a very young age. I always felt a calling to help those in need, those people less fortunate who did not have anyone to advocate for their basic human rights. I shared this with you my sweet Aliza and even though you were young, I knew that you understood and empathized with people who were less fortunate. I took you to the soup kitchen and you were barely old enough to serve food but you warmly smiled and said hello to all the strangers who passed by us as though they were your intimate friends. Hungry dirty human beings who were not afforded the dignity that all humans are entitled to experience. The irony of Shafik being a rich man with many powerful and political connections did not save him nor afford him respect or dignity. He was killed simply because he was a Jewish scapegoat blamed for the many ills other people experienced. I still smile when I think of the times when Shafiq came to our house and brought me and Marcel small pieces of candy: I clearly remember the fateful day he was hanged and executed in the name of hate.

Later in life, this hate ironically made me a believer in the common good of mankind and I made it my goal to search this out and be an agent for it as well

I know you will too my sweet Aliza

MYPOETRY.COM

Family

Brooke G.O.

★ ★ ★

I like you in all your funny ways
A wait so long finally pays
I will never let you go away
Let's learn, laugh, love n play
I found with whom to grow wise n old
You're mine to love n hold

★ ★ ★

♡ 192   240

 JN24:   now
Swastikas painted on synagogue in France are found to be the work of an anit-Semitic youth group centered in Northern Paris neighborhood.
Jewish News You Can Use

Freedom 📩 Inbox ×

👤 **Dahlia** <FreeDahlia@mail.com>   4:30AM ☆ ↰ ▾
to EL ▾

One more thin' Sugah. God created men for two things – sperm n protection. Y' don't need his sperm n you don't need his protection. Y' have money, a brain n talent - all y' need for your life. But y' do need a good lovin' partner in life.

BOKER TOV

Goodman Family!

Welcome to day five of your Holy Land excursion!
Here is today's schedule:

We are off to the Kibbutz!

Today we will depart the hotel at 10am and drive one hour south to the kibbutz for your family reunion. The kibbutzim, communal settlements, were started all over Israel in the beginning of the 20th Century to help settle the desert land and create residential communities where early pioneers and immigrants could work and live. The original formula for a successful kibbutz was a healthy combination of Zionism and socialism; however, in recent years this model society has adapted to be more pluralistic and capitalistic. You will experience the beautiful blend of all these diverse systems at work on the modern kibbutz. Mostly it will feel like a relaxing day in the countryside.

Please bring insect repellent. There will be plenty of cold water on the bus. Our bus will return to the hotel at 5:30pm. Please be in the lobby at 8pm to depart for dinner at the Eucalyptus Restaurant.

Today's Temperature:

 The temperature will be 30˚c / 85˚f and humid

Moshe

Rimon Tours

JN24:   now

92-year-old grandfather became a bar mitzvah in Odessa along side his youngest of 20 grandchildren. This bnei mitzvah brought villagers and Jews from across the region together for a joyful celebration.

Jewish News You Can Use

Andy Orser   •••
Now · Israel

GOY IN THE HOLY LAND PART 2

Fresh Jerusalem early morning air fills my room; I look out from my open window enamored by the illuminating spectacle of the luminous sun rising over the still sleepy Old City. I slowly wake as I drink my first cup of fresh mint tea – green leaves float in the glass cup. My still slumbering eyes widen as the ancient, story filled walls warm with intense light and a wave of brilliant excitement invites me to embark on exploration of the ancient sites and stories first hand. The mystical city streets below are still quiet but will soon wake to locals preparing for Shabbat. A great sense of serenity saturates this ancient holy city known for bloody turmoil. I am jubilant and grateful for the magical journey I have commenced.

Dear Friends, for those of you who feared for me traveling to this part of the world, I could only say that the Holy Land feels calm and healthy: I do not feel hate and there are no sirens or bombs exploding. #Israel #Holylandtravel #amazingJerusalem #Shalom

👍 Like   💬 Comment   ↗ Share

📶 cellcom   7:00 AM   100% 🔋

Israel Family Group

‹   EL, Kate, Andy, Teddy, Aliza, Brooke,…

EL
Hi Everyone! I'm so happy we are here together to celebrate Aliza's bat mitzvah. I want to give a little background on my Israeli family before we go to visit them on the kibbutz today. Aunt Marcel is my mom's twin sister. Her husband died many years ago + she never remarried.

+ (   ) 📷 🎤

Israel Family Group

EL, Kate, Andy, Teddy, Aliza, Brooke,...

EL

Aunt Marcel is a successful painter; her paintings have sold in Israeli galleries over the years + she is a well-respected artist in this small country. Today you will meet 2 of her 3 children: Raffi who is a pharmacist + lives near Tel Aviv with his wife Iris + three kids; and Miri who still lives on the kibbutz with her husband Nimrod. Miri's three kids are all grown + have moved away. Rinat who is my baby cousin lives in the West Bank with her husband + seven children. Yes, I wrote seven! Her eldest is twelve years old. Rinat does not visit the kibbutz as she cannot eat or drink in her mother's non-kosher kibbutz house. She + her husband Gilad will not come to the bat mitzvah because they believe that it is blasphemy for a girl to read from the Torah or even have a religious bat mitzvah ceremony. We do not speak about Rinat as it makes Aunt Marcel cry.

EL

One more thing.

My cousin Raffi asked me to tell you about his youngest son Noam who will be with us today. While he is a bit different, we should treat him like everyone else apart from touching him. He does not like to be touched.

Aliza

Why can't you just say he is autistic? Is this a bad word?

EL

My bad. Naom is autistic + does not like to be touched. Other than this please treat him the same as the others.

Aliza

Maybe I should not have a bat mitzvah if it is blasphemy? Rinat is religious & may have a better relationship w God? Does she know something we don't?

Israel Family Group

EL, Kate, Andy, Teddy, Aliza, Brooke,...

<

EL
I think God is more tolerant than Rinat + respects all forms of religious belief.

Aliza
Please send proof that God exists & I will accept your answer

Teddy
Yes EL please send us your proof of God's existence this would be greatly appreciated.

Kate
We are so happy to be here with you all! Thank you. Sending all our love.

EL
We are very happy too! See you soon. In the meantime, I will look for God and bring my children happiness.

Aliza
Let me know when u find her

Teddy
Try googling 'God'!

EL
Thank you for your 17-year-old expert advice. I am quite familiar with Professor Google. You have proven to be quite a computer wiz Tricky Teddy. Maybe you have some special relationship with God that you have been hiding as well? Please feel free to share with us all!

Lucas
Haha Tricky Teddy she got you! Mom you should call him Lucky Leonardo – get it? Leonardo Da Vinci Award. Funny right? LMAO

+

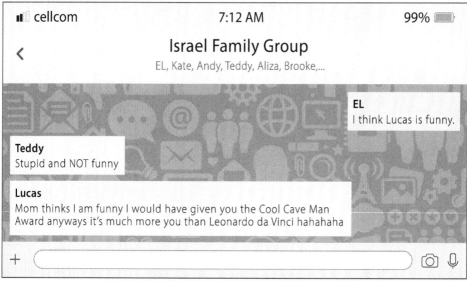

cellcom   7:12 AM   99%

Israel Family Group
EL, Kate, Andy, Teddy, Aliza, Brooke,...

EL
I think Lucas is funny.

Teddy
Stupid and NOT funny

Lucas
Mom thinks I am funny I would have given you the Cool Cave Man Award anyways it's much more you than Leonardo da Vinci hahahaha

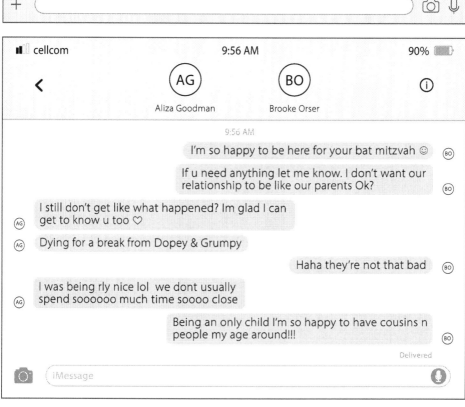

cellcom   9:56 AM   90%

AG   BO
Aliza Goodman   Brooke Orser

9:56 AM

I'm so happy to be here for your bat mitzvah ☺

If u need anything let me know. I don't want our relationship to be like our parents Ok?

I still don't get like what happened? Im glad I can get to know u too ♡

Dying for a break from Dopey & Grumpy

Haha they're not that bad

I was being rly nice lol we dont usually spend soooooo much time soooo close

Being an only child I'm so happy to have cousins n people my age around!!!

Delivered

iMessage

94

AG
Aliza Goodman

BO
Brooke Orser

9:57 AM

Have U been to the kibbutz where we're going???

when I was little we visited the kibbutz and met Grama Shula's twin sister Aunt Marcel. She freaked me out and I cried cuz she looked exactly like my grandmother but she was fatter and only spoke Hebrew. I remember it was creepy

lol what's it like on a kibbutz???

like a big farm I remember there were lots of cakes nuts and watermelon on the table. I remember cows & chickens & swimming in a large pool w lots of kids who only spoke Hebrew they wanted to play w me & I didn't understand a word of what they said

EL always tells me stories from her summers on the kibbutz & how spending time on the kibbutz shaped her her first boyfriend was from the kibbutz but she doesnt talk about him much.

how do U know about him then???

I discovered love letters he wrote to her & when I asked her about them she blushed & told me a little she made it seem rly small, but from her red face & secret smile I knew there was more than what she shared w me

does he still live there???

not sure? like to find out

wow!!! love letters real old fashioned hand written notes like in the movies now everything is made public immediately on a screen - nothing personal about romance like in the old days

but in the movies it ends happy & I don't think it is for EL

happy endings are for the movies not real life. How come you guys call your parents by their first names?

Teddy called them by their first names when he was a baby & I just followed him it always seemed funny but natural w them they are just EL & Benj not mom & dad

☺

iMessage

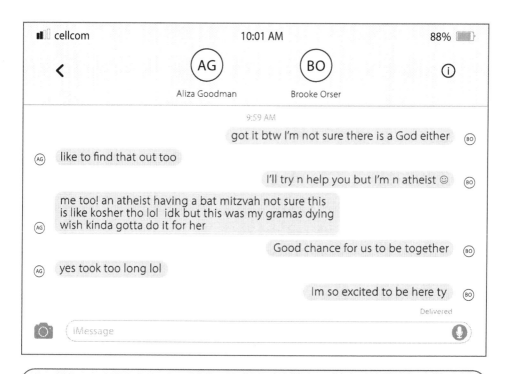

Aliza Goodman's Daily Motivational Quote #1:   now

"I refuse to accept the view that mankind is so tragically bound to the starless midnight of racism and war that the bright daybreak of peace and brotherhood can never become a reality... I believe that unarmed truth and unconditional love will have the final word."
Martin Luther King, Jr.

MotiQuote.com

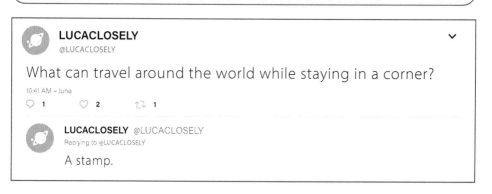

LUCACLOSELY   ∨
@LUCACLOSELY

What can travel around the world while staying in a corner?

10:41 AM – June

💬 1   ♡ 2   ⟲ 1

LUCACLOSELY @LUCACLOSELY
Replying to @LUCACLOSELY

A stamp.

Andy Orser

Now · Israel

GOY IN THE HOLY LAND PART 3

Today I am visiting relatives who live on a beautiful kibbutz. I have read extensively on the grit and guts of kibbutzes: communal farming communities established all over Israel to populate and develop the harsh desert lands of the nascent nation. What an ideal egalitarian way to live surrounded by close family and dear friends, fresh green grass and clean air, birds singing and dogs barking, and cows grazing and children running free. Small, simple, uniform houses: no signs of the modern world I recognize where people incessantly race for bigger, better and more. The natural, calm and collective community accents the chasm of the big cities' quality of life where congestion, snarling traffic and character anonymity identify one's existence.

Dear Friends, I feel an abundance of refreshing joy; I do not feel hate and there are no sirens or bombs exploding. #Israel #HolylandTravel #kibbutzlife

    👍 Like   💬 Comment   ↪ Share

Kibbutz

EL <ELGood@mail.com>   12:01PM
to Shirl

At the kibbutz.

Nothing has changed + at the same time everything seems different: Aunt Marcel still lives in the same little house where I stayed all those summers; she has gotten old + is quite large, but she still has the delightful sparkle in her sky-blue eyes just like Mom had. Funny to think mom stayed so fit in her city life + her sister on the kibbutz got so fat. Everything about the kibbutz seems so small today except for Aunt Marcel. Haha. She is also still painting incredibly fine impressionist vistas of the kibbutz (she's an Israeli Monet!) + her hands are just as I remember with specks of paint like colored freckles all over them that haven't washed out.

Returning to the kibbutz reminds me of all the summers I spent running around free with my cousins + Hezzi. My summers here were the closest I ever got to the fancy summer camps you + all the other kids loved. I was so jealous each summer when you left me + my father told me that summer camps were for fake Jews + goyim. Haha. Finally, when I was 13, they sent me to the kibbutz for the summer + I still felt I was missing out.

Returning here makes me realize all I had back then - shit it took so long for this appreciation.

I'm so slow!

Ugh!

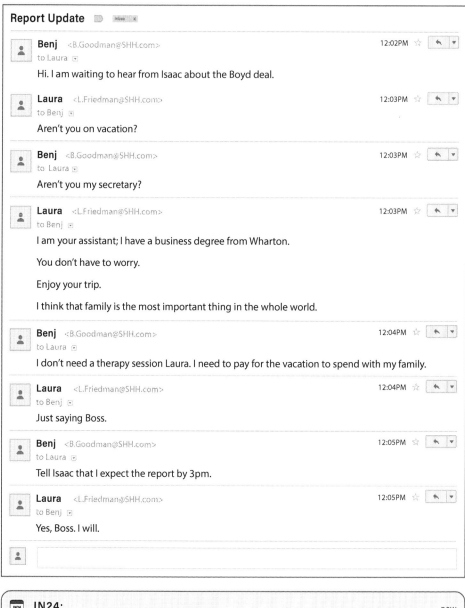

Report Update 📩 inbox x

👤	**Benj** <B.Goodman@SHH.com> to Laura ▾	12:02PM ☆ ↰ ▾
	Hi. I am waiting to hear from Isaac about the Boyd deal.	

👤	**Laura** <L.Friedman@SHH.com> to Benj ▾	12:03PM ☆ ↰ ▾
	Aren't you on vacation?	

👤	**Benj** <B.Goodman@SHH.com> to Laura ▾	12:03PM ☆ ↰ ▾
	Aren't you my secretary?	

👤	**Laura** <L.Friedman@SHH.com> to Benj ▾	12:03PM ☆ ↰ ▾
	I am your assistant; I have a business degree from Wharton.	
	You don't have to worry.	
	Enjoy your trip.	
	I think that family is the most important thing in the whole world.	

👤	**Benj** <B.Goodman@SHH.com> to Laura ▾	12:04PM ☆ ↰ ▾
	I don't need a therapy session Laura. I need to pay for the vacation to spend with my family.	

👤	**Laura** <L.Friedman@SHH.com> to Benj ▾	12:04PM ☆ ↰ ▾
	Just saying Boss.	

👤	**Benj** <B.Goodman@SHH.com> to Laura ▾	12:05PM ☆ ↰ ▾
	Tell Isaac that I expect the report by 3pm.	

👤	**Laura** <L.Friedman@SHH.com> to Benj ▾	12:05PM ☆ ↰ ▾
	Yes, Boss. I will.	

👤

JN24:   now

Four yeshiva students attack Arab store owner on outskirts of Jerusalem.
Jewish News You Can Use

Kibbutz

Brooke G.O.

Fear invades my deepest thread
Jets roar overhead
Danger believing all is fair
A hateful rainbow fills the air

Where Im going, anyone's bet
Far from my safety blanket

Love and kindness all too rare
A life where people share
Engaged in games of trust to play
What their neighbors feel each day

Far from my comfort room
Vulnerable in a foreign womb

Had lost my way
Till stumbled on a new breadth today
A strange pattern yes
Where I'm going is anyone's guess

♡ 202　　　　　　　　　　　　600 ◉

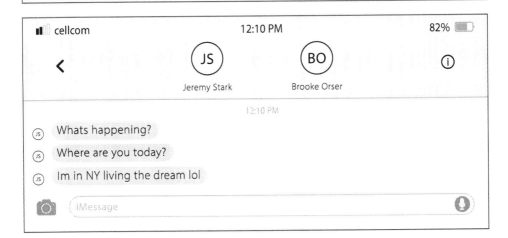

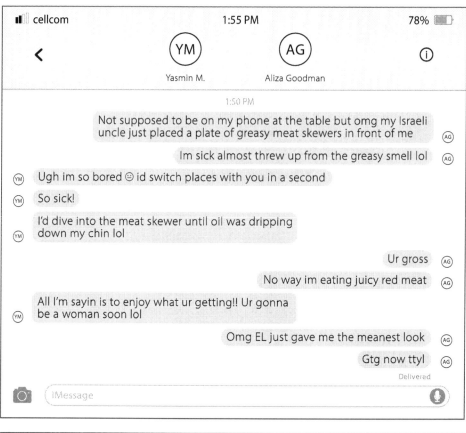

cellcom   1:55 PM   78%

YM   **AG**

Yasmin M.   Aliza Goodman

1:50 PM

Not supposed to be on my phone at the table but omg my Israeli uncle just placed a plate of greasy meat skewers in front of me

Im sick almost threw up from the greasy smell lol

Ugh im so bored ☺ id switch places with you in a second

So sick!

I'd dive into the meat skewer until oil was dripping down my chin lol

Ur gross

No way im eating juicy red meat

All I'm sayin is to enjoy what ur getting!! Ur gonna be a woman soon lol

Omg EL just gave me the meanest look

Gtg now ttyl

Delivered

iMessage

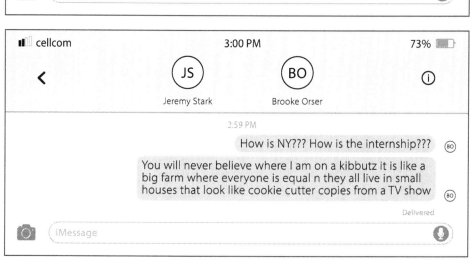

cellcom   3:00 PM   73%

JS   **BO**

Jeremy Stark   Brooke Orser

2:59 PM

How is NY??? How is the internship???

You will never believe where I am on a kibbutz it is like a big farm where everyone is equal n they all live in small houses that look like cookie cutter copies from a TV show

Delivered

iMessage

3:00 PM

"Love this fresh air," dad kept saying until there was a breeze carrying the scent of cow shit that hit us n mom mimicked him n said, "Love this fresh air!" We all laughed. Even dad!!! Then he said, "Love the peace n quiet of the kibbutz" n a few minutes later, a team of fighter jets flew overhead in the blue skies with such a roar that we had to wait for them to pass before we could speak again they told us that there is a secret military base near by n this terrible noise is a common occurrence. Not sure how secret it can be with all the intense noise the fighter jets make??? Not sure if I should feel safe or be scared???

I had lunch with this very cool girl Tomer who is 18 n just finished her basic training for the army n she learned to shoot an M16 gun she is Teddy's cousin

In Israel, all the 18-year-olds go in the army for a few years before they g2 college she has a job in the army in a special intelligence division where she works on classified information n is sworn to secrecy so cool!!! She plans to go to college only after her service in the army n get this - between the army n college she will go to India for 6 months with a backpack n friends. She told me that all the young people travel after the army if I told my parents that I was joining the army traveling the world with a backpack n then going to college they would freak. Kate n Andy my liberal 'hang loose' parents would never go for this!!!

My cousin Teddy is cool too but a bit shy at least I'm happy to have young people to hang out with here I was sure I'd be partnered with Grama Rose the whole time don't get me wrong– I LOVE Grama Rose n I know she's paying for this trip but I'm relieved to have people my age

Oh n my evil Uncle Benj has said a total of 10 words to me since we met!!! I think he's said 5 words to mom so I'm ahead of the game it's a bit creepy he's worse than teenagers with his Blackberry obsession not sure if he is antisocial or just busy working but he's not here – not part of the group!

Aunt EL seems really nice

Delivered

iMessage

3:05 PM

She gave me a necklace with a hamsa to ward off evil aka suicide bombers I will not take it off!! ☺ I sat on the bus coming here with Aliza she is super smart n super sweet says she's also an atheist! I know we will be friends soon I could use a little sister n I'm sure she could use a break from being sandwiched in between two brothers (BO)

Ok more later I miss you! I love you Xxx Brooke ☻ (BO)

Standing in line at Starbucks with a list of coffee drinks for the office. Very glamourous internship I have here they have me filing papers (yes, there are still papers passing around this office), buying coffees (fun and challenging work); picked up my boss' dry cleaning (and his daughter's personalized ballet slippers too), and my favorite, I took the office's town car across the city to buy a special suppository for my boss' shitzu named Saki. I do sit in meetings and theyre very interesting so I bite my tongue with the rest of the bullshit. I think this is what they call "Paying my dues?" (JS)

Your trip sounds great I'm a bit envious but so happy that you get this adventure and get to know your estranged family I'm not sure I would want to go to the army before college – I can't wait to start my studies at Columbia in the fall but I'm sure they have a lot to do to protect their country from all the enemies that surround them (JS)

I would go to India with you for 6 months...I have no idea how we could afford this but I know there is no one I would rather eat Naan and Raita with over looking the Taj Mahal than you! (JS)

Keep writing to me I'll have plenty of free time standing in lines and you'll keep me occupied with your stories (JS)

I know we agreed that I had to start a new life in New York and I'm trying but Brooke I still think of you all the time and miss you. xJ (JS)

Miss you too J!!! Love you (BO)

Delivered

📷 (iMessage) 🎤

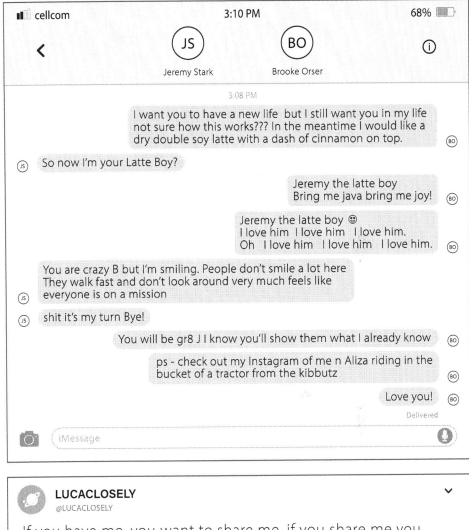

3:08 PM

> I want you to have a new life but I still want you in my life not sure how this works??? In the meantime I would like a dry double soy latte with a dash of cinnamon on top.

So now I'm your Latte Boy?

> Jeremy the latte boy
> Bring me java bring me joy!

> Jeremy the latte boy 😊
> I love him I love him   I love him.
> Oh I love him   I love him   I love him.

You are crazy B but I'm smiling. People don't smile a lot here They walk fast and don't look around very much feels like everyone is on a mission

shit it's my turn Bye!

> You will be gr8 J I know you'll show them what I already know

> ps - check out my Instagram of me n Aliza riding in the bucket of a tractor from the kibbutz

> Love you!

Delivered

iMessage

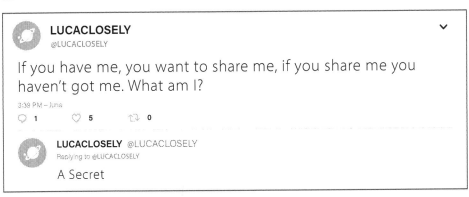

LUCACLOSELY
@LUCACLOSELY

If you have me, you want to share me, if you share me you haven't got me. What am I?

3:39 PM – June

♡ 1   ♡ 5   ↻ 0

LUCACLOSELY @LUCACLOSELY
Replying to @LUCACLOSELY

A Secret

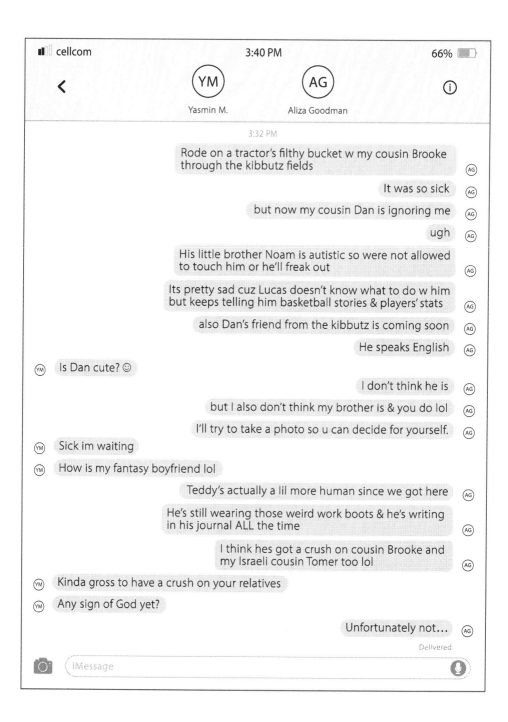

Andy Orser
Now · Israel

GOY IN THE HOLY LAND PART 4

Can't imagine living on a more divine piece of land where all mortals are equal and life is not based on a combination of "Keeping up with the Joneses" and Darwin's "Survival of the Fittest." This is an authentic utopia where you can live faithfully and enjoy the valuable quality of life without having to worry about where the next meal is coming from or knowing your kids are safe to roam around by themselves. Feeling a part of a loving, treasured community, I have experienced this incredible light from the moment we arrived at the kibbutz. This returns me to the simple days of Ollie Haskell's Summer Camp circa 1972 where I was free to explore, create, and dream - all in the framework of a safe and loving community.

I just had the best meditation in the middle of a watermelon field.

Dear Friends, I am feeling so much love on this adventure. #Kibbutz #heavenlyplaceonearth #newjourney #Israeltravels

   △ Like   💬 Comment   ↗ Share

LIFEEXPRESSIONS.COM

JN24:   now

Terror attack at Jaffa Port shortly after two attacks by the Southern Tel Aviv bus station: eight injured and no reported fatalities.

Jewish News You Can Use

Dear Lucas Goodman, Astronaut in Training –

@JUNIORNASAUSA

| Crew | About | Photos |

TODAY ON THE INTERNATIONAL SPACE STATION:

Every day on the International Space Station (@ISS), astronauts conduct amazing experiments in biology, physics, astronomy and meteorology and take many beautiful pictures of earth. Today we captured in broad daylight the impressive and majestic snow capped Himalayas in Nepal. The Himalayas have 14 peaks over 26,000 feet tall and over 100 peaks that are over 20,000 feet tall. The Himalaya Range is not only the tallest, but also the youngest mountain range created by a continental collision between the Indian and Eurasian tectonic plates approximately 70 million years ago. The Himalayas continue to grow 5 mm per year due to the great amount of tectonic movement experienced daily.

On this clear and crispy day, we also see three other powerful and very large countries: India, Pakistan and China that surround the proud Himalayas and our incredible view from space look very close indeed.

 JN24:   now

Palestinian Authority has reduced incitement on its official media outlet, working with local personnel to ease confrontation with the IDF.

Jewish News You Can Use

Aliza Goodman's Daily Motivational Quote #2:   now

"Fight for the things that you care about, but do it in a way that will lead others to join you."   Ruth Bader Ginsburg

MotiQuote.com

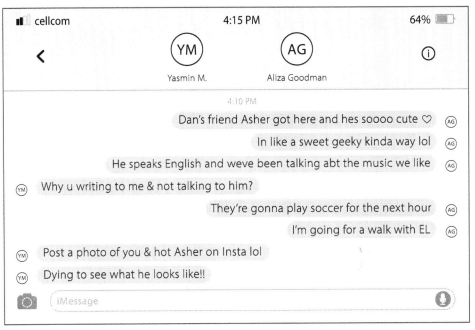

cellcom   4:15 PM   64%

(YM) Yasmin M.   (AG) Aliza Goodman

4:10 PM

Dan's friend Asher got here and hes soooo cute ♡ (AG)

In like a sweet geeky kinda way lol (AG)

He speaks English and weve been talking abt the music we like (AG)

(YM) Why u writing to me & not talking to him?

They're gonna play soccer for the next hour (AG)

I'm going for a walk with EL (AG)

(YM) Post a photo of you & hot Asher on Insta lol

(YM) Dying to see what he looks like!!

iMessage

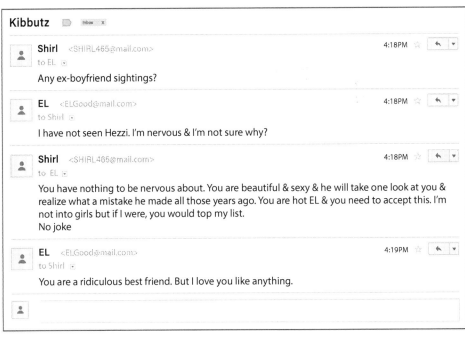

Kibbutz   Inbox x

Shirl <SHIRL465@mail.com>   4:18PM
to EL

Any ex-boyfriend sightings?

EL <ELGood@mail.com>   4:18PM
to Shirl

I have not seen Hezzi. I'm nervous & I'm not sure why?

Shirl <SHIRL465@mail.com>   4:18PM
to EL

You have nothing to be nervous about. You are beautiful & sexy & he will take one look at you & realize what a mistake he made all those years ago. You are hot EL & you need to accept this. I'm not into girls but if I were, you would top my list.
No joke

EL <ELGood@mail.com>   4:19PM
to Shirl

You are a ridiculous best friend. But I love you like anything.

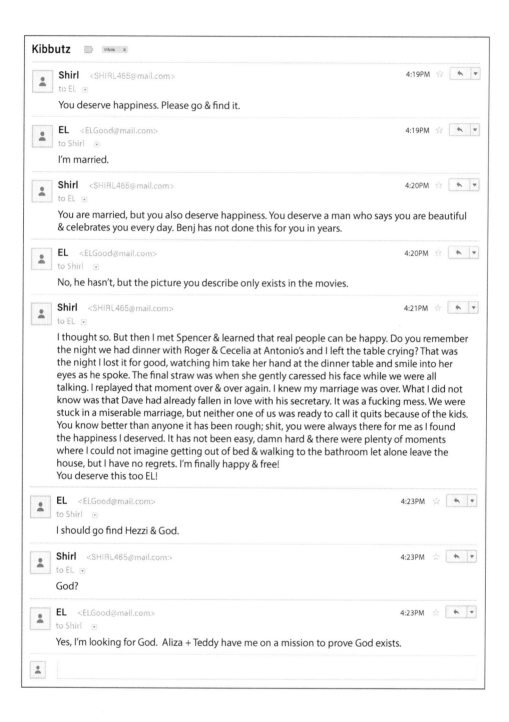

Shirl <SHIRL465@mail.com> 4:19PM
to EL

You deserve happiness. Please go & find it.

EL <ELGood@mail.com> 4:19PM
to Shirl

I'm married.

Shirl <SHIRL465@mail.com> 4:20PM
to EL

You are married, but you also deserve happiness. You deserve a man who says you are beautiful & celebrates you every day. Benj has not done this for you in years.

EL <ELGood@mail.com> 4:20PM
to Shirl

No, he hasn't, but the picture you describe only exists in the movies.

Shirl <SHIRL465@mail.com> 4:21PM
to EL

I thought so. But then I met Spencer & learned that real people can be happy. Do you remember the night we had dinner with Roger & Cecelia at Antonio's and I left the table crying? That was the night I lost it for good, watching him take her hand at the dinner table and smile into her eyes as he spoke. The final straw was when she gently caressed his face while we were all talking. I replayed that moment over & over again. I knew my marriage was over. What I did not know was that Dave had already fallen in love with his secretary. It was a fucking mess. We were stuck in a miserable marriage, but neither one of us was ready to call it quits because of the kids. You know better than anyone it has been rough; shit, you were always there for me as I found the happiness I deserved. It has not been easy, damn hard & there were plenty of moments where I could not imagine getting out of bed & walking to the bathroom let alone leave the house, but I have no regrets. I'm finally happy & free!
You deserve this too EL!

EL <ELGood@mail.com> 4:23PM
to Shirl

I should go find Hezzi & God.

Shirl <SHIRL465@mail.com> 4:23PM
to EL

God?

EL <ELGood@mail.com> 4:23PM
to Shirl

Yes, I'm looking for God. Aliza + Teddy have me on a mission to prove God exists.

Debating Parents
Teddy Goodman

We are on a kibbutz in the middle of Israel. Originally the kibbutz was a socialist paradise, but this one appears to have become a Mecca of capitalism and the political atmosphere at the table is very lefty liberal. My father, Benj, does not pick up on this or just does not give a fuck and has joined in the table conversation to declare his paradoxical support for the Israeli government's continuing policy of settlement expansion. He does not trust nor believe that the Palestinians are going to ever make peace. He lectures us all on how the Israeli pullout of Gaza did not make peace with the Palestinians but instead resulted in thousands of rockets being sent into Israel and subsequent wars. The Palestinians are no angels, but neither are the Israelis. The settlements that the Israeli Right continues building are just 'fuck you' messages to the Palestinians and perpetuate hate and distrust.

And shit, EL is forever foolish and jumps in to dilute her crazy husband and comes to the rescue of her kibbutz family: she suggests that we have no right to comment, not being Israelis and not living with this terribly difficult situation daily. I think this is her way of apologizing to her Israeli relatives at the table, but mostly preventing World War 3 with her asshole husband: I know that EL agrees with me that the Palestinians need to run their own country and live their own independent lives. EL generally drinks the liberal MSNBC news bullshit Kool-Aid and is basically in a constant state of opposition with right wing, revisionist, Fox News watching Benj - another layer in their fucked up discourse that we are abused by daily. My parents are like the battling Jews and Palestinians - there is no end to the violence in sight.

When we arrived at the kibbutz, EL looked so happy and now she looks hurt. Benj walks away in a state of disgust clutching his Blackberry. Just another round in the EPW - Eternal Parental War.

Aliza Goodman's Daily Motivational Quote #3:   *now*

"Peace is not absence of conflict, it is the ability to handle conflict by peaceful means."
President Ronald Reagan

MotiQuote.com

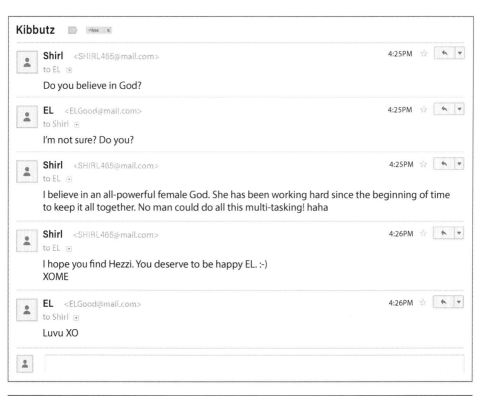

Kibbutz

Shirl <SHIRL465@mail.com>	4:25PM	
to EL		
Do you believe in God?		

EL <ELGood@mail.com>	4:25PM	
to Shirl		
I'm not sure? Do you?		

Shirl <SHIRL465@mail.com>	4:25PM	
to EL		
I believe in an all-powerful female God. She has been working hard since the beginning of time to keep it all together. No man could do all this multi-tasking! haha		

Shirl <SHIRL465@mail.com>	4:26PM	
to EL		
I hope you find Hezzi. You deserve to be happy EL. :-) XOME		

EL <ELGood@mail.com>	4:26PM	
to Shirl		
Luvu XO		

Andy Orser

Now · Israel

GOY IN THE HOLY LAND PART 5

Just encountered two graceful peacocks proudly roaming the tranquil kibbutz with their plumage, spotted with iridescent green-blue powerful eyes, wide open like a royal fan. No peahens in sight, just the dominant, picturesque male peacocks. A group of young boys with World Cup enthusiasm play soccer on the rundown dirt field and elder white haired residents slowly pass by on their electric golf carts in no apparent rush to go anywhere. Everyone I have met here is warm and friendly; they all speak English. I feel as though I have returned to a time when simplicity was valued and the pace of life was gentle. It feels like Little House on the Prairie meets The Andy Griffith Show in the Middle East where everyone is Jewish.

Dear Friends, I see no fighting and feel no hate. Why doesn't CNN cover this? #noconflict #kibbutz #heavenonearth #holylandadventure

👍 Like   💬 Comment   ↗ Share

No Going Back   Inbox X

Ethan <RoamingRoman@mail.com>   4:30PM
to Teddy

I arrive tomorrow evening. Will text when I get to the hotel & see where you all are. How's the trip so far? How is Aliza? Your mom? Strangely exciting this whole thing. Long over due.

Teddy <GoodTeddy@mail.com>   4:32PM
to Ethan

See you tomorrow. It will be interesting! Hope no one ends up in the hospital.

Ethan <RoamingRoman@mail.com>   4:33PM
to Teddy

Hospital? Why so dramatic?

Teddy <GoodTeddy@mail.com>   4:33PM
to Ethan

You do not know my mother.

Ethan <RoamingRoman@mail.com>   4:33PM
to Teddy

I wish I did.

Teddy <GoodTeddy@mail.com>   4:34PM
to Ethan

Soon you will.
There will be no going back.

Ethan <RoamingRoman@mail.com>   4:34PM
to Teddy

I can't wait to get there.

Aliza Goodman's Daily Motivational Quote #4:   now

"I know nothing with any certainty but the sight of the stars makes me dream."
Vincent van Gogh

MotiQuote.com

JN24:   now

Hamas operatives arrested near Ramallah after increase in stabbings.
Jewish News You Can Use

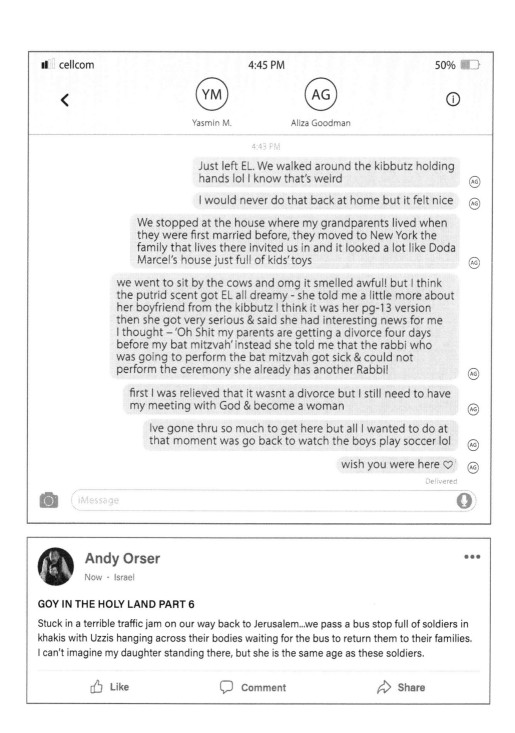

Andy Orser
Now · Israel

GOY IN THE HOLY LAND PART 6

Stuck in a terrible traffic jam on our way back to Jerusalem...we pass a bus stop full of soldiers in khakis with Uzzis hanging across their bodies waiting for the bus to return them to their families. I can't imagine my daughter standing there, but she is the same age as these soldiers.

👍 Like   💬 Comment   ↪ Share

FOOD AFFAIR WITH KATE

Love at First Sight

★ ★ ★ ★ ★

A toasty afternoon lounging on an unmowed, weed filled kibbutz lawn – the feeling of a summer romance novel envelops the small picnic lunch. I have fallen hard for the Israeli cuisine so hospitably introduced to me; my palate pleasantly welcomes flavors I am eager to engage and enjoy. The air is fresh and the food delightful and plentiful; surrounded by the people I love the most in this world creates an ideal setting to live out my delicious love affair with Israeli cuisine. Seventy years ago, a youthful nation, and a barren desert welcomed persecuted Diaspora Jews to its shores and now a rich, bountiful oasis entices and encourages hungry travelers with a warm invitation.

An array of tantalizing foods tease my appetite: floral trimmed plates piled high with chopped vegetables, tart eggplants, sweet beets, bitter couscous, bright corn and peppers, powerfully pickled cucumbers, soft creamy hummus and doughy pita, and Israeli chopped salad with cucumbers, tomatoes, a bit of parsley gently flavored with olive oil, a sprig of lemon, snowwhite flaky sea salt and topped with robust pomegranate seeds. I have never relished a chopped salad this mouth watering. The irresistible salad's simple produce originates from the kibbutz' organic garden (picked this morning) and robust olive oil (straight from a nearby Arab-Israeli village) and tart lemon (fresh from the tree) dressed with a dash of sea salt; and all ingredients are lightly tossed at the final moment before serving. Many Israelis add onions, but the perfect blend of fragrant cucumbers and vine ripe tomatoes needs little support to serenade its simple genius. No need to travel to the Holy Land to take pleasure in this treat, you can create this divine salad easily in your home after visiting your own vegetable garden or farmer's market.

See the photos below and check out Food Affair with Kate on Instagram and Facebook. #Kibbutzcuisine #loveatfirstbite #heavenlyhummus #choppedsaladlover

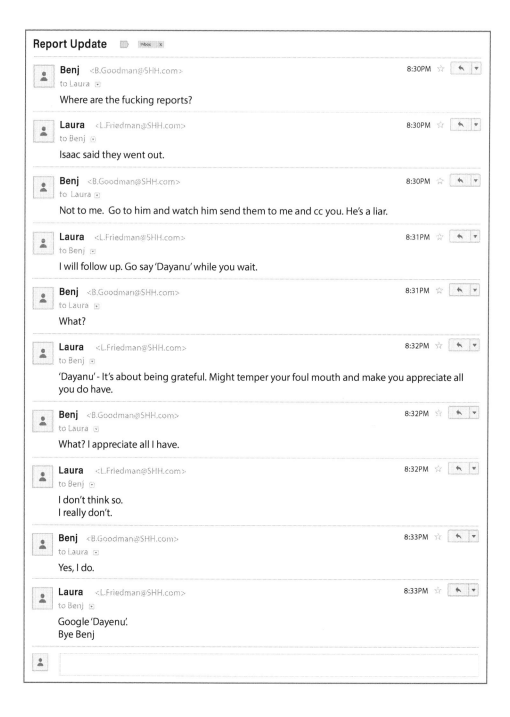

Report Update

Benj <B.Goodman@SHH.com>   8:30PM
to Laura
Where are the fucking reports?

Laura <L.Friedman@SHH.com>   8:30PM
to Benj
Isaac said they went out.

Benj <B.Goodman@SHH.com>   8:30PM
to Laura
Not to me. Go to him and watch him send them to me and cc you. He's a liar.

Laura <L.Friedman@SHH.com>   8:31PM
to Benj
I will follow up. Go say 'Dayanu' while you wait.

Benj <B.Goodman@SHH.com>   8:31PM
to Laura
What?

Laura <L.Friedman@SHH.com>   8:32PM
to Benj
'Dayanu' - It's about being grateful. Might temper your foul mouth and make you appreciate all you do have.

Benj <B.Goodman@SHH.com>   8:32PM
to Laura
What? I appreciate all I have.

Laura <L.Friedman@SHH.com>   8:32PM
to Benj
I don't think so.
I really don't.

Benj <B.Goodman@SHH.com>   8:33PM
to Laura
Yes, I do.

Laura <L.Friedman@SHH.com>   8:33PM
to Benj
Google 'Dayenu'.
Bye Benj

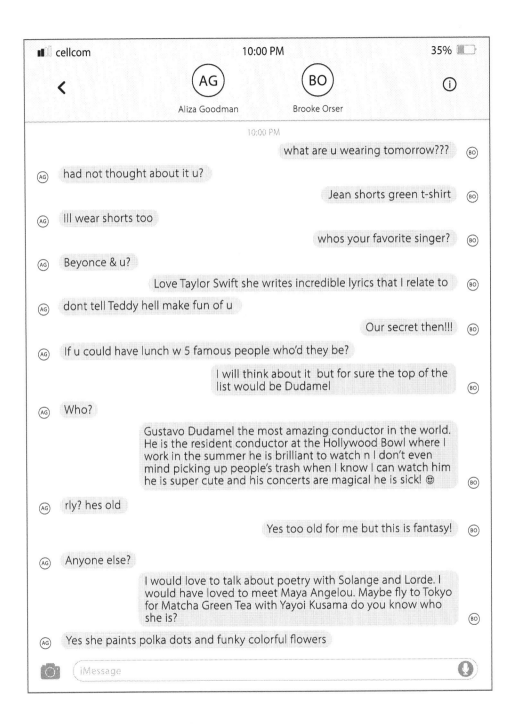

AG Aliza Goodman   **BO** Brooke Orser

10:00 PM

what are u wearing tomorrow??? (BO)

(AG) had not thought about it u?

Jean shorts green t-shirt (BO)

(AG) Ill wear shorts too

whos your favorite singer? (BO)

(AG) Beyonce & u?

Love Taylor Swift she writes incredible lyrics that I relate to (BO)

(AG) dont tell Teddy hell make fun of u

Our secret then!!! (BO)

(AG) If u could have lunch w 5 famous people who'd they be?

I will think about it but for sure the top of the list would be Dudamel (BO)

(AG) Who?

Gustavo Dudamel the most amazing conductor in the world. He is the resident conductor at the Hollywood Bowl where I work in the summer he is brilliant to watch n I don't even mind picking up people's trash when I know I can watch him he is super cute and his concerts are magical he is sick! 😊 (BO)

(AG) rly? hes old

Yes too old for me but this is fantasy! (BO)

(AG) Anyone else?

I would love to talk about poetry with Solange and Lorde. I would have loved to meet Maya Angelou. Maybe fly to Tokyo for Matcha Green Tea with Yayoi Kusama do you know who she is? (BO)

(AG) Yes she paints polka dots and funky colorful flowers

iMessage

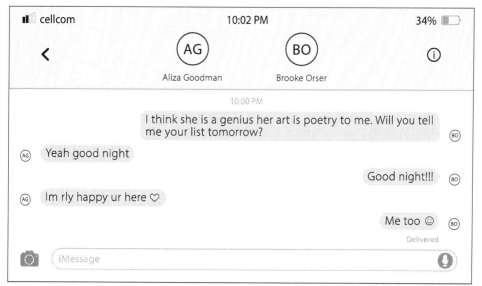

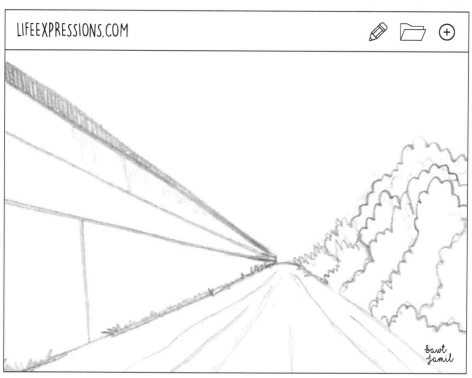

HM — Hezzi Mandel   **EG** — EL Goodman

10:40 PM

> It was great to see you today

> Many questions circling in my head from the last time we were together on the kibbutz. I felt young, once again, next to you.

We are young. We still kiss like teenagers.

> We are not teenagers. Two grown adults kissing each other + holding hands, but married to other people. It was wrong.

It was still nice EL.

> I was happy to kiss you. I cannot lie. But I feel guilty.

Guilty about kissing me?

> No, guilty that I don't feel guilty about kissing you.

EL, I'm sorry I hurt you all those years ago. I was terrible. Really terrible. I have thought about what I did to you so many times and have not been able to forgive myself.

> Why didn't you call me that last summer while I waited on the kibbutz for you? Hello. You need to answer me.

I made a decision that was not easy. And I am not sure it was correct.

> What decision?

I chose my country over you.

> Huh?

I was romanced by my vital role in Israel's security. I was young and believed my country needed all of me. I knew I could not have both of you. It would not be fair to you.

> So, you dumped me for your country?

I know you cannot understand this decision.

> I guess it's better than for another woman. Haha

Delivered

iMessage

117

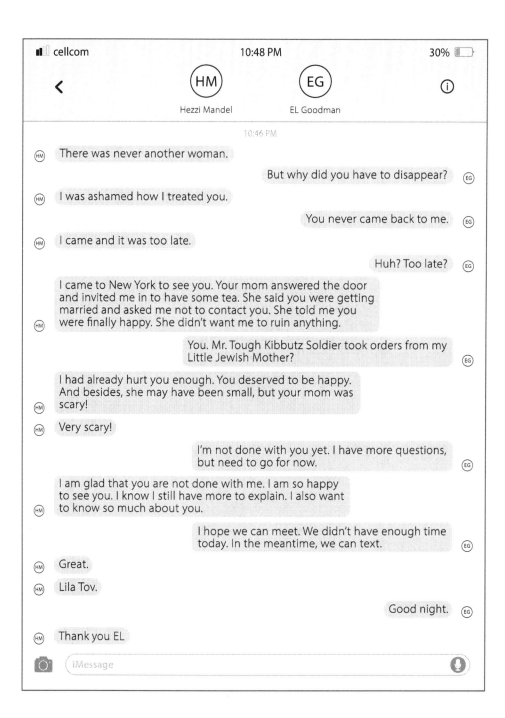

(HM) Hezzi Mandel   (EG) EL Goodman

10:46 PM

(HM) There was never another woman.

But why did you have to disappear? (EG)

(HM) I was ashamed how I treated you.

You never came back to me. (EG)

(HM) I came and it was too late.

Huh? Too late? (EG)

(HM) I came to New York to see you. Your mom answered the door and invited me in to have some tea. She said you were getting married and asked me not to contact you. She told me you were finally happy. She didn't want me to ruin anything.

You. Mr. Tough Kibbutz Soldier took orders from my Little Jewish Mother? (EG)

(HM) I had already hurt you enough. You deserved to be happy. And besides, she may have been small, but your mom was scary!

(HM) Very scary!

I'm not done with you yet. I have more questions, but need to go for now. (EG)

(HM) I am glad that you are not done with me. I am so happy to see you. I know I still have more to explain. I also want to know so much about you.

I hope we can meet. We didn't have enough time today. In the meantime, we can text. (EG)

(HM) Great.

(HM) Lila Tov.

Good night. (EG)

(HM) Thank you EL

iMessage 🎤

Dearest Aliza,

Safta Shula's LOVE. After we arrived in Israel, we lived in a large tent camp set up on sand dunes near Hadera. We were shocked to move from a comfortable city house to a barren tent in the middle of nowhere. There were many other Iraqi immigrant children to play with and this made the days pass nicely. We were also reunited with our wonderful brothers. The nights were terribly difficult as we all slept together: four children, two parents and four grandparents all in one tent. We closely shared a lot of snoring and bad dreams. What little food we had was cooked on a small pot over an open fire. Interestingly, while it was terribly hard, the love our family shared was enough to bond us and keep us positive. I could see from my parents' faces that they were worried but when we all sat together and ate our meals, we laughed and talked as one tightly bound family.

After 6 months, we moved to the kibbutz. My brothers Nissim and Reuben enlisted in the IDF and did not come home very often. Nissim was killed one night while guarding an outpost surrounded by Arab villages. His death almost tore our family apart. Nissim was the person who always made jokes and gave the warmest hugs. He would tease me and just when I was very angry he could make me laugh so hard that I peed in my pants. Mother used to get so mad at him as she had to wash my pants! After Nissim died, no one laughed for a long time. Reuben was a wonderful older brother with a very serious character. After the army, he studied engineering in the Technion and helped build bridges and roads, but never built a family. Reuben died of cancer when he was 50. Both of my grandfathers died of broken hearts within 5 years of arriving in Israel. They were so sad to leave their Iraqi homeland and never felt at home living in Israel and speaking Hebrew. They had small jobs on the kibbutz but never made a living again or felt valued in Israel. My grandmothers were the pioneers of their families; they arrived at the kibbutz and worked very hard in the kibbutz' dining hall. Quite the opposite, back in Basra, the women stayed home and the men went to work. My beautiful grandmothers lived together for a long time like two old maids in a small kibbutz house. Many afternoons, Marcel and I would undoubtedly wind up at their home looking for cookies and conversation. While serving us sweet baked treats we loved back in Iraq, they would indulge us with incredible stories about life in Basra and Baghdad. They also shared the local kibbutz gossip, which we excitedly listened to while eating our cookies. We never wanted to leave but after awhile they would kick us out with a promise of more sweets and stories in the new day. We lived with the other kids on the kibbutz and our afternoons were free to visit our family.

Mother and father always knew that they would find us at our grandmothers' house.

‹   **Theo & Rose**

Rose
I miss you.

Theo
I miss you too.

Rose
What did you do today?

Theo
Played golf.

Rose
Was it warm? Sunny?

Theo
Had a great round. It was sunny. Fresh air helped replenish the good with which you nurture my spirit when you are here by my side.

Rose
What are you doing now?

Theo
Lying on the couch reading. Thinking of you desperately. Missing you.

+ ⟨   ⟩ 📷 🎤

Theo & Rose

Rose
I'm in bed. I'm very tired. This jet lag is killing me.

Theo
I wish I were lying next to you, my hands wrapped around & holding you tightly, listening to you breath & feeling your heartbeat.

Rose
Kissing my neck?

Theo
Warm, wet kisses all over you.

Rose
I miss you so much. I cannot believe how much I want you right now. But you are so far away.

Theo
Close your eyes. I will be there caressing & kissing you.

Rose
Theo.

Theo
Enjoy Rosie. Close your eyes & feel me taking over your body. Rosie? Rosie?

Rose
Your words make me feel amazing.

Theo
You are amazing.

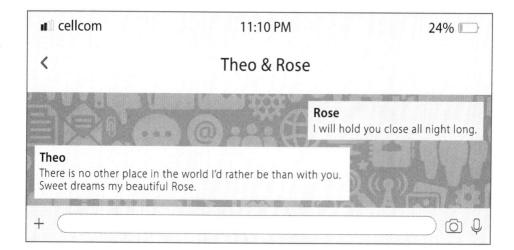

cellcom 11:10 PM 24%

Rose
I will hold you close all night long.

Theo
There is no other place in the world I'd rather be than with you.
Sweet dreams my beautiful Rose.

Aliza Goodman's Daily Motivational Quote #5: now

"We can change the world and make it a better place. It is in your hands to make a difference." Nelson Mandela

MotiQuote.com

MYPOETRY.COM

Forever Grateful

Brooke G.O.

You are my deeper half,
You opened the door,
Let me out from the hidden room,
Opened my site to more,

You stole my heart,
You ignored the height,
Pleaded with reason,
Held myths to light,

Forever grateful,
Growing strong,
Separated by miles,
Hope not too long.

♡ 119

150

Dearest Aliza,

Safta Shula's LOVE. March 11, 1954 was the day that would change my life. I was working in the kibbutz' vegetable garden, this was my after school weekend job. I loved being outdoors weeding and picking vegetables. On this afternoon, an old blue truck arrived at the fields to pick up crates of freshly picked vegetables. Two men jumped out of the truck, one older round fellow with orange fuzzy hair we called 'Jinjee' and a thin young man with large sparkly blue eyes who I had never seen before. I felt within seconds, as I could not take my eyes off this dreamy eyed new comer, that something strange was happening to me. I would stare at him as he loaded crates into the rear of the truck sure that I remained anonymous to him. Each week I worried that when the blue truck backed into the field,' Jinjee' would be with some other person. Then one week, blue eyes looked right at me and told me to stop staring and help him. He had a funny accent, as did my parents when they spoke Hebrew, but his was different I helped him load the truck and when we were finished, he smiled and said "todah" and disappeared into the front of the truck and drove away. I had butterflies in my stomach for a week until he returned. Before he could ask, I was by his side loading the crates. He asked my name and told me his, Yacov. This was April 29, 1954. I knew it was the first day of the beginning of my life.

Yacov lived in Ashdod. He had no family. He arrived in Israel and fought in Israel's War of Independence. Slowly Yacov became a part of our family. He was like a third son and when Nissim died, he took care of my devastated parents lovingly as though they were his own. Yacov spoke endlessly of his passion for the State of Israel but spoke little of his life in Poland and his trauma of the Holocaust.

Your grandfather Yacov was born in Lodz, Poland in 1928. He spent most of the war in the Lodz Ghetto. In 1941 when he was 13 years old, he and his father were working in a German factory producing German officer uniforms. One day he left for work and his mother, 2 little brothers and baby sister were deported to the Chelmno Camp where they were killed. His father and he stayed together and worked very hard until August 1944 when the Nazis decided to destroy the Lodz Ghetto and they were deported to Auschwitz-Birkenau. Yacov's father was quite ill and Yacov kept him alive by trading sewing services to the Nazis for little bits of food. In early January 1945, Yacov's father was sent on a death march and when

Yacov offered to go in his place, he was refused. On January 27, 1945, Soviet troops liberated Auschwitz and Yacov was freed. He was alone. He lost his whole family and had nowhere to go. He could not return to Lodz where the Poles were still treating the Jews terribly. Yacov travelled over Europe for a few years with odd sewing jobs until he made his way to the South of France. He finally arrived at the shores of Israel where he fought in Israel's War of Independence against the Arab nations. He did this even before he could speak Hebrew. After the army, he looked for work. He had experience in sewing but refused to take on this work as it reminded him of his job making uniforms for the Nazis. He went to work for a market in Ashdod and became a partner after a few years. He was responsible for the produce and when he came to the kibbutz, he was checking the quality of the produce. There had been some complaints by customers and he informed the kibbutz that he would be taking over the deliveries to verify that we were sending his market our best produce and not old vegetables. This was my luck. Our kibbutz had been cheating his market and he was there to set things straight. I remain thankful to the cheating system or we never would have met each other.

Your grandfather was warm and caring and even though he was older, mother and father trusted him to take good care of me. We were married when I was 18 and he was almost 29 years old. I was not ready to leave my family and we lived on the kibbutz in our own small house. I was in heaven. I had my parents and sister near to me; and the man of my dreams living on a beautiful farmland in a country where we were free to live. Yacov continued to work in the market but had to give his earnings to the kibbutz. This was the rule of the kibbutz. My husband was happy to make this sacrifice for me.

11:15 PM

(JS) Thank you for our poem

📷 (iMessage) 🎤

Kibbutz

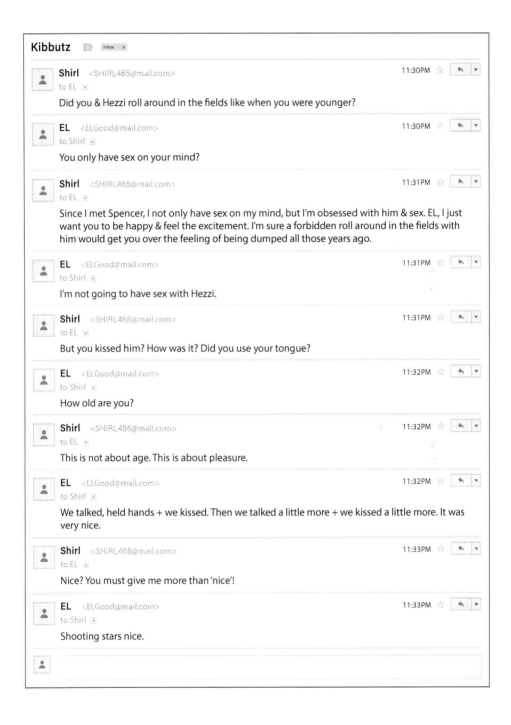

Shirl ‹SHIRL465@mail.com›
to EL
11:30PM

Did you & Hezzi roll around in the fields like when you were younger?

EL ‹ELGood@mail.com›
to Shirl
11:30PM

You only have sex on your mind?

Shirl ‹SHIRL465@mail.com›
to EL
11:31PM

Since I met Spencer, I not only have sex on my mind, but I'm obsessed with him & sex. EL, I just want you to be happy & feel the excitement. I'm sure a forbidden roll around in the fields with him would get you over the feeling of being dumped all those years ago.

EL ‹ELGood@mail.com›
to Shirl
11:31PM

I'm not going to have sex with Hezzi.

Shirl ‹SHIRL465@mail.com›
to EL
11:31PM

But you kissed him? How was it? Did you use your tongue?

EL ‹ELGood@mail.com›
to Shirl
11:32PM

How old are you?

Shirl ‹SHIRL465@mail.com›
to EL
11:32PM

This is not about age. This is about pleasure.

EL ‹ELGood@mail.com›
to Shirl
11:32PM

We talked, held hands + we kissed. Then we talked a little more + we kissed a little more. It was very nice.

Shirl ‹SHIRL465@mail.com›
to EL
11:33PM

Nice? You must give me more than 'nice'!

EL ‹ELGood@mail.com›
to Shirl
11:33PM

Shooting stars nice.

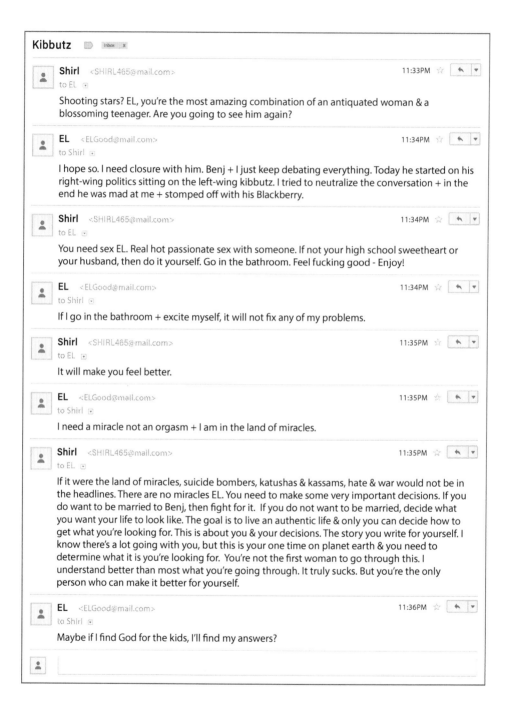

Kibbutz Inbox x

Shirl <SHIRL465@mail.com>   11:33PM
to EL

Shooting stars? EL, you're the most amazing combination of an antiquated woman & a blossoming teenager. Are you going to see him again?

EL <ELGood@mail.com>   11:34PM
to Shirl

I hope so. I need closure with him. Benj + I just keep debating everything. Today he started on his right-wing politics sitting on the left-wing kibbutz. I tried to neutralize the conversation + in the end he was mad at me + stomped off with his Blackberry.

Shirl <SHIRL465@mail.com>   11:34PM
to EL

You need sex EL. Real hot passionate sex with someone. If not your high school sweetheart or your husband, then do it yourself. Go in the bathroom. Feel fucking good - Enjoy!

EL <ELGood@mail.com>   11:34PM
to Shirl

If I go in the bathroom + excite myself, it will not fix any of my problems.

Shirl <SHIRL465@mail.com>   11:35PM
to EL

It will make you feel better.

EL <ELGood@mail.com>   11:35PM
to Shirl

I need a miracle not an orgasm + I am in the land of miracles.

Shirl <SHIRL465@mail.com>   11:35PM
to EL

If it were the land of miracles, suicide bombers, katushas & kassams, hate & war would not be in the headlines. There are no miracles EL. You need to make some very important decisions. If you do want to be married to Benj, then fight for it. If you do not want to be married, decide what you want your life to look like. The goal is to live an authentic life & only you can decide how to get what you're looking for. This is about you & your decisions. The story you write for yourself. I know there's a lot going with you, but this is your one time on planet earth & you need to determine what it is you're looking for. You're not the first woman to go through this. I understand better than most what you're going through. It truly sucks. But you're the only person who can make it better for yourself.

EL <ELGood@mail.com>   11:36PM
to Shirl

Maybe if I find God for the kids, I'll find my answers?

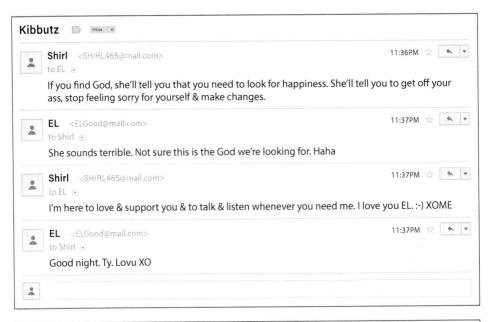

Kibbutz Inbox x

Shirl <SHIRL465@mail.com>   11:36PM
to EL

If you find God, she'll tell you that you need to look for happiness. She'll tell you to get off your ass, stop feeling sorry for yourself & make changes.

EL <ELGood@mail.com>   11:37PM
to Shirl

She sounds terrible. Not sure this is the God we're looking for. Haha

Shirl <SHIRL465@mail.com>   11:37PM
to EL

I'm here to love & support you & to talk & listen whenever you need me. I love you EL. :-) XOME

EL <ELGood@mail.com>   11:37PM
to Shirl

Good night. Ty. Lovu XO

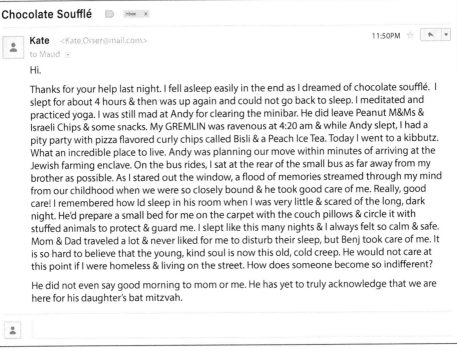

Chocolate Soufflé Inbox x

Kate <Kate.Orser@mail.com>   11:50PM
to Maud

Hi.

Thanks for your help last night. I fell asleep easily in the end as I dreamed of chocolate soufflé. I slept for about 4 hours & then was up again and could not go back to sleep. I meditated and practiced yoga. I was still mad at Andy for clearing the minibar. He did leave Peanut M&Ms & Israeli Chips & some snacks. My GREMLIN was ravenous at 4:20 am & while Andy slept, I had a pity party with pizza flavored curly chips called Bisli & a Peach Ice Tea. Today I went to a kibbutz. What an incredible place to live. Andy was planning our move within minutes of arriving at the Jewish farming enclave. On the bus rides, I sat at the rear of the small bus as far away from my brother as possible. As I stared out the window, a flood of memories streamed through my mind from our childhood when we were so closely bound & he took good care of me. Really, good care! I remembered how Id sleep in his room when I was very little & scared of the long, dark night. He'd prepare a small bed for me on the carpet with the couch pillows & circle it with stuffed animals to protect & guard me. I slept like this many nights & I always felt so calm & safe. Mom & Dad traveled a lot & never liked for me to disturb their sleep, but Benj took care of me. It is so hard to believe that the young, kind soul is now this old, cold creep. He would not care at this point if I were homeless & living on the street. How does someone become so indifferent?

He did not even say good morning to mom or me. He has yet to truly acknowledge that we are here for his daughter's bat mitzvah.

Chocolate Soufflé 📁 Inbox x

Maud <Maud@yogavilla.com>   11:52PM ☆ ↰ ▾
to Kate ▾

Kate, your brother is obviously a very unhappy man. Do not let his negative energy ruin this time with the family for you. I know it is a great challenge but feel gratitude for where you are and what you are experiencing. The safe and caring brother from your childhood is a beautiful memory and one that I would hold tight with vigilance. No one can take this truth away from you, but it has been many years and you do not need your brother to keep you safe anymore from the night, you are now a mature adult and can do this for yourself.

If he comes around, then you will welcome him with a full heart and open arms. If he does not appear in that light, then you will accept this and move on. There is no magical secret; there is only acceptance.

You can only be responsible for your behavior.

Follow your own words from the Blog Post yesterday-

"I realize that it is time to fully enjoy my experiences".

Kate <Kate.Orser@mail.com>   11:54PM ☆ ↰ ▾
to Maud ▾

I was writing about food & travel, not my personal feelings.

Maud <Maud@yogavilla.com>   11:55PM ☆ ↰ ▾
to Kate ▾

You were writing the truth. Be in the moment. Enjoy what you are experiencing. It will only happen once in this life.

If you make this trip about your angry brother then you will lose all the flavors, tastes, scents and sights you flew across the world to indulge in and enjoy.

This is your time and won't get it back so make the most of it.

Kate <Kate.Orser@mail.com>   11:55PM ☆ ↰ ▾
to Maud ▾

I know. You are right. Thank You.

Maud <Maud@yogavilla.com>   11:57PM ☆ ↰ ▾
to Kate ▾

Hold gratitude in your heart.

Kate <Kate.Orser@mail.com>   11:57PM ☆ ↰ ▾
to Maud ▾

I will.
Good night.

Dearest Aliza,

Safta Shula's LOVE.

July 27, 1959 a fateful letter arrived. It was from Yacov's uncle who he believed had died in the Holocaust. Samuel Pasternak was Yacov's mother's brother who managed to survive the war in hiding. Samuel had searched his whole family after the war and assumed everyone had been killed, when one day he was at a barber in New York, and met a young Israeli diplomat who had served in the army with a Yacov Bernard from Lodz. He helped the uncle locate Yacov. Samuel Pasternak arrived a poor immigrant to New York in 1950 and started a bra making business. Nine years later the business was quite large and in discovering he had family, he invited your grandfather to come and join his business.

I knew that this was our next stage as a married couple. I was sad to leave my family but I knew that I had to make this sacrifice for my husband who had lost everything and now had a chance to gain some family. We left the kibbutz and moved to Ashdod for a couple of months as we prepared to leave for America. We sold the market and brought the money with us to start our new life in New York. October 19, 1959, we boarded a plane to America. I was excited for this new life and at the same time I was terribly sad to say goodbye to my family. I had never been away from them and now we would be 6000 miles apart.

I remember saying goodbye to mother and father at the airport and tears streaming down all of our faces. Reuben was there and he tried to smile. Marcel did not cry - My twin, in her typical stoic form, was strong for me, as tears flooded my face. The last time I left my home, I was leaving Basra with my family and now I was leaving my Israeli home with my husband for America. I was very adventurous and ready to start my life with Yacov but I also had never felt such a deep pang of sadness saying goodbye as on that day. I already felt that I was missing the warmth of their bodies near to me.

I wanted to turn around and run to them, but Yacov held me close and we kept walking away toward the waiting airplane.

My new life began.

America was my home now.

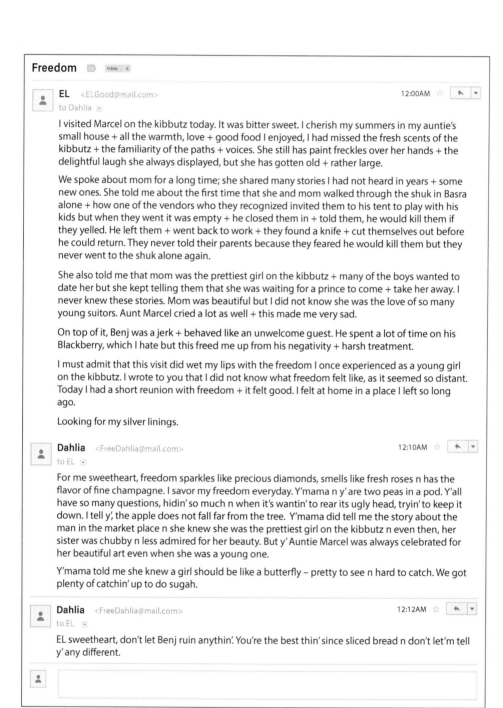

Freedom Inbox x

EL <ELGood@mail.com>   12:00AM
to Dahlia

I visited Marcel on the kibbutz today. It was bitter sweet. I cherish my summers in my auntie's small house + all the warmth, love + good food I enjoyed, I had missed the fresh scents of the kibbutz + the familiarity of the paths + voices. She still has paint freckles over her hands + the delightful laugh she always displayed, but she has gotten old + rather large.

We spoke about mom for a long time; she shared many stories I had not heard in years + some new ones. She told me about the first time that she and mom walked through the shuk in Basra alone + how one of the vendors who they recognized invited them to his tent to play with his kids but when they went it was empty + he closed them in + told them, he would kill them if they yelled. He left them + went back to work + they found a knife + cut themselves out before he could return. They never told their parents because they feared he would kill them but they never went to the shuk alone again.

She also told me that mom was the prettiest girl on the kibbutz + many of the boys wanted to date her but she kept telling them that she was waiting for a prince to come + take her away. I never knew these stories. Mom was beautiful but I did not know she was the love of so many young suitors. Aunt Marcel cried a lot as well + this made me very sad.

On top of it, Benj was a jerk + behaved like an unwelcome guest. He spent a lot of time on his Blackberry, which I hate but this freed me up from his negativity + harsh treatment.

I must admit that this visit did wet my lips with the freedom I once experienced as a young girl on the kibbutz. I wrote to you that I did not know what freedom felt like, as it seemed so distant. Today I had a short reunion with freedom + it felt good. I felt at home in a place I left so long ago.

Looking for my silver linings.

Dahlia <FreeDahlia@mail.com>   12:10AM
to EL

For me sweetheart, freedom sparkles like precious diamonds, smells like fresh roses n has the flavor of fine champagne. I savor my freedom everyday. Y'mama n y' are two peas in a pod. Y'all have so many questions, hidin' so much n when it's wantin' to rear its ugly head, tryin' to keep it down. I tell y', the apple does not fall far from the tree. Y'mama did tell me the story about the man in the market place n she knew she was the prettiest girl on the kibbutz n even then, her sister was chubby n less admired for her beauty. But y' Auntie Marcel was always celebrated for her beautiful art even when she was a young one.

Y'mama told me she knew a girl should be like a butterfly – pretty to see n hard to catch. We got plenty of catchin' up to do sugah.

Dahlia <FreeDahlia@mail.com>   12:12AM
to EL

EL sweetheart, don't let Benj ruin anythin'. You're the best thin' since sliced bread n don't let'm tell y' any different.

BOKER TOV

Goodman Family!

Welcome to day three of your Holy Land excursion!
Here is today's schedule:

We are off to explore the Ancient and Modern Desert!

5 AM - We will depart the hotel for Masada in the Judean Desert. This incredible mountaintop fortress is a symbol of Israeli freedom and independence. The walk up the Snake Path will take one hour or you can take a short ride up on the funicular. There will be plenty of cold water to take with you on the hike.

After retracing the steps of the ancient Israelites, we will travel a short distance to the shore of the Yam HaMelakh (Dead Sea) for mud baths and a float in the dense, salty sea.

We are here to make your stay in the Holy Land comfortable, exciting and challenging. We are sure that this will be a trip of a lifetime. Please bring a hat, lots of sunblock, and a bathing suit. We will return to the hotel for dinner.

Today's Temperature:

 The weather today will be a warm 35°c / 95°f

Yom Tov!

Moshe
Rimon Tours

Andy Orser

Now · Israel

· · ·

GOY IN THE HOLY LAND PART 7

Dark morning. Driving back in time to 35 BCE when Herod constructed the ancient community Masada atop a mountain in the Judean Desert. I will visit the tragic site where 1000 Jewish zealots, who had escaped religious persecution in Jerusalem, lived surrounded by the powerful Roman enemy before in a final tragic act to bravely defend their honor, they dramatically took their lives in a mass suicide.

Dear Friends, this is an adventure of a lifetime! #Holylandadventures #israeltravel #heavenonearth #Masada

👍 Like	💬 Comment	↗ Share

📶 cellcom　　　　　　　6:35 AM　　　　　　100% 🔋

‹　　　　　**YM**　　　　　**AG**　　　　　ⓘ

Yasmin M.　　　Aliza Goodman

6:30 AM

Are you still up? (AG)

Im driving to Masada I barely slept jetlag is fkn killing me (AG)

EL + Benj started debating at like 5 in the morning about how long the hike up Masada is & if the sunrise that morning 20 years ago when they last hiked Masada was orange or pink omg want to kill myself listening to them ☹ (AG)

Now the bus is silent everyones sleeping but Benj's doing that annoying humming while he checks his emails (AG)

Its driving me crazy ugh (AG)

I miss u & hope volleyball camps is fun how r the supermodel roommates? Do they eat? haha (AG)

Wish you were here (AG)

Delivered

📷　iMessage　　　　　　　　　🎤

135

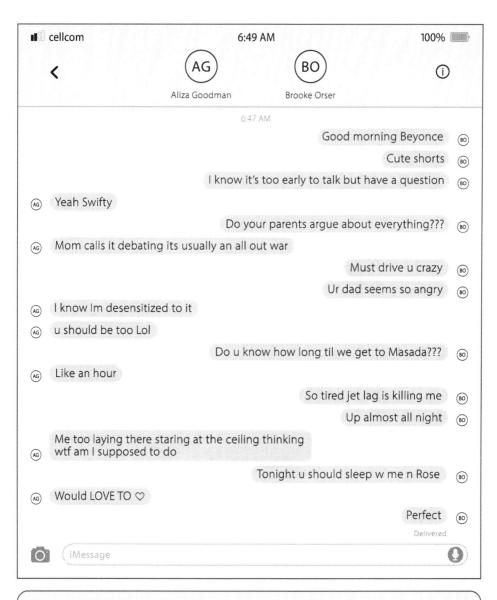

AG
Aliza Goodman

BO
Brooke Orser

6:47 AM

Good morning Beyonce

Cute shorts

I know it's too early to talk but have a question

Yeah Swifty

Do your parents argue about everything???

Mom calls it debating its usually an all out war

Must drive u crazy

Ur dad seems so angry

I know Im desensitized to it

u should be too Lol

Do u know how long til we get to Masada???

Like an hour

So tired jet lag is killing me

Up almost all night

Me too laying there staring at the ceiling thinking wtf am I supposed to do

Tonight u should sleep w me n Rose

Would LOVE TO ♡

Perfect

Delivered

iMessage

Aliza Goodman's Daily Motivational Quote #1:   now

"For the sake of peace one may lie, but peace itself shall never be a lie."
Talmud

MotiQuote.com

Kindness Lost

Brooke G.O.

Angry rain clouds hover
A picnic of kindness takes cover
Thunder and lightning wait by the door
The numbing champagne waiting to pour

An angry fox circles the hen house
Panic inside thrills and chills
An attack will come after the pleasure
Desperate souls wait in measure

An angry man pockets full
Love and kindness lost their pull
Power from destruction grows
Victims all he knows

An angry stare takes its toll
Your DNA fills my soul
Perilous anger strikes me deep
I shall never weep

♡ 209   367 ◉

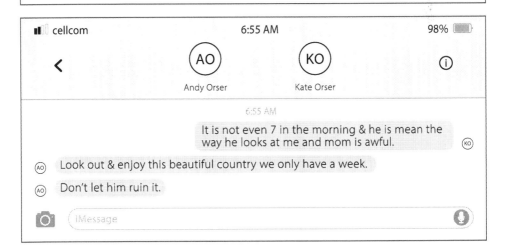

Israel Family Group

EL, Kate, Andy, Teddy, Aliza, Brooke,...

EL
Good morning.
I conferred with Professor Google on the question of "Does God Exist?" He provided 434,000,000 results in .61 seconds. I then tried the negative "Does God Not Exist?" and had 18,200,000 results in .31 seconds. Then the professor + I simplified our search to just "God" and had 339,000,000 results in .43 seconds. Based on my conference with Professor Google, God's existence is quite favorable.

Teddy
EL what do you personally think?

Andy
I know you didn't ask me Teddy, but I think God exists. I joined an incredible meditation retreat last year and by the 3rd day of intense meditation away from the powerful Internet and other modern day social ills, I felt very spiritually moved. I was in the presence of another being - it was warm and comforting, not physical but very much present.

I decided this was some sort of validation for me of God's existence once I was emotionally able to receive him.

Kate
I think that God is everywhere all the time. He fills the universe; he knows what we're doing and he's aware of all that's going on. He's not a God just for Jews but for everyone.

+ 🔲 📷 🎤

Aliza Goodman's Daily Motivational Quote #2:   now

"On the last day of the world, I would want to plant a tree."
W.S. Merwin

MotiQuote.com

JS Jeremy Stark   **BO** Brooke Orser

6:58 AM

Being in Israel makes me think about the half n half we talk about. I always knew I was half jewish n half christian, but here it feels very black n white omg I can't believe I just wrote that! You have told me how hard it is but you have always acted cool with it. Guess I'm saying it confuses me n I'm sorry I wasn't so understanding. I just love you for who you are not for your skin color but for your heart n soul n smile. Here in Israel it feels like being half n half is challenging, makes me question more n more who I am!

Delivered

iMessage

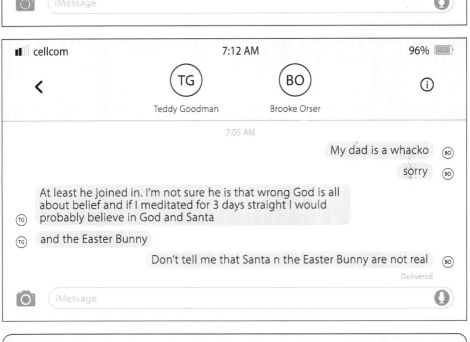

TG Teddy Goodman   **BO** Brooke Orser

7:05 AM

My dad is a whacko

sorry

At least he joined in. I'm not sure he is that wrong God is all about belief and if I meditated for 3 days straight I would probably believe in God and Santa

and the Easter Bunny

Don't tell me that Santa n the Easter Bunny are not real

Delivered

iMessage

JN24:   now
Soldier gravely wounded by sniper fire in West Bank.
Jewish News You Can Use

139

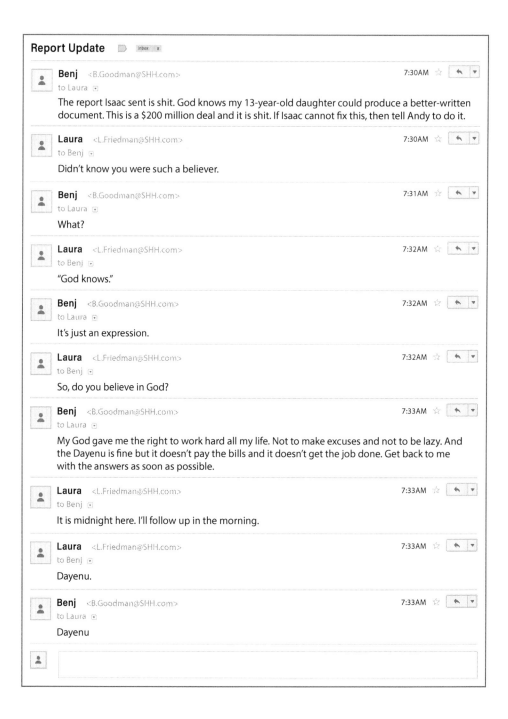

Report Update inbox x

Benj <B.Goodman@SHH.com>   7:30AM ☆
to Laura

The report Isaac sent is shit. God knows my 13-year-old daughter could produce a better-written document. This is a $200 million deal and it is shit. If Isaac cannot fix this, then tell Andy to do it.

Laura <L.Friedman@SHH.com>   7:30AM ☆
to Benj

Didn't know you were such a believer.

Benj <B.Goodman@SHH.com>   7:31AM ☆
to Laura

What?

Laura <L.Friedman@SHH.com>   7:32AM ☆
to Benj

"God knows."

Benj <B.Goodman@SHH.com>   7:32AM ☆
to Laura

It's just an expression.

Laura <L.Friedman@SHH.com>   7:32AM ☆
to Benj

So, do you believe in God?

Benj <B.Goodman@SHH.com>   7:33AM ☆
to Laura

My God gave me the right to work hard all my life. Not to make excuses and not to be lazy. And the Dayenu is fine but it doesn't pay the bills and it doesn't get the job done. Get back to me with the answers as soon as possible.

Laura <L.Friedman@SHH.com>   7:33AM ☆
to Benj

It is midnight here. I'll follow up in the morning.

Laura <L.Friedman@SHH.com>   7:33AM ☆
to Benj

Dayenu.

Benj <B.Goodman@SHH.com>   7:33AM ☆
to Laura

Dayenu

LUCACLOSELY
@LUCACLOSELY

What gets broken without being held?

7:35 AM – June

💬 1 ♡ 3 ↻ 1

LUCACLOSELY @LUCACLOSELY
Replying to @LUCACLOSELY

A Promise

Aliza Goodman's Daily Motivational Quote #3:   now

"There is a future for the man of peace."
Psalms 37:37

MotiQuote.com

LIFEEXPRESSIONS.COM   ✏️ 🗂️ ⊕

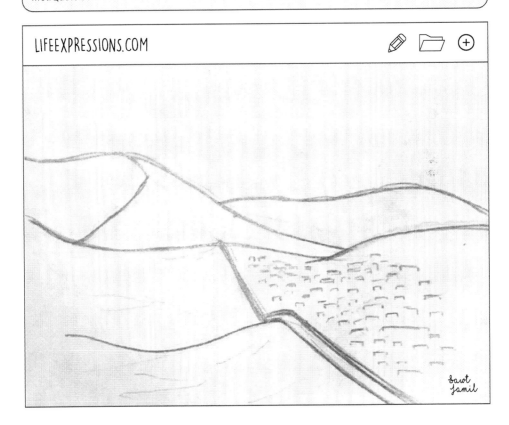

JN24:
LGBT groups to march from Tel Aviv to Jerusalem before the Gay Pride Parade.
Jewish News You Can Use

cellcom 8:13 AM

< Theo & Rose

Rose
I'm on top of Masada. Waiting for the others; they're hiking up the snake path. I rode the funicular with our sweet guide, Moshe. It's so quiet up here. Moshe is a big talker but it is even too early for him to say much. The desert views as the sun rises are beautiful.

Theo
Alone in the desert with Moses? Should I be jealous?

Rose
Yes. Of course, you should

Theo
You play unfair Rosie

Rose
Moses and I are exploring the vast shining desert and shortly the rest of our tribal clan will join us in search of our Holy Land. I have never felt so much like an adventurer. How I wish you were here next to me.

Theo
Then you would not be focused on your family. If I were there it would still be our honeymoon & we would not leave our desert tent. I would hold you so tight & not let you leave me for a second. The rest of the world would start to worry that the Roman Army had kidnapped you.

Rose
I would miss the whole family experience?

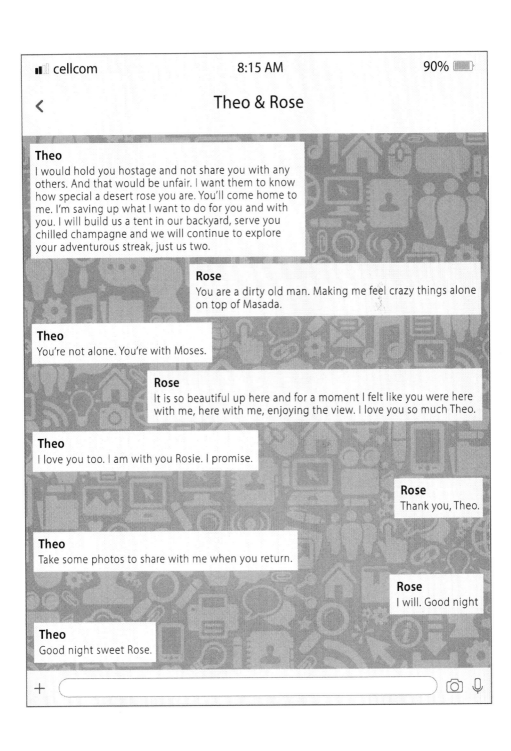

Theo & Rose

Theo
I would hold you hostage and not share you with any others. And that would be unfair. I want them to know how special a desert rose you are. You'll come home to me. I'm saving up what I want to do for you and with you. I will build us a tent in our backyard, serve you chilled champagne and we will continue to explore your adventurous streak, just us two.

Rose
You are a dirty old man. Making me feel crazy things alone on top of Masada.

Theo
You're not alone. You're with Moses.

Rose
It is so beautiful up here and for a moment I felt like you were here with me, here with me, enjoying the view. I love you so much Theo.

Theo
I love you too. I am with you Rosie. I promise.

Rose
Thank you, Theo.

Theo
Take some photos to share with me when you return.

Rose
I will. Good night

Theo
Good night sweet Rose.

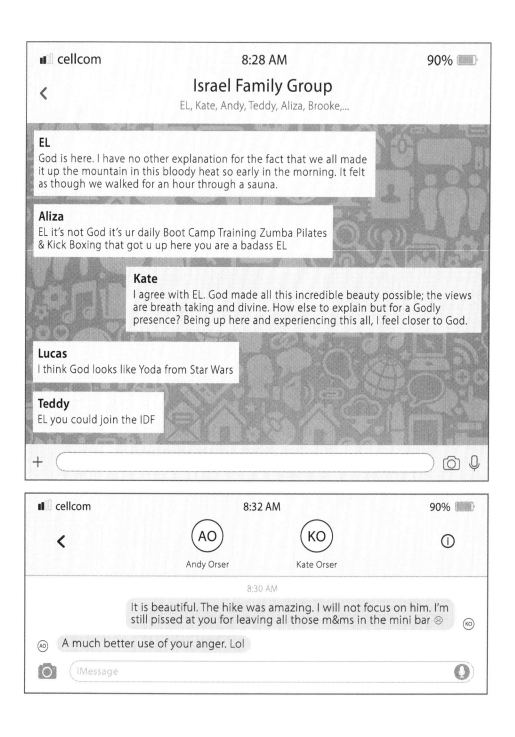

EL
God is here. I have no other explanation for the fact that we all made it up the mountain in this bloody heat so early in the morning. It felt as though we walked for an hour through a sauna.

Aliza
EL it's not God it's ur daily Boot Camp Training Zumba Pilates & Kick Boxing that got u up here you are a badass EL

Kate
I agree with EL. God made all this incredible beauty possible; the views are breath taking and divine. How else to explain but for a Godly presence? Being up here and experiencing this all, I feel closer to God.

Lucas
I think God looks like Yoda from Star Wars

Teddy
EL you could join the IDF

AO Andy Orser   **KO** Kate Orser

8:30 AM

It is beautiful. The hike was amazing. I will not focus on him. I'm still pissed at you for leaving all those m&ms in the mini bar ☹

A much better use of your anger. Lol

Andy Orser

Now · Israel

•••

GOY IN THE HOLY LAND PART 8

Just hiked up the small dark dirt Snake Path and arrived atop majestic Masada as the sun slowly illuminated the mountain side and proudly rose over the Judean Desert plains spreading powerful rays of bright light in all directions. This is the same illumination that radiated over the Jewish residents who lived, prayed, farmed and fought for their lives on this flat desert mountain top 2000 years ago escaping from the hateful Romans who surrounded them. Masada serves as a modern metaphor for the nation's current survival and principles while surrounded by the enemies' outspoken disdain for its existence; the profound lesson the modern Jews learned about survival and not falling into deadly enemy hands or arriving at a place where a mass suicide would be a more prudent response.

Dear Friends, I am extremely humbled by this experience and feel so small in this vast, historical and powerful desert. #Israelnature #Masada #jewishrebellion #amazingviews

---

👍 Like   💬 Comment   ↗ Share

📶 cellcom   8:36 AM   88% 🔋

‹

Israel Family Group

EL, Kate, Andy, Teddy, Aliza, Brooke,...

Teddy
If there is a God why did he make it so hot?

EL
God is all powerful.
She is testing us. She wants to push us hard to discover our limits.

Teddy
I didn't know that God was a woman?

EL
So, you just assumed God was a man all this time? If God were a man everything would only be half done + half as beautiful

➕ ⸺⸺⸺⸺⸺⸺⸺⸺⸺⸺⸺ 📷 🎤

Masada
Teddy Goodman

My cheery Californian cousin Brooke and I just explored Masada, an incredible fortress originally built by Herod in 35 BCE where Jews escaping the Roman enemies lived 2000 years ago. We walked on dusty dirt paths by and through Herod's original palace, residences, bathhouses, a mikvah, a synagogue, and even a Byzantine church. It is awesome. No textbook could accurately provide this learning experience. I'm wasting my fucking time in school and my parents fucking money. The visit with history I encountered today will remain with me for life. Brooke and I barely said a word to each other. We both were very focused on the moment and even though we did not speak, the silence did not seem strange.

When I went back to the entrance Benj was on his fucking Blackberry. I am not sure he ever took a walk around to explore this amazing place. My father is like a modern-day Herod; busy building his empire, yelling at his slaves and workers and only gratified by his abounding ambition for success and more. I wonder if Herod was also too busy to stop and appreciate the beauty in front of his very eyes or he just worked compulsively to build more and more monuments?

My dad could possibly be a cool guy if he wasn't such an asshole. I'm sure that Herod was an asshole too.

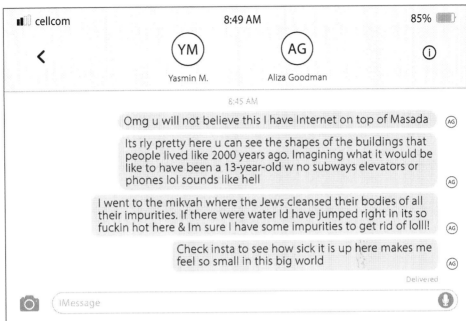

YM   AG

Yasmin M.   Aliza Goodman

8:45 AM

Omg u will not believe this I have Internet on top of Masada

Its rly pretty here u can see the shapes of the buildings that people lived like 2000 years ago. Imagining what it would be like to have been a 13-year-old w no subways elevators or phones lol sounds like hell

I went to the mikvah where the Jews cleansed their bodies of all their impurities. If there were water Id have jumped right in its so fuckin hot here & Im sure I have some impurities to get rid of lolll!

Check insta to see how sick it is up here makes me feel so small in this big world

Delivered

iMessage

Andy Orser

Now · Israel

GOY IN THE HOLY LAND PART 9

Leaving powerful Masada by cable car high above the wind sculpted cliffs with the motionless beige and blue Dead Sea down below. After the violent siege and mass suicide in 74 CE, 2 brave women and 5 innocent children hid and survived to keep their community's history alive. Stories of passionate conviction are engraved in the ruins - prompting us to never allow for stories to disappear even after so many years.

Dear Friends, I witnessed the remains of Ancient Siege and Hate. A modern reminder. #NeverAgain! #Deadsea #Masada #Israeltravel

Like   Comment   Share

JN24:   now

Smoke can be seen following an explosion last night on the Syrian side of the Israeli-Syrian border.

Jewish News You Can Use

Andy Orser
Now · Israel

GOY IN THE HOLY LAND PART 10

Masada is the symbol for freedom and independence under terrible circumstances. Almost 1000 Jews committed suicide rather than be killed, raped and taken as prisoners by the 15,000 Roman soldiers who surrounded Masada. The Romans built a huge ramp to reach the mountaintop and when they finally attacked, they found the corpses of the Jewish community. Masada commemorates fallen Jews in their struggle against oppression and reminds all to be vigilant against modern extremism and the refusal to compromise with our relentless enemies in current times.

Dear Friends, how I wish that after all these years, that hate for fellow man would be eradicated and all people would be free to live their lives in peace. I meditated on this mountaintop overlooking the Judean Desert and felt peaceful and hopeful. #Liveinpeace #Masada #masssuicide #judeandesert

    👍 Like   💬 Comment   ↗ Share

Divine Desert 📥 Inbox ×

EL <ELGood@mail.com>   11:13AM ☆ ↩ ▾
to Shiri ▾

I'm in the bathroom. Still shaking. Lucas disappeared on top of Masada. We almost left him.

Benj was so busy on his damn Blackberry (love this country – there is Internet everywhere creating a mobile office for the man) typing away when Teddy realized his younger brother was missing. He never even looked up - he had no idea what was going on.

I grabbed the Blackberry from Benj's hands + threw it over the edge of Masada. I screamed, "You Asshole, your son is fucking missing!" He looked at me with the meanest eyes, but this wasn't an ideal time for him to scream back at me.

Every worst nightmare crossed my mind about what could have happened to my baby + of course I was the worst mother in the whole world for that endless 20 minutes before Teddy found him + brought him back to me.

Lucas had been hiding out in one of the cisterns reliving the history of the Jews on top of Masada. Interestingly it was Teddy who took control + knew where to look.

Now I need to go back out there + face the group + Blackberry-less Benj. When will this start being fun?

Ugh!

Rose
Are you up? Just left the cistern where the witch swam with her lover in The Dove Keeper's Wife. I imagined you and I were swimming naked in the cool water under the full moon.

Theo
Yes. Love your imagination.

Rose
I have gotten good at this - considering the sun is shining, it is bloody hot, the cistern is dry and you are not here!

Theo
Our imaginations guide our reality. Keep dreaming.

Rose
I have not stopped dreaming of you since I got here.

Theo
I have not stopped dreaming of you since you left. Last night I wokefor a pit stop & while I tried to go back to sleep, I kept remembering the afternoon we drove to the vineyards & we were too drunk to drive home. We checked into the small B&B with the fireplace & made love all night on the fur rug with the flames dancing in the dark.

Rose
I remember that night. Missing you so much.

Theo
Soon you will be back. I love you.

Rose
I love you.

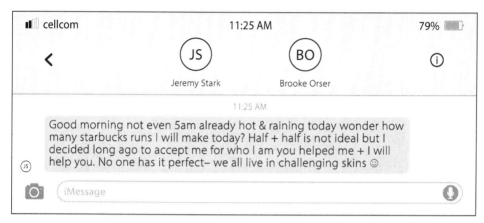

JS
Jeremy Stark

BO
Brooke Orser

11:25 AM

Good morning not even 5am already hot & raining today wonder how many starbucks runs I will make today? Half + half is not ideal but I decided long ago to accept me for who I am you helped me + I will help you. No one has it perfect– we all live in challenging skins ☺

iMessage

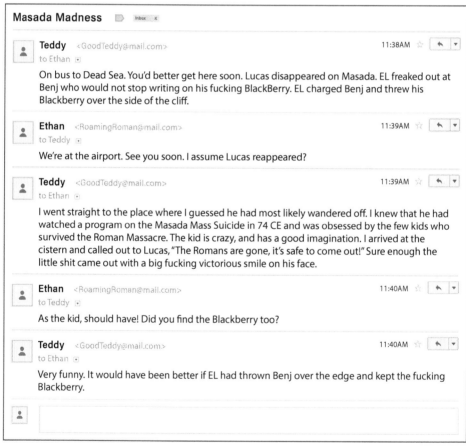

Masada Madness   Inbox   x

Teddy <GoodTeddy@mail.com>   11:38AM
to Ethan

On bus to Dead Sea. You'd better get here soon. Lucas disappeared on Masada. EL freaked out at Benj who would not stop writing on his fucking BlackBerry. EL charged Benj and threw his Blackberry over the side of the cliff.

Ethan <RoamingRoman@mail.com>   11:39AM
to Teddy

We're at the airport. See you soon. I assume Lucas reappeared?

Teddy <GoodTeddy@mail.com>   11:39AM
to Ethan

I went straight to the place where I guessed he had most likely wandered off. I knew that he had watched a program on the Masada Mass Suicide in 74 CE and was obsessed by the few kids who survived the Roman Massacre. The kid is crazy, and has a good imagination. I arrived at the cistern and called out to Lucas, "The Romans are gone, it's safe to come out!" Sure enough the little shit came out with a big fucking victorious smile on his face.

Ethan <RoamingRoman@mail.com>   11:40AM
to Teddy

As the kid, should have! Did you find the Blackberry too?

Teddy <GoodTeddy@mail.com>   11:40AM
to Ethan

Very funny. It would have been better if EL had thrown Benj over the edge and kept the fucking Blackberry.

Masada Madness 📥 Inbox ×

Ethan <RoamingRoman@mail.com>   11:41AM ☆ ↩ ▾
to Teddy ▾

Didn't know that anyone still used a Blackberry?

Teddy <GoodTeddy@mail.com>   11:41AM ☆ ↩ ▾
to Ethan ▾

You don't know my father.

Ethan <RoamingRoman@mail.com>   11:41AM ☆ ↩ ▾
to Teddy ▾

I'm looking forward to getting to know him. See you tonight.

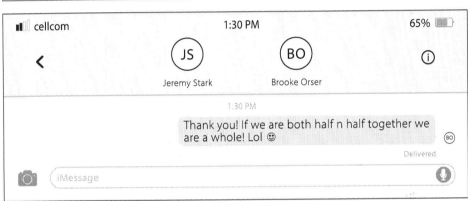

▫▫ cellcom   1:30 PM   65% 🔋

‹   (JS)   (BO)   ⓘ
          Jeremy Stark   Brooke Orser

1:30 PM

Thank you! If we are both half n half together we
are a whole! Lol ☺   (BO)

Delivered

📷 iMessage   ⬇

Andy Orser   •••
Now · Israel

GOY IN THE HOLY LAND PART 11

Just floated in the Dead Sea, 1400 feet below sea level (also earth's lowest level on land); the rich salt water permeated my skin and stung a shaving nick on my neck. Then I covered my entire body with dark brown mud only exposing my eyes. The desert sun quickly dried the mud hard on to my skin. After, I took a cold freshwater shower leaving my skin reinvigorated and refreshed.

Dear Friends, I am revitalized. This is a desert paradise. #lowestplaceonearth #hotterthanhell

👍 Like   💬 Comment   ➦ Share

Familiar and Unknown

<u>Brooke G.O.</u>

I walked these paths
Unrecognizable
Faintly familiar
Not clear where they lead
I feel at home
Destruction
Withering welcome
Returning from where I came

Every day I run away

Misunderstood
Too tired to explain
Applause soon to wane
My audience stopped listening
Keep the message short I'm told
Depth of thought long been sold

We must move on
I saw it on a bus stop at a red light
Don't be a sucker
I am reminded as I get off the highway
Love thy Neighbor
The torn bumper sticker reads

Hiking boots make their mark
Strong steps lead others
Your shadow keeps them fresh
Strength in silence
Till words build upon your lips
Shooting your thoughts
Like bullets gently landing on a grassy field

I flew across the sky to meet you
I have only one regret
Why it took so long to take flight
Relieved it was not another night

FOOD AFFAIR WITH KATE

DIVINE, DELICIOUS, AND DELIGHTFUL   ABOUT   RECIPES   CONTACT

Limonana
★ ★ ★ ★ ☆

Bloody hot here.... Today I fell in love with a simple drink – Limonana, a refreshing combination of tart lemonade, a touch of sugar, and fresh mint blended with ice. Slowly sipping this celestial frozen blend contrasts the brutal dry desert heat and refreshingly hits the spot; it revives me after a sweltering tour of Masada high in the Judean Desert and just before I prepare for a full body mud wrap and a Dead Sea float. This heavenly mint infused bittersweet drink is simple to prepare - no caffeine, few calories and all natural ingredients from your garden and ideal for an afternoon pool party. Fresh lemon and mint blended with ice can offer a healthy cleanse and gives a boost to your digestion. I highly recommend you dive head first into a fresh Limonana! To see more photos, check out Food Affair with Kate on Instagram and Facebook. #refreshingdrinks #limonana

---

Andy Orser
Now · Israel

•••

GOY IN THE HOLY LAND PART 12

Shared my afternoon with a beautiful camel named Hercules. The desert majesty with her royal wobble carried me through the Judean Desert on my way to a spectacular Bedouin tent set alone in the wicked hot orange venue. This experience shares the desert dwellers' journey offering a view of a very different life style.

Dear Friends, this is a dream: I have ridden a camel, dined in a Bedouin tent and for a moment experienced the life of a nomadic desert dweller. The dream lives on. #camelrides #bedouin

👍 Like   💬 Comment   ↪ Share

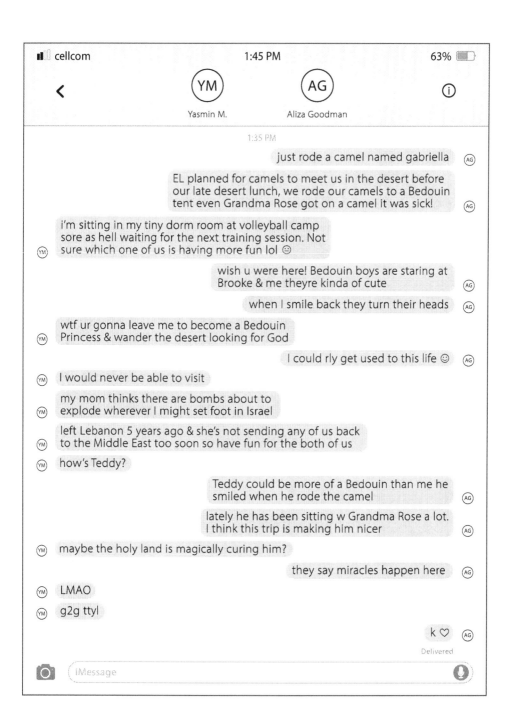

1:35 PM

just rode a camel named gabriella (AG)

EL planned for camels to meet us in the desert before our late desert lunch, we rode our camels to a Bedouin tent even Grandma Rose got on a camel it was sick! (AG)

(YM) i'm sitting in my tiny dorm room at volleyball camp sore as hell waiting for the next training session. Not sure which one of us is having more fun lol ☺

wish u were here! Bedouin boys are staring at Brooke & me theyre kinda of cute (AG)

when I smile back they turn their heads (AG)

(YM) wtf ur gonna leave me to become a Bedouin Princess & wander the desert looking for God

I could rly get used to this life ☺ (AG)

(YM) I would never be able to visit

(YM) my mom thinks there are bombs about to explode wherever I might set foot in Israel

(YM) left Lebanon 5 years ago & she's not sending any of us back to the Middle East too soon so have fun for the both of us

(YM) how's Teddy?

Teddy could be more of a Bedouin than me he smiled when he rode the camel (AG)

lately he has been sitting w Grandma Rose a lot. I think this trip is making him nicer (AG)

(YM) maybe the holy land is magically curing him?

they say miracles happen here (AG)

(YM) LMAO

(YM) g2g ttyl

k ♡ (AG)

Delivered

iMessage

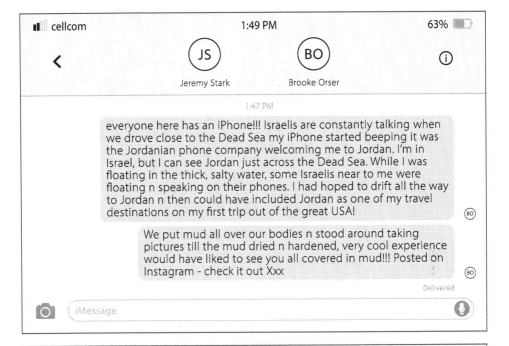

Bedouins

Brooke G.O.

You dance as if each song may be the last
Your wings are clipped
You still fly high
I am filled with awe

You dwell in the desert since ancient days
Your time is endless
You forge on with glory and pride
I wish to steal a piece of your devotion

Soft sand burns
Winds carry warm records
Strong spices awaken
Secrets from the desert floor

♡ 163   250 ◉

Judean Desert Experience
Teddy Goodman

My mother has purchased the perfect tourist's Judean Desert Experience.

It is like an attraction at Disney World where you ride a giant camel, sit in a desert tent on brightly colored dusty floor pillows, and are served a genuine Bedouin feast by men dressed in decorative costumes. No fucking Mickey Mouse or Aladdin here to pop out and hug you for a selfie! Most of the men serving us are my age. There are no women, and these young men are checking out cousin Brooke and even my little sister Aliza.

I am reminded what a jaded life I lead living in the City and attending a prestigious college preparatory school. I do no manual work; I barely break a sweat each day and live like a fucking prince in our Manhattan high rise. I am going through all the correct motions that will catapult me to an Ivy League college in a year. But I look at these young men working hard and they seem to have so little (no iPhones, no Polo T shirts and no Doormen), and at the same time, they appear fucking happy with their lives. I watch as they work fast and hard as a team and proudly serve us. I am both inspired and a bit depressed at the same time. I feel like I'm stuck.

I am busting my ass for good grades, and walk around fucking miserable. Maybe I will take a gap year and join a Bedouin tribe? This would give EL and Benj a combined heart attack, but perhaps something that could unite them and shit, maybe they would get along for once.

Either way I would be free - far away riding camels living in a tent with my biblical cousins and I wouldn't have to give a shit about anyone or anything.

I need to do something different.

 JN24:   now

Explosive device detonates near Israel - Lebanon border. No reported injuries. Border guards have been deployed to patrol the area.

Jewish News You Can Use

Dear Lucas Goodman, Astronaut in Training –

@JUNIORNASAUSA

Crew | About | Photos

TODAY ON THE INTERNATIONAL SPACE STATION:

On the International Space Station (@ISS) astronauts have a daily two-hour workout with exercise on a treadmill, a cycling machine, and a resistive device. We all need to stay in good shape in space and be ready to return to Earth's gravity at the end of our missions. Today we are passing over the Great Barrier Reef off the coast of Eastern Australia. The Great Barrier Reef is the biggest single structure made by living organisms, 1,600 miles long and a total area of 130,000 square miles, and the world's largest reef system composed of over 2,900 independent reefs. The Great Barrier Reef is a protected natural habitat and home to one of the most dynamic natural ecosystems: more than 600 different corals and over 1,500 species of fish ranging from tiny plankton to whales live in the reef.

LIFEEXPRESSIONS.COM

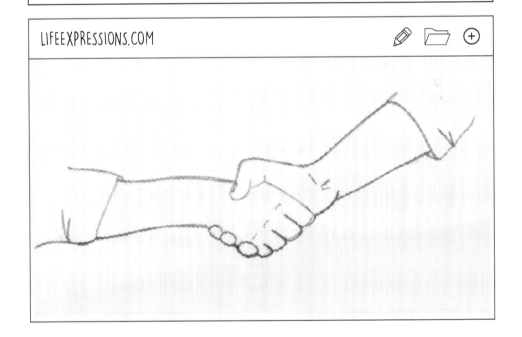

FOOD AFFAIR WITH KATE

DIVINE, DELICIOUS, AND DELIGHTFUL

A Whole New World
★ ★ ★ ☆ ☆

A Whole New World.... Sitting in a Bedouin Tent in the Judean Desert. After an early morning exploration atop burning hot Masada and a swim in the salty Dead Sea, the colorful and festive Bedouin Tent offers traveling pilgrims greatly welcomed shade from the blazing desert sun. Seated upon dusty fabric cushions at low wooden tables, we eat a feast meant for nomadic royalty: large platters of rich, yellow rice garnished with spices, nuts and raisins, fragrant mixed vegetables and charcoaled grilled meats on skewers lay atop fresh fluffy white rice. Overwhelmed by the incredible flavors, I invite myself for a kitchen visit to thank the chef wishing to learn the spice's names and origins. Chef Amir, a small and intense looking man, speaks no English and controls the array of spices. I promise myself at that very moment to return to the Holy Land – a pilgrimage all must make in their lifetime - for Bedoiun cooking lessons. Chef Amir is a culinary magician and I watch with awe as he prepares our beautiful meal.

The star of the meal is Ahmed, an older gentleman who sits cross legged by the round flat oven (over a burning flame) preparing large fragrant flatbread one by one; he then spreads white milky lebneh over the fresh, warm bread and drizzles it with za'atar, an aromatic and alluringly tangy spice. Finally, Ahmed craftly folds the creation into a Bedouin burrito. Doughy Arab flatbread melts in my mouth as lebana drips down my chin. It is a messy delight and a memorable, cherished culinary experience. (Arab flatbread, as well, can be baked in a traditional oven at a very high temperature). One main difference between Jews and Arabs is the shape of the bread - Jews serve pita or pocket bread with their meals and Arabs serve lafa or flat doughy bread. Both cultures' culinary worlds have many crossovers and are enriched by similar scents and flavors. See the photos below and check out Food Affair with Kate on Instagram and Facebook. #bedouindining #ilovezatar #pitaandlafa #holylanddining

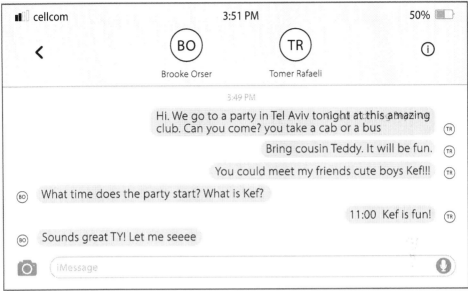

cellcom   3:51 PM   50%

(BO)   (TR)   (i)

Brooke Orser   Tomer Rafaeli

3:49 PM

Hi. We go to a party in Tel Aviv tonight at this amazing club. Can you come? you take a cab or a bus (TR)

Bring cousin Teddy. It will be fun. (TR)

You could meet my friends cute boys Kef!!! (TR)

(BO) What time does the party start? What is Kef?

11:00 Kef is fun! (TR)

(BO) Sounds great TY! Let me seeee

iMessage

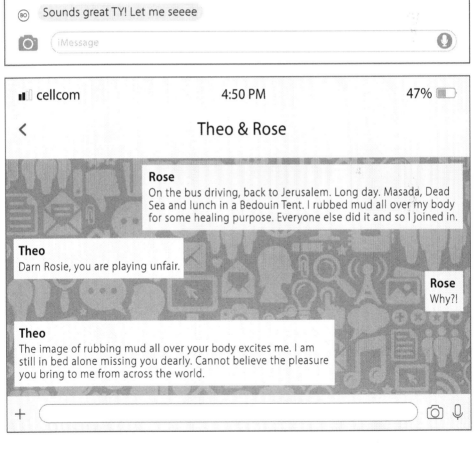

cellcom   4:50 PM   47%

Theo & Rose

Rose
On the bus driving, back to Jerusalem. Long day. Masada, Dead Sea and lunch in a Bedouin Tent. I rubbed mud all over my body for some healing purpose. Everyone else did it and so I joined in.

Theo
Darn Rosie, you are playing unfair.

Rose
Why?!

Theo
The image of rubbing mud all over your body excites me. I am still in bed alone missing you dearly. Cannot believe the pleasure you bring to me from across the world.

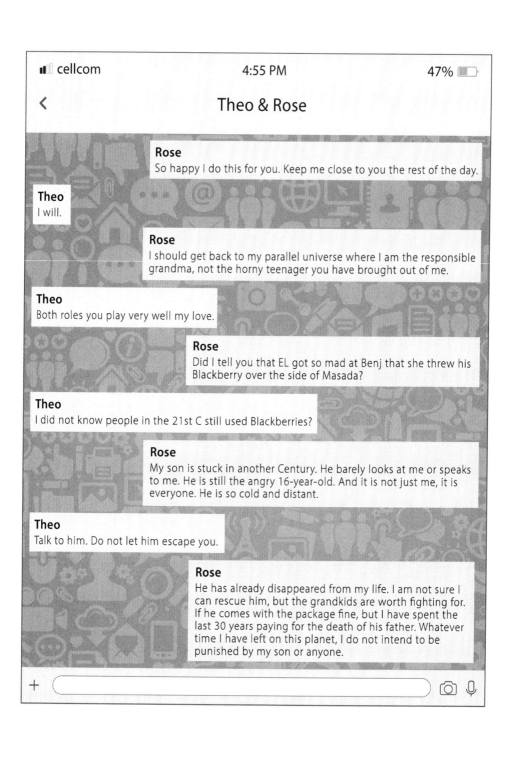

Rose
So happy I do this for you. Keep me close to you the rest of the day.

Theo
I will.

Rose
I should get back to my parallel universe where I am the responsible grandma, not the horny teenager you have brought out of me.

Theo
Both roles you play very well my love.

Rose
Did I tell you that EL got so mad at Benj that she threw his Blackberry over the side of Masada?

Theo
I did not know people in the 21st C still used Blackberries?

Rose
My son is stuck in another Century. He barely looks at me or speaks to me. He is still the angry 16-year-old. And it is not just me, it is everyone. He is so cold and distant.

Theo
Talk to him. Do not let him escape you.

Rose
He has already disappeared from my life. I am not sure I can rescue him, but the grandkids are worth fighting for. If he comes with the package fine, but I have spent the last 30 years paying for the death of his father. Whatever time I have left on this planet, I do not intend to be punished by my son or anyone.

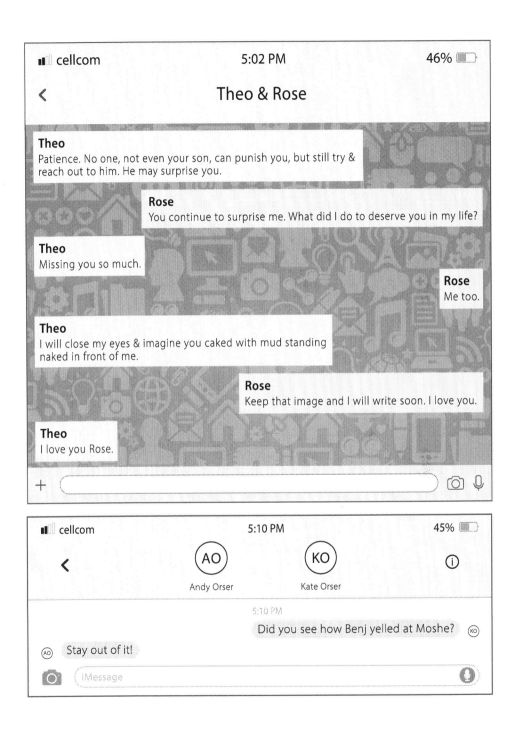

Theo
Patience. No one, not even your son, can punish you, but still try & reach out to him. He may surprise you.

Rose
You continue to surprise me. What did I do to deserve you in my life?

Theo
Missing you so much.

Rose
Me too.

Theo
I will close my eyes & imagine you caked with mud standing naked in front of me.

Rose
Keep that image and I will write soon. I love you.

Theo
I love you Rose.

Andy Orser   **Kate Orser**

5:10 PM

Did you see how Benj yelled at Moshe?

Stay out of it!

iMessage

AG
Aliza Goodman

BO
Brooke Orser

5:13 PM

Glad we didn't lose your little brother this morning

Ik he tends to walk off and like disappear

One time we couldn't find him at Target EL was hysterically screaming one man thought she'd been shot & called 911. We found Lucas in the lawn mower section picking out the machine he wanted for his 8th birthday present

We live in a cement city & the only green around us is Central Park. Lucas is an adventurous dreamer & EL tends to overreact

I once disappeared for a week n no one noticed

Where did u go

Grandma Rose's house but she was on vacation

Omg

u were alone at her house?

Yes, n it was fun! Don't think Lucas would like living on Masada for a week. No iPad No Playstation

He wouldn't survive ur right hes rly an addict. how come no one knew U were missing?

It's a long story will tell U later but I had the best time.

If u gave me a good book, paper n pen n a volleyball Id survive anywhere in the world alone n happy

Id need a book, my music & my iPhone - not to talk but to look things up

Want to go swimming back at the hotel???

yessssss omg so hot here

cool ☺

Delivered

iMessage

162

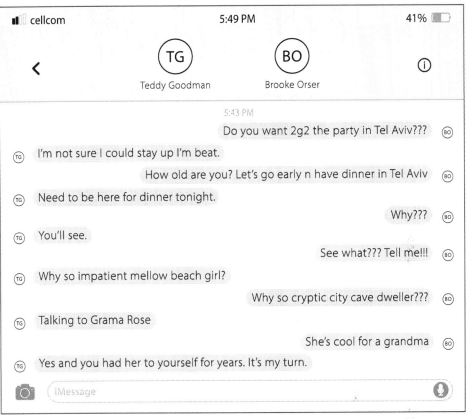

TG — Teddy Goodman   BO — Brooke Orser

5:43 PM

BO: Do you want 2g2 the party in Tel Aviv???

TG: I'm not sure I could stay up I'm beat.

BO: How old are you? Let's go early n have dinner in Tel Aviv

TG: Need to be here for dinner tonight.

BO: Why???

TG: You'll see.

BO: See what??? Tell me!!!

TG: Why so impatient mellow beach girl?

BO: Why so cryptic city cave dweller???

TG: Talking to Grama Rose

BO: She's cool for a grandma

TG: Yes and you had her to yourself for years. It's my turn.

iMessage

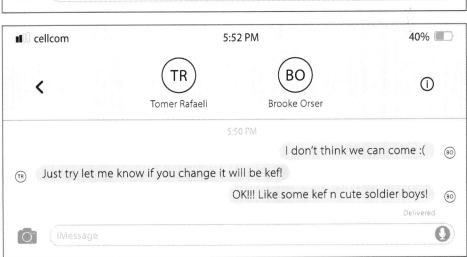

cellcom   5:52 PM   40%

TR — Tomer Rafaeli   BO — Brooke Orser

5:50 PM

BO: I don't think we can come :(

TR: Just try let me know if you change it will be kef!

BO: OK!!! Like some kef n cute soldier boys!

Delivered

iMessage

Masada

Brooke G.O.

Desert winds tell a hollow story
Lives taken, fallen glory
Ruins mark life long passed
History travels fast
Glory and darkness are the game
Each grain carries a forgotten name
Human choices are they wise
Sand flies burning eyes
Looking back the air clears
History repeats, one fears
Hope and glory
Same old story
Masada stands
Jewish Lands

♡ 151   246 ◉

ıl cellcom   6:00 PM   38% ▭

‹ Theo & Rose

Rose
Aliza just asked me to name five famous people I would like to eat lunch with if I could. I told her that you were my favorite living partner but she said that was not a fair answer. I should think. Who would your five-famous people be? Please tell me.

\+   ( )

JN24:   now
301 Ukranian Olim touch down as they make Aliyah in Israel. Last week 239 American Olim arrived in Israel to start their Aliyah journey.
Jewish News You Can Use

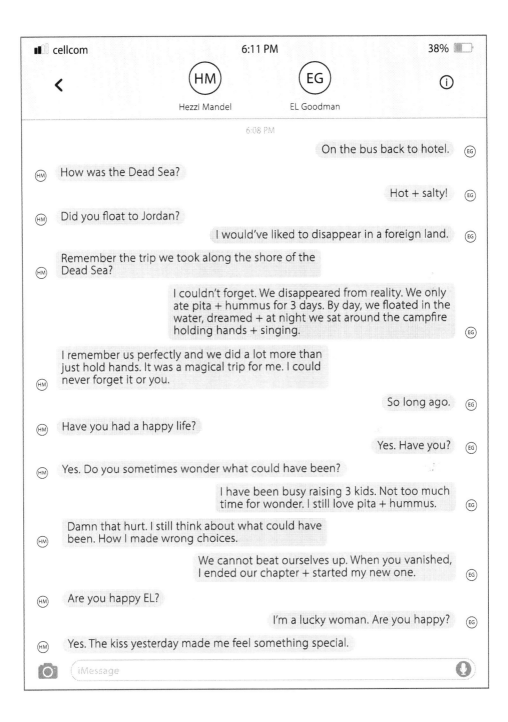

HM — Hezzi Mandel   EG — EL Goodman

6:08 PM

On the bus back to hotel. (EG)

(HM) How was the Dead Sea?

Hot + salty! (EG)

(HM) Did you float to Jordan?

I would've liked to disappear in a foreign land. (EG)

(HM) Remember the trip we took along the shore of the Dead Sea?

I couldn't forget. We disappeared from reality. We only ate pita + hummus for 3 days. By day, we floated in the water, dreamed + at night we sat around the campfire holding hands + singing. (EG)

(HM) I remember us perfectly and we did a lot more than just hold hands. It was a magical trip for me. I could never forget it or you.

So long ago. (EG)

(HM) Have you had a happy life?

Yes. Have you? (EG)

(HM) Yes. Do you sometimes wonder what could have been?

I have been busy raising 3 kids. Not too much time for wonder. I still love pita + hummus. (EG)

(HM) Damn that hurt. I still think about what could have been. How I made wrong choices.

We cannot beat ourselves up. When you vanished, I ended our chapter + started my new one. (EG)

(HM) Are you happy EL?

I'm a lucky woman. Are you happy? (EG)

(HM) Yes. The kiss yesterday made me feel something special.

iMessage

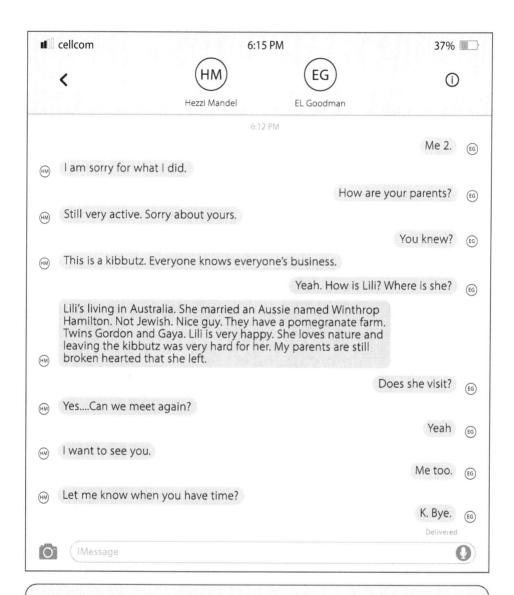

(HM) Hezzi Mandel   (EG) EL Goodman   (i)

6:12 PM

Me 2. (EG)

(HM) I am sorry for what I did.

How are your parents? (EG)

(HM) Still very active. Sorry about yours.

You knew? (EG)

(HM) This is a kibbutz. Everyone knows everyone's business.

Yeah. How is Lili? Where is she? (EG)

(HM) Lili's living in Australia. She married an Aussie named Winthrop Hamilton. Not Jewish. Nice guy. They have a pomegranate farm. Twins Gordon and Gaya. Lili is very happy. She loves nature and leaving the kibbutz was very hard for her. My parents are still broken hearted that she left.

Does she visit? (EG)

(HM) Yes....Can we meet again?

Yeah (EG)

(HM) I want to see you.

Me too. (EG)

(HM) Let me know when you have time?

K. Bye. (EG)

Delivered

iMessage

Aliza Goodman's Daily Motivational Quote #4:   now

"Not one of you is a believer unless he desires for his brother that which he desires for himself."
Prophet Muhammad

MotiQuote.com

Andy Orser
Now · Israel

•••

GOY IN THE HOLY LAND PART 13

Sitting at the delightful rooftop hotel restaurant after a long day touring; bright lights illuminate the ancient Old City walls; a slight breeze cools the air and a glass of chilled white wine feels heavenly. My dear family and fellow enthusiastic travelers surround me. Everyone's excitement and passion to be in the world's holiest city is palpable tonight.

Today we traveled through Jerusalem, Bedouin villages and the Palestinian city of Jericho on our way to Masada and the Dead Sea. Everything is so close in this uplifting nation. So many diverse people share a small limited land. On the surface, it appears to work, in the news we are told the opposite. The truth must be somewhere in between.

This Holy Land Adventure is awesome and inspiring. Each moment is better than the last and time is passing very quickly.

Dear Friends, this is one of those perfect picture moments captured in one's mind. There is no violence. There is no hate. There is love. #Jerusalemnights #amazing

👍 Like   💬 Comment   ↪ Share

 JN24:   now

Palestinian and Jewish writers' conference in Jerusalem leads efforts to bring young Jewish, Muslim and Christian writers together to share their work and collaborate for peace efforts.

Jewish News You Can Use

MYJOURNAL.COM

Arrival in the Holy Land
Roaming Roman

Bruno & I safely arrived in the Holy Land. My mission has commenced. I need to repair the damage I caused many years earlier. In the magical Holy Land, perhaps I can make things right. I have already waited too long. I could not do this without Bruno by my side.
Wish me luck. I think I will need it.

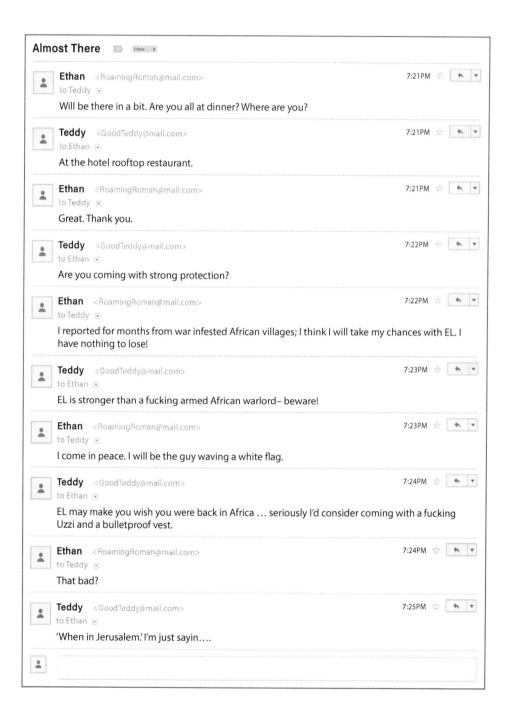

Almost There Inbox x

Ethan <RoamingRoman@mail.com>
to Teddy
7:21PM

Will be there in a bit. Are you all at dinner? Where are you?

Teddy <GoodTeddy@mail.com>
to Ethan
7:21PM

At the hotel rooftop restaurant.

Ethan <RoamingRoman@mail.com>
to Teddy
7:21PM

Great. Thank you.

Teddy <GoodTeddy@mail.com>
to Ethan
7:22PM

Are you coming with strong protection?

Ethan <RoamingRoman@mail.com>
to Teddy
7:22PM

I reported for months from war infested African villages; I think I will take my chances with EL. I have nothing to lose!

Teddy <GoodTeddy@mail.com>
to Ethan
7:23PM

EL is stronger than a fucking armed African warlord– beware!

Ethan <RoamingRoman@mail.com>
to Teddy
7:23PM

I come in peace. I will be the guy waving a white flag.

Teddy <GoodTeddy@mail.com>
to Ethan
7:24PM

EL may make you wish you were back in Africa … seriously I'd consider coming with a fucking Uzzi and a bulletproof vest.

Ethan <RoamingRoman@mail.com>
to Teddy
7:24PM

That bad?

Teddy <GoodTeddy@mail.com>
to Ethan
7:25PM

'When in Jerusalem.' I'm just sayin….

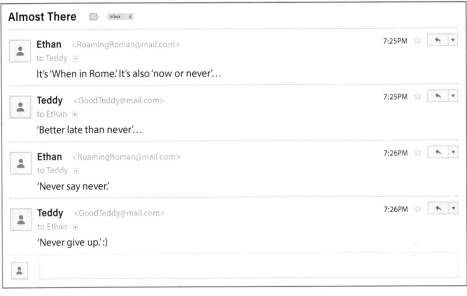

Almost There 📁 Inbox ✕

👤 **Ethan** <RoamingRoman@mail.com> 7:25PM ☆ ↩ ▾
to Teddy ▾

It's 'When in Rome.' It's also 'now or never'…

👤 **Teddy** <GoodTeddy@mail.com> 7:25PM ☆ ↩ ▾
to Ethan ▾

'Better late than never'…

👤 **Ethan** <RoamingRoman@mail.com> 7:26PM ☆ ↩ ▾
to Teddy ▾

'Never say never.'

👤 **Teddy** <GoodTeddy@mail.com> 7:26PM ☆ ↩ ▾
to Ethan ▾

'Never give up.' :)

👤

WTF 📁 Inbox ✕

👤 **EL** <ELGood@mail.com> 8:15PM ☆ ↩ ▾
to Shirl ▾

WTF!

I'm sitting at dinner on the beautiful hotel rooftop gulping down chilled white wine to recover from my 10-year-old son's dramatic disappearance + the violent death of my husband's best friend (which has resulted in the longest adult temper tantrum possible) + oh my God WTF…. As I'm drowning in alcohol - who shows up but my brother Ethan. My long-lost brother.

Aliza gets up + gives him a big hug. Teddy gets up + gives him a big hug. Traitors! Then Ethan walks over to me + calmly says, "Hi EL." I froze Shirl. I didn't say anything. My partially estranged mother-in-law introduced herself to my fully estranged brother - It was so odd like a Fellini movie. Even Benj got up + shook his hand + then introduced him to the others.

Then a very handsome man came out from behind of Ethan + he introduced him as his partner, Bruno Bocaccio. He was stunning. My head was spinning so fast at this point + I could not say a word.

Bruno Bocaccio – WTF.

👤 **Shirl** <SHIRL465@mail.com> 8:17PM ☆ ↩ ▾
to EL ▾

Where are you now?

👤

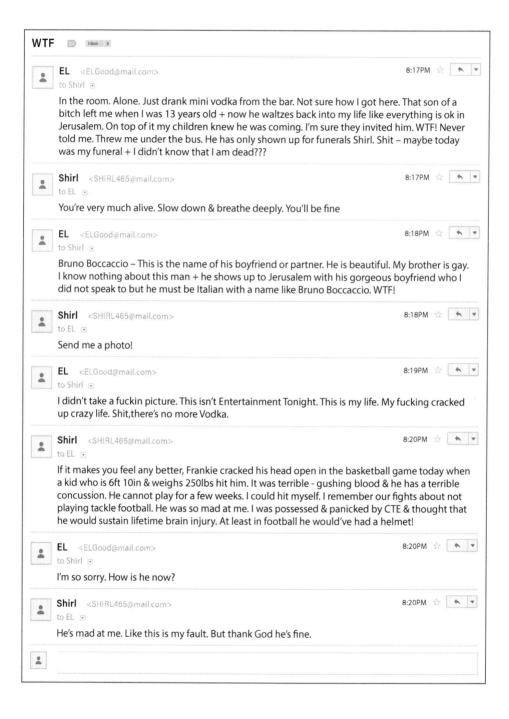

WTF 📋 Inbox x

EL <ELGood@mail.com>
to Shirl   8:17PM

In the room. Alone. Just drank mini vodka from the bar. Not sure how I got here. That son of a bitch left me when I was 13 years old + now he waltzes back into my life like everything is ok in Jerusalem. On top of it my children knew he was coming. I'm sure they invited him. WTF! Never told me. Threw me under the bus. He has only shown up for funerals Shirl. Shit – maybe today was my funeral + I didn't know that I am dead???

Shirl <SHIRL465@mail.com>
to EL   8:17PM

You're very much alive. Slow down & breathe deeply. You'll be fine

EL <ELGood@mail.com>
to Shirl   8:18PM

Bruno Boccaccio – This is the name of his boyfriend or partner. He is beautiful. My brother is gay. I know nothing about this man + he shows up to Jerusalem with his gorgeous boyfriend who I did not speak to but he must be Italian with a name like Bruno Boccaccio. WTF!

Shirl <SHIRL465@mail.com>
to EL   8:18PM

Send me a photo!

EL <ELGood@mail.com>
to Shirl   8:19PM

I didn't take a fuckin picture. This isn't Entertainment Tonight. This is my life. My fucking cracked up crazy life. Shit,there's no more Vodka.

Shirl <SHIRL465@mail.com>
to EL   8:20PM

If it makes you feel any better, Frankie cracked his head open in the basketball game today when a kid who is 6ft 10in & weighs 250lbs hit him. It was terrible - gushing blood & he has a terrible concussion. He cannot play for a few weeks. I could hit myself. I remember our fights about not playing tackle football. He was so mad at me. I was possessed & panicked by CTE & thought that he would sustain lifetime brain injury. At least in football he would've had a helmet!

EL <ELGood@mail.com>
to Shirl   8:20PM

I'm so sorry. How is he now?

Shirl <SHIRL465@mail.com>
to EL   8:20PM

He's mad at me. Like this is my fault. But thank God he's fine.

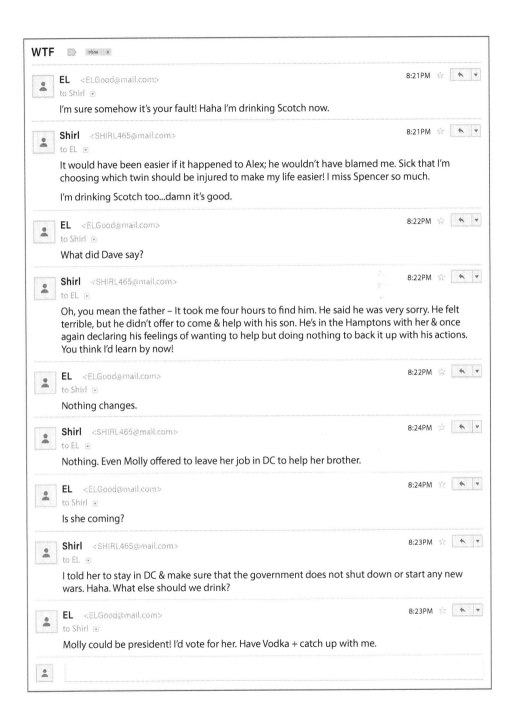

WTF

EL <ELGood@mail.com>
to Shirl
8:21PM

I'm sure somehow it's your fault! Haha I'm drinking Scotch now.

Shirl <SHIRL465@mail.com>
to EL
8:21PM

It would have been easier if it happened to Alex; he wouldn't have blamed me. Sick that I'm choosing which twin should be injured to make my life easier! I miss Spencer so much.

I'm drinking Scotch too...damn it's good.

EL <ELGood@mail.com>
to Shirl
8:22PM

What did Dave say?

Shirl <SHIRL465@mail.com>
to EL
8:22PM

Oh, you mean the father – It took me four hours to find him. He said he was very sorry. He felt terrible, but he didn't offer to come & help with his son. He's in the Hamptons with her & once again declaring his feelings of wanting to help but doing nothing to back it up with his actions. You think I'd learn by now!

EL <ELGood@mail.com>
to Shirl
8:22PM

Nothing changes.

Shirl <SHIRL465@mail.com>
to EL
8:24PM

Nothing. Even Molly offered to leave her job in DC to help her brother.

EL <ELGood@mail.com>
to Shirl
8:24PM

Is she coming?

Shirl <SHIRL465@mail.com>
to EL
8:23PM

I told her to stay in DC & make sure that the government does not shut down or start any new wars. Haha. What else should we drink?

EL <ELGood@mail.com>
to Shirl
8:23PM

Molly could be president! I'd vote for her. Have Vodka + catch up with me.

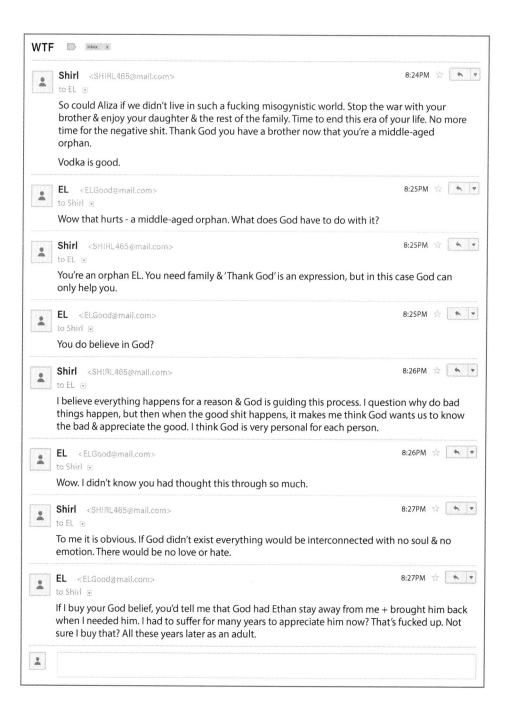

WTF ▷ Inbox x

Shirl <SHIRL465@mail.com>   8:24PM ☆
to EL

So could Aliza if we didn't live in such a fucking misogynistic world. Stop the war with your brother & enjoy your daughter & the rest of the family. Time to end this era of your life. No more time for the negative shit. Thank God you have a brother now that you're a middle-aged orphan.

Vodka is good.

EL <ELGood@mail.com>   8:25PM ☆
to Shirl

Wow that hurts - a middle-aged orphan. What does God have to do with it?

Shirl <SHIRL465@mail.com>   8:25PM ☆
to EL

You're an orphan EL. You need family & 'Thank God' is an expression, but in this case God can only help you.

EL <ELGood@mail.com>   8:25PM ☆
to Shirl

You do believe in God?

Shirl <SHIRL465@mail.com>   8:26PM ☆
to EL

I believe everything happens for a reason & God is guiding this process. I question why do bad things happen, but then when the good shit happens, it makes me think God wants us to know the bad & appreciate the good. I think God is very personal for each person.

EL <ELGood@mail.com>   8:26PM ☆
to Shirl

Wow. I didn't know you had thought this through so much.

Shirl <SHIRL465@mail.com>   8:27PM ☆
to EL

To me it is obvious. If God didn't exist everything would be interconnected with no soul & no emotion. There would be no love or hate.

EL <ELGood@mail.com>   8:27PM ☆
to Shirl

If I buy your God belief, you'd tell me that God had Ethan stay away from me + brought him back when I needed him. I had to suffer for many years to appreciate him now? That's fucked up. Not sure I buy that? All these years later as an adult.

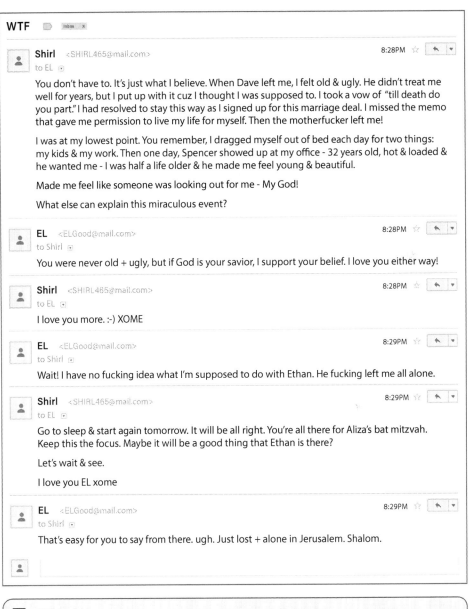

WTF 📁 Inbox ×

Shirl <SHIRL465@mail.com>   8:28PM ☆
to EL

You don't have to. It's just what I believe. When Dave left me, I felt old & ugly. He didn't treat me well for years, but I put up with it cuz I thought I was supposed to. I took a vow of "till death do you part." I had resolved to stay this way as I signed up for this marriage deal. I missed the memo that gave me permission to live my life for myself. Then the motherfucker left me!

I was at my lowest point. You remember, I dragged myself out of bed each day for two things: my kids & my work. Then one day, Spencer showed up at my office - 32 years old, hot & loaded & he wanted me - I was half a life older & he made me feel young & beautiful.

Made me feel like someone was looking out for me - My God!

What else can explain this miraculous event?

EL <ELGood@mail.com>   8:28PM ☆
to Shirl

You were never old + ugly, but if God is your savior, I support your belief. I love you either way!

Shirl <SHIRL465@mail.com>   8:28PM ☆
to EL

I love you more. :-) XOME

EL <ELGood@mail.com>   8:29PM ☆
to Shirl

Wait! I have no fucking idea what I'm supposed to do with Ethan. He fucking left me all alone.

Shirl <SHIRL465@mail.com>   8:29PM ☆
to EL

Go to sleep & start again tomorrow. It will be all right. You're all there for Aliza's bat mitzvah. Keep this the focus. Maybe it will be a good thing that Ethan is there?

Let's wait & see.

I love you EL xome

EL <ELGood@mail.com>   8:29PM ☆
to Shirl

That's easy for you to say from there. ugh. Just lost + alone in Jerusalem. Shalom.

JN24:   now

Jewish, Muslim and Christian young people enjoy same night clubs across Israel.

Jewish News You Can Use

An Overdue Reunion
Roaming Roman

The long overdue reunion took place. Not a full apocalypse: Aliza & Teddy (my niece and nephew) were so happy to see me. Genuine hugs and warmth. I felt so excited to have them in life. My sister EL was a different story. Not a word to me before she left the table very drunk & angry. I am not sure she will ever forgive me but I must try to appeal to her for absolution. Bruno and I sat with the rest of my family at the beautiful hotel rooftop. The cool Jerusalem night air refreshing as I breathed in so much new air. A city accustomed to the arrival of visitors ready to conquer and conquest; their restless hearts and souls share the pioneer's DNA that has no time or place for simple contentment. I am not the first to arrive in the holy city with so much to resolve; I will use the power of this extraordinary place to fill my sails as I seek asylum in the life I once denounced and so dearly want to regain as my own. I have found true love in my life and yet feel the vacuum of my past prevents me from fully embracing joy and fulfillment. I could not have made it without Bruno holding my hand - he is my true sunshine. He is my life partner. He deserves a whole me, and this is the conquest I desperately yearn for now in my life - to close and fill my life's circle.

LIFEEXPRESSIONS.COM

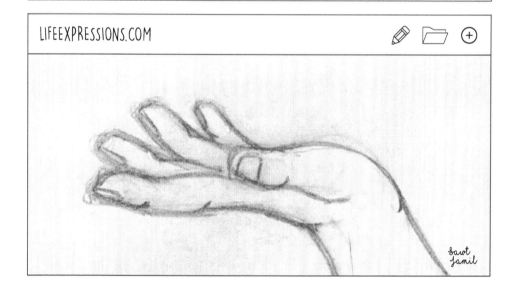

The Black Sheep
Teddy Goodman

Uncle Ethan, EL's older brother, is the black sheep of the family. When my mom was 13, Uncle Ethan was 18. He graduated high school, went off to college and then disappeared. My mother still vehemently hates him for abandoning her and the family. I have only met Ethan on two occasions: at each of my grandparent's funerals. Both times EL did not speak to him: she said hello and then walked away. Last year at Grandma Shula's funeral, I finally spoke with Uncle Ethan. He seemed nice and interesting. He gave me his email address and since then, we have been emailing. He is a journalist and lives in Rome with his partner Bruno. Aliza has also been emailing with uncle Ethan and invited him to her bat mitzvah. When he wrote that he planned to attend, I knew this could cause WW3, and I also knew if EL knew ahead of time that she would forbid him from coming. It has been a secret between Aliza and me. We don't have much in common so this has been a unifying sibling experience. It was time for the truth to come out. Ethan seems like a nice enough guy: we do not exactly have a lot of relatives and the ones we do have, we are not supposed to like, kind of a fucked up dysfunctional 21st Century family. I want to learn the real reason that he left home at 18; there are plenty of days when I think about leaving home and disappearing myself. But in the end, I cannot imagine doing something so fucking dramatic and crazy.

When Ethan and Bruno arrived at our table, EL and Benj were still debating about where "The best hummus originated from" and "If Israel was a true democracy, if Judaism is the official religion." EL and Benj have made debating a marital pastime and as usual this debate was full of deep anger and frustration to back up senseless arguments. When EL saw uncle Ethan she literally took her full glass of wine and chugged it like a shot glass. EL looked at her brother Ethan with overwhelming shock in her eyes. A long minute later, she got up from the table and stammered away, a little drunk and very angry. WW3 has begun!

Aliza Goodman's Daily Motivational Quote #5:　　　　　　　　now

"The universe took its time on you, crafted you precisely so you could offer the world something distinct from everyone else. So when you doubt how you were created, you doubt an energy greater than us both."　　*Rupi Kaur*

MotiQuote.com

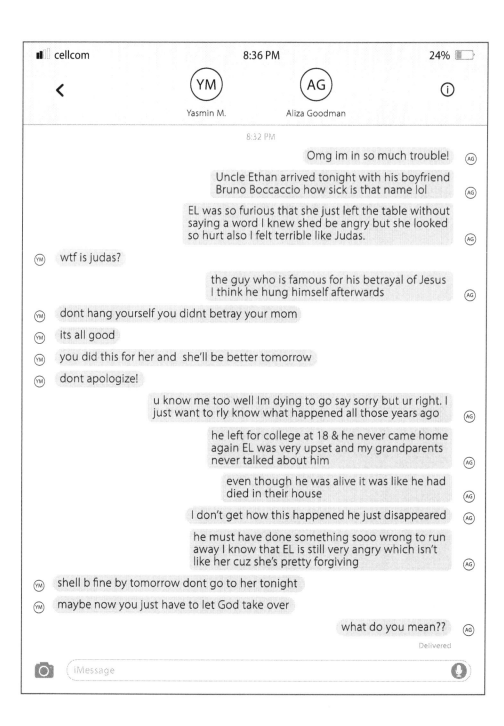

8:32 PM

Omg im in so much trouble!

Uncle Ethan arrived tonight with his boyfriend Bruno Boccaccio how sick is that name lol

EL was so furious that she just left the table without saying a word I knew shed be angry but she looked so hurt also I felt terrible like Judas.

wtf is judas?

the guy who is famous for his betrayal of Jesus I think he hung himself afterwards

dont hang yourself you didnt betray your mom

its all good

you did this for her and she'll be better tomorrow

dont apologize!

u know me too well Im dying to go say sorry but ur right. I just want to rly know what happened all those years ago

he left for college at 18 & he never came home again EL was very upset and my grandparents never talked about him

even though he was alive it was like he had died in their house

I don't get how this happened he just disappeared

he must have done something sooo wrong to run away I know that EL is still very angry which isn't like her cuz she's pretty forgiving

shell b fine by tomorrow dont go to her tonight

maybe now you just have to let God take over

what do you mean??

Delivered

iMessage

176

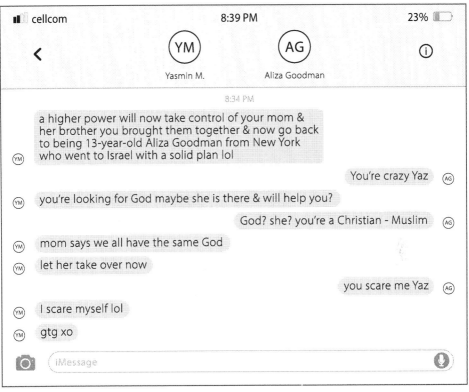

YM Yasmin M.   **AG** Aliza Goodman

8:34 PM

(YM) a higher power will now take control of your mom & her brother you brought them together & now go back to being 13-year-old Aliza Goodman from New York who went to Israel with a solid plan lol

You're crazy Yaz **(AG)**

(YM) you're looking for God maybe she is there & will help you?

God? she? you're a Christian - Muslim **(AG)**

(YM) mom says we all have the same God

(YM) let her take over now

you scare me Yaz **(AG)**

(YM) I scare myself lol

(YM) gtg xo

iMessage

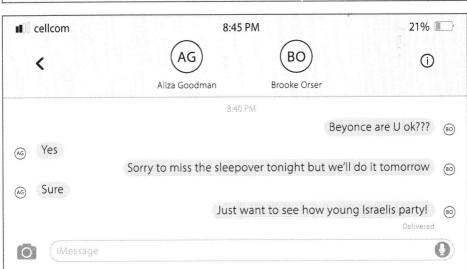

AG Aliza Goodman   **BO** Brooke Orser

8:40 PM

Beyonce are U ok??? **(BO)**

(AG) Yes

Sorry to miss the sleepover tonight but we'll do it tomorrow **(BO)**

(AG) Sure

Just want to see how young Israelis party! **(BO)**

Delivered

iMessage

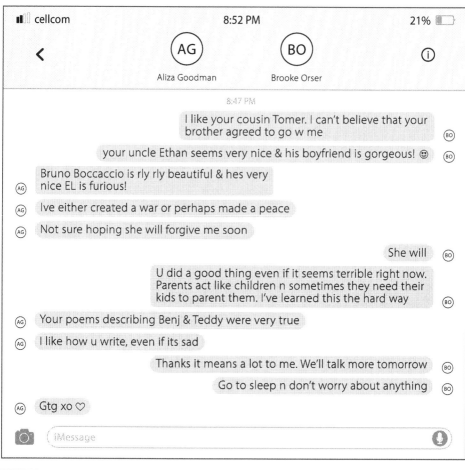

cellcom   8:52 PM   21% ▭

AG   **BO**
Aliza Goodman   Brooke Orser

8:47 PM

I like your cousin Tomer. I can't believe that your brother agreed to go w me

your uncle Ethan seems very nice & his boyfriend is gorgeous! ☺

Bruno Boccaccio is rly rly beautiful & hes very nice EL is furious!

Ive either created a war or perhaps made a peace

Not sure hoping she will forgive me soon

She will

U did a good thing even if it seems terrible right now. Parents act like children n sometimes they need their kids to parent them. I've learned this the hard way

Your poems describing Benj & Teddy were very true

I like how u write, even if its sad

Thanks it means a lot to me. We'll talk more tomorrow

Go to sleep n don't worry about anything

Gtg xo ♡

iMessage

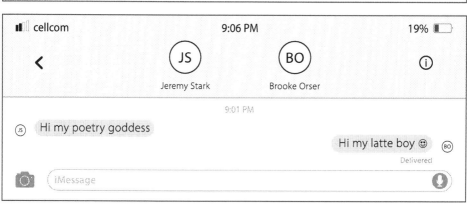

cellcom   9:06 PM   19% ▭

JS   **BO**
Jeremy Stark   Brooke Orser

9:01 PM

Hi my poetry goddess

Hi my latte boy ☺

Delivered

iMessage

JS — Jeremy Stark

BO — Brooke Orser

9:06 PM

JS Ugh! That hurts

Wish you were here BO

JS The humidity here feels like mud caked on my skin and I didnt go to the dead sea lol

Sorry! Wish you were here 😊 BO

JS Me too. My turn at Starbucks BYE

BYE BO

♡ BO

Delivered

iMessage

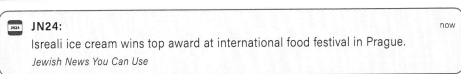

JN24: now

Isreali ice cream wins top award at international food festival in Prague.

Jewish News You Can Use

Report Update Inbox x

Benj <B.Goodman@SHH.com> 9:22PM
to Laura

Did Isaac fix the report?

Laura <L.Friedman@SHH.com> 9:22PM
to Benj

Isaac is away for the weekend with his family.

Benj <B.Goodman@SHH.com> 9:22PM
to Laura

WTF. Does he know how crazy tight our timing is on this?

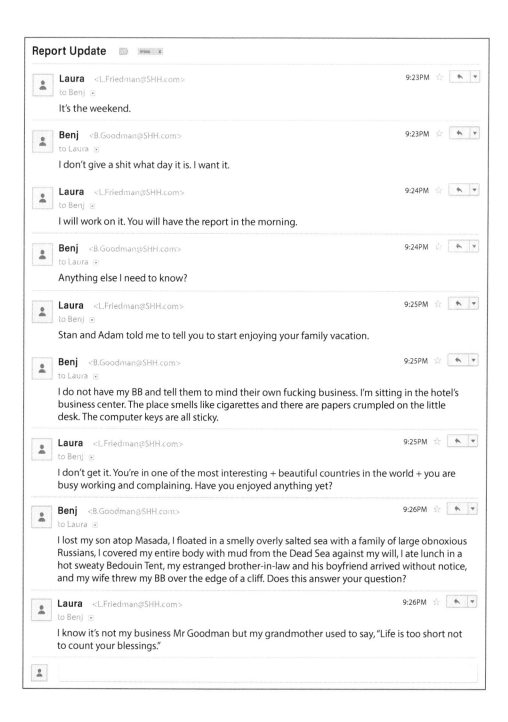

Report Update Inbox x

Laura <L.Friedman@SHH.com>
to Benj
9:23PM

It's the weekend.

Benj <B.Goodman@SHH.com>
to Laura
9:23PM

I don't give a shit what day it is. I want it.

Laura <L.Friedman@SHH.com>
to Benj
9:24PM

I will work on it. You will have the report in the morning.

Benj <B.Goodman@SHH.com>
to Laura
9:24PM

Anything else I need to know?

Laura <L.Friedman@SHH.com>
to Benj
9:25PM

Stan and Adam told me to tell you to start enjoying your family vacation.

Benj <B.Goodman@SHH.com>
to Laura
9:25PM

I do not have my BB and tell them to mind their own fucking business. I'm sitting in the hotel's business center. The place smells like cigarettes and there are papers crumpled on the little desk. The computer keys are all sticky.

Laura <L.Friedman@SHH.com>
to Benj
9:25PM

I don't get it. You're in one of the most interesting + beautiful countries in the world + you are busy working and complaining. Have you enjoyed anything yet?

Benj <B.Goodman@SHH.com>
to Laura
9:26PM

I lost my son atop Masada, I floated in a smelly overly salted sea with a family of large obnoxious Russians, I covered my entire body with mud from the Dead Sea against my will, I ate lunch in a hot sweaty Bedouin Tent, my estranged brother-in-law and his boyfriend arrived without notice, and my wife threw my BB over the edge of a cliff. Does this answer your question?

Laura <L.Friedman@SHH.com>
to Benj
9:26PM

I know it's not my business Mr Goodman but my grandmother used to say, "Life is too short not to count your blessings."

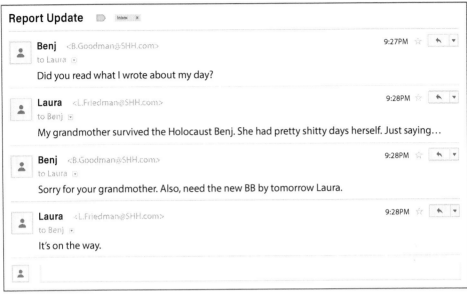

Report Update Inbox ×

Benj <B.Goodman@SHH.com>　　　　　　　　　　9:27PM
to Laura

Did you read what I wrote about my day?

Laura <L.Friedman@SHH.com>　　　　　　　　　　9:28PM
to Benj

My grandmother survived the Holocaust Benj. She had pretty shitty days herself. Just saying…

Benj <B.Goodman@SHH.com>　　　　　　　　　　9:28PM
to Laura

Sorry for your grandmother. Also, need the new BB by tomorrow Laura.

Laura <L.Friedman@SHH.com>　　　　　　　　　　9:28PM
to Benj

It's on the way.

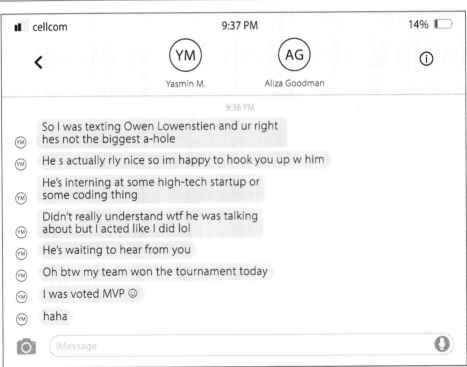

cellcom　　　　　　9:37 PM　　　　　　14%

‹　　　　**YM**　　　　**AG**　　　　ⓘ
　　　Yasmin M.　　Aliza Goodman

9:36 PM

So I was texting Owen Lowenstien and ur right hes not the biggest a-hole

He s actually rly nice so im happy to hook you up w him

He's interning at some high-tech startup or some coding thing

Didn't really understand wtf he was talking about but I acted like I did lol

He's waiting to hear from you

Oh btw my team won the tournament today

I was voted MVP ☺

haha

iMessage

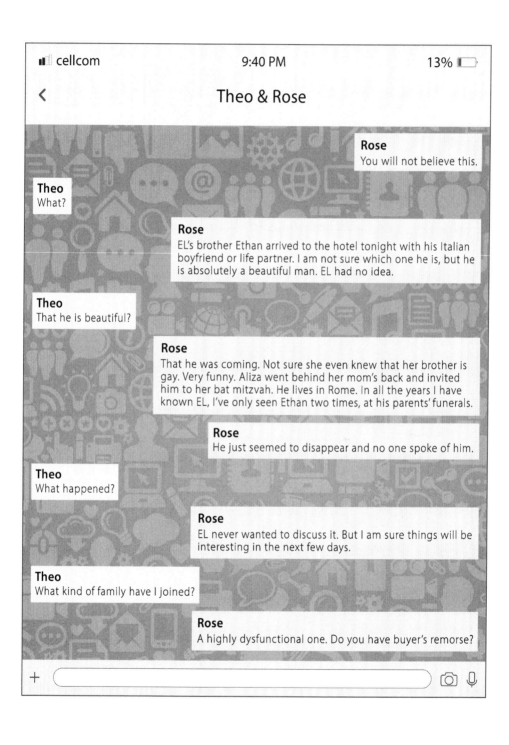

Theo & Rose

Rose
You will not believe this.

Theo
What?

Rose
EL's brother Ethan arrived to the hotel tonight with his Italian boyfriend or life partner. I am not sure which one he is, but he is absolutely a beautiful man. EL had no idea.

Theo
That he is beautiful?

Rose
That he was coming. Not sure she even knew that her brother is gay. Very funny. Aliza went behind her mom's back and invited him to her bat mitzvah. He lives in Rome. In all the years I have known EL, I've only seen Ethan two times, at his parents' funerals.

Rose
He just seemed to disappear and no one spoke of him.

Theo
What happened?

Rose
EL never wanted to discuss it. But I am sure things will be interesting in the next few days.

Theo
What kind of family have I joined?

Rose
A highly dysfunctional one. Do you have buyer's remorse?

‹   **Theo & Rose**

Theo
Not for a second. Before I met you, I never thought I would be happy again in my life. I lost everything I had enjoyed for 35 years. You have given me a new lease on life. I have truly never been happier than I am now. I live to love you Rosie. I take you for good & bad, thick & thin, soft & hard despiteyour dysfunctional family dynamics. We are in sync & I'm yours forever.

Rose
You make me complete. I feel the same way. Living with you. Loving you deeply makes me fulfilled in every way. Thank you. Thank God

Theo
You think God brought us together?

Rose
If we both were not at the bbq the same day with friends, not even good friends, we would never have met. I lived in Santa Barbara and you in Los Angeles. If not God, then what?

Theo
Luck. Good timing?

Rose
Some force brought us together and I just refer to it as God.

Theo
I think that God is more than a force; he is like a super human man.

Rose
What?

Theo
He is imperfect like man, but all-powerful.

\+

Rose
Why?

Theo
He causes wars, he allows for killing & death; he also allows for great things & pure happiness. He has more power & greater influence but all in the same parameters of humans - just bolder.

Rose
Wow. Your God brings about all these challenges for my family and me so I will appreciate all the good?

Theo
Perhaps now your role is to bring your stories, your wit & your love to a family that is hungry for this - focus on why you went on this trip. Do not get involved in their negative business. Keep being the positive and beautiful Rose that God brought into my life & who I fell hard in love with at first sight.

Rose
Yes, I will. I will try to play this role but with all the sexting you are doing, I am not sure I can act my age or give them the time they require.

Theo
Sexting I am doing? I thought we were doing?

Rose
I can barely keep my eyes open

Theo
Seriously Rosie - I'm here & love texting with you, but if I take too much of your time we can take a break & let you focus on your family.

+ ⬭   ▢ ⬤

Theo & Rose

Rose
Don't be ridiculous. I need you. I love you.

Theo
I miss you Rosie. I love you

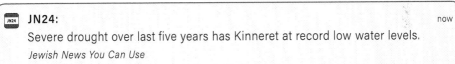

JN24:   now
Severe drought over last five years has Kinneret at record low water levels.
Jewish News You Can Use

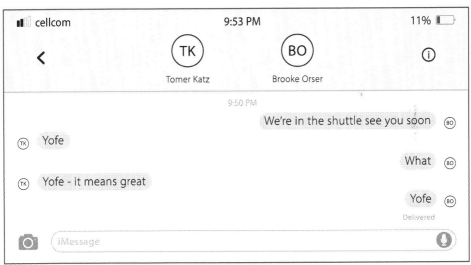

Tomer Katz   **Brooke Orser**

9:50 PM

We're in the shuttle see you soon

Yofe

What

Yofe - it means great

Yofe

Delivered

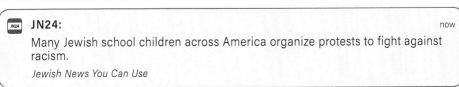

JN24:   now
Many Jewish school children across America organize protests to fight against racism.
Jewish News You Can Use

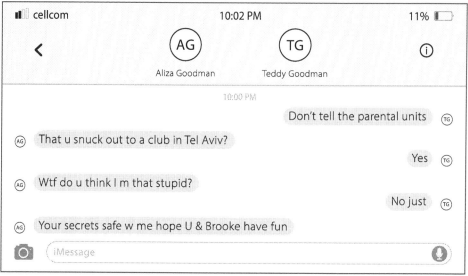

AG Aliza Goodman   **TG** Teddy Goodman

10:00 PM

Don't tell the parental units

That u snuck out to a club in Tel Aviv?

Yes

Wtf do u think I m that stupid?

No just

Your secrets safe w me hope U & Brooke have fun

iMessage

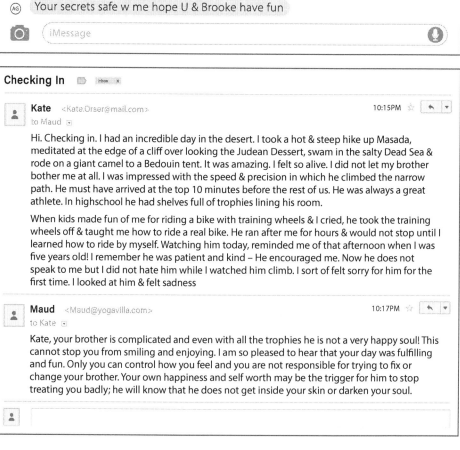

Checking In   inbox x

Kate <Kate.Orser@mail.com>   10:15PM
to Maud

Hi. Checking in. I had an incredible day in the desert. I took a hot & steep hike up Masada, meditated at the edge of a cliff over looking the Judean Dessert, swam in the salty Dead Sea & rode on a giant camel to a Bedouin tent. It was amazing. I felt so alive. I did not let my brother bother me at all. I was impressed with the speed & precision in which he climbed the narrow path. He must have arrived at the top 10 minutes before the rest of us. He was always a great athlete. In highschool he had shelves full of trophies lining his room.

When kids made fun of me for riding a bike with training wheels & I cried, he took the training wheels off & taught me how to ride a real bike. He ran after me for hours & would not stop until I learned how to ride by myself. Watching him today, reminded me of that afternoon when I was five years old! I remember he was patient and kind – He encouraged me. Now he does not speak to me but I did not hate him while I watched him climb. I sort of felt sorry for him for the first time. I looked at him & felt sadness

Maud <Maud@yogavilla.com>   10:17PM
to Kate

Kate, your brother is complicated and even with all the trophies he is not a very happy soul! This cannot stop you from smiling and enjoying. I am so pleased to hear that your day was fulfilling and fun. Only you can control how you feel and you are not responsible for trying to fix or change your brother. Your own happiness and self worth may be the trigger for him to stop treating you badly; he will know that he does not get inside your skin or darken your soul.

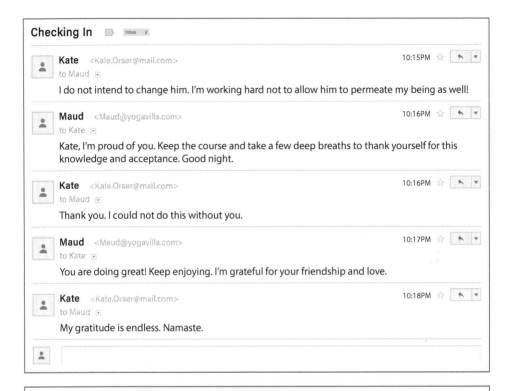

Checking In Inbox ×

Kate \<Kate.Orser@mail.com\> 10:15PM
to Maud

I do not intend to change him. I'm working hard not to allow him to permeate my being as well!

Maud \<Maud@yogavilla.com\> 10:16PM
to Kate

Kate, I'm proud of you. Keep the course and take a few deep breaths to thank yourself for this knowledge and acceptance. Good night.

Kate \<Kate.Orser@mail.com\> 10:16PM
to Maud

Thank you. I could not do this without you.

Maud \<Maud@yogavilla.com\> 10:17PM
to Kate

You are doing great! Keep enjoying. I'm grateful for your friendship and love.

Kate \<Kate.Orser@mail.com\> 10:18PM
to Maud

My gratitude is endless. Namaste.

MYPOETRY.COM   • • •

Bruno Boccacio

Brooke G.O.

Fruit from the earth
Italian angels danced at your birth
Discovering the next adventure
Red wine sweet and pure
Renaissance beauty ideal
Italian black truffle's meal
Prosecco passion pours
Love what's not yours
A taste hard to place
A foreign space
Sweet sensation leaves one's lips
Holy and sacred trips

♡ 160   301 ◎

Dear Aliza,

Safta Shula's HAPPINESS. We arrived in New York and Uncle Samuel met us at the airport. Yacov fell into his arms and sobbed. The two grown men wept in each other's arms for months. I joined them in crying many times myself.

Yacov quickly took his place by Uncle Samuel learning his bra and lingerie manufacturing business. Yacov who swore he would never sew again, now used his talent and expertise to partner with his uncle. This time his efforts produced positive joyful wardrobe for women. He loved his work and loved his Uncle Samuel.

We both learned English quickly and assimilated into the American big city life. We had a large apartment twice as big as the house we lived in on the kibbutz. The first year I wandered the streets learning my new city, finding markets that sold products I recognized and learning the foods, spices and supplies of my new country. I missed the green, gentle kibbutz but quickly learned what an incredible fast paced, dynamic city I was living in. After a year, I enrolled in Hunter College to get my teaching degree. On the weekends when Samuel and Yacov were not working we went to museums, shows and spent time picnicking in Central Park.

As soon as I finished my studies, I was pregnant with my first child and never began a career as a teacher. May 31, 1965 my son Eitan was born, but we quickly called him Ethan, his American name. I was the happiest when I became a mother and our lives' focus was all about our son. We planned his future as an American Jew. We prayed he would not see war, conflict and experience hate and persecution as Yacov and I had. I dedicated myself to my son, who was beautiful, happy and very intelligent. Five years later May 26, 1970, your mother EL was born and I had the perfect family I always dreamed of: A husband, a son and a daughter.

I missed my family in Israel dearly. We spoke by phone once a week, but the lines were not always available and the calls were very expensive. There was no Internet or wifi so we had no way to check in or call unexpectedly just to say hi. Our calls were planned and organized in advance. Sending a letter could take two weeks to arrive. The pace was slower and much more thought went into the relationships as we had great appreciation for the time we did spend sharing stories over a crackling phone line. After each baby my parents came to New York to stay with us for a few weeks and I remember how happy I was that they were in my home and part of my life.

Each trip I realized that my parents were getting older and I valued their love and time so much more. All the sacrifices they had made for me to have a better life and they wanted nothing but love and warmth in return. They were sad that I lived far away but so happy that I found a home with Yacov in a free country.

I found the perfect balance between being a mom, a wife and a daughter.

Freedom Inbox x

Dahlia ‹FreeDahlia@mail.com›   11:29PM
to EL

Freedom also feels powerful like waves crashin' on a sandy shore. Y'asked how I knew I was finished with my marriage? I recalled that snowy night in college n the woman I enjoyed bein' back then had disappeared. I woke one mornin' n said to myself, "My mama didn't raise a fool." It hit me hard. I cried for a good straight hour that mornin'.

Then I took a shower n got dressed to start a new day. I never looked back. I made peace with myself n forgave myself for not bein' the perfect Southern Belle who stood by her man no matter what.

My children were grown up n they were very supportive of me. I was an arrested girl finally set free in New York City with a great appetite to enjoy the life I had ahead of me.

Y' mama n I met years earlier workin' at the shelter. After your father's death n my divorce, we started spendin' time together; our special bond gave a surprisin' richness at the end of her life n as part of my older years. Who thought a Southern Belle n an Iraqi/Israeli immigrant would forge a special bond? I'm forever grateful for this short n beautiful period in my life.

EL, I'm here to support y' no matter what y' decide. Y'can count on me for cryin' out loud n just don't let that man get the best of y'!

EL ‹ELGood@mail.com›   11:57PM
to Dahlia

Thank you, Dahlia for sharing this with me. Today I threw Benj's Blackberry off the cliff + it felt a lot like Freedom. I came back to the hotel secretly feeling incredibly victorious + this lasted for a short time. Until I sat at dinner + had a completely unexpected surprise. Guess who shows up at the table? My long lost big brother Ethan. I lost it. I went crazy + now I'm in the room batshit drunk.

HELP!!!

WTF

Shirl <SHIRL.465@mail.com>   1:15AM
to EL

Are you still up? I'm drunk & sharing a room with two smelly 16-year-old boys. We are listening to
their shitty music. It is horrible misogynistic crap that terrifies me - 'And my dick so hard it makes
the metal detector go off, this that sauce, this that dressing, Givency, n***a bless you, If having a
bad bitch was a crime, I'd be arrested.' If this is what the future leaders of America are listening
to, we are screwed.

BOKER TOV

Goodman Family!

Welcome to day four of your Holy Land excursion!
Here is today's schedule:

Exploring International Cross Roads.

10AM– We will depart the hotel for the tour of Jerusalem's Old City.

Today we will visit the historical Western Wall, the Western Wall Tunnel, and the Church of the Holy Sepulchre. Our lunch will be at Abu Massan, a wonderful local Arab restaurant in the Muslim Quarter of the Old City. In Jerusalem, a UNESCO world heritage site, you will connect with the world's Abrahamic faiths: Judaism, Christianity, and Islam. You will experience first hand how close everyone is and how despite the news coverage, most people here get along and are free to believe as they wish.

Please dress modestly: women cover your shoulders and legs.

Today's Temperature:

 The weather today will be a warm 30°c / 86°f

Yom Tov!

Moshe
Rimon Tours

Andy Orser
Now · Israel

GOY IN THE HOLY LAND PART 14

Just back from an invigorating early morning run. It is a glorious new day in the Holy City. Even at this early warm hour, the city is alive and bustling with energy: exuberant children with cartoon decorated backpacks on their way to school darting past the solemn religious man in a disheveled black suit yelling on his cell phone and shaking his free hand as the dark-skinned trash collectors methodically pick up overly stuffed bags piled high on the street corner and dump them in the truck's rear. Passed a bakery with the scent of fresh cheese bread wafting through the air, church bells rang as the Muzzin called Muslims at the Mosque to early Morning Prayer.

Looking around, the ancient city famous for discord and dissonance, feels fresh and alive with positive energy.

Dear Friends, it is still early but I am happy and safe. No bombs, no sirens and no hate. I have entered one of my own documentaries. #Jerusalemmorning #holylandadventures #peace

 Like   Comment   Share

JN24:   now

Jewish and Arab student orchestra performs Mozart's 5th Symphony in Milan's La Scala Theater.

Jewish News You Can Use

WTF   Inbox x

 EL <ELGood@mail.com>   8:01AM
to Shirl

Fainted drunk last night. My head is so heavy this morning. Not sure how I can make it through the day? Shocking that Ethan is here. I just want to hide in my dark room. The image of a dick so hard it sets off a metal detector is fucking funny though. I'd laugh but my head hurts too much.

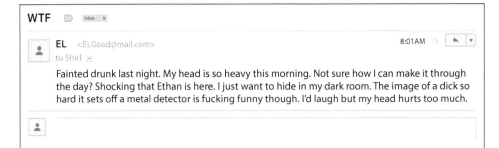

Aliza Goodman's Daily Motivational Quote #1:   now

"When the power of love overcomes the love of power the world will know peace."
Jimi Hendrix

MotiQuote.com

FOOD AFFAIR WITH KATE

DIVINE, DELICIOUS, AND DELIGHTFUL

The Breakfast of Champions

★ ★ ★ ★ ★

A breakfast of Olympic proportions summons me this morning. The Israeli breakfast buffet, a culinary marathon feast with endless choices: the real dilemma narrowing down options to fill one's plate and not to appear gluttonous with eyes much grander than one's stomach. This morning buffet's divine temptations reflect the most diverse dietary desires of all religious pilgrims and tourists. Breakfast, lunch, and dinner foods - pizza, fried chicken, meatloaf, salads, lasagna and pasta, cakes, puddings and soufflés (it is not 9am yet!) - fill grand tables of the multifaceted presentation alongside customary breakfast yogurts, pancakes, cereals, cold cuts, eggs, vegetables, fresh fruit, cheese and breads. Even after I fill my plate to the brim, I'm tempted to go back for seconds and thirds. This meal is inspiring!

Israeli dairy offerings are my dietary focus: the perfect consistency of local cottage cheese, slightly chunky while very creamy with a mild, faintly tangy taste. I devour bowls of this incredibly delicious cottage cheese garnished with fresh cut fruit and generously spread on moist multigrain toast. My second divine dairy discovery is warm cheesecake; sweet creamy cheese pudding melts in my mouth sending tingles of pure dessert joy through my entire body- an orgasmic breakfast dessert that has all day long to burn off the effects of its tremendous caloric count. I counted 18 cheese options with a multitude of shapes, colors and scents on one table; equally as many appealing salad combinations on the next table over. 18 characterizes an incredible quantity of food choices and as well in Judaism, CHAI, or the number 18 represents "life" and "good luck". One certainly needs a bit of mazel tov "good luck" navigating the heavenly food choices and carefully filling a dinner size plate with just the right number of flavorsome items to satisfy a healthy and curious appetite!

See the photos below and check out Food Affair with Kate on Instagram and Facebook. #Israelibreakfastmarathon #orgasmicfood #divinedining

Road to Redemption
Roaming Roman

Hungry religious pilgrims push their way through the vast breakfast buffet and pile incredible quantities of food on their plates as if this were indeed the real 'Last Supper'; a few of these crazy tourists stop and stare at Bruno and wonder how do they know this beautiful man? Why is he here? I want to shout - he is mine! This divine man is all mine!

📶 cellcom   8:31 AM   92% 🔋

<   (JS)   (BO)   ⓘ

Jeremy Stark   Brooke Orser

9:27 AM

Hi (BO)

Cousin Tomer invited us to an amazing nightclub last night in Tel Aviv we left at 10 n did not get home til 4 this morning. Mom n Dad don't know (BO)

I told Grama Rose I was hanging out w Teddy n Aliza! (BO)

We took a bus Tel Aviv is a very cool city the club was in an old marina n packed w kids they drink n smoke a lot NO ONE needs id!!! The music was amazing n everyone was so happy. One of Tomer's friends hooked up w Teddy I don't think he ever had a girlfriend. At first he looked a little like a deer in headlights lol then they were kissing (BO)

I'm so tired today but it was so much fun I danced n felt so free no one knew me n I didn't have any cares (BO)

Grama Rose had no idea what time I slipped in she takes sleeping pills n nothing can wake her up (BO)

Will write more later n have a good morning! (BO)

Delivered

📷 (iMessage) 🎙️

LUCACLOSELY
@LUCACLOSELY

Feed me and I live, yet give me a drink and I die. Who am I?

8:45 AM – June

💬 1   ♡ 3   ⟲ 0

LUCACLOSELY @LUCACLOSELY
Replying to @LUCACLOSELY

Fire

MYPOETRY.COM

Ironic

Brooke G.O.

Young and bound
Lost and found
Khaki uniform by day
Techno nights to play
Committed helping hand
Protect the land
Scream and shout
Need to get out
Out of war, all is fair
Love is in the air

♡ 192   240 👁

📶 cellcom   8:51 AM   90% 🔋

‹   **Israel Family Group**
                EL, Kate, Andy, Teddy, Aliza, Brooke,…

Kate
That was the most amazing breakfast I have ever laid my
eyes upon.Thank you EL for the divine culinary experience.
My new favorite breakfast foods are cottage cheese and
warm cheesecake.

+ (   ) 📷 🎤

Israel Family Group
EL, Kate, Andy, Teddy, Aliza, Brooke,...

Andy
Wow. I have never seen so much food in one buffet. Amazing choices.

Lucas
I love the pizza & chocolate pudding!

Aliza
since when are those breakfast foods

Lucas
Since this morning when they were on the Israeli breakfast buffet!

Rose
Lucas may have a point there, Aliza.

Lucas
Finally something special about Jewish food

Brooke
YOLO!

Rose
What is YOLO?

Brooke
You Only Live Once!

Rose
YOLO sounds good to me.

Lucas
Christians get everything good - Santa's gifts on Christmas and Easter Bunnies' chocolate we don't get any of the good things

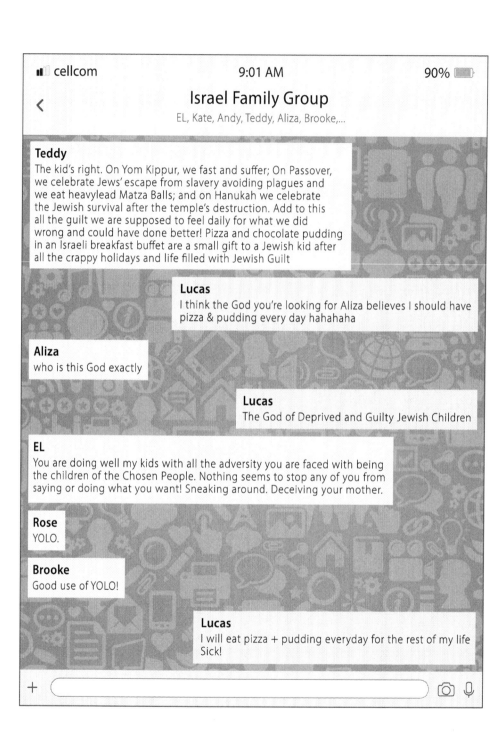

Israel Family Group

EL, Kate, Andy, Teddy, Aliza, Brooke,...

Teddy
The kid's right. On Yom Kippur, we fast and suffer; On Passover, we celebrate Jews' escape from slavery avoiding plagues and we eat heavylead Matza Balls; and on Hanukah we celebrate the Jewish survival after the temple's destruction. Add to this all the guilt we are supposed to feel daily for what we did wrong and could have done better! Pizza and chocolate pudding in an Israeli breakfast buffet are a small gift to a Jewish kid after all the crappy holidays and life filled with Jewish Guilt

Lucas
I think the God you're looking for Aliza believes I should have pizza & pudding every day hahahaha

Aliza
who is this God exactly

Lucas
The God of Deprived and Guilty Jewish Children

EL
You are doing well my kids with all the adversity you are faced with being the children of the Chosen People. Nothing seems to stop any of you from saying or doing what you want! Sneaking around. Deceiving your mother.

Rose
YOLO.

Brooke
Good use of YOLO!

Lucas
I will eat pizza + pudding everyday for the rest of my life Sick!

9:10 AM

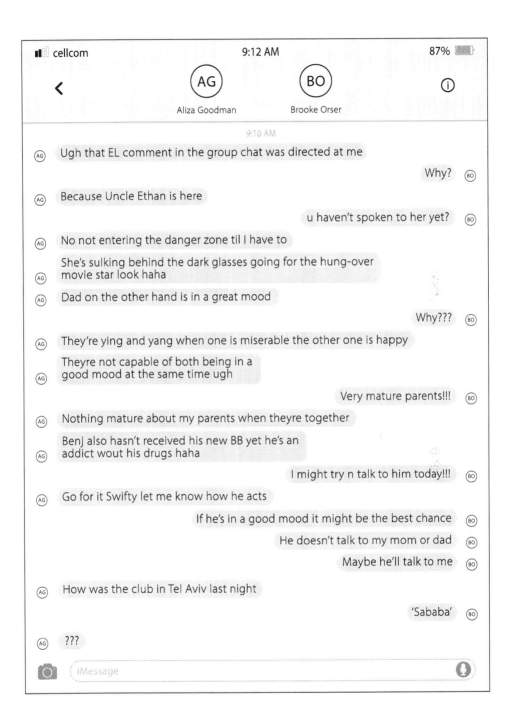

Ugh that EL comment in the group chat was directed at me

Why?

Because Uncle Ethan is here

u haven't spoken to her yet?

No not entering the danger zone til I have to

She's sulking behind the dark glasses going for the hung-over movie star look haha

Dad on the other hand is in a great mood

Why???

They're ying and yang when one is miserable the other one is happy

Theyre not capable of both being in a good mood at the same time ugh

Very mature parents!!!

Nothing mature about my parents when theyre together

Benj also hasn't received his new BB yet he's an addict wout his drugs haha

I might try n talk to him today!!!

Go for it Swifty let me know how he acts

If he's in a good mood it might be the best chance

He doesn't talk to my mom or dad

Maybe he'll talk to me

How was the club in Tel Aviv last night

'Sababa'

???

iMessage

AG Aliza Goodman BO Brooke Orser

9:12 AM

'Sababa' means great BO

everyone kept saying 'Sababa' BO

AG So u had fun

The best time BO

AG happy for u ♡ g2g meet the new rabbi & enter the danger zone

AG wish me good luck bye

AG ☺

Good luck ☺ BO

AG I need it

iMessage

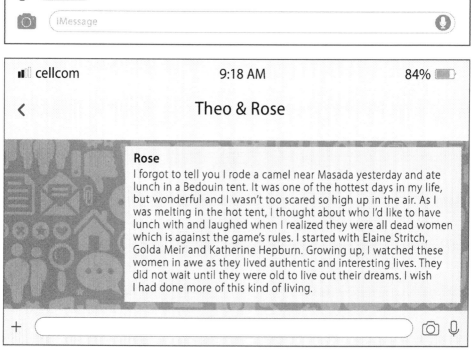

Theo & Rose

Rose
I forgot to tell you I rode a camel near Masada yesterday and ate lunch in a Bedouin tent. It was one of the hottest days in my life, but wonderful and I wasn't too scared so high up in the air. As I was melting in the hot tent, I thought about who I'd like to have lunch with and laughed when I realized they were all dead women which is against the game's rules. I started with Elaine Stritch, Golda Meir and Katherine Hepburn. Growing up, I watched these women in awe as they lived authentic and interesting lives. They did not wait until they were old to live out their dreams. I wish I had done more of this kind of living.

The Rabbi
Teddy Goodman

It is too early to write in detail, but worth commenting once again that my parents are truly fucked up people. We have been here for a few days and this morning appears to be their first truce brought on by last night's revolutionary reunion of EL and her brother Ethan. EL is wearing dark sunglasses with a completely fake half-smile plastered on her face. Benj is sitting with a big (rarely seen I might add) almost devious smile on his face; this also may have to do with his involuntary disconnection from technology or the fact that his wife has assumed the suffering martyr role in their relationship, which allows him to surface as the good angelic guy. Aliza, EL, and Benj are interviewing the new rabbi, who happens to be a young female, which is cool for a non-religious girl who does not believe in God and is having a bat mitzvah in the Holy Land only because this was her dead grandmother's dying wish.

Honestly, I would say that Aliza is conducting the interview and our parents are simply robots that shake their heads like puppets from side to the side and up and down. Aliza may only be 13 but she is more mature than both of our childish parents put together. She is also a far better debater than either one of them pretend to be. She wins awards and warms hearts; they create tension and break hearts. I revel in the fact that we three kids are not more fucked up. I guess there is still time for this.

Road to Redemption cont.
Roaming Roman

EL sits across the room sulking in large, dark glasses that cover her face. Reminds me of when she was a little girl & did not get her way, she would sit on the small living room couch cross legged, hands under her chin & sulk for hours. The image is still vivid after all these years. She was so darn cute & incredibly manipulative that in the end, my parents both broke down & she always got her way. Looks like some things don't change.

YM
Yasmin M.

AG
Aliza Goodman

10:01 AM

Are you up? AG

Just met the new rabbi AG

Shes cool her name is Iris pronounced "ear-iss" AG

Grama Shula would've loved her a smart & powerful female rabbi AG

Still no sign of God anywhere! ☹ AG

btw thanks for making sure I didn't apologize to EL last night AG

she seems to have recovered from Uncle Ethan's arrival she hasn't spoken to him but she's back from the land of the dead AG

😊 AG

Uncle Ethan must've rly done some bad shit years ago but now he's on his own. I brought them back together & thats the most I can do AG

We are in the Holiest City so maybe God'll show up & work some magic lol AG

oops sorry but youll laugh at this next one AG

Teddy's in the best mood…he's whistling & smiling & has been talking to all of us AG

its so strange AG

I'm so excited for this afternoon!! I've waited sooo long to meet Lady Gaga. Thanks for texting Owen ☺ AG

sorry i know its 3 in the morning there AG

NP I'm so jealous that ur going to meet her. Owen thinks he can enter the system & send 300,000 in like one second he said there is no one else he would do it for. What's this about? YM

We're friends from religious school AG

at regular school he is too cool to talk to us but at Jew school I'm all he's got AG

Delivered

📷 (iMessage 　　　　　　　　　　　　　　🎤)

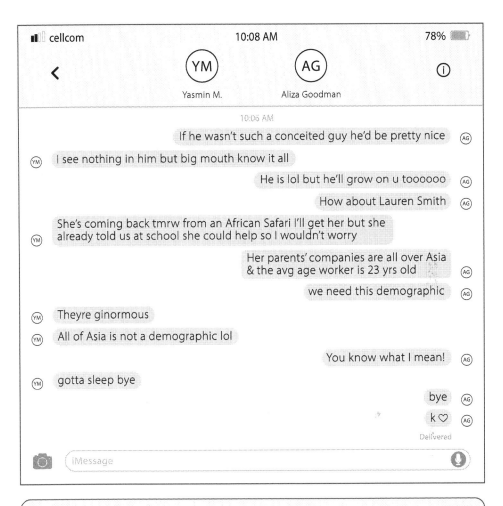

YM   **AG**

Yasmin M.   Aliza Goodman

10:06 AM

If he wasn't such a conceited guy he'd be pretty nice

I see nothing in him but big mouth know it all

He is lol but he'll grow on u toooooo

How about Lauren Smith

She's coming back tmrw from an African Safari I'll get her but she already told us at school she could help so I wouldn't worry

Her parents' companies are all over Asia & the avg age worker is 23 yrs old

we need this demographic

Theyre ginormous

All of Asia is not a demographic lol

You know what I mean!

gotta sleep bye

bye

k ♡

Delivered

iMessage

 JN24:   now

Israeli orthodox and rabbinical group meets to discuss acceptance of gays and lesbians.

Jewish News You Can Use

Aliza Goodman's Daily Motivational Quote #2:   now

"If you want peace, you don't talk to your friends. You talk to your enemies."
Archbishop Desmond Tutu

MotiQuote.com

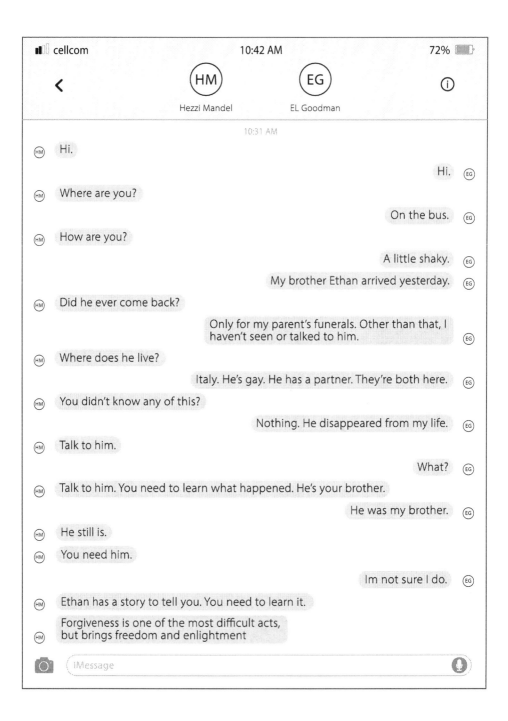

cellcom   10:42 AM   72% ▰

(HM)   **(EG)**

Hezzi Mandel   EL Goodman

10:31 AM

(HM) Hi.

Hi. (EG)

(HM) Where are you?

On the bus. (EG)

(HM) How are you?

A little shaky. (EG)

My brother Ethan arrived yesterday. (EG)

(HM) Did he ever come back?

Only for my parent's funerals. Other than that, I haven't seen or talked to him. (EG)

(HM) Where does he live?

Italy. He's gay. He has a partner. They're both here. (EG)

(HM) You didn't know any of this?

Nothing. He disappeared from my life. (EG)

(HM) Talk to him.

What? (EG)

(HM) Talk to him. You need to learn what happened. He's your brother.

He was my brother. (EG)

(HM) He still is.

(HM) You need him.

Im not sure I do. (EG)

(HM) Ethan has a story to tell you. You need to learn it.

(HM) Forgiveness is one of the most difficult acts, but brings freedom and enlightment

iMessage

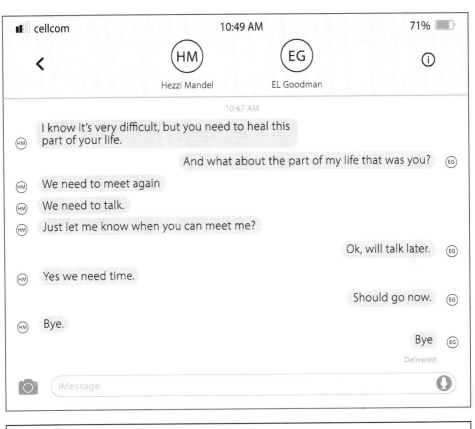

(HM)   **(EG)**   ⓘ

Hezzi Mandel   EL Goodman

10:47 AM

(HM) I know it's very difficult, but you need to heal this part of your life.

And what about the part of my life that was you? (EG)

(HM) We need to meet again

(HM) We need to talk.

(HM) Just let me know when you can meet me?

Ok, will talk later. (EG)

(HM) Yes we need time.

Should go now. (EG)

(HM) Bye.

Bye (EG)

Delivered

iMessage

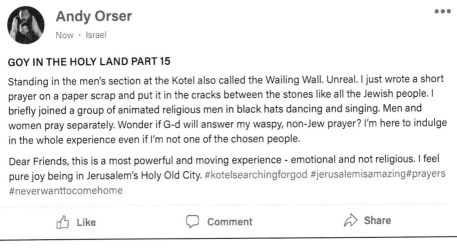

Andy Orser   •••

Now · Israel

GOY IN THE HOLY LAND PART 15

Standing in the men's section at the Kotel also called the Wailing Wall. Unreal. I just wrote a short prayer on a paper scrap and put it in the cracks between the stones like all the Jewish people. I briefly joined a group of animated religious men in black hats dancing and singing. Men and women pray separately. Wonder if G-d will answer my waspy, non-Jew prayer? I'm here to indulge in the whole experience even if I'm not one of the chosen people.

Dear Friends, this is a most powerful and moving experience - emotional and not religious. I feel pure joy being in Jerusalem's Holy Old City. #kotelsearchingforgod #jerusalemisamazing#prayers #neverwanttocomehome

👍 Like   💬 Comment   ↪ Share

Where Are You?

<u>Brooke G.O.</u>

The Wall calls me to approach
I stand lost in its cold rough power
Fearful I will not relate to its majesty
A failed travesty

Surrounded by strangers
Alone in my thoughts
Mumbled prayers relaxing sound
Spray scents all around

Where are you?
Please send a signal
Where are you?
Strong reassurances

Reach a hand
Feel your warmth
Glance my way
Save myself today

♡ 192

240 ◉

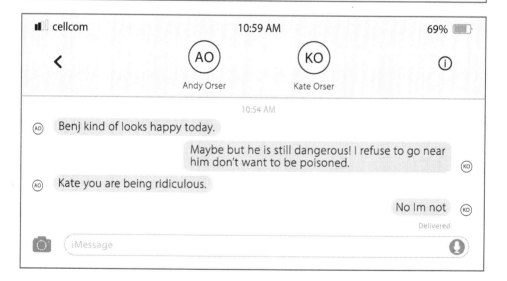

Road to Redemption cont.
Roaming Roman

At the astonishing spectacular Kotel. The last remnants of the Holy 2nd Jewish Temple destroyed in 70 CE. Above where we are standing is the Al-Aqsa Mosque in the Palestinian territory reminding me of the closeness of warring cousins and neighbors in this small crowded country. My sister & I metaphorically are these untrusting relatives. Years filled with so many misunderstandings & great distance - how to begin repairing all the historical rifts?

A warm Jerusalem morning hopes to thaw the cold layers of hate & mistrust at least between siblings in our small fractured family.

The Little Shit
Teddy Goodman

Yesterday Lucas disappeared on top of Masada.

Today you would have thought that he would be on a fucking leash. But no, Benj and EL were too absorbed in their new roles: Benj playing the oddly happy man and EL playing the suffering woman. Neither performance is quite convincing. We were finally at the amazing Wailing Wall where men and women gather separately for prayer. When we all came back together, EL realized that Lucas was fucking missing again. She was just about to go into freak out mode when I looked up and saw Lucas across the plaza high in the sky.

Twenty men in jeans, prayer shawls and yarmulkes in a circle were passing Lucas from one to the other as they danced and sang in Hebrew. He was beaming the little shit! Like the New York Knicks had just won the NBA finals, and he had shot the fucking game winning three-point fade away with one second left to go.

One of these days, the little shit is going to truly disappear.

Andy Orser
Now · Israel

GOY IN THE HOLY LAND PART 16

Walking in the cold damp tunnel under the Wailing Wall: Dark, cavernous dungeon with small narrow passages deeply carved underground as water drips along stonewalls. Imagining thousands of courageous workers slowly moving heavy stones, methodically building wonderous walls with their defiant hands, creating a lasting monument to Judaism and all of mankind that still survives thousands of years later.

The closest to G-d I may ever be in this life the guide tells me.

Dear Friends, This is a very powerful and passionate moment where I am surrounded by many others and yet feel all alone and so small and insignificant. #wailingwalltunnels #closetogod #godspresence #prayforme

   👍 Like   💬 Comment   ↪ Share

MYPOETRY.COM

Kotel

Brooke G.O.

A wall

Hope

History

Heaven

Honor

Pray

A new day

♡ 146   202 ◉

 JN24:   now

Increase in violence by Anti-Israel groups on US university campuses against Israel and its supporters rises to record levels.

Jewish News You Can Use

Hope 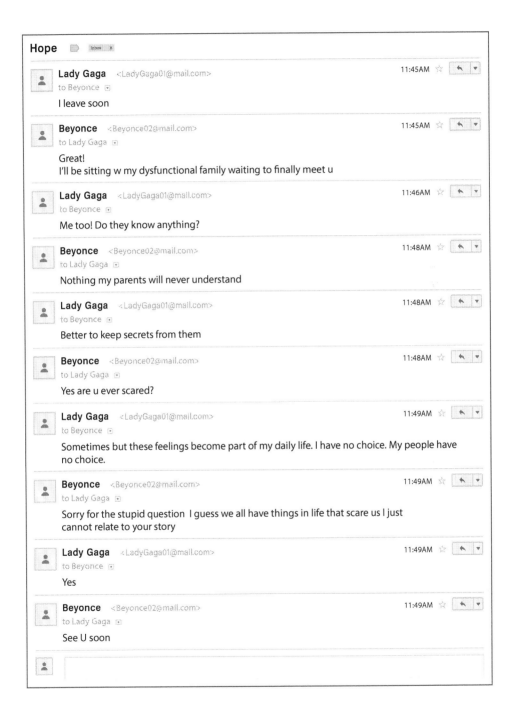 Inbox ✕

Lady Gaga <LadyGaga01@mail.com>	11:45AM ☆
to Beyonce	
I leave soon	

Beyonce <Beyonce02@mail.com>	11:45AM ☆
to Lady Gaga	
Great!	
I'll be sitting w my dysfunctional family waiting to finally meet u	

Lady Gaga <LadyGaga01@mail.com>	11:46AM ☆
to Beyonce	
Me too! Do they know anything?	

Beyonce <Beyonce02@mail.com>	11:48AM ☆
to Lady Gaga	
Nothing my parents will never understand	

Lady Gaga <LadyGaga01@mail.com>	11:48AM ☆
to Beyonce	
Better to keep secrets from them	

Beyonce <Beyonce02@mail.com>	11:48AM ☆
to Lady Gaga	
Yes are u ever scared?	

Lady Gaga <LadyGaga01@mail.com>	11:49AM ☆
to Beyonce	
Sometimes but these feelings become part of my daily life. I have no choice. My people have no choice.	

Beyonce <Beyonce02@mail.com>	11:49AM ☆
to Lady Gaga	
Sorry for the stupid question I guess we all have things in life that scare us I just cannot relate to your story	

Lady Gaga <LadyGaga01@mail.com>	11:49AM ☆
to Beyonce	
Yes	

Beyonce <Beyonce02@mail.com>	11:49AM ☆
to Lady Gaga	
See U soon	

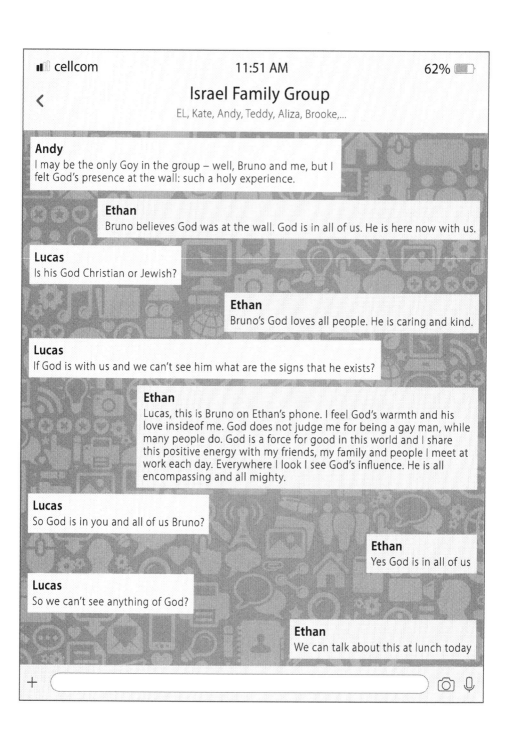

Israel Family Group

EL, Kate, Andy, Teddy, Aliza, Brooke,...

Andy
I may be the only Goy in the group – well, Bruno and me, but I felt God's presence at the wall: such a holy experience.

Ethan
Bruno believes God was at the wall. God is in all of us. He is here now with us.

Lucas
Is his God Christian or Jewish?

Ethan
Bruno's God loves all people. He is caring and kind.

Lucas
If God is with us and we can't see him what are the signs that he exists?

Ethan
Lucas, this is Bruno on Ethan's phone. I feel God's warmth and his love insideof me. God does not judge me for being a gay man, while many people do. God is a force for good in this world and I share this positive energy with my friends, my family and people I meet at work each day. Everywhere I look I see God's influence. He is all encompassing and all mighty.

Lucas
So God is in you and all of us Bruno?

Ethan
Yes God is in all of us

Lucas
So we can't see anything of God?

Ethan
We can talk about this at lunch today

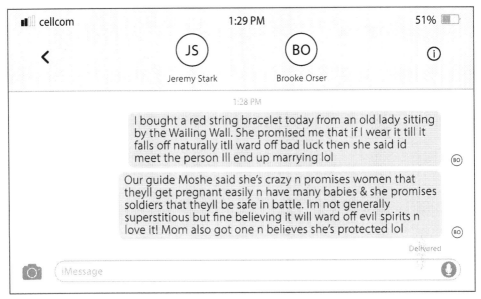

JS
Jeremy Stark

BO
Brooke Orser

1:28 PM

I bought a red string bracelet today from an old lady sitting by the Wailing Wall. She promised me that if I wear it till it falls off naturally itll ward off bad luck then she said id meet the person Ill end up marrying lol

Our guide Moshe said she's crazy n promises women that theyll get pregnant easily n have many babies & she promises soldiers that theyll be safe in battle. Im not generally superstitious but fine believing it will ward off evil spirits n love it! Mom also got one n believes she's protected lol

Delivered

iMessage

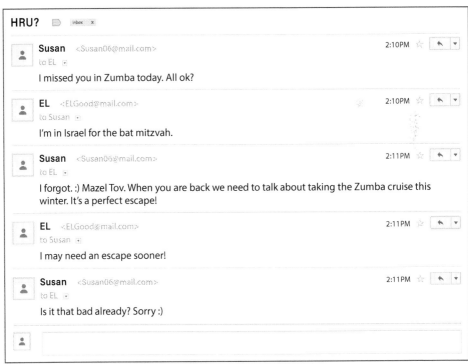

HRU?   Inbox x

Susan <Susan06@mail.com>
to EL

2:10PM

I missed you in Zumba today. All ok?

EL <ELGood@mail.com>
to Susan

2:10PM

I'm in Israel for the bat mitzvah.

Susan <Susan06@mail.com>
to EL

2:11PM

I forgot. :) Mazel Tov. When you are back we need to talk about taking the Zumba cruise this winter. It's a perfect escape!

EL <ELGood@mail.com>
to Susan

2:11PM

I may need an escape sooner!

Susan <Susan06@mail.com>
to EL

2:11PM

Is it that bad already? Sorry :)

213

FOOD AFFAIR WITH KATE

DIVINE, DELICIOUS, AND DELIGHTFUL   ABOUT   RECIPES   CONTACT

When in Jerusalem

★ ★ ★ ★ ★

Small and narrow streets guide us through the Old City until we arrive at a cozy restaurant set deep in a stone cave. Welcomed as visiting royalty by a Palestinian family: one congenial brother greets us in Arabic-English, another quite serious serves and two delightful, boisterous cousins prepare food in a small open kitchen and clanking pots and pans under the watchful eye of the family patriarch and restaurant owner.

Loud Middle Eastern music mixed with vivacious gutteral banter among the proprietors serenades us as our table fills with an incredible array of Middle Eastern salads adorned by olive oil, zatar, lebanah and pickles. The falafel is ideally fried: perfectly light and fluffy - green on the inside and crispy golden brown on the outside, not oily and appropriately spicy. There are three ideal dips for the fresh falafel - lebanah, a slightly sour, watery yogurt with a tangy essence; creamy hummus doused with olive oil; or smooth sesame tahina sauce. Either combination is a symphony of flavors truly magnificent and gastronomically stimulating.

The Israeli Jewish and Palestinian culinary offerings are so similar, yet with each bite, I realize just how each has its own distinct culinary flair. I am not a politician but I have a feeling that this is a perfect metaphor for these two people: falafels and hummus could break down the barriers of warring cousins offering opportunities to sit together to bridge differences with a meal both loved and appreciated. See the photos below and check out Food Affair with Kate on Instagram and Facebook. #fabulousfalafel #peacefood #hummusharmony #Jerusalemdining

Dysfunctional Family
Teddy Goodman

I think all families are fucking dysfunctional and mine is no exception.

A long table separates EL and Benj - this distance calms the perpetual snapping and attacking that plagues our regular daily lives. The cycle of constant contradictions is firmly ingrained in their beings and we all pay the price for this fucked up condition they have by default agreed to accept as a family norm.

Benj just received a new Blackberry and is already shooting off demanding emails with demonic speed; I can see him giving orders with his fingers to his foot soldiers thousands of miles away on the capital war front. He is oblivious to the family he sits amongst.

EL happily chats with Grandma Rose and Kate, two women she has been estranged from due to my father's obvious lifelong contempt for his mom and sister. Lucas tells uncle Ethan and Bruno about his school trip to Washington DC last month. They listen and care to hear what he is telling them.

Aliza, who is usually quite talkative, sits nervously fidgeting not eating and looking all around. She is usually the calm and collected one in our dysfunctional group. She has been to the bathroom twice already. I am sure she has nerves about her bat mitzvah, but I think something is up with her. I have pretty much ignored my family for a few years, but I still know their fucked-up behavior and patterns very well. Aliza's eyes follow a young girl with dark skin and curly brown hair who walks past our table. She carefully watches her disappear into the back of the restaurant. A minute later, she goes to the bathroom again.

Brooke and her father are debating the merits of Instagram vs Twitter next to me.

My head is spinning with real and important subjects that are so vast and answerless, I need to stay focused on the surface issues at our table so I do not vanish into my own dark and dangerous world. Stay present I warn myself.

Do not fucking get lost in the dense weeds filling my brain and clogging my dreams as though they are dealing with life changing issues.

Stay present I remind myself. Stay present.

YM   **AG**

Yasmin M.   Aliza Goodman

3:14 PM

OMG

We just met at lunch and I was beginning to think she wouldn't make it. She promised to take me there so im not scared im actually pretty excited

it's sick!

shes awesome

cant wait

Delivered

iMessage

Andy Orser

Now · Israel

GOY IN THE HOLY LAND PART 17

Just walked along Via Dolorosa from the Church of the Holy Sepulchre through the 13 Stations of the Cross tracing the painful path that Jesus took carrying the heavy wooden cross on his back to his crucifixion. We followed a group of devout Christian pilgrims. This is not a Hollywood movie; this feature takes place in real time and with real people.

Dear Friends, I'm overwhelmed with new and unrecognizable feelings reflecting the power of this transformational city. #13stationsforJesus #churchoftheholysepulchre #biblicallifein21stcentury

👍 Like   💬 Comment   ↪ Share

Aliza Goodman's Daily Motivational Quote #3:   now

"What's important for my daughter to know is that... if you are fortunate to have opportunity, it is your duty to make sure other people have those opportunities as well."
Senator Kamala Harris

MotiQuote.com

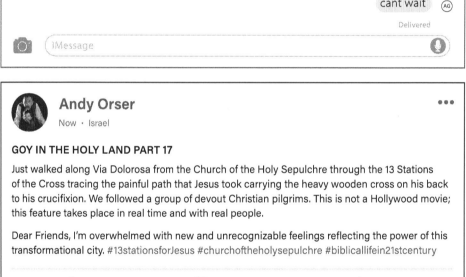

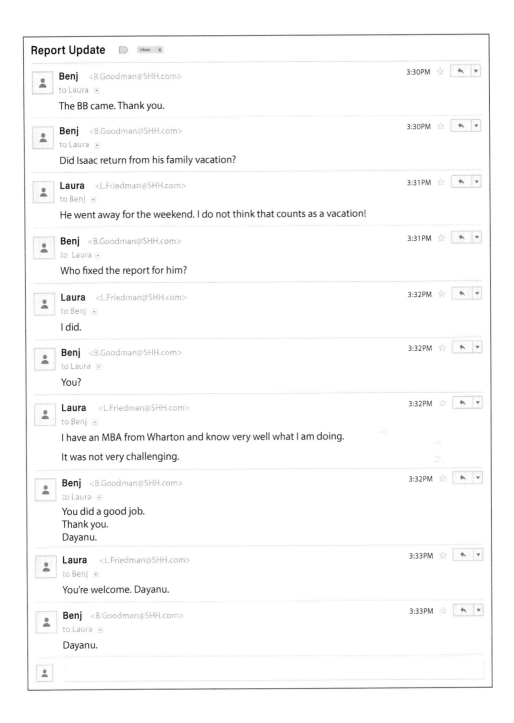

Report Update Inbox x

Benj <B.Goodman@SHH.com>
to Laura
3:30PM

The BB came. Thank you.

Benj <B.Goodman@SHH.com>
to Laura
3:30PM

Did Isaac return from his family vacation?

Laura <L.Friedman@SHH.com>
to Benj
3:31PM

He went away for the weekend. I do not think that counts as a vacation!

Benj <B.Goodman@SHH.com>
to Laura
3:31PM

Who fixed the report for him?

Laura <L.Friedman@SHH.com>
to Benj
3:32PM

I did.

Benj <B.Goodman@SHH.com>
to Laura
3:32PM

You?

Laura <L.Friedman@SHH.com>
to Benj
3:32PM

I have an MBA from Wharton and know very well what I am doing.

It was not very challenging.

Benj <B.Goodman@SHH.com>
to Laura
3:32PM

You did a good job.
Thank you.
Dayanu.

Laura <L.Friedman@SHH.com>
to Benj
3:33PM

You're welcome. Dayanu.

Benj <B.Goodman@SHH.com>
to Laura
3:33PM

Dayanu.

Dear Lucas Goodman, Astronaut in Training –

@JUNIORNASAUSA

Crew | About | Photos

TODAY ON THE INTERNATIONAL SPACE STATION:

Looking down from the International Space Station (@ISS) astronauts take many beautiful pictures of earth. Today, we are passing over Alaska's Hubbard Glacier, the largest tidewater glacier in North America. Our stunning view demonstrates that this glacier has been growing thicker and larger as opposed to other shrinking Alaskan glaciers and so many of the world's thinning and retreating glaciers due to global warming. Hubbard Glacier's growth happens as a result of snow fall and the flowing sediment - rocks and other debris - that loosen from the Earth's surface.

Our view of the majestic glacier is stunning from up here. It appears like a soft, bright white blanket during the day. At night, this region with no man made light is pitch black. The only faint light comes from cities in the distance. The contrast is awesome from our view 250 miles above the earth's surface. Each time we circle the globe we encounter different characteristics and many beautiful vistas.

Andy Orser

Now · Israel

· · ·

GOY IN THE HOLY LAND PART 18

Standing speechless in the very spot in the Church of the Holy Sepulchre where Jesus is believed to have been buried after his crucifixion. Not clear if he was? But very clear that many enamored pilgrims believe so and are in awe of the mind-blowing experience. This sensational moment reminds me that the power of the human soul is much more forceful than historical facts.

Dear Friends, there is such adoration and excitement in this house of worship by crossroads of people - a beautiful confluence of race, religion and respect. There is no hate. I'm in love with this encounter. #Isjesusburiedhere #religiouspilgrim #worshipinholyland #jesuschrist

👍 Like   💬 Comment   ↪ Share

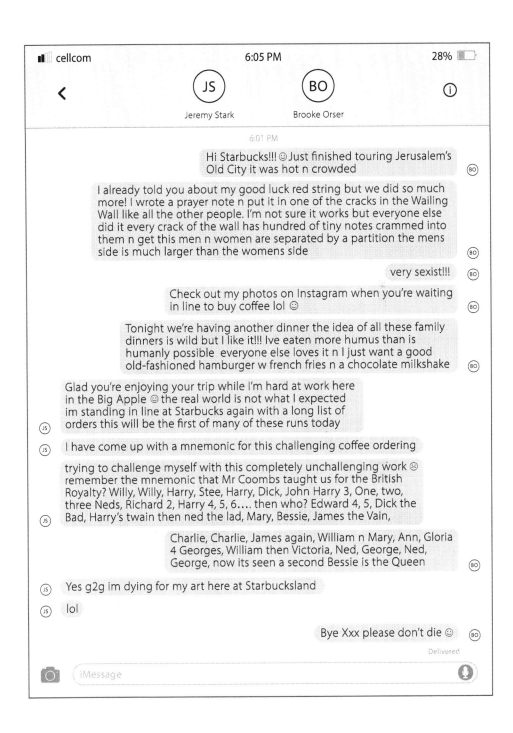

JS
Jeremy Stark

BO
Brooke Orser

6:01 PM

Hi Starbucks!!! ☺ Just finished touring Jerusalem's Old City it was hot n crowded

I already told you about my good luck red string but we did so much more! I wrote a prayer note n put it in one of the cracks in the Wailing Wall like all the other people. I'm not sure it works but everyone else did it every crack of the wall has hundred of tiny notes crammed into them n get this men n women are separated by a partition the mens side is much larger than the womens side

very sexist!!!

Check out my photos on Instagram when you're waiting in line to buy coffee lol ☺

Tonight we're having another dinner the idea of all these family dinners is wild but I like it!!! Ive eaten more humus than is humanly possible everyone else loves it n I just want a good old-fashioned hamburger w french fries n a chocolate milkshake

Glad you're enjoying your trip while I'm hard at work here in the Big Apple ☺ the real world is not what I expected im standing in line at Starbucks again with a long list of orders this will be the first of many of these runs today

I have come up with a mnemonic for this challenging coffee ordering

trying to challenge myself with this completely unchallenging work ☹ remember the mnemonic that Mr Coombs taught us for the British Royalty? Willy, Willy, Harry, Stee, Harry, Dick, John Harry 3, One, two, three Neds, Richard 2, Harry 4, 5, 6.... then who? Edward 4, 5, Dick the Bad, Harry's twain then ned the lad, Mary, Bessie, James the Vain,

Charlie, Charlie, James again, William n Mary, Ann, Gloria 4 Georges, William then Victoria, Ned, George, Ned, George, now its seen a second Bessie is the Queen

Yes g2g im dying for my art here at Starbucksland

lol

Bye Xxx please don't die ☺

Delivered

iMessage

Road to Redemption
Roaming Roman

Via Dolorosa in the Old City of Jerusalem means "Way of Suffering". EL is completely in character as she suffers with each painful step she makes. EL was always dramatic & today she just may have given an Academy Award level performance as the modern-day martyr burdened by the invisible yet heavy wooden cross she drags through the ancient city where Jesus first initiated this ceremony two thousand years ago.

 JN24: now

Jewish and Arab students compete in soccer matches sponsored by the Peres Center designed to teach collaboration and respect.

Jewish News You Can Use

Aliza Goodman's Daily Motivational Quote #4: now

"Here are the values that I stand for: honesty, equality, kindness, compassion, treating people the way you want to be treated and helping those in need. To me, those are traditional values."
Ellen DeGeneres

MotiQuote.com

Road to Redemption cont.
Roaming Roman

Bruno is enthralled by the rich religious history as we slowly make our way through the 13 Stations alongside the zestful religious pilgrims. It is remarkable the incongruence of my dear partner's deeply rooted love of the Catholic Church stemming from his pious youth & yet the church's abandonment & lack of recognition for his adult existence.

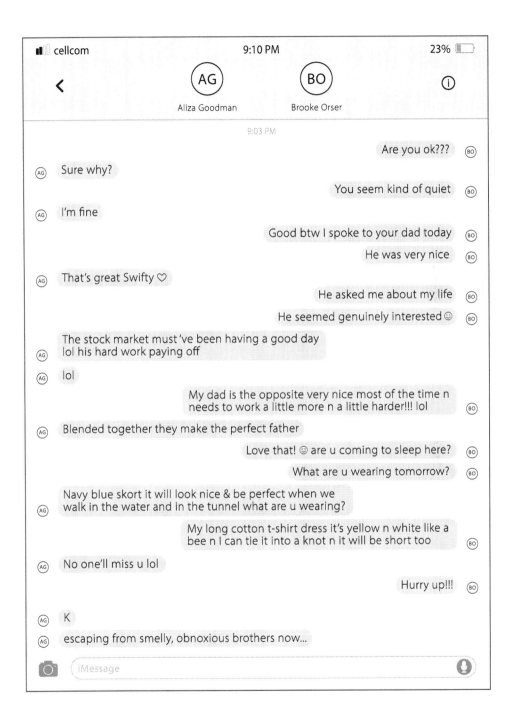

cellcom   9:10 PM   23% 🔋

AG Aliza Goodman   **BO** Brooke Orser

9:03 PM

Are you ok??? **BO**

AG Sure why?

You seem kind of quiet **BO**

AG I'm fine

Good btw I spoke to your dad today **BO**

He was very nice **BO**

AG That's great Swifty ♡

He asked me about my life **BO**

He seemed genuinely interested ☺ **BO**

AG The stock market must've been having a good day lol his hard work paying off

AG lol

My dad is the opposite very nice most of the time n needs to work a little more n a little harder!!! lol **BO**

AG Blended together they make the perfect father

Love that! ☺ are u coming to sleep here? **BO**

What are u wearing tomorrow? **BO**

AG Navy blue skort it will look nice & be perfect when we walk in the water and in the tunnel what are u wearing?

My long cotton t-shirt dress it's yellow n white like a bee n I can tie it into a knot n it will be short too **BO**

AG No one'll miss u lol

Hurry up!!! **BO**

AG K

AG escaping from smelly, obnoxious brothers now...

📷 (iMessage   🎤)

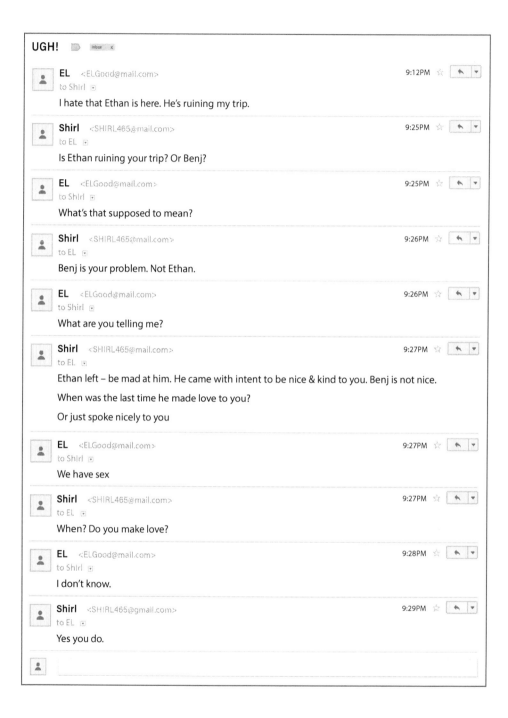

UGH! Inbox x

EL <ELGood@mail.com>   9:12PM
to Shirl

I hate that Ethan is here. He's ruining my trip.

Shirl <SHIRL465@mail.com>   9:25PM
to EL

Is Ethan ruining your trip? Or Benj?

EL <ELGood@mail.com>   9:25PM
to Shirl

What's that supposed to mean?

Shirl <SHIRL465@mail.com>   9:26PM
to EL

Benj is your problem. Not Ethan.

EL <ELGood@mail.com>   9:26PM
to Shirl

What are you telling me?

Shirl <SHIRL465@mail.com>   9:27PM
to EL

Ethan left – be mad at him. He came with intent to be nice & kind to you. Benj is not nice.

When was the last time he made love to you?

Or just spoke nicely to you

EL <ELGood@mail.com>   9:27PM
to Shirl

We have sex

Shirl <SHIRL465@mail.com>   9:27PM
to EL

When? Do you make love?

EL <ELGood@mail.com>   9:28PM
to Shirl

I don't know.

Shirl <SHIRL465@gmail.com>   9:29PM
to EL

Yes you do.

Andy Orser

Now · Israel

GOY IN THE HOLY LAND PART 19

Just drove with the most charming and enlightened Arab cab driver named Fuad. He spoke perfect English and could not have been more congenial. He is a journalist by day and drives a cab at night to make extra money. His wife is a doctor and he has three children: a daughter in dental school and two sons in high school.

Dear Friends, this trip makes me realize how, no matter where in the world, people are all the same. We care for our families; we go to work and we want to be happy. Simple concepts yet so elusive. #liveinpeace #shalom #salam

    👍 Like   💬 Comment   ↗ Share

LIFEEXPRESSIONS.COM

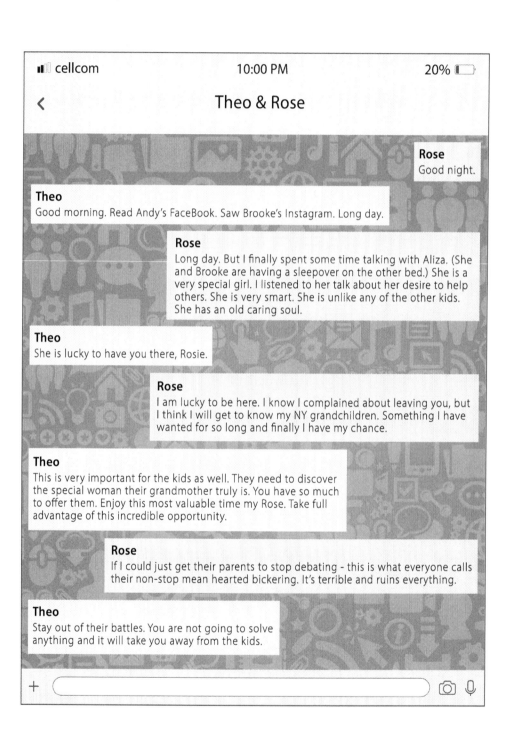

Theo & Rose

Rose
Good night.

Theo
Good morning. Read Andy's FaceBook. Saw Brooke's Instagram. Long day.

Rose
Long day. But I finally spent some time talking with Aliza. (She and Brooke are having a sleepover on the other bed.) She is a very special girl. I listened to her talk about her desire to help others. She is very smart. She is unlike any of the other kids. She has an old caring soul.

Theo
She is lucky to have you there, Rosie.

Rose
I am lucky to be here. I know I complained about leaving you, but I think I will get to know my NY grandchildren. Something I have wanted for so long and finally I have my chance.

Theo
This is very important for the kids as well. They need to discover the special woman their grandmother truly is. You have so much to offer them. Enjoy this most valuable time my Rose. Take full advantage of this incredible opportunity.

Rose
If I could just get their parents to stop debating - this is what everyone calls their non-stop mean hearted bickering. It's terrible and ruins everything.

Theo
Stay out of their battles. You are not going to solve anything and it will take you away from the kids.

Theo & Rose

Rose
Kate and Andy ask more questions than even a bunch of impatient little children. It's embarrassing. Brooke is their mother keeping them in line. She and her cousin Teddy have struck up a friendship. I do not know Teddy well enough yet, but he is an interesting young man. He is a bit quiet. I will give him a few days to open. My Brooke will take care of that. Tomorrow I will try and work on Lucas. He looks at me as though I am a dinosaur that has risen from the tar pits. I will use the basketball information that you drilled into me.

Theo
Drilled into you? Happy I could help.

Rose
You are a sick man. You go from basketball stats to sex in one line.

Theo
I know how much you like it. I miss you. Cold here without you.

Rose
Put on the electric blanket.

Theo
Wow - what a cold shower!

Rose
No cold shower. Just stay warm until I get back.

Theo
I love you. Good night. Sweet dreams.

Rose
I love you too.

+ (　　　　　　　　　　　　　　　　) 📷 🎤

Dearest Aliza,

Safta Shula's FREEDOM.

"We the people of the United States, in order to form a more perfect union, establish Justice, ensure domestic tranquility, provide for the common defense, promote the general welfare, and secure the blessings of liberty to ourselves and our posterity, do ordain and establish the Constitution for the United States of America."

These words held great meaning for my life as they were the safety net I had not truly felt until I set foot on American soil. America was an incredible country for two immigrants to build a business and raise a family. We knew that we were safe and protected; we would not have to leave in the middle of the night or go to work and return home to find that family had been deported. We were safe.

I never took my freedom for granted. Once the kids went off to school, I knew that I wanted to give back to the country that had embraced us and welcomed us. Yacov and I had our health, we had wealth and our family was prospering. I found my calling — I volunteered to help homeless and abused women. These women needed love and support and I believed I could give it to them. I would leave my kids at school and work all day in shelters with these beautiful women, talking to them about their lives, their children and their dreams. I was someone who they met along their way who believed in them. The freedom I attained living in America gave me this opportunity; I believe this was a way of mending my childhood experiences of adversity and injustice. Giving back each day was in a way my therapy, a way to heal my soul.

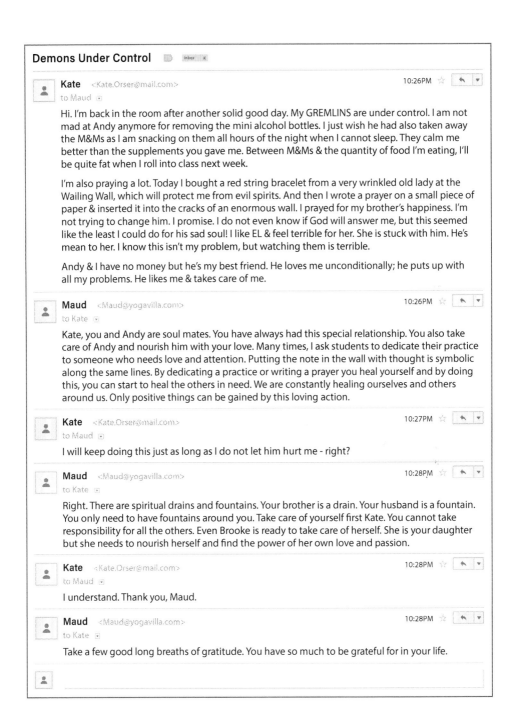

Demons Under Control inbox X

Kate <Kate.Orser@mail.com>   10:26PM
to Maud

Hi. I'm back in the room after another solid good day. My GREMLINS are under control. I am not mad at Andy anymore for removing the mini alcohol bottles. I just wish he had also taken away the M&Ms as I am snacking on them all hours of the night when I cannot sleep. They calm me better than the supplements you gave me. Between M&Ms & the quantity of food I'm eating, I'll be quite fat when I roll into class next week.

I'm also praying a lot. Today I bought a red string bracelet from a very wrinkled old lady at the Wailing Wall, which will protect me from evil spirits. And then I wrote a prayer on a small piece of paper & inserted it into the cracks of an enormous wall. I prayed for my brother's happiness. I'm not trying to change him. I promise. I do not even know if God will answer me, but this seemed like the least I could do for his sad soul! I like EL & feel terrible for her. She is stuck with him. He's mean to her. I know this isn't my problem, but watching them is terrible.

Andy & I have no money but he's my best friend. He loves me unconditionally; he puts up with all my problems. He likes me & takes care of me.

Maud <Maud@yogavilla.com>   10:26PM
to Kate

Kate, you and Andy are soul mates. You have always had this special relationship. You also take care of Andy and nourish him with your love. Many times, I ask students to dedicate their practice to someone who needs love and attention. Putting the note in the wall with thought is symbolic along the same lines. By dedicating a practice or writing a prayer you heal yourself and by doing this, you can start to heal the others in need. We are constantly healing ourselves and others around us. Only positive things can be gained by this loving action.

Kate <Kate.Orser@mail.com>   10:27PM
to Maud

I will keep doing this just as long as I do not let him hurt me - right?

Maud <Maud@yogavilla.com>   10:28PM
to Kate

Right. There are spiritual drains and fountains. Your brother is a drain. Your husband is a fountain. You only need to have fountains around you. Take care of yourself first Kate. You cannot take responsibility for all the others. Even Brooke is ready to take care of herself. She is your daughter but she needs to nourish herself and find the power of her own love and passion.

Kate <Kate.Orser@mail.com>   10:28PM
to Maud

I understand. Thank you, Maud.

Maud <Maud@yogavilla.com>   10:28PM
to Kate

Take a few good long breaths of gratitude. You have so much to be grateful for in your life.

Israel

<u>Brooke G.O.</u>

Surrounded for being different
Attacked for being defiant
Starved for being full
Never compliant

An orphan
Loved by many and feared by most
You survive where not welcome
A hospitable host

Harsh and untrusting
Defeated and defended
Harboring immigrants
Nothing pretended

Foreigners embraced
Far from their native home
Welcomed with love
No longer need to roam

Rough like a diamond
Sweet like honey
Opaque as quartz
Warm and sunny

♡ 199   261 ◉

Freedom 📩 inbox ✕

EL <ElGood@mail.com>   11:29PM ☆ ↩ ▾
to Dahlia ▾

Ethan is here. I am sure mom told you plenty more than she shared with me. This appears to be an ongoing theme. Do you want to fill me in? Maybe you could help me figure out how to deal with my ex-brother? More pressing than my fucked-up marriage at this moment.

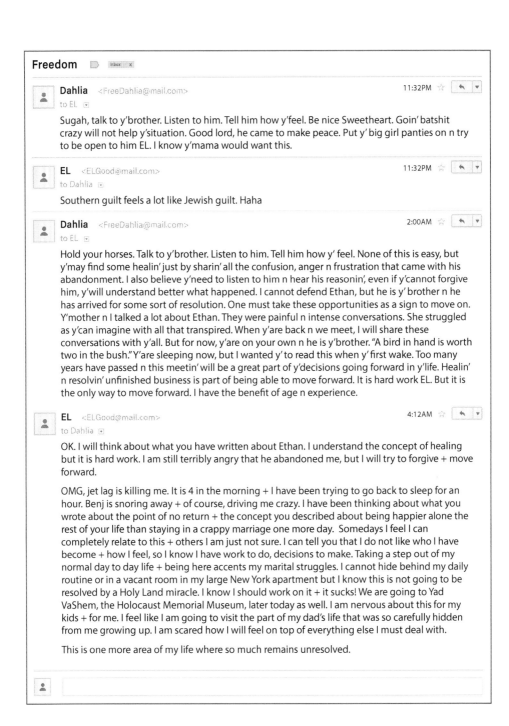

Freedom

Dahlia <FreeDahlia@mail.com>   11:32PM
to EL

Sugah, talk to y'brother. Listen to him. Tell him how y'feel. Be nice Sweetheart. Goin' batshit crazy will not help y'situation. Good lord, he came to make peace. Put y' big girl panties on n try to be open to him EL. I know y'mama would want this.

EL <ELGood@mail.com>   11:32PM
to Dahlia

Southern guilt feels a lot like Jewish guilt. Haha

Dahlia <FreeDahlia@mail.com>   2:00AM
to EL

Hold your horses. Talk to y'brother. Listen to him. Tell him how y' feel. None of this is easy, but y'may find some healin' just by sharin' all the confusion, anger n frustration that came with his abandonment. I also believe y'need to listen to him n hear his reasonin', even if y'cannot forgive him, y'will understand better what happened. I cannot defend Ethan, but he is y' brother n he has arrived for some sort of resolution. One must take these opportunities as a sign to move on. Y'mother n I talked a lot about Ethan. They were painful n intense conversations. She struggled as y'can imagine with all that transpired. When y'are back n we meet, I will share these conversations with y'all. But for now, y'are on your own n he is y'brother. "A bird in hand is worth two in the bush." Y'are sleeping now, but I wanted y' to read this when y' first wake. Too many years have passed n this meetin' will be a great part of y'decisions going forward in y'life. Healin' n resolvin' unfinished business is part of being able to move forward. It is hard work EL. But it is the only way to move forward. I have the benefit of age n experience.

EL <ELGood@mail.com>   4:12AM
to Dahlia

OK. I will think about what you have written about Ethan. I understand the concept of healing but it is hard work. I am still terribly angry that he abandoned me, but I will try to forgive + move forward.

OMG, jet lag is killing me. It is 4 in the morning + I have been trying to go back to sleep for an hour. Benj is snoring away + of course, driving me crazy. I have been thinking about what you wrote about the point of no return + the concept you described about being happier alone the rest of your life than staying in a crappy marriage one more day. Somedays I feel I can completely relate to this + others I am just not sure. I can tell you that I do not like who I have become + how I feel, so I know I have work to do, decisions to make. Taking a step out of my normal day to day life + being here accents my marital struggles. I cannot hide behind my daily routine or in a vacant room in my large New York apartment but I know this is not going to be resolved by a Holy Land miracle. I know I should work on it + it sucks! We are going to Yad VaShem, the Holocaust Memorial Museum, later today as well. I am nervous about this for my kids + for me. I feel like I am going to visit the part of my dad's life that was so carefully hidden from me growing up. I am scared how I will feel on top of everything else I must deal with.

This is one more area of my life where so much remains unresolved.

BOKER TOV

Goodman Family!

Welcome to day five of your Holy Land excursion!
Here is today's schedule:

Returning to a painful history...

Our first visit this morning is at the David Citadel where we will walk through the underground waterways. As we cannot guarantee the water levels that you will encounter and walk through, please bring your water shoes and wear shorts. We can buy mini flashlights in their gift shop, but they do not sell water shoes. From there, we will continue with a strolling adventure through the famous Jerusalem Shuk Market Place and arrive at Mahane Yehuda Restaurant for a very special lunch. I recommend that you also bring a hat for the walk around the Shuk.

We will change clothing before lunch and for our afternoon visit to Yad Vashem, the official memorial to the victims of the Holocaust. This is always a very emotional and sad experience for all visitors and holds even deeper meaning to your family's personal history. We will also visit the Children's Memorial and the Hall of Remembrance. "Yad Vashem" comes from a verse in the Book of Isaiah – "Even unto them will I give in mine house and within my walls a place and a name (yad vashem) better than of sons and of daughters: I will give them an everlasting name, that shall not be cut off" (Isaiah 56:5)

Today's Temperature:

 The weather today will be a warm 30˚c / 86˚f

Moshe

Rimon Tours

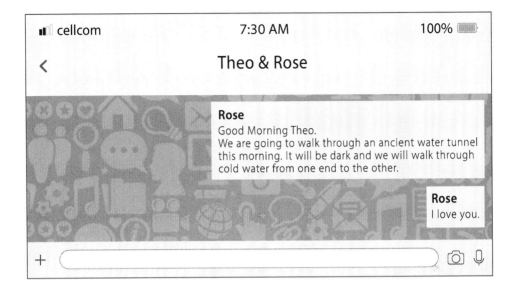

Rose
Good Morning Theo.
We are going to walk through an ancient water tunnel this morning. It will be dark and we will walk through cold water from one end to the other.

Rose
I love you.

Andy Orser
Now · Israel

GOY IN THE HOLY LAND PART 20

Walked through Hezekiah's Tunnel in Jerusalem's City of David. Dating back to the 8th Century BCE, the underground tunnel was intended to provide the city Jews with fresh water when they were under enemy siege by the Assyrians. The walk is a delightful and invigorating half kilometer where we escaped daylight, fresh air, and walked through two feet of cold water along a dark, narrow path.

Dear Friends, it was pitch black and mini flashlights produced tiny specks of light barely guiding us through two feet of cold water. We had to trust ourselves and keep moving forward! #Hezekiahstunnel #israeliadventureforme

   👍 Like   💬 Comment   ↪ Share

Aliza Goodman's Daily Motivational Quote #1:   now

"As long as there are those who are willing to shed blood and take innocent life in the name of religion - in the name of God - the world will never know a true and lasting peace."
Hillary Clinton

MotiQuote.com

Light at the End of the Tunnel
Roaming Roman

I just walked through Hezekiah's Tunnel with Bruno & the family. Interesting, the tunnel was built by digging from two opposite sides that met in the middle; people underground used sound generated hammering to guide themselves through the dark tunnel. Perhaps, EL & I are not unlike the two different sides & this trip together is guiding us closer. Will we shortly meet in the middle? Will there be light at the end of the tunnel? Will I get my little sister back in my life?

UGH! Inbox x

Shirl <Shirl465@mail.com> 9:00AM
to EL

How are you doing?

EL <ELGood@mail.com> 9:00AM
to Shirl

Why aren't you sleeping?

Shirl <Shirl465@mail.com> 9:01AM
to EL

On a sleep break! Where are you?

EL <ELGood@mail.com> 9:01AM
to Shirl

On the bus. Running out of people who I like on this tour over the age of 11.

Shirl <Shirl465@mail.com> 9:01AM
to EL

More than just your renegade brother & your detached husband?

EL <ELGood@mail.com> 9:01AM
to Shirl

I know this is petty, but I can't stand watching Kate + Andy hold hands + smile when they look at each other. On top of that, Rose has become best friends with Ethan + Bruno - UGH!

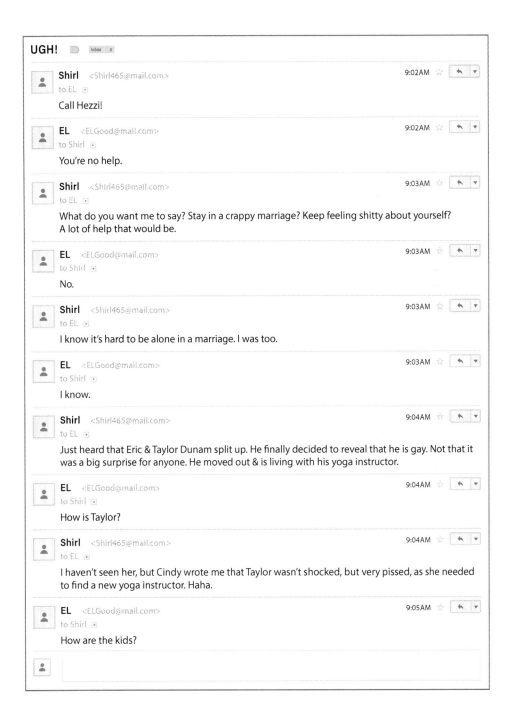

UGH! Inbox ×

Shirl <Shirl465@mail.com> 9:02AM
to EL

Call Hezzi!

EL <ELGood@mail.com> 9:02AM
to Shirl

You're no help.

Shirl <Shirl465@mail.com> 9:03AM
to EL

What do you want me to say? Stay in a crappy marriage? Keep feeling shitty about yourself?
A lot of help that would be.

EL <ELGood@mail.com> 9:03AM
to Shirl

No.

Shirl <Shirl465@mail.com> 9:03AM
to EL

I know it's hard to be alone in a marriage. I was too.

EL <ELGood@mail.com> 9:03AM
to Shirl

I know.

Shirl <Shirl465@mail.com> 9:04AM
to EL

Just heard that Eric & Taylor Dunam split up. He finally decided to reveal that he is gay. Not that it
was a big surprise for anyone. He moved out & is living with his yoga instructor.

EL <ELGood@mail.com> 9:04AM
to Shirl

How is Taylor?

Shirl <Shirl465@mail.com> 9:04AM
to EL

I haven't seen her, but Cindy wrote me that Taylor wasn't shocked, but very pissed, as she needed
to find a new yoga instructor. Haha.

EL <ELGood@mail.com> 9:05AM
to Shirl

How are the kids?

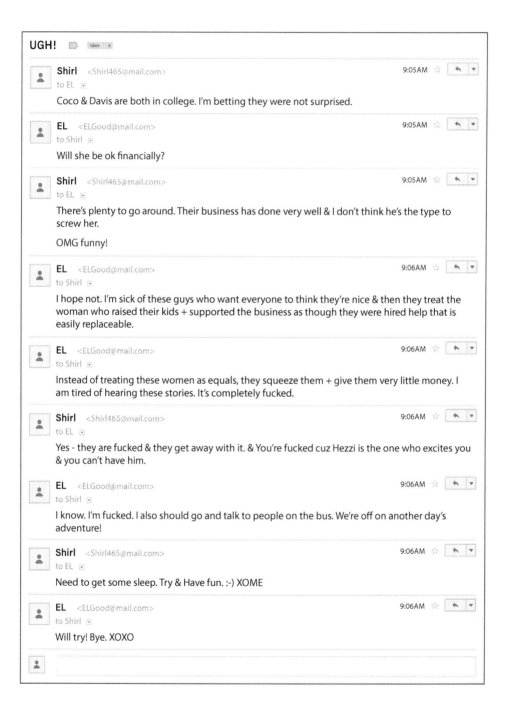

UGH! Inbox x

Shirl <Shirl465@mail.com>   9:05AM
to EL

Coco & Davis are both in college. I'm betting they were not surprised.

EL <ELGood@mail.com>   9:05AM
to Shirl

Will she be ok financially?

Shirl <Shirl465@mail.com>   9:05AM
to EL

There's plenty to go around. Their business has done very well & I don't think he's the type to screw her.

OMG funny!

EL <ELGood@mail.com>   9:06AM
to Shirl

I hope not. I'm sick of these guys who want everyone to think they're nice & then they treat the woman who raised their kids + supported the business as though they were hired help that is easily replaceable.

EL <ELGood@mail.com>   9:06AM
to Shirl

Instead of treating these women as equals, they squeeze them + give them very little money. I am tired of hearing these stories. It's completely fucked.

Shirl <Shirl465@mail.com>   9:06AM
to EL

Yes - they are fucked & they get away with it. & You're fucked cuz Hezzi is the one who excites you & you can't have him.

EL <ELGood@mail.com>   9:06AM
to Shirl

I know. I'm fucked. I also should go and talk to people on the bus. We're off on another day's adventure!

Shirl <Shirl465@mail.com>   9:06AM
to EL

Need to get some sleep. Try & Have fun. :-) XOME

EL <ELGood@mail.com>   9:06AM
to Shirl

Will try! Bye. XOXO

LUCACLOSELY
@LUCACLOSELY

What is greater than God, more evil than the devil, the poor have it, the rich need it and if you eat it, you will die?

9:20 AM – June

💬 1   ♡ 2   ⟲ 1

LUCACLOSELY @LUCACLOSELY
Replying to @LUCACLOSELY

Nothing.

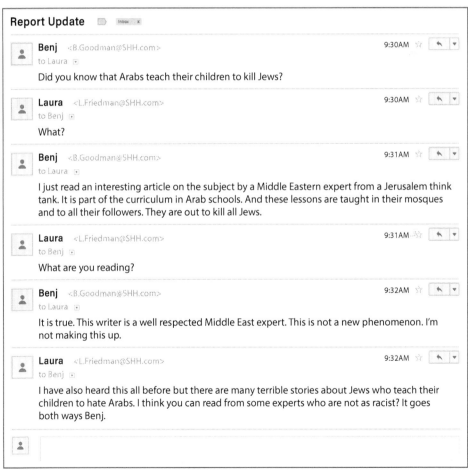

Report Update

Benj <B.Goodman@SHH.com>   9:30AM
to Laura

Did you know that Arabs teach their children to kill Jews?

Laura <L.Friedman@SHH.com>   9:30AM
to Benj

What?

Benj <B.Goodman@SHH.com>   9:31AM
to Laura

I just read an interesting article on the subject by a Middle Eastern expert from a Jerusalem think tank. It is part of the curriculum in Arab schools. And these lessons are taught in their mosques and to all their followers. They are out to kill all Jews.

Laura <L.Friedman@SHH.com>   9:31AM
to Benj

What are you reading?

Benj <B.Goodman@SHH.com>   9:32AM
to Laura

It is true. This writer is a well respected Middle East expert. This is not a new phenomenon. I'm not making this up.

Laura <L.Friedman@SHH.com>   9:32AM
to Benj

I have also heard this all before but there are many terrible stories about Jews who teach their children to hate Arabs. I think you can read from some experts who are not as racist? It goes both ways Benj.

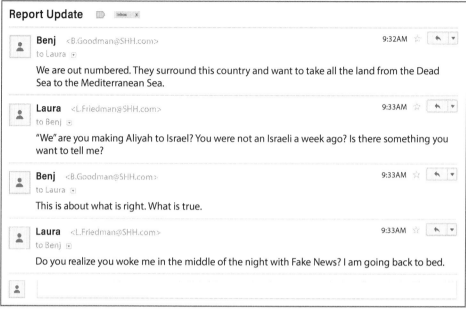

Report Update Inbox

Benj <B.Goodman@SHH.com> · to Laura — 9:32AM

We are out numbered. They surround this country and want to take all the land from the Dead Sea to the Mediterranean Sea.

Laura <L.Friedman@SHH.com> · to Benj — 9:33AM

"We" are you making Aliyah to Israel? You were not an Israeli a week ago? Is there something you want to tell me?

Benj <B.Goodman@SHH.com> · to Laura — 9:33AM

This is about what is right. What is true.

Laura <L.Friedman@SHH.com> · to Benj — 9:33AM

Do you realize you woke me in the middle of the night with Fake News? I am going back to bed.

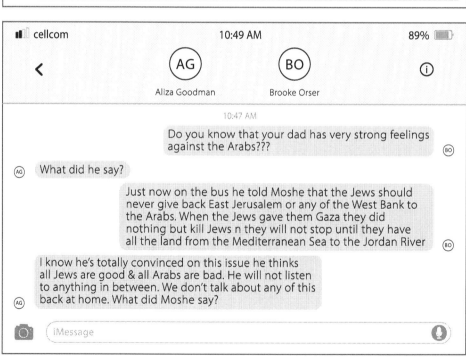

cellcom · 10:49 AM · 89%

AG — Aliza Goodman   BO — Brooke Orser

10:47 AM

Do you know that your dad has very strong feelings against the Arabs??? (BO)

What did he say? (AG)

Just now on the bus he told Moshe that the Jews should never give back East Jerusalem or any of the West Bank to the Arabs. When the Jews gave them Gaza they did nothing but kill Jews n they will not stop until they have all the land from the Mediterranean Sea to the Jordan River (BO)

I know he's totally convinced on this issue he thinks all Jews are good & all Arabs are bad. He will not listen to anything in between. We don't talk about any of this back at home. What did Moshe say? (AG)

iMessage

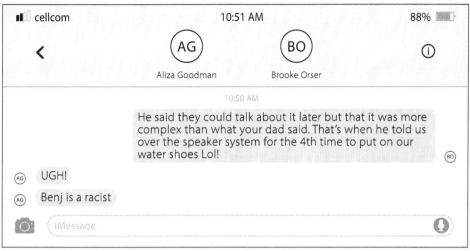

cellcom 10:51 AM 88%

(AG) Aliza Goodman (BO) Brooke Orser

10:50 AM

He said they could talk about it later but that it was more complex than what your dad said. That's when he told us over the speaker system for the 4th time to put on our water shoes Lol! (BO)

(AG) UGH!

(AG) Benj is a racist

iMessage

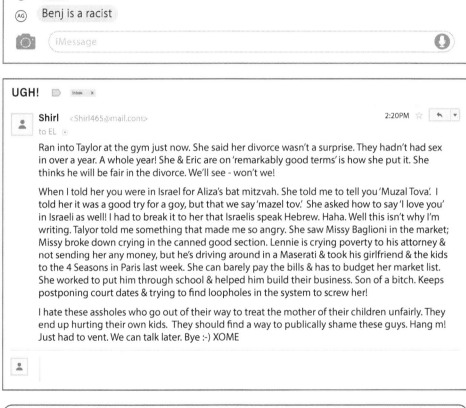

UGH! 📁 Inbox ×

 Shirl <Shirl465@mail.com> 2:20PM
to EL

Ran into Taylor at the gym just now. She said her divorce wasn't a surprise. They hadn't had sex in over a year. A whole year! She & Eric are on 'remarkably good terms' is how she put it. She thinks he will be fair in the divorce. We'll see - won't we!

When I told her you were in Israel for Aliza's bat mitzvah. She told me to tell you 'Muzal Tova'. I told her it was a good try for a goy, but that we say 'mazel tov.' She asked how to say 'I love you' in Israeli as well! I had to break it to her that Israelis speak Hebrew. Haha. Well this isn't why I'm writing. Talyor told me something that made me so angry. She saw Missy Baglioni in the market; Missy broke down crying in the canned good section. Lennie is crying poverty to his attorney & not sending her any money, but he's driving around in a Maserati & took his girlfriend & the kids to the 4 Seasons in Paris last week. She can barely pay the bills & has to budget her market list. She worked to put him through school & helped him build their business. Son of a bitch. Keeps postponing court dates & trying to find loopholes in the system to screw her!

I hate these assholes who go out of their way to treat the mother of their children unfairly. They end up hurting their own kids. They should find a way to publically shame these guys. Hang m! Just had to vent. We can talk later. Bye :-) XOME

📋 **JN24:** now

Israeli leaders believed to be in secret meetings with top Iranian officials.

Jewish News You Can Use

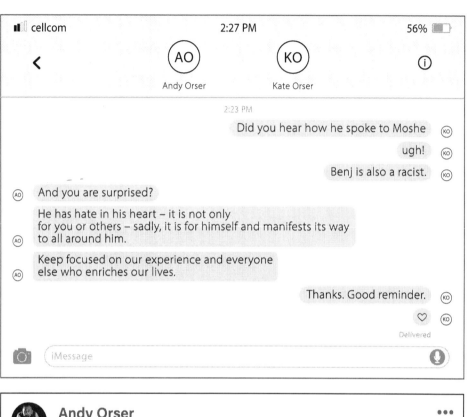

iMessage conversation:

2:23 PM

> Did you hear how he spoke to Moshe (KO)

> ugh! (KO)

> Benj is also a racist. (KO)

(AO) And you are surprised?

(AO) He has hate in his heart – it is not only for you or others – sadly, it is for himself and manifests its way to all around him.

(AO) Keep focused on our experience and everyone else who enriches our lives.

> Thanks. Good reminder. (KO)

> ♡ (KO)

> Delivered

Andy Orser
Now · Israel

GOY IN THE HOLY LAND PART 21

Mahane Yehuda Market. Just enjoyed the loud and very lively outdoor shuk/market in Jerusalem that feels like a beautifully designed movie set: row after row of bright booths full of products and proud Israelis yelling out in Hebrew and Palestinians in Arabic: they all switch to English as we pass by knowing who their customers are at each minute. I hated to disappoint them all and not buy from each passionate vendor, all charming characters in the real-life movie I am living. I am inspired by the collaborative, diverse community represented in this microcosm.

Dear Friends, the market was incredibly fun: Kate enthusiastically took photos for her Blog, Brooke for her Instagram and I sampled delicious food all along the way. We were surrounded by very aggressive shoppers and vendors fondly screaming at us in Hebrew and Arabic; it was hot, dusty and sweaty, but no war. #Mahaneyehudamarket #shuk #nohate

👍 Like   💬 Comment   ↪ Share

FOOD AFFAIR WITH KATE

DIVINE, DELICIOUS, AND DELIGHTFUL

Shop Til I Drop

★ ★ ★ ★ ★

Mahane Yehuda Market, a delicious open air market, pleasingly presents bountiful, bright, juicy fruits and vegetables, countless bins of brown and orange grains and spices, colorful, multishaped bottles of oils and wines, smelly cheeses and fragrant breads, buckets of green and brown olives and pickled vegetables, trays of flaky baklava and flavored halvah, large bowls of salted nuts and dried fruits, foggy glass counters of pink meats and poultry and shaved ice embracing fresh fish and seafood. My taste buds dance as I sample their cooked delicacies, rotisserie chicken, burekas, humus, falafel, shwarma, rice, pasta, soups and more. I could spend hours delightfully lost, discovering, sampling and endulging my taste senses at endless tempting booths. I learn so much absorbing the essence of this market place and realize I could spend days here fully enraptured in this culinary world – a cross roads of religious and cultural food. There is so much to learn and experience. A culinary Mecca, a food lover's paradise and a feast of incredible magnitude for the human senses; not to mention the crazy contagious energy that pulsates through all the aisles asas vendors scream and laugh convincing us all to indulge in their products and guaranteeing the hungry travelers not only the best quality but the best prices. Bloody hot today, but everyone passionately shops and fills bags and carts to the brim. This is what heaven must feel, smell and look like.

See the incredible photos below and check out Food Affair with Kate on Instagram and Facebook. #shuk #israelifood #holylandcuisine #israelisforfoodlovers #isrealifoodies #farmersmarket

Roman God in the Market Place

Brooke G.O.

Heads turn to catch his essence
A godly figure in their presence
Roman full of pride
Humble footsteps carry stride
One cannot help but stare
Fruit sweetens the warm air
Owners pray in their stall
Holy market graced by all

♡ 194   261 ◉

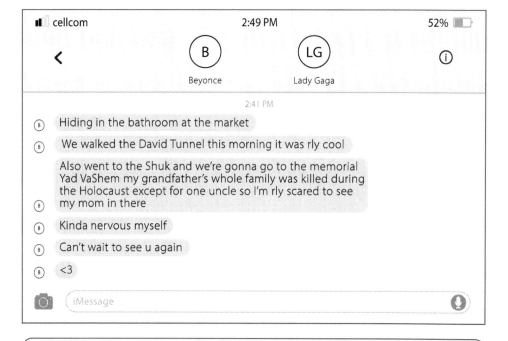

il cellcom   2:49 PM   52% 🔋

‹   **B**   **LG**   ⓘ

Beyonce   Lady Gaga

2:41 PM

Ⓑ Hiding in the bathroom at the market

Ⓑ We walked the David Tunnel this morning it was rly cool

Ⓑ Also went to the Shuk and we're gonna go to the memorial Yad VaShem my grandfather's whole family was killed during the Holocaust except for one uncle so I'm rly scared to see my mom in there

Ⓑ Kinda nervous myself

Ⓑ Can't wait to see u again

Ⓑ <3

📷 (iMessage)   🎙

 JN24:   now
Two teenagers finish their bicycle journey from Nehariya in Northern Israel to Eilat in the south raising money to pay for a friend's kidney transplant.
Jewish News You Can Use

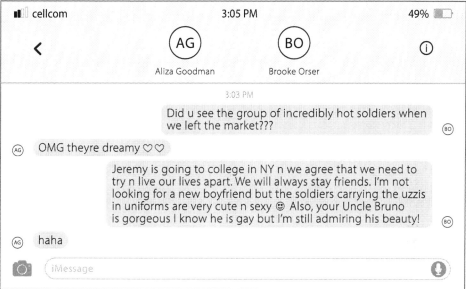

AG Aliza Goodman   **BO** Brooke Orser

3:03 PM

> Did u see the group of incredibly hot soldiers when we left the market???

OMG theyre dreamy ♡♡

> Jeremy is going to college in NY n we agree that we need to try n live our lives apart. We will always stay friends. I'm not looking for a new boyfriend but the soldiers carrying the uzzis in uniforms are very cute n sexy ☺ Also, your Uncle Bruno is gorgeous I know he is gay but I'm still admiring his beauty!

haha

iMessage

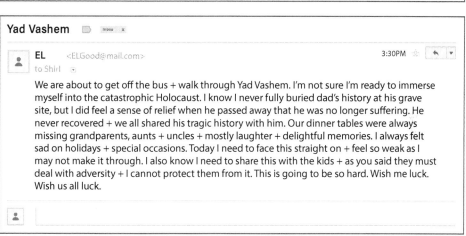

Yad Vashem Inbox x

EL <ELGood@mail.com>   3:30PM
to Shirl

We are about to get off the bus + walk through Yad Vashem. I'm not sure I'm ready to immerse myself into the catastrophic Holocaust. I know I never fully buried dad's history at his grave site, but I did feel a sense of relief when he passed away that he was no longer suffering. He never recovered + we all shared his tragic history with him. Our dinner tables were always missing grandparents, aunts + uncles + mostly laughter + delightful memories. I always felt sad on holidays + special occasions. Today I need to face this straight on + feel so weak as I may not make it through. I also know I need to share this with the kids + as you said they must deal with adversity + I cannot protect them from it. This is going to be so hard. Wish me luck. Wish us all luck.

Aliza Goodman's Daily Motivational Quote #2:   now

"We can forgive the Arabs for killing our children. We cannot forgive them for forcing us to kill their children. We will only have peace with the Arabs when they love their children more than they hate us."
Golda Meir

MotiQuote.com

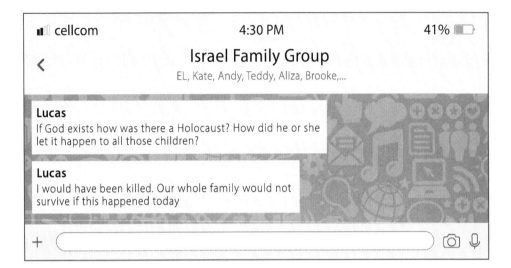

Lucas
If God exists how was there a Holocaust? How did he or she let it happen to all those children?

Lucas
I would have been killed. Our whole family would not survive if this happened today

Andy Orser
Now · Israel

GOY IN THE HOLY LAND PART 22

Just experienced Yad Vashem, the Holocaust Memorial Museum. I am not a Jew but today my heart and soul did not need to be Jewish. They just needed to be human to experience the inhumane atrocities. I have seen countless movies and studied the Holocaust on paper. Today I breathed the stories of millions of murdered human beings for no other reason than they were Jewish. Their faith was different and this difference was their marking for killing: Human hatred so pervasive.

Yad Vashem gives the Jewish victims a meaningful place for their proud names to live on after their barbaric deaths. The museum is shaped like a triangular concrete 'prism' that is illuminated by a long skylight. We walked amidst these murdered victims' belongings, clothing, books, and toys.

Next we visited Yad Vashem Children's Memorial. How could anyone kill an innocent child? I looked deep into their eyes today and saw the toys they played with and the shoes they wore. The hall was packed with other visitors. It was almost silent as no one spoke a word out loud.

Dear Friends, I was not prepared for this misery - before my understanding was clinical, today it permeated my soul and changed me forever. In this exhibit tears poured from my troubled eyes uncontrollably. Hate is here. A concentrated exhibit for the world to keep hold of and declare 'Never Again'! #Yadvashem #holocaustmemorialjerusalem #neveragain

👍 Like   💬 Comment   ➦ Share

Hell
Teddy Goodman

Nothing in the last 17 years could have prepared me for this monumental moment. I just visited Yad Vashem, the Holocaust Memorial Museum in Jerusalem.

Today I changed.

I have studied the Holocaust over the years at school making me familiar with what I saw, but it did not prepare me for how drained I felt physically walking through and seeing the clothes, books and toys of kids who were killed. Witnessing their young and fresh eyes hit me so hard; I was shocked by how so many of them were familiar to me and looked like the kids that I go to school with in NY. All these innocent human beings were killed for no other reason than hate - hate of the Jewish people. It was a living memorial to 6 million dead Jews.

My whole family was quiet. All our crazy dysfunctional qualities disappeared for a couple of hours. Even my Aunt Kate and Uncle Andy, who ask endless stupid questions, were quiet and listened. Finally, Benj joined us and turned off his fucking BB.

EL and Ethan grew up in a house with a father, who was a Holocaust survivor, inhaling daily the severity and utmost cruelty imaginable that scarred his beautiful character: my grandfather's parents and siblings were all killed - today we saw the faces of our relatives as well. EL and Ethan have been estranged for their entire adult lives, but after the couple of hours shared in this depressing place, I cannot see how they can continue to hate each other.

Even at 17, this experience helps me understand that the need for human compassion, understanding, tolerance, love and forgiveness is beckoning each person who allows himself to be vulnerable and make sure that this never fucking happens again.

In a couple of days, my little sister will celebrate her bat mitzvah and become a woman. Having experienced a bar mitzvah, I know that no one at the age of 13 is a real adult. It is only the beginning. I'm about to turn 18 and start to take my life more seriously. Today was a huge catalyst for me to live and experience in a different way. I have spent so much time in my room and school learning but the real world is out there waiting for me and I for it.

I fucking better get going.

Finality
Roaming Roman

My father was a Holocaust survivor. Today I visited Yad Vashem & feel as if I was finally able to honor my aunts, uncles & grandparents whose faces I only imagined & whose voices I never heard. I know this hollow sadness will haunt me for the rest of my life. My father was a good and kind man ruined by the Holocaust at an early age. The shadow of a man lived his life on earth but the Nazis killed his kind soul. I have no doubt that my father was a victim and yet even after all these years I struggle to accept my father's treatment of me. How badly I want to forgive him; and today I moved much closer to finish this chapter to excuse the pain he caused me.

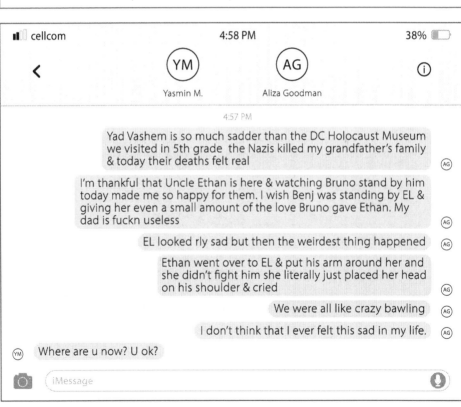

cellcom   4:58 PM   38%

YM   **AG**
Yasmin M.   Aliza Goodman

4:57 PM

Yad Vashem is so much sadder than the DC Holocaust Museum we visited in 5th grade the Nazis killed my grandfather's family & today their deaths felt real

I'm thankful that Uncle Ethan is here & watching Bruno stand by him today made me so happy for them. I wish Benj was standing by EL & giving her even a small amount of the love Bruno gave Ethan. My dad is fuckn useless

EL looked rly sad but then the weirdest thing happened

Ethan went over to EL & put his arm around her and she didn't fight him she literally just placed her head on his shoulder & cried

We were all like crazy bawling

I don't think that I ever felt this sad in my life.

Where are u now? U ok?

iMessage

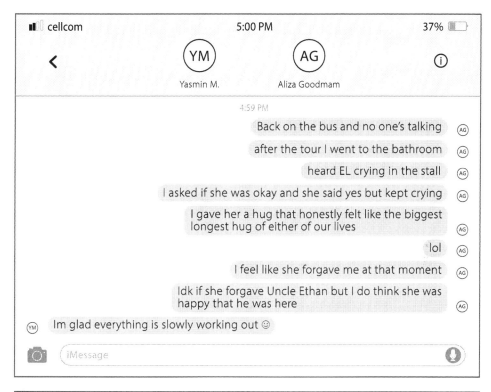

4:59 PM

Back on the bus and no one's talking

after the tour I went to the bathroom

heard EL crying in the stall

I asked if she was okay and she said yes but kept crying

I gave her a hug that honestly felt like the biggest longest hug of either of our lives

lol

I feel like she forgave me at that moment

Idk if she forgave Uncle Ethan but I do think she was happy that he was here

Im glad everything is slowly working out ☺

iMessage

MYJOURNAL.COM

Finality cont.
Roaming Roman

Dad lost his whole family through no fault of his own & lived with this terrible truth his entire life; I lost my sister but this was my entire fault & I regret this every day. I am an orphan; I lost both of my estranged parents over the last few years. Today as we buried our Polish family, I am so keenly aware that EL & I need to bury our differences & distrust. I feel like we are being given a second chance. I need to stop crying & think how I speak with EL. Life has never felt more precious and today was a solemn reminder that each day alive is a gift that I cannot waste. I cannot change my past but I can lead my future. I say, "To Life" with a renewed spirit.

War

Brooke G.O.

No one came home at the end of the day
No one took off his winter coat
No one kissed goodnight
No one smiled and said I love you

You stole our hearts
You stabbed our souls
You stopped our belief
I alone cannot stop you

We live on
We share our memories
We can never forget
We remember

5:28 PM

(HM) I'm on my way. I will meet you at 6:00.

Ok. (EG)

(HM) How was your day?

Surreal. (EG)

(HM) Why?

We just came back from Yad Vashem. It was one of the most heartbreaking experiences in my entire life. I just kept seeing my father + the one little photo he had of his family before the war that he hid in his bureau. (EG)

We never talked about it. It was a forbidden subject in our house. But all I saw today were their faces. I felt like I was looking at my murdered family. Their eyes were so powerful. I cried more than I can remember. Then Ethan came over + put his arm around me. I cried more. (EG)

(HM) He loves you EL. You need to talk to him. Alone. Just the two of you. He has a story and you need to learn it.

I will. I'm scared. I have hated him for so long. How do I just stop hating him? (EG)

(HM) Human healing requires you to stop the hate. He is not your enemy. He is your brother. He would not have come to the bat mitzvah if he wanted to stay apart. You lost your parents. You need your brother.

When will you be here? (EG)

(HM) In half an hour.

Waiting. I want to see you. (EG)

(HM) I want to see you.

Hurry. (EG)

(HM) Bye

📷 (iMessage) 🎤

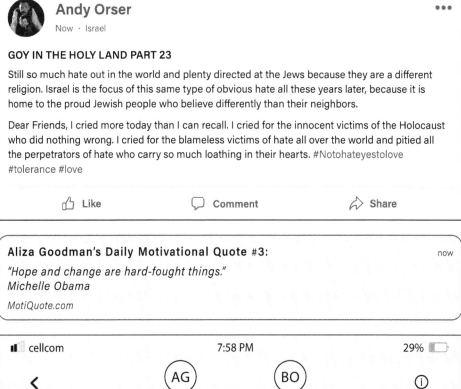

Andy Orser
Now · Israel

GOY IN THE HOLY LAND PART 23

Still so much hate out in the world and plenty directed at the Jews because they are a different religion. Israel is the focus of this same type of obvious hate all these years later, because it is home to the proud Jewish people who believe differently than their neighbors.

Dear Friends, I cried more today than I can recall. I cried for the innocent victims of the Holocaust who did nothing wrong. I cried for the blameless victims of hate all over the world and pitied all the perpetrators of hate who carry so much loathing in their hearts. #Notohateyestolove #tolerance #love

    👍 Like   💬 Comment   ↗ Share

Aliza Goodman's Daily Motivational Quote #3:   now

"Hope and change are hard-fought things."
Michelle Obama

MotiQuote.com

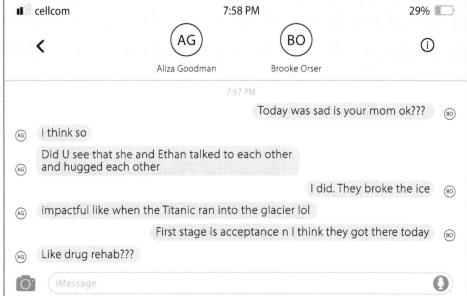

cellcom   7:58 PM   29%

AG   **BO**

Aliza Goodman   Brooke Orser

7:57 PM

Today was sad is your mom ok??? (BO)

(AG) I think so

(AG) Did U see that she and Ethan talked to each other and hugged each other

I did. They broke the ice (BO)

(AG) impactful like when the Titanic ran into the glacier lol

First stage is acceptance n I think they got there today (BO)

(AG) Like drug rehab???

iMessage

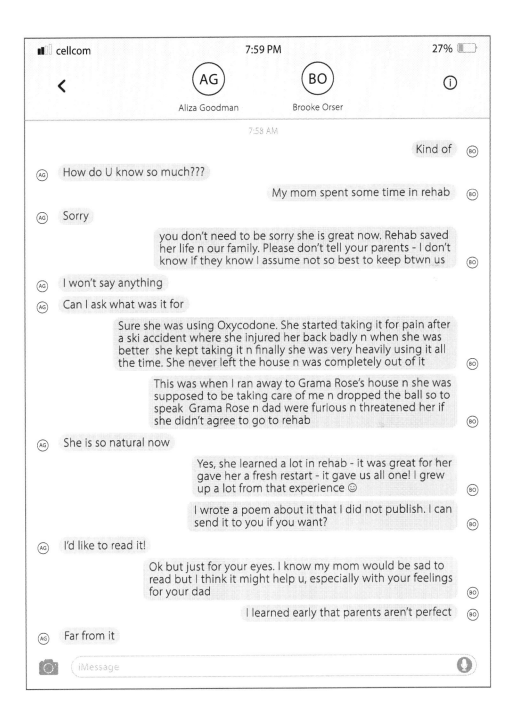

AG — Aliza Goodman
BO — Brooke Orser

7:58 AM

Kind of

AG: How do U know so much???

My mom spent some time in rehab

AG: Sorry

you don't need to be sorry she is great now. Rehab saved her life n our family. Please don't tell your parents - I don't know if they know I assume not so best to keep btwn us

AG: I won't say anything

AG: Can I ask what was it for

Sure she was using Oxycodone. She started taking it for pain after a ski accident where she injured her back badly n when she was better she kept taking it n finally she was very heavily using it all the time. She never left the house n was completely out of it

This was when I ran away to Grama Rose's house n she was supposed to be taking care of me n dropped the ball so to speak Grama Rose n dad were furious n threatened her if she didn't agree to go to rehab

AG: She is so natural now

Yes, she learned a lot in rehab - it was great for her gave her a fresh restart - it gave us all one! I grew up a lot from that experience ☺

I wrote a poem about it that I did not publish. I can send it to you if you want?

AG: I'd like to read it!

Ok but just for your eyes. I know my mom would be sad to read but I think it might help u, especially with your feelings for your dad

I learned early that parents aren't perfect

AG: Far from it

iMessage

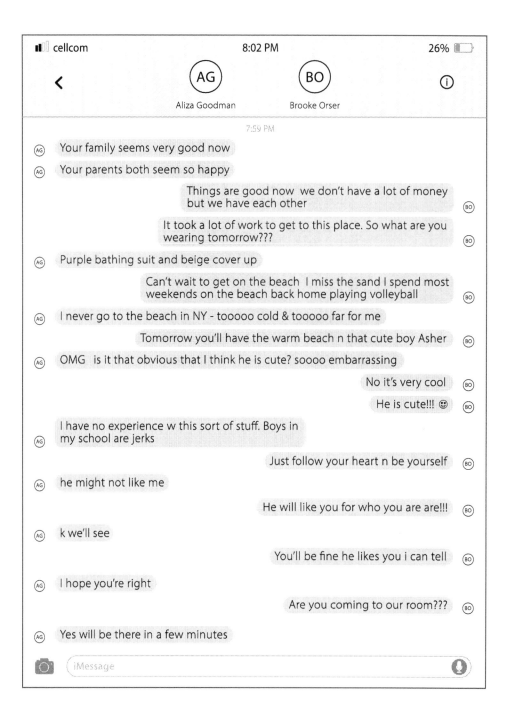

cellcom   8:02 PM   26%

(AG) Aliza Goodman   (BO) Brooke Orser   ⓘ

7:59 PM

(AG) Your family seems very good now

(AG) Your parents both seem so happy

Things are good now we don't have a lot of money but we have each other (BO)

It took a lot of work to get to this place. So what are you wearing tomorrow??? (BO)

(AG) Purple bathing suit and beige cover up

Can't wait to get on the beach I miss the sand I spend most weekends on the beach back home playing volleyball (BO)

(AG) I never go to the beach in NY - tooooo cold & tooooo far for me

Tomorrow you'll have the warm beach n that cute boy Asher (BO)

(AG) OMG is it that obvious that I think he is cute? soooo embarrassing

No it's very cool (BO)

He is cute!!! ☺ (BO)

(AG) I have no experience w this sort of stuff. Boys in my school are jerks

Just follow your heart n be yourself (BO)

(AG) he might not like me

He will like you for who you are!!! (BO)

(AG) k we'll see

You'll be fine he likes you i can tell (BO)

(AG) I hope you're right

Are you coming to our room??? (BO)

(AG) Yes will be there in a few minutes

📷 (iMessage) 🎤

Dear Lucas Goodman, Astronaut in Training —

@JUNIORNASAUSA

| Crew | About | Photos |

TODAY ON THE INTERNATIONAL SPACE STATION:

Our crew members on the International Space Station (@ISS) are from many different countries. We all have different backgrounds and expertise and each day we work closely together to complete our objectives and missions. We are now traveling over the Southern Patagonian Icefield, over 12,000 square kilometers on the southern border of Chile and Argentina. The icefield is the largest temperate ice sheet in the Southern Hemisphere. Today is a rare, clear day and the views of the snow and ice juxtaposed to blue lakes and brown landmasses are stunning. Since the end of the little Ice Age in the 19th Century, these South America glaciers have been shrinking as global temperatures have increased.

 JN24:   now

Unrest in East Jerusalem neighborhood after tax collectors locked residents out of their properties for delinquent accounts.

Jewish News You Can Use

LIFEEXPRESSIONS.COM

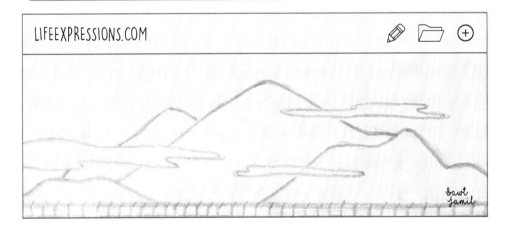

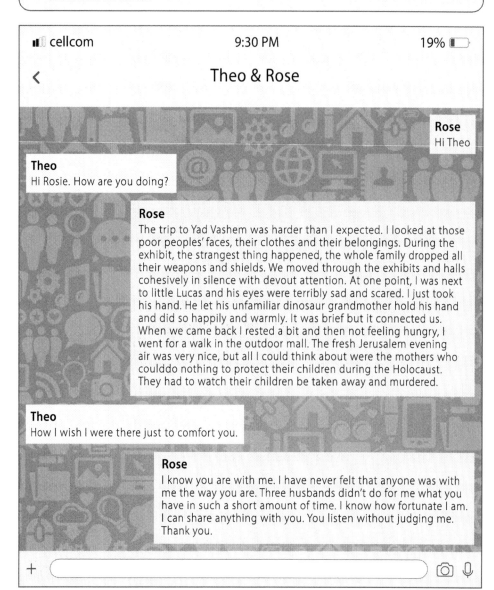

cellcom   9:30 PM   19%

Theo & Rose

Rose
Hi Theo

Theo
Hi Rosie. How are you doing?

Rose
The trip to Yad Vashem was harder than I expected. I looked at those poor peoples' faces, their clothes and their belongings. During the exhibit, the strangest thing happened, the whole family dropped all their weapons and shields. We moved through the exhibits and halls cohesively in silence with devout attention. At one point, I was next to little Lucas and his eyes were terribly sad and scared. I just took his hand. He let his unfamiliar dinosaur grandmother hold his hand and did so happily and warmly. It was brief but it connected us. When we came back I rested a bit and then not feeling hungry, I went for a walk in the outdoor mall. The fresh Jerusalem evening air was very nice, but all I could think about were the mothers who coulddo nothing to protect their children during the Holocaust. They had to watch their children be taken away and murdered.

Theo
How I wish I were there just to comfort you.

Rose
I know you are with me. I have never felt that anyone was with me the way you are. Three husbands didn't do for me what you have in such a short amount of time. I know how fortunate I am. I can share anything with you. You listen without judging me. Thank you.

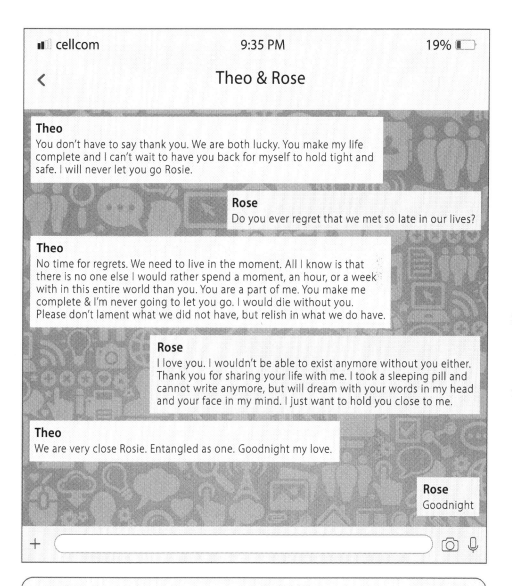

Theo & Rose

Theo
You don't have to say thank you. We are both lucky. You make my life complete and I can't wait to have you back for myself to hold tight and safe. I will never let you go Rosie.

Rose
Do you ever regret that we met so late in our lives?

Theo
No time for regrets. We need to live in the moment. All I know is that there is no one else I would rather spend a moment, an hour, or a week with in this entire world than you. You are a part of me. You make me complete & I'm never going to let you go. I would die without you. Please don't lament what we did not have, but relish in what we do have.

Rose
I love you. I wouldn't be able to exist anymore without you either. Thank you for sharing your life with me. I took a sleeping pill and cannot write anymore, but will dream with your words in my head and your face in my mind. I just want to hold you close to me.

Theo
We are very close Rosie. Entangled as one. Goodnight my love.

Rose
Goodnight

Aliza Goodman's Daily Motivational Quote #4:   now

"If you want to end the war then, instead of sending guns, send books. Instead of sending tanks, send pens. Instead of sending soldiers, send teachers."
Malala Yousafzai

MotiQuote.com

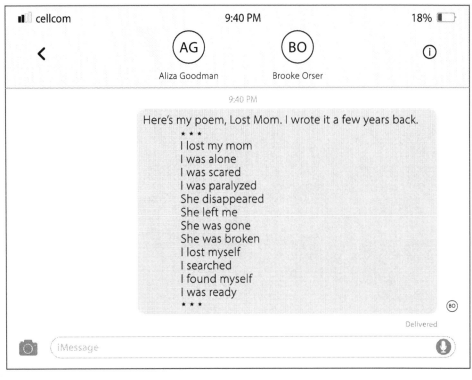

Here's my poem, Lost Mom. I wrote it a few years back.

★ ★ ★
I lost my mom
I was alone
I was scared
I was paralyzed
She disappeared
She left me
She was gone
She was broken
I lost myself
I searched
I found myself
I was ready
★ ★ ★

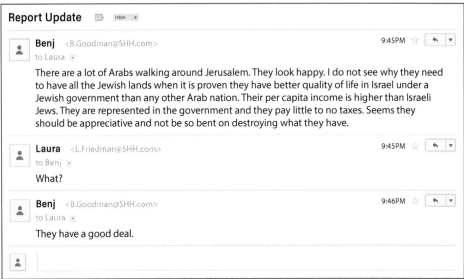

Report Update Inbox x

Benj <B.Goodman@SHH.com> 9:45PM
to Laura

There are a lot of Arabs walking around Jerusalem. They look happy. I do not see why they need to have all the Jewish lands when it is proven they have better quality of life in Israel under a Jewish government than any other Arab nation. Their per capita income is higher than Israeli Jews. They are represented in the government and they pay little to no taxes. Seems they should be appreciative and not be so bent on destroying what they have.

Laura <L.Friedman@SHH.com> 9:45PM
to Benj

What?

Benj <B.Goodman@SHH.com> 9:46PM
to Laura

They have a good deal.

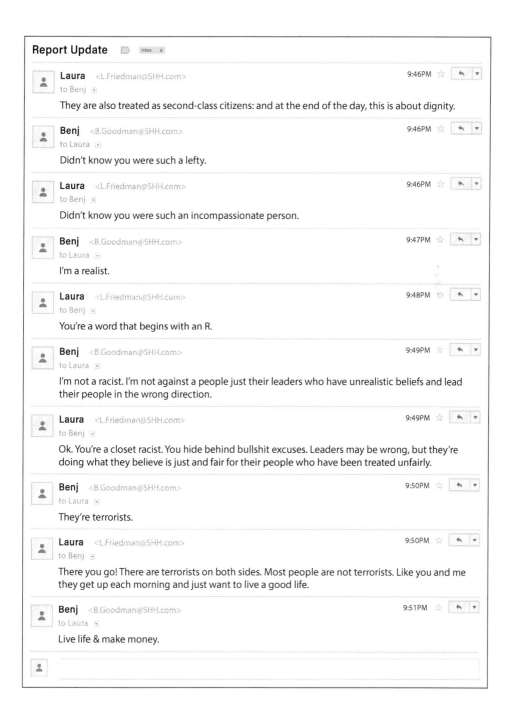

Report Update Inbox x

Laura <L.Friedman@SHH.com> 9:46PM
to Benj

They are also treated as second-class citizens: and at the end of the day, this is about dignity.

Benj <B.Goodman@SHH.com> 9:46PM
to Laura

Didn't know you were such a lefty.

Laura <L.Friedman@SHH.com> 9:46PM
to Benj

Didn't know you were such an incompassionate person.

Benj <B.Goodman@SHH.com> 9:47PM
to Laura

I'm a realist.

Laura <L.Friedman@SHH.com> 9:48PM
to Benj

You're a word that begins with an R.

Benj <B.Goodman@SHH.com> 9:49PM
to Laura

I'm not a racist. I'm not against a people just their leaders who have unrealistic beliefs and lead their people in the wrong direction.

Laura <L.Friedman@SHH.com> 9:49PM
to Benj

Ok. You're a closet racist. You hide behind bullshit excuses. Leaders may be wrong, but they're doing what they believe is just and fair for their people who have been treated unfairly.

Benj <B.Goodman@SHH.com> 9:50PM
to Laura

They're terrorists.

Laura <L.Friedman@SHH.com> 9:50PM
to Benj

There you go! There are terrorists on both sides. Most people are not terrorists. Like you and me they get up each morning and just want to live a good life.

Benj <B.Goodman@SHH.com> 9:51PM
to Laura

Live life & make money.

Report Update 📩 Inbox x

👤 **Laura** <L.Friedman@SHH.com>   9:51PM ☆ ↰ ▾
   to Benj ▾

We all need money but we all need to treat each other fairly. No labels. No judgement.
No cruelty.

👤 **Benj** <B.Goodman@SHH.com>   9:52PM ☆ ↰ ▾
   to Laura ▾

Then they need to stand up against the terrorists and say NO to violence.

👤

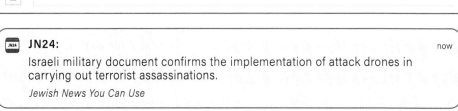

📰 **JN24:**   now
Israeli military document confirms the implementation of attack drones in
carrying out terrorist assassinations.
Jewish News You Can Use

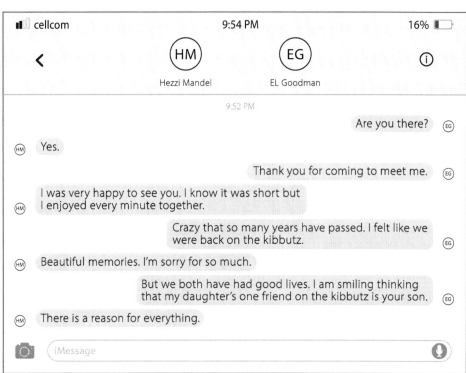

📶 cellcom   9:54 PM   16% 🔋

‹   (HM)   (EG)   ⓘ
     Hezzi Mandel   EL Goodman

                    9:52 PM

                                    Are you there? (EG)

(HM) Yes.

                            Thank you for coming to meet me. (EG)

(HM) I was very happy to see you. I know it was short but
      I enjoyed every minute together.

                            Crazy that so many years have passed. I felt like we
                            were back on the kibbutz. (EG)

(HM) Beautiful memories. I'm sorry for so much.

                            But we both have had good lives. I am smiling thinking
                            that my daughter's one friend on the kibbutz is your son. (EG)

(HM) There is a reason for everything.

📷 (iMessage   🎤)

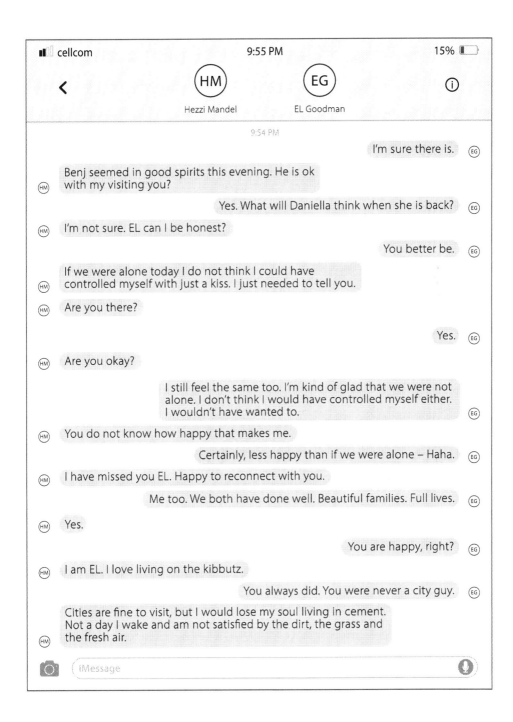

9:54 PM

I'm sure there is.

Benj seemed in good spirits this evening. He is ok with my visiting you?

Yes. What will Daniella think when she is back?

I'm not sure. EL can I be honest?

You better be.

If we were alone today I do not think I could have controlled myself with just a kiss. I just needed to tell you.

Are you there?

Yes.

Are you okay?

I still feel the same too. I'm kind of glad that we were not alone. I don't think I would have controlled myself either. I wouldn't have wanted to.

You do not know how happy that makes me.

Certainly, less happy than if we were alone – Haha.

I have missed you EL. Happy to reconnect with you.

Me too. We both have done well. Beautiful families. Full lives.

Yes.

You are happy, right?

I am EL. I love living on the kibbutz.

You always did. You were never a city guy.

Cities are fine to visit, but I would lose my soul living in cement. Not a day I wake and am not satisfied by the dirt, the grass and the fresh air.

iMessage

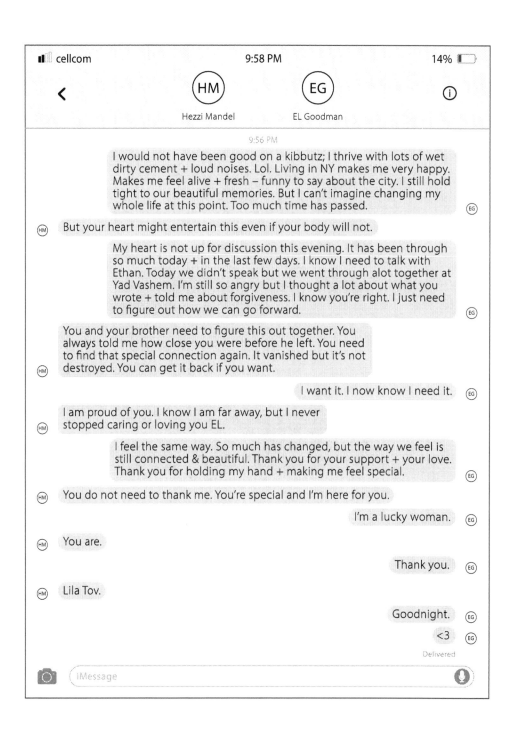

HM
Hezzi Mandel

EG
EL Goodman

9:56 PM

I would not have been good on a kibbutz; I thrive with lots of wet dirty cement + loud noises. Lol. Living in NY makes me very happy. Makes me feel alive + fresh – funny to say about the city. I still hold tight to our beautiful memories. But I can't imagine changing my whole life at this point. Too much time has passed. EG

But your heart might entertain this even if your body will not. HM

My heart is not up for discussion this evening. It has been through so much today + in the last few days. I know I need to talk with Ethan. Today we didn't speak but we went through alot together at Yad Vashem. I'm still so angry but I thought a lot about what you wrote + told me about forgiveness. I know you're right. I just need to figure out how we can go forward. EG

You and your brother need to figure this out together. You always told me how close you were before he left. You need to find that special connection again. It vanished but it's not destroyed. You can get it back if you want. HM

I want it. I now know I need it. EG

I am proud of you. I know I am far away, but I never stopped caring or loving you EL. HM

I feel the same way. So much has changed, but the way we feel is still connected & beautiful. Thank you for your support + your love. Thank you for holding my hand + making me feel special. EG

You do not need to thank me. You're special and I'm here for you. HM

I'm a lucky woman. EG

You are. HM

Thank you. EG

Lila Tov. HM

Goodnight. EG

<3 EG

Delivered

iMessage

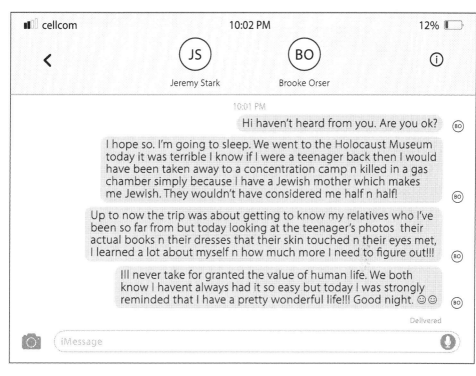

JS
Jeremy Stark

BO
Brooke Orser

10:01 PM

Hi haven't heard from you. Are you ok?

I hope so. I'm going to sleep. We went to the Holocaust Museum today it was terrible I know if I were a teenager back then I would have been taken away to a concentration camp n killed in a gas chamber simply because I have a Jewish mother which makes me Jewish. They wouldn't have considered me half n half!

Up to now the trip was about getting to know my relatives who I've been so far from but today looking at the teenager's photos their actual books n their dresses that their skin touched n their eyes met, I learned a lot about myself n how much more I need to figure out!!!

Ill never take for granted the value of human life. We both know I havent always had it so easy but today I was strongly reminded that I have a pretty wonderful life!!! Good night. ☺☺

Delivered

iMessage

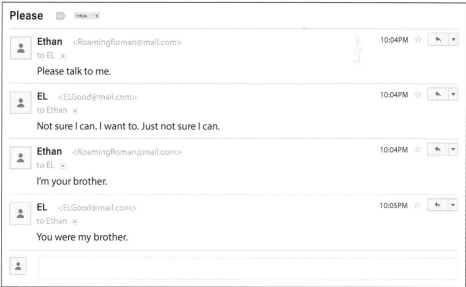

Please Inbox x

Ethan <RoamingRoman@mail.com>
to EL
10:04PM

Please talk to me.

EL <ELGood@mail.com>
to Ethan
10:04PM

Not sure I can. I want to. Just not sure I can.

Ethan <RoamingRoman@mail.com>
to EL
10:04PM

I'm your brother.

EL <ELGood@mail.com>
to Ethan
10:05PM

You were my brother.

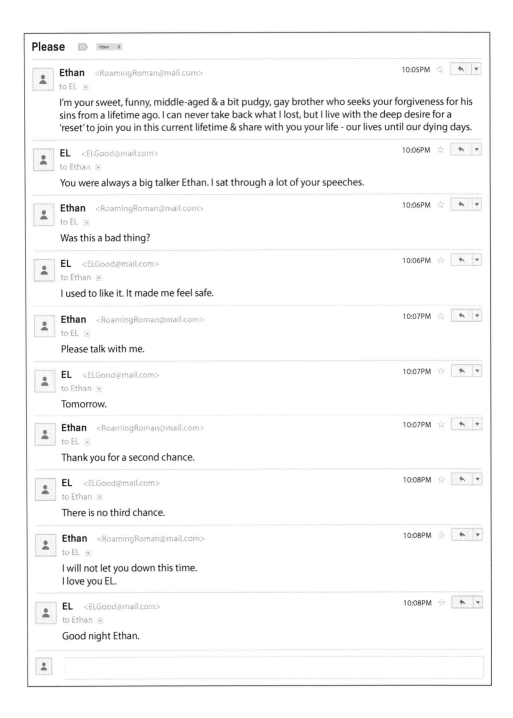

Please Inbox ×

Ethan <RoamingRoman@mail.com> 10:05PM
to EL

I'm your sweet, funny, middle-aged & a bit pudgy, gay brother who seeks your forgiveness for his sins from a lifetime ago. I can never take back what I lost, but I live with the deep desire for a 'reset' to join you in this current lifetime & share with you your life - our lives until our dying days.

EL <ELGood@mail.com> 10:06PM
to Ethan

You were always a big talker Ethan. I sat through a lot of your speeches.

Ethan <RoamingRoman@mail.com> 10:06PM
to EL

Was this a bad thing?

EL <ELGood@mail.com> 10:06PM
to Ethan

I used to like it. It made me feel safe.

Ethan <RoamingRoman@mail.com> 10:07PM
to EL

Please talk with me.

EL <ELGood@mail.com> 10:07PM
to Ethan

Tomorrow.

Ethan <RoamingRoman@mail.com> 10:07PM
to EL

Thank you for a second chance.

EL <ELGood@mail.com> 10:08PM
to Ethan

There is no third chance.

Ethan <RoamingRoman@mail.com> 10:08PM
to EL

I will not let you down this time.
I love you EL.

EL <ELGood@mail.com> 10:08PM
to Ethan

Good night Ethan.

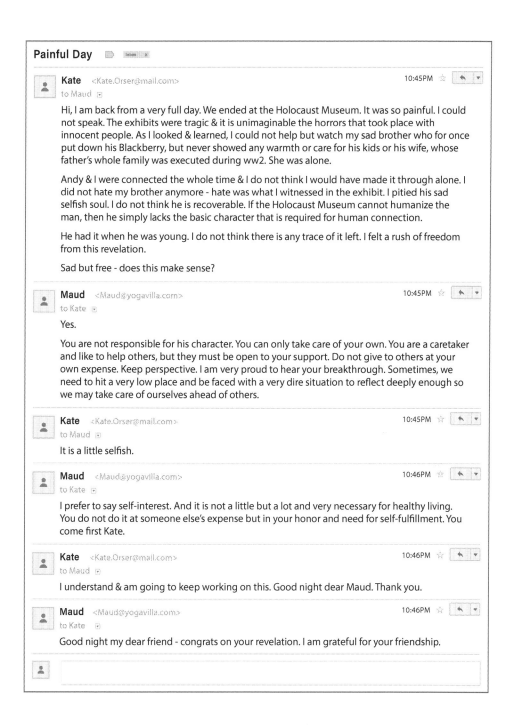

Painful Day Inbox x

Kate <Kate.Orser@mail.com> 10:45PM
to Maud

Hi, I am back from a very full day. We ended at the Holocaust Museum. It was so painful. I could not speak. The exhibits were tragic & it is unimaginable the horrors that took place with innocent people. As I looked & learned, I could not help but watch my sad brother who for once put down his Blackberry, but never showed any warmth or care for his kids or his wife, whose father's whole family was executed during ww2. She was alone.

Andy & I were connected the whole time & I do not think I would have made it through alone. I did not hate my brother anymore - hate was what I witnessed in the exhibit. I pitied his sad selfish soul. I do not think he is recoverable. If the Holocaust Museum cannot humanize the man, then he simply lacks the basic character that is required for human connection.

He had it when he was young. I do not think there is any trace of it left. I felt a rush of freedom from this revelation.

Sad but free - does this make sense?

Maud <Maud@yogavilla.com> 10:45PM
to Kate

Yes.

You are not responsible for his character. You can only take care of your own. You are a caretaker and like to help others, but they must be open to your support. Do not give to others at your own expense. Keep perspective. I am very proud to hear your breakthrough. Sometimes, we need to hit a very low place and be faced with a very dire situation to reflect deeply enough so we may take care of ourselves ahead of others.

Kate <Kate.Orser@mail.com> 10:45PM
to Maud

It is a little selfish.

Maud <Maud@yogavilla.com> 10:46PM
to Kate

I prefer to say self-interest. And it is not a little but a lot and very necessary for healthy living. You do not do it at someone else's expense but in your honor and need for self-fulfillment. You come first Kate.

Kate <Kate.Orser@mail.com> 10:46PM
to Maud

I understand & am going to keep working on this. Good night dear Maud. Thank you.

Maud <Maud@yogavilla.com> 10:46PM
to Kate

Good night my dear friend - congrats on your revelation. I am grateful for your friendship.

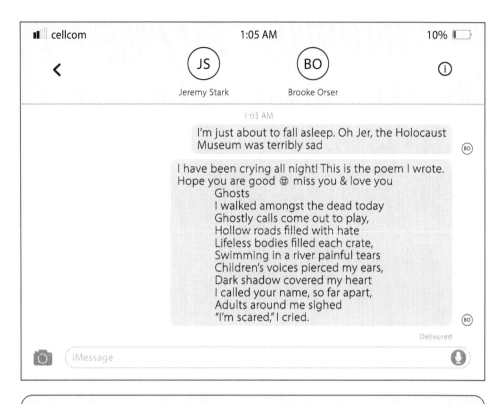

JS — Jeremy Stark
BO — Brooke Orser

1:03 AM

I'm just about to fall asleep. Oh Jer, the Holocaust Museum was terribly sad (BO)

I have been crying all night! This is the poem I wrote. Hope you are good ☺ miss you & love you
    Ghosts
    I walked amongst the dead today
    Ghostly calls come out to play,
    Hollow roads filled with hate
    Lifeless bodies filled each crate,
    Swimming in a river painful tears
    Children's voices pierced my ears,
    Dark shadow covered my heart
    I called your name, so far apart,
    Adults around me sighed
    "I'm scared," I cried. (BO)

Delivered

iMessage

Aliza Goodman's Daily Motivational Quote #5:   now

"I was once asked why I don't participate in anti-war demonstrations. I said that I will never do that, but as soon as you have a pro-peace rally, I'll be there."
Mother Teresa

MotiQuote.com

JS — Jeremy Stark
BO — Brooke Orser

2:31 AM

(JS) I wish I could be there with you I am sorry

iMessage

Dearest Aliza,

In 1979 Uncle Samuel passed away a week after his 80th birthday. He had lived over two centuries, survived the war in hiding, lost all but one member of his family and came to America and built a successful business. He was incredibly smart and very charming, but he never married. He treated all the employees, many who were also immigrants in his company, like family; he knew the names of their husbands, wives and children. He never talked about it, but I am sure he paid for their kids to go to college as well. Many weekends he went to church or temple with his workers to celebrate birthdays and weddings. The workers' kids called him Uncle Sam! He took us in and made our lives in New York wonderful. Yacov worked long and hard hours and absorbed his uncle's love and care. Uncle Sam filled a deep dark emptiness that I knew lived in my husband. I never complained that he worked long hours and sometimes 7 days a week as I knew his lifeline was working along side his only family member in the world alive and breathing.

Your grandfather was such a good man, who was so damaged by his early years. He was a good husband and father but he also could not ever recover from all the murder he watched and all the tragedy he experienced. He was a victim of indescribable abuse by the Nazis. His mother and siblings murdered, his friends as well. He lost his father to the cruelty of the Nazis also: he was so close to being free when he died that Yacov blamed himself for not keeping his dad alive. I tried to get him to go for therapy, but this was not something our generation of immigrants accepted. When Uncle Sam died in 1979 there were thousands at his funeral. It was incredible as he had literally spent 30 years building his American family and they all came out to celebrate his life. Yacov did not recover from his sadness. His uncle was his life support and when he was gone, Yacov focused on his work and barely could be present in our lives. We had money and a warm house, but he could not participate. The company thrived, as this was his focus, I took over the family as best I could alone and we lived this way.

I never looked back, just forward. I had the family I dreamed of and this was more than I imagined I would have in my life. I also saw the struggles of the women I met each day who did not have a roof over their heads and did not know where their kids' next meal would come from. I told myself repeatedly that I did not have the right to complain. I had my family in

Israel My sister had a family and was a beautiful and successful painter. My parents were getting old and they lived on the kibbutz where aging could be protected and graceful I would take my little kids to Israel.

EL was young and her life was charmed.

She was smart, beautiful and very social. She played the flute and sang for her father on the weekends, she spent hours reading teen fashion magazines and watching television. She was the perfect American girl. When she was thirteen we sent her to Israel for the summer to be with her cousins. Ethan was growing very fast; he was an excellent student, a good athlete and played the piano beautifully.

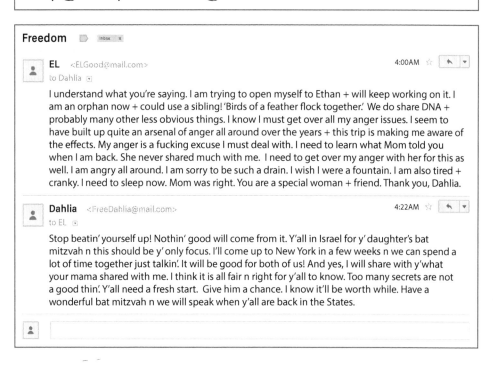

Freedom 〉 Inbox x

EL <ELGood@mail.com> to Dahlia ⊙   4:00AM ☆ ↩ ▾

I understand what you're saying. I am trying to open myself to Ethan + will keep working on it. I am an orphan now + could use a sibling! 'Birds of a feather flock together.' We do share DNA + probably many other less obvious things. I know I must get over all my anger issues. I seem to have built up quite an arsenal of anger all around over the years + this trip is making me aware of the effects. My anger is a fucking excuse I must deal with. I need to learn what Mom told you when I am back. She never shared much with me. I need to get over my anger with her for this as well. I am angry all around. I am sorry to be such a drain. I wish I were a fountain. I am also tired + cranky. I need to sleep now. Mom was right. You are a special woman + friend. Thank you, Dahlia.

Dahlia <FreeDahlia@mail.com> to EL ⊙   4:22AM ☆ ↩ ▾

Stop beatin' yourself up! Nothin' good will come from it. Y'all in Israel for y' daughter's bat mitzvah n this should be y' only focus. I'll come up to New York in a few weeks n we can spend a lot of time together just talkin'. It will be good for both of us! And yes, I will share with y' what your mama shared with me. I think it is all fair n right for y'all to know. Too many secrets are not a good thin'. Y'all need a fresh start. Give him a chance. I know it'll be worth while. Have a wonderful bat mitzvah n we will speak when y'all are back in the States.

BOKER TOV

Goodman Family!

Welcome to day six of your Holy Land excursion!
Here is today's schedule:

A Mediterranean Sea Sojourn.

We are off to spend the day on the white sandy beach in Herzelia Pituah, a suburb north of Tel Aviv. We will join local Israelis at the Gazebbo Beach Club for a day of leisure and sports including paddle boarding, surfing, canoeing, and sailing. Lunch will be served at the water's edge featuring fresh salads, local seafood, watermelon and cold drinks.

The Mediterranean Sea serves as a beautiful escape for city residents on very hot summer days. Be on the lookout for stunning, translucent jellyfish that bathe in the shallow waters and wash up to the shore. Beware, they can sting just by brushing up against your skin. We will return to Jerusalem in the late afternoon

Please bring a bathing suit, hat, beach shoes, towels and lots of sunblock. There will be umbrellas to offer shade and clean bathrooms.

Today's Temperature:

 The weather today will be a warm 33˚c / 92˚f

Moshe
Rimon Tours

Aliza Goodman's Daily Motivational Quote #1:   now

"The best thing about your life is that it is constantly in a state of design, this means that you have at all times, the power to redesign it. Make moves, allow shifts, smile more, do more, do less, say no, say yes – just remember when it comes to your life, you are not only the artist but the masterpiece as well."   Cleo Wade

MotiQuote.com

‹   (YM)   (AG)   ⓘ

Yasmin M.   Aliza Goodman

8:46 AM

(YM) just finished watching the scariest movie ever ☺

(YM) don't know if I hated or loved it lol

(YM) It's sooo late here where are u?

On the bus to the beach to meet the Israeli cousins (AG)

I rly need a break from religion history & tragedy lol (AG)

I'm also excited because Asher is coming too he is soo hot ♡♡ (AG)

Hopefully I get a photo of us to send to you (AG)

Big news, we left EL & Benj in Jerusalem they've pretty much gotten on everyone's nerves (AG)

they debate over everything & honestly we all needed a break so we left them to spend the day alone (AG)

they'll either kill themselves or make up lol (AG)

(YM) How tf did u get away w out them?

Cancelled their wake-up call lol (AG)

Grama Rose & Teddy were in on it (AG)

Found out that Grama Rose & Benj havent gotten along forever and that she's on her 4th husband Theo (AG)

She told me that he's her soul mate and that they text all the time ☺ (AG)

Delivered

📷 (iMessage   🎤)

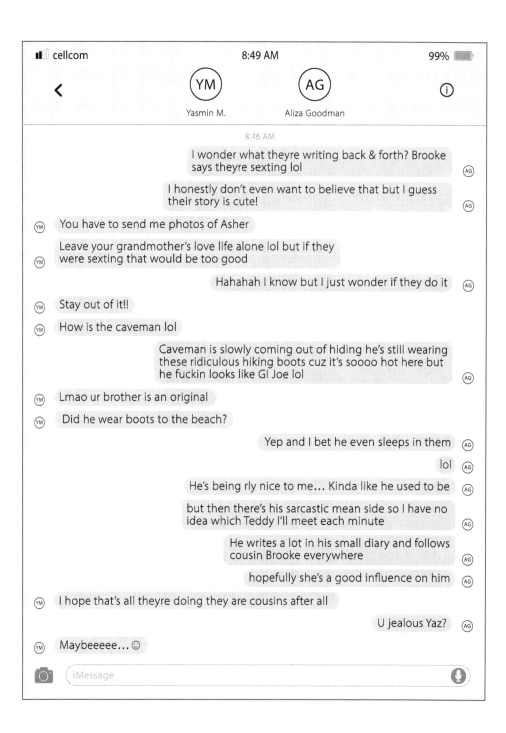

YM
Yasmin M.

AG
Aliza Goodman

8:46 AM

I wonder what theyre writing back & forth? Brooke says theyre sexting lol

I honestly don't even want to believe that but I guess their story is cute!

You have to send me photos of Asher

Leave your grandmother's love life alone lol but if they were sexting that would be too good

Hahahah I know but I just wonder if they do it

Stay out of it!!

How is the caveman lol

Caveman is slowly coming out of hiding he's still wearing these ridiculous hiking boots cuz it's soooo hot here but he fuckin looks like GI Joe lol

Lmao ur brother is an original

Did he wear boots to the beach?

Yep and I bet he even sleeps in them

lol

He's being rly nice to me... Kinda like he used to be

but then there's his sarcastic mean side so I have no idea which Teddy I'll meet each minute

He writes a lot in his small diary and follows cousin Brooke everywhere

hopefully she's a good influence on him

I hope that's all theyre doing they are cousins after all

U jealous Yaz?

Maybeeeee... ☺

iMessage

272

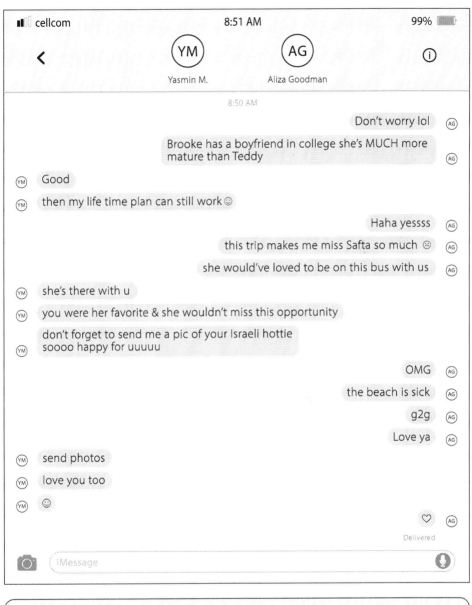

cellcom   8:51 AM   99% ▮

YM   **AG**   ⓘ

Yasmin M.   Aliza Goodman

8:50 AM

Don't worry lol (AG)

Brooke has a boyfriend in college she's MUCH more mature than Teddy (AG)

(YM) Good

(YM) then my life time plan can still work ☺

Haha yessss (AG)

this trip makes me miss Safta so much ☹ (AG)

she would've loved to be on this bus with us (AG)

(YM) she's there with u

(YM) you were her favorite & she wouldn't miss this opportunity

(YM) don't forget to send me a pic of your Israeli hottie soooo happy for uuuuu

OMG (AG)

the beach is sick (AG)

g2g (AG)

Love ya (AG)

(YM) send photos

(YM) love you too

(YM) ☺

♡ (AG)

Delivered

📷   (iMessage)   🎤

JN24:   now

Hamas' desire to increase West Bank attacks could trigger new war.

Jewish News You Can Use

Andy Orser
Now · Israel

GOY IN THE HOLY LAND PART 24

Our drive this morning took us along the windy mountain road from Jerusalem to the Herzelia Beach. We passed the densely green forests, stone monuments and old, rusted military vehicles that serve as profound reminders of the deathly battles that took place when the Jews were desperately fighting for their independence and the advancing Arab enemies blocked the route to the Holy City. Many of the strong, powerful trees were planted since the country's creation by foreign donations to help populate the barren desert lands with greenery and life. In complete contrast, on our drive through Tel Aviv, we passed a modern cosmopolitan city with skyscrapers, billboards and traffic. We will spend the weekend after the bat mitzvah in Tel Aviv before we fly home. We are arriving at the beach. A glorious day!

Dear Friends, this country is a living monument to its ancient right to exist and a celebration of its modern creation. Today there is no fighting. There is no hate. #Herzeliabeach

   👍 Like   💬 Comment   ↪ Share

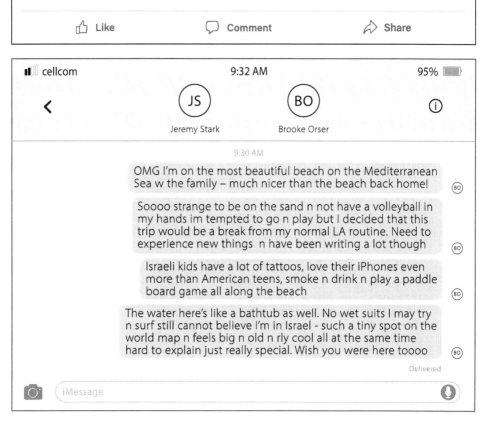

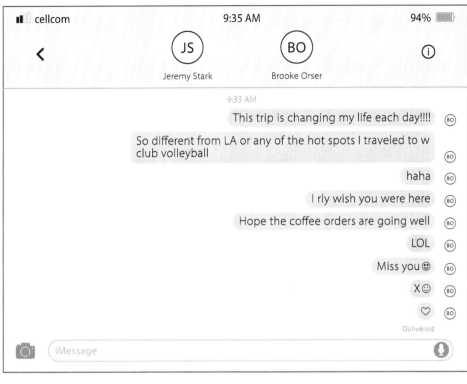

JS — Jeremy Stark   BO — Brooke Orser

9:33 AM

This trip is changing my life each day!!!!

So different from LA or any of the hot spots I traveled to w club volleyball

haha

I rly wish you were here

Hope the coffee orders are going well

LOL

Miss you ☺

X ☺

♡

Delivered

iMessage

Andy Orser
Now · Israel

GOY IN THE HOLY LAND PART 25

Herzelia Beach. A Mediterranean paradise - deep sandy shores and the warm shimmering sea chock full of sailboats, paddle boarders, surfers and swimmers. We are spending the day at Gazebbo, a small, charming beach club with our Israeli relatives. Not like the fancy beach clubs back home in Santa Monica where the price tag prohibits my entry and members dress like fancy polo players; here the people are down to earth and incredibly friendly. Earlier Kate and I meditated on the sand, I just returned from paddle boarding tour of the Herzelia coast with Simon, a cool surfer with blond dreadlocks.

Dear Friends, this is a day of incredible peace and harmony, breathing in the holy sea life and enjoying the rhythmic sounds of gently crashing waves. #Gazebbo #Herzeliabeach #Mediterraneandream

👍 Like   💬 Comment   ↪ Share

FOOD AFFAIR WITH KATE

DIVINE, DELICIOUS, AND DELIGHTFUL

ABOUT   RECIPES   CONTACT

Down By The Sea

★ ★ ★ ★ ★

Comfortably seated on the fine, soft Herzelia sand, inhaling the fresh sea breeze, and tasting the salty mist of the crashing waves. Meditation on Mediterranean shores, a dream come true; my entire being at one with natural elements while Holy Land spirituality enhances my existence here fully enraptured in this culinary world – a crossroads of religious and cultural food. There is so much to learn and experience.

Juxtaposed to my calm meditation, Israelis excitedly play and yell out loud as they enjoy the refreshing, salty water. Many Israeli families and friends lounge in large groups on the sand and eat bright red watermelon slices accompanied by thin white slices of bulgarite salty cheese. Contrasting flavors, a time-honored Mediterranean blend for the locals, a non-traditional taste I gratefully experience.

See the photos below and check out Food Affair with Kate on Instagram and Facebook. #Watermelonhitsthespot #meditation #foodaffair #Mediterraneanmeditation

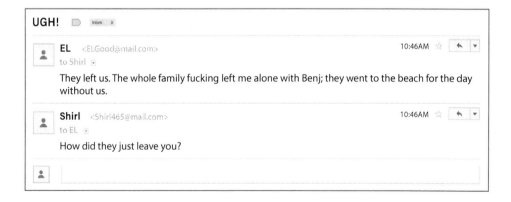

UGH!   Inbox x

EL <ELGood@mail.com>   10:46AM
to Shirl

They left us. The whole family fucking left me alone with Benj; they went to the beach for the day without us.

Shirl <Shirl465@mail.com>   10:46AM
to EL

How did they just leave you?

UGH! 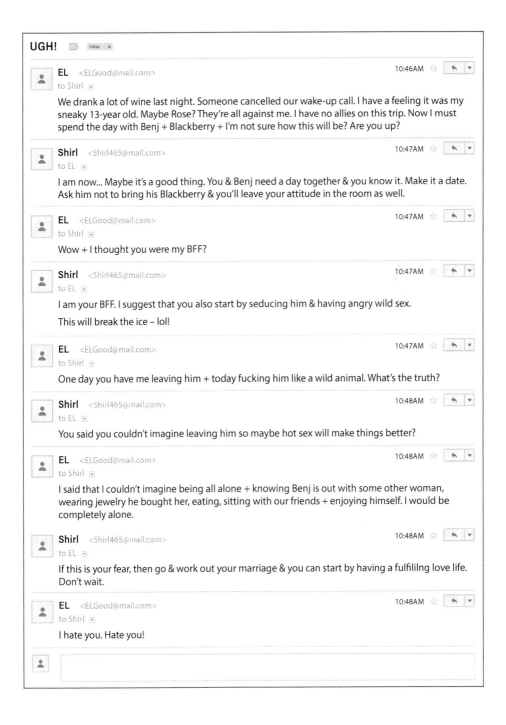 Inbox ×

EL <ELGood@mail.com> 10:46AM
to Shirl

We drank a lot of wine last night. Someone cancelled our wake-up call. I have a feeling it was my sneaky 13-year old. Maybe Rose? They're all against me. I have no allies on this trip. Now I must spend the day with Benj + Blackberry + I'm not sure how this will be? Are you up?

Shirl <Shirl465@mail.com> 10:47AM
to EL

I am now... Maybe it's a good thing. You & Benj need a day together & you know it. Make it a date. Ask him not to bring his Blackberry & you'll leave your attitude in the room as well.

EL <ELGood@mail.com> 10:47AM
to Shirl

Wow + I thought you were my BFF?

Shirl <Shirl465@mail.com> 10:47AM
to EL

I am your BFF. I suggest that you also start by seducing him & having angry wild sex.

This will break the ice – lol!

EL <ELGood@mail.com> 10:47AM
to Shirl

One day you have me leaving him + today fucking him like a wild animal. What's the truth?

Shirl <Shirl465@mail.com> 10:48AM
to EL

You said you couldn't imagine leaving him so maybe hot sex will make things better?

EL <ELGood@mail.com> 10:48AM
to Shirl

I said that I couldn't imagine being all alone + knowing Benj is out with some other woman, wearing jewelry he bought her, eating, sitting with our friends + enjoying himself. I would be completely alone.

Shirl <Shirl465@mail.com> 10:48AM
to EL

If this is your fear, then go & work out your marriage & you can start by having a fulfililng love life. Don't wait.

EL <ELGood@mail.com> 10:48AM
to Shirl

I hate you. Hate you!

UGH! 📬 Inbox ✕

Shirl <Shirl465@mail.com>   10:49AM
to EL

I hate you too. Go for it. Enjoy yourself EL. Will write later. Take care of yourself. :) XOME

EL <ELGood@mail.com>   10:50 AM
to Shirl

There's no one else who will.
Ugh!

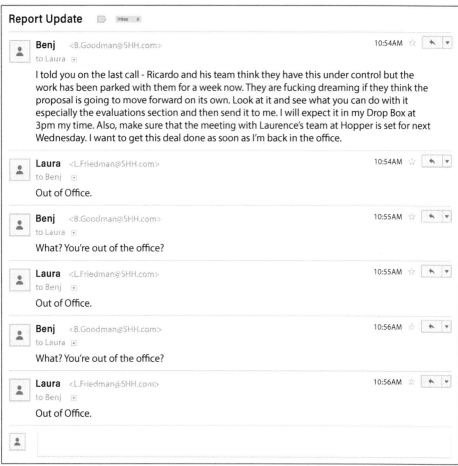

Report Update 📬 Inbox ✕

Benj <B.Goodman@SHH.com>   10:54AM
to Laura

I told you on the last call - Ricardo and his team think they have this under control but the work has been parked with them for a week now. They are fucking dreaming if they think the proposal is going to move forward on its own. Look at it and see what you can do with it especially the evaluations section and then send it to me. I will expect it in my Drop Box at 3pm my time. Also, make sure that the meeting with Laurence's team at Hopper is set for next Wednesday. I want to get this deal done as soon as I'm back in the office.

Laura <L.Friedman@SHH.com>   10:54AM
to Benj

Out of Office.

Benj <B.Goodman@SHH.com>   10:55AM
to Laura

What? You're out of the office?

Laura <L.Friedman@SHH.com>   10:55AM
to Benj

Out of Office.

Benj <B.Goodman@SHH.com>   10:56AM
to Laura

What? You're out of the office?

Laura <L.Friedman@SHH.com>   10:56AM
to Benj

Out of Office.

AG   **BO**

Aliza Goodman   Brooke Orser

11:02 AM

Good job leaving your parents behind (BO)

☺ (BO)

(AG) Debate Free Day

You look cute! (BO)

(AG) TY! Wonder if Asher is coming?

He's coming he likes you! (BO)

(AG) How do u know

I can just tell all you can do is be yourself n smile (BO)

(AG) How is the beach here compared to California

the beach here is insane n the water is so warm even in the summer our beach water is freezing! (BO)

I think I'm going to try surfing wanna come? (BO)

(AG) crashing in salty seawater is not my thing

Have fun with Asher (BO)

☺ (BO)

(AG) What if he tries to kiss me

Kiss him back! (BO)

(AG) K not sure I know how

Your lips press against his lips n your body feels a tingle all throughout it then you'll melt into it – you'll feel magical it is very simple (BO)

(AG) I can do that???

don't be scared it's very fun you'll be fine (BO)

(AG) not sure but ill try

📷 (iMessage) 🎤

LUCACLOSELY
@LUCACLOSELY   ⌄

Forward I'm heavy, but backwards I'm not. What am I?

11:26 AM – June

♡ 1   ♡ 2   ↻ 1

LUCACLOSELY @LUCACLOSELY
Replying to @LUCACLOSELY

A ton.

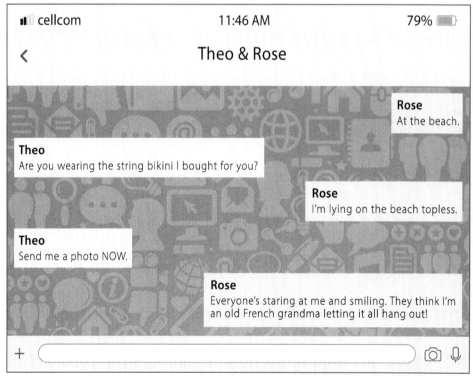

.ıl cellcom   11:46 AM   79% ▭

< **Theo & Rose**

Rose
At the beach.

Theo
Are you wearing the string bikini I bought for you?

Rose
I'm lying on the beach topless.

Theo
Send me a photo NOW.

Rose
Everyone's staring at me and smiling. They think I'm an old French grandma letting it all hang out!

<   **Theo & Rose**

Theo
Lucky everyone. Do I need to worry?

Rose
No. I've made it clear that I'm saving myself for the man of my wildest dreams.

Theo
So, you're wearing the sign around your neck that says 'taken'?

Rose
My sign says 'obsessed' I haven't stopped thinking of you since I arrived.

Theo
We're in sync. I think of you 24-7. I want you to have a great time. But I miss you dearly. Not sure how I'll make it the next few days without your kiss.

Rose
Cannot think too much about this or I start to miss you too deeply. I'm crazy for you Theo. I'm a better grandmother to my grandchildren because of you. I cannot explain it, but it's going so much easier than I could've dreamed. Benj's the only huge obstacle here in the Middle East where I cannot seem to make any progress.

Theo
Keep focusing on the kids. Enjoy them. Benj may come around but do not let him get in the way of enjoying your grandchildren. This is your opportunity

Rose
I won't. Got to go now. I love you.

Theo
I love you too. I will sleep now and dream of us.

\+

Andy Orser

GOY IN THE HOLY LAND PART 26

Met two young Arab men with wives and kids on the beach. The men were standing on the sand while the women fully hidden in black burqas and hijabs were wading in the warm water with jubilant, small children splashing around them. Mohammad and Hussein both in their early 40s spoke English very well. They curiously asked if movie stars were all over the streets of Los Angeles? I told them that people who wished they were movie stars filled the LA streets. LOL. I questioned them on what life is like for Arabs living in Israel. Their response was that life is not easy for many Arabs, but they were happy: they had their families, good health and jobs. Their greatest complaint was being stereotyped as dangerous because their different language and darker skin color set them apart. They acknowledged that racism exists and clearly Jewish Israelis considered them second-class citizens. By contrast, in their village life was good and they were free to be themselves with no one looking down at them. These fine gentlemen shared that the beach was a safe place where they felt neutral and equal with the other Israelis.

Dear Friends, See my Instagram with photos of my new friends Mohammad and Hussein. #beachclub #mediterraneansea&sun #deepsandyshores

👍 Like   💬 Comment   ↗ Share

MYPOETRY.COM

Beach

Brooke G.O.

I know where equality dwells
I have seen her at the shore
There's always an open door
She encourages all to share
Her abundance of fresh air

Wealth and power do not reign
Millions of grains of precious sand
Walking down the beach in hand
True riches money cannot buy
Never question why

♡ 129   204 👁

Differences
Teddy Goodman

Today we are at the beach. The Israelis arrived two hours after we did. They were busy sleeping. It is summer and Israeli kids go to sleep late and do not get up early. Not a bad life, but then at 18, they go into the army. Cousin Tomer is in the army for two years. She is excited about her service and talks about it like a rite of passage. She does not even think about going to college.

She did not spend her senior year writing college applications and essays like the purgatory I will enter in September. Listening to her makes me question if I am ready to go to college in a year? If I even want to go to college? One thing I am certain is that I need to get out of my parents' house and do something interesting with my life. I cannot wait to leave my parents' fucking Eternal Parent War that we have all defined as 'debating' to ease the severity of the situation. They make me crazy. I cannot imagine being excited to join the army. I love my country but not the same way that she does. I have no idea what I fucking want and this is making me crazy. I have so many choices. The Israeli kids have no choice. Little Noam has no choice. I watch, as Lucas desperately wants to play with him – a little boy about his size who barely speaks, moves slowly and sort of stares out into space. He is in his own closed off, distant world. I can relate to this having secluded myself over the last few years from my family and lived in my own world. Even at school, I have never been the one to join each club and be super congenial like my little sister Aliza. I am involved but very selfishly on my own terms and not in a group setting. While Noam has no choice, I have made this choice myself and lived with it.

Spending the last few days with Sunny Brooke from California and Cheerful Tomer from Israel, I have begun to question what the heck I am doing. I am light years better educated than the two of them, but they are happy and content with their lives. I know I am not. I'm fucked.

Lucas is sitting once again next to Noam. He inspired me – my funny little brother. Today he is directing Noam to look at a group of surfers out in the water. Lucas talks and Noam is listening to him and staring at the surfers. Lucas is like "Wow?" "Did you see that?" Then I see Lucas tap Noam on the shoulder and I wait to see if Noam freaks out as uncle Raffi advised. But there is no reaction from Noam and Lucas continues his dynamic monologue.

Differences
Teddy Goodman

I watched an incredible documentary on small children with Autism who did not like to be touched by humans, but when they were in the water, they welcomed the frisky dolphins' kisses and pushes. The dolphins helped them. I think Lucas is like a dolphin for Noam. Lucas likes his cousin and is not freaked out that he is different and not the type of kid he normally likes to play with back at home. He enjoys the moment no matter what the circumstance. My little brother fucking impresses me and inspires me.

LIFEEXPRESSIONS.COM

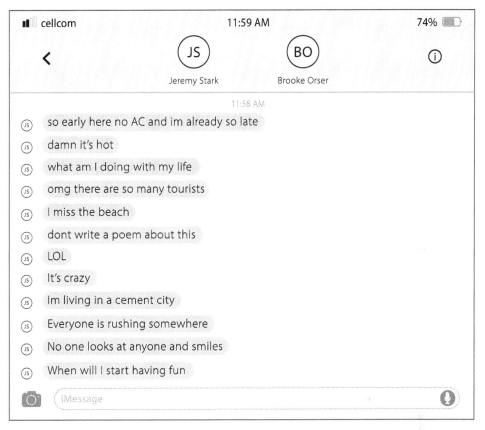

JS — Jeremy Stark   BO — Brooke Orser

11:58 AM

so early here no AC and im already so late

damn it's hot

what am I doing with my life

omg there are so many tourists

I miss the beach

dont write a poem about this

LOL

It's crazy

Im living in a cement city

Everyone is rushing somewhere

No one looks at anyone and smiles

When will I start having fun

iMessage

MYJOURNAL.COM

The Beach
Roaming Roman

Bruno & I just walked up the beautiful beach. The aqua blue water is incredibly warm. White transparent jellyfish swept ashore now lay melting in the hot sun. An older Israeli woman in a pink floral bathing suit came up to us & asked Bruno for his autograph & without waiting for an answer, took a selfie with him. She was sure she had seen him in a movie last week on the TV. Bruno was happy to oblige & was not bothered by her instrusion.

JN24:   now

Israeli army investigates officer who killed fleeing Palestinian stone-throwing teenagers near Hebron.

Jewish News You Can Use

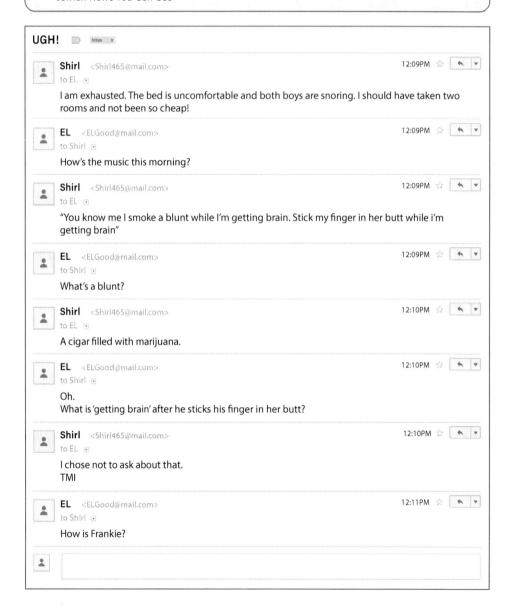

UGH! Inbox x

Shirl <Shirl465@mail.com>   12:09PM
to EL

I am exhausted. The bed is uncomfortable and both boys are snoring. I should have taken two rooms and not been so cheap!

EL <ELGood@mail.com>   12:09PM
to Shirl

How's the music this morning?

Shirl <Shirl465@mail.com>   12:09PM
to EL

"You know me I smoke a blunt while I'm getting brain. Stick my finger in her butt while i'm getting brain"

EL <ELGood@mail.com>   12:09PM
to Shirl

What's a blunt?

Shirl <Shirl465@mail.com>   12:10PM
to EL

A cigar filled with marijuana.

EL <ELGood@mail.com>   12:10PM
to Shirl

Oh.
What is 'getting brain' after he sticks his finger in her butt?

Shirl <Shirl465@mail.com>   12:10PM
to EL

I chose not to ask about that.
TMI

EL <ELGood@mail.com>   12:11PM
to Shirl

How is Frankie?

UGH! 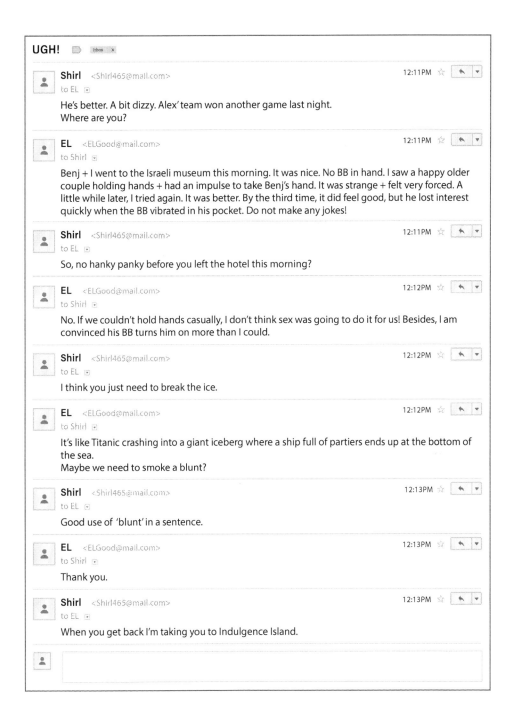 Inbox x

Shirl <Shirl465@mail.com>   12:11PM
to EL

He's better. A bit dizzy. Alex' team won another game last night.
Where are you?

EL <ELGood@mail.com>   12:11PM
to Shirl

Benj + I went to the Israeli museum this morning. It was nice. No BB in hand. I saw a happy older couple holding hands + had an impulse to take Benj's hand. It was strange + felt very forced. A little while later, I tried again. It was better. By the third time, it did feel good, but he lost interest quickly when the BB vibrated in his pocket. Do not make any jokes!

Shirl <Shirl465@mail.com>   12:11PM
to EL

So, no hanky panky before you left the hotel this morning?

EL <ELGood@mail.com>   12:12PM
to Shirl

No. If we couldn't hold hands casually, I don't think sex was going to do it for us! Besides, I am convinced his BB turns him on more than I could.

Shirl <Shirl465@mail.com>   12:12PM
to EL

I think you just need to break the ice.

EL <ELGood@mail.com>   12:12PM
to Shirl

It's like Titanic crashing into a giant iceberg where a ship full of partiers ends up at the bottom of the sea.
Maybe we need to smoke a blunt?

Shirl <Shirl465@mail.com>   12:13PM
to EL

Good use of 'blunt' in a sentence.

EL <ELGood@mail.com>   12:13PM
to Shirl

Thank you.

Shirl <Shirl465@mail.com>   12:13PM
to EL

When you get back I'm taking you to Indulgence Island.

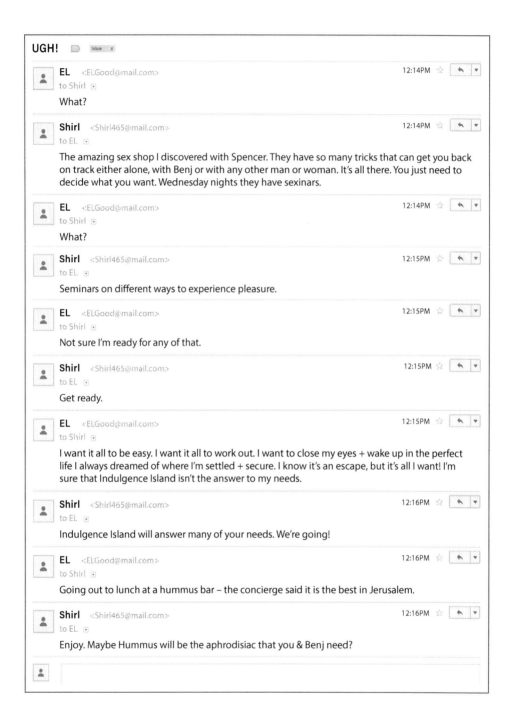

UGH! Inbox x

EL <ELGood@mail.com> 12:14PM
to Shirl

What?

Shirl <Shirl465@mail.com> 12:14PM
to EL

The amazing sex shop I discovered with Spencer. They have so many tricks that can get you back on track either alone, with Benj or with any other man or woman. It's all there. You just need to decide what you want. Wednesday nights they have sexinars.

EL <ELGood@mail.com> 12:14PM
to Shirl

What?

Shirl <Shirl465@mail.com> 12:15PM
to EL

Seminars on different ways to experience pleasure.

EL <ELGood@mail.com> 12:15PM
to Shirl

Not sure I'm ready for any of that.

Shirl <Shirl465@mail.com> 12:15PM
to EL

Get ready.

EL <ELGood@mail.com> 12:15PM
to Shirl

I want it all to be easy. I want it all to work out. I want to close my eyes + wake up in the perfect life I always dreamed of where I'm settled + secure. I know it's an escape, but it's all I want! I'm sure that Indulgence Island isn't the answer to my needs.

Shirl <Shirl465@mail.com> 12:16PM
to EL

Indulgence Island will answer many of your needs. We're going!

EL <ELGood@mail.com> 12:16PM
to Shirl

Going out to lunch at a hummus bar – the concierge said it is the best in Jerusalem.

Shirl <Shirl465@mail.com> 12:16PM
to EL

Enjoy. Maybe Hummus will be the aphrodisiac that you & Benj need?

UGH! 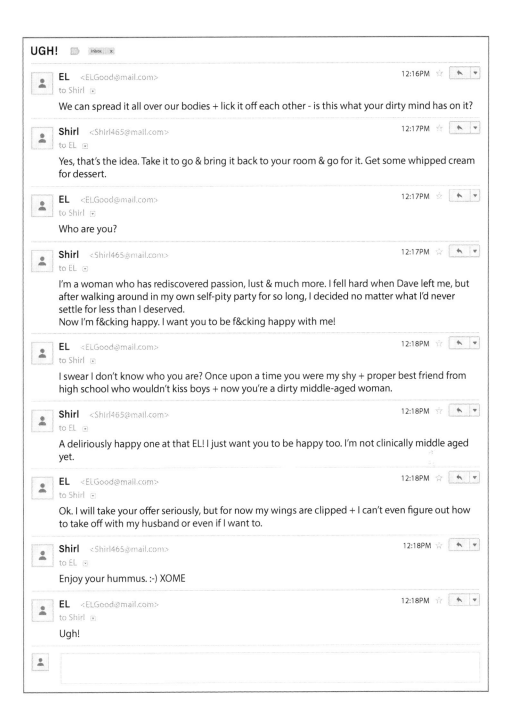 Inbox ×

EL <ELGood@mail.com>   12:16PM
to Shirl

We can spread it all over our bodies + lick it off each other - is this what your dirty mind has on it?

Shirl <Shirl465@mail.com>   12:17PM
to EL

Yes, that's the idea. Take it to go & bring it back to your room & go for it. Get some whipped cream for dessert.

EL <ELGood@mail.com>   12:17PM
to Shirl

Who are you?

Shirl <Shirl465@mail.com>   12:17PM
to EL

I'm a woman who has rediscovered passion, lust & much more. I fell hard when Dave left me, but after walking around in my own self-pity party for so long, I decided no matter what I'd never settle for less than I deserved.
Now I'm f&cking happy. I want you to be f&cking happy with me!

EL <ELGood@mail.com>   12:18PM
to Shirl

I swear I don't know who you are? Once upon a time you were my shy + proper best friend from high school who wouldn't kiss boys + now you're a dirty middle-aged woman.

Shirl <Shirl465@mail.com>   12:18PM
to EL

A deliriously happy one at that EL! I just want you to be happy too. I'm not clinically middle aged yet.

EL <ELGood@mail.com>   12:18PM
to Shirl

Ok. I will take your offer seriously, but for now my wings are clipped + I can't even figure out how to take off with my husband or even if I want to.

Shirl <Shirl465@mail.com>   12:18PM
to EL

Enjoy your hummus. :-) XOME

EL <ELGood@mail.com>   12:18PM
to Shirl

Ugh!

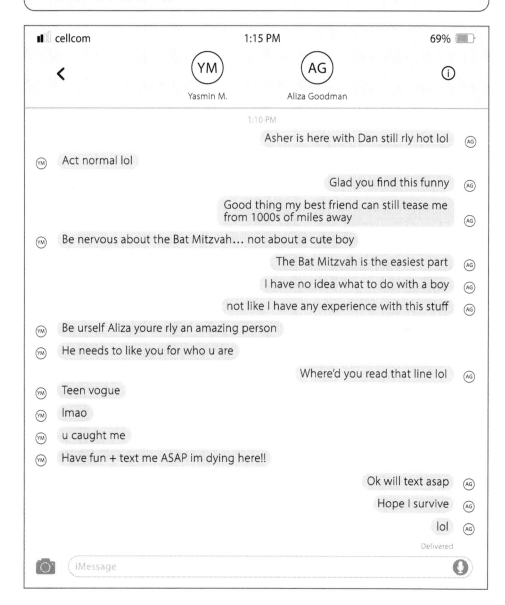

JN24:   now

Israel cuts power to parts of West Bank in response to $500 million debt the Palestinian Authority owes to the Israeli Electric Company.

Jewish News You Can Use

---

cellcom   1:15 PM   69%

YM   **AG**

Yasmin M.   Aliza Goodman

1:10 PM

> Asher is here with Dan still rly hot lol

Act normal lol

> Glad you find this funny

> Good thing my best friend can still tease me from 1000s of miles away

Be nervous about the Bat Mitzvah... not about a cute boy

> The Bat Mitzvah is the easiest part

> I have no idea what to do with a boy

> not like I have any experience with this stuff

Be urself Aliza youre rly an amazing person

He needs to like you for who u are

> Where'd you read that line lol

Teen vogue

lmao

u caught me

Have fun + text me ASAP im dying here!!

> Ok will text asap

> Hope I survive

> lol

Delivered

iMessage

290

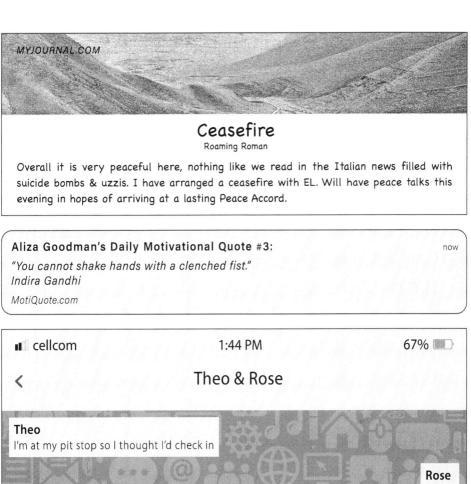

MYJOURNAL.COM

Ceasefire
Roaming Roman

Overall it is very peaceful here, nothing like we read in the Italian news filled with suicide bombs & uzzis. I have arranged a ceasefire with EL. Will have peace talks this evening in hopes of arriving at a lasting Peace Accord.

Aliza Goodman's Daily Motivational Quote #3:   now
"You cannot shake hands with a clenched fist."
Indira Gandhi

MotiQuote.com

📶 cellcom   1:44 PM   67% 🔋

<   Theo & Rose

Theo
I'm at my pit stop so I thought I'd check in

Rose
Hi.

Theo
Hi my love. What are you doing?

Rose
Went for a walk on the beach with Kate and Andy. Finally left them on their own. They stopped to photograph every shell they saw and talked to everyone they passed on the sand. Then they sat down and meditated in the middle of the beach. They are unique individuals.

\+

< 　　　　　　　**Theo & Rose**

Theo
I am happy you are enjoying yourself.

Rose
It's beautiful here. Very peaceful without EL and Benj. Also, spoke more to Teddy. He just sat down next to me and asked if I was having a good time. He was very nice

Theo
What did you tell him?

Rose
I'm having a very good time. I'm so happy to be with my grandchildren. I've always been the crazy, distant visiting grandmother. EL's mom Shula was the grandmother that they knew and loved. I always felt like an outsider. Now I feel like an insider. Terrible to say that I'm happy that Shula isn't here. I never stood a chance when she was around.

Theo
Be yourself. Do not try to be Shula.

Rose
I will. I am.
Teddy is sweet even with his gruff outside. He is curious and very observant. I see him writing in his journal with pen and paper. Not like most of the kids his age. He won an award at school this year for his accomplishments. He speaks slowly and thoughtfully. I thought it was arrogance, but I think he is very sensitive and insecure: he is not sure what he wants to be when he grows up. He has so many ideas flying around his head and I can see that this bothers him greatly. He asked me many questions about when I was young.

Theo
What did you say to him about this?

＋　⟨　　　　　　　　　　　　⟩　📷 🎤

< **Theo & Rose**

Rose
I told him that when I was 18 my goal was to get out of my house and start living.

Theo
Does not sound like after all these years, your grandson is much different from you.

Rose
But I was not scared. I was excited. It feels like he is running away; I was running to something. I wanted to be a nurse, get married and live in Los Angeles. Teddy is very worried. He doesn't say as much but I can tell he is anxious.

Theo
He has you now. You do not need to give him directions; sounds like he is a smart young man who mostly needs love & support. Just listen to him Rosie. Be there for him and the others.

Rose
I will. I have you to help me – I mean with the listening part. I'm not very good at this. I'm much better at giving advice.

Theo
He will ask if he wants.

Rose
What if he doesn't ask and makes mistakes I could have saved him from? What if he fails?

Theo
You will be there to help him, but he needs to take steps on his own. This is the best gift you can give him. It will not take that long. We have all made mistakes & we hopefully figure them out. If we do it for them, they learn nothing.

+ ⬜ 📷 🎤

Theo & Rose

Rose
Took me three husbands to get to you. I'm a slow learner. haha

Theo
But in the end, you did learn & we are happy.

Rose
Don't want it to take him 50 years.

Theo
He needs to do this at his pace and on his own.

Theo
I'm here for you Rosie.

Rose
He asked who I keep texting?

Theo
Did you tell him the man you are crazy in love with?

Rose
I did.

Theo
You said "crazy in love?"

Rose
Yes, and the words 'Love of my Life'.

Theo
You do not know how happy those words make me.

< **Theo & Rose**

Rose
I know how happy you make me.

Theo
We make each other.

Rose
Yes. I don't think I can travel without you again.

Theo
We will consider this as we plan our future together. I think I quite agree with you. Much more fun to be together.

Rose
Thank You. I love you. Now go back to sleep.

Theo
I will. I love you

\+

LIFEEXPRESSIONS.COM

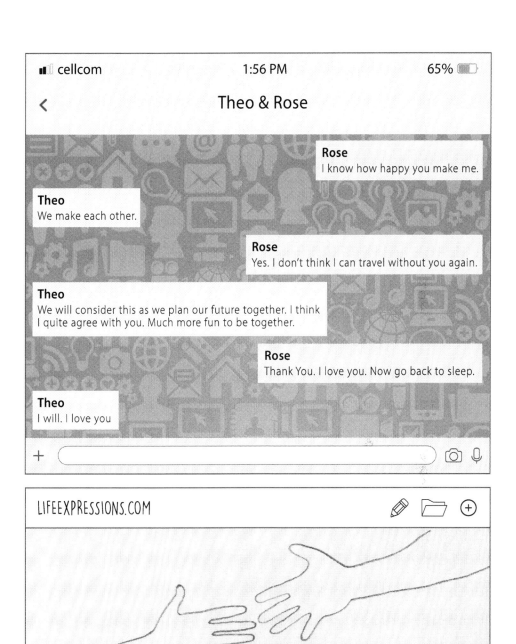

Sawt
Jamil

FOOD AFFAIR WITH KATE

DIVINE, DELICIOUS, AND DELIGHTFUL   ABOUT   RECIPES   CONTACT

Heaven On Earth

★ ★ ★ ★ ★

Perched comfortably on a bluff along the Mediterranean shore at a simple, rustic beach club. A gentle breeze battles a fierce, dominant sun; vibrant waves crash below along the soft, sandy beach. Exuberant swimmers, surfers and sailors frolic in the refreshing salty sea. Sitting on a plastic white chair under a simple umbrella advertising Heineken Beer as Techno music blares from the speakers overhead.

Gentle, soft sand massages my feet as I savor an incredible, light lunch featuring sunflower seed crusted whole wheat bread, Israeli chopped salad, hummus, tahina, and fresh grilled branzino fish caught by local fishermen hours earlier. Today I fall in love with tahina, a creamy ground sesame sauce, Israelis drizzle over a fresh chopped vegetable salad and with olive oil over hummus. Tahina, a calorically dense food has many health and immune benefits. A fresh Mediterranean ambience, accompanied by the perfectly chilled glass of Israeli wine seduce me while divine Branzino literally melts like butter in my mouth. This tranquil fish looks me in the eyes, not horrified by his expression; his glance suggests that he is here for my enjoyment.

This is a Mediterranean paradise. I cannot more highly recommend a day at Gazebbo Beach Club as a break from all the touring in the Holy Land - A real highlight to visiting and understanding Israel.

See the photos below and check out Food Affair with Kate on Instagram and Facebook. #foodiesheaven #bestinIsrael #Mediterranianmeal #yolo

UGH!

EL <ELGood@mail.com>
to Shirl

4:08PM ☆ ↰ ▾

Just back from walking around the Old City with Benj.

Shirl <Shirl465@mail.com>
to EL

4:08PM ☆ ↰ ▾

How was it?

EL <ELGood@mail.com>
to Shirl

4:08PM ☆ ↰ ▾

It was fun. It felt a little like the old EL + Benj on an adventure. No plans. No BB. No kids. We discovered small little roads + alleys; just walked till we arrived at this amazing hole in the wall hummus bar run by Arabs. We sat at a table with some men who only spoke Arabic. The food was amazing. We stuffed ourselves with the best hummus + falafel that I can remember eating in my whole life. Benj + I agreed on something. Lol. We ate so much + we even laughed together. Sorry we didn't follow your instruction with the hummus. I did think of your idea. Made me smile.

Shirl <Shirl465@mail.com>
to EL

4:08PM ☆ ↰ ▾

Why are you writing to me? You should be fucking your husband right now.

EL <ELGood@mail.com>
to Shirl

4:09PM ☆ ↰ ▾

Why is everything about sex with you?

Shirl <Shirl465@mail.com>
to EL

4:09PM ☆ ↰ ▾

Sex is everything. Lol. Just sayin….

EL <ELGood@mail.com>
to Shirl

4:09PM ☆ ↰ ▾

I know what you're saying. I know you're right too. But you still piss me off.

Shirl <Shirl465@mail.com>
to EL

4:09PM ☆ ↰ ▾

So, did you talk with him?

EL <ELGood@mail.com>
to Shirl

4:09PM ☆ ↰ ▾

Not really. We barely spoke, but he was nice to me + this was a break from his snapping + anger. We sort of were together w/out the dark, thunder cloud that always lingers above us.

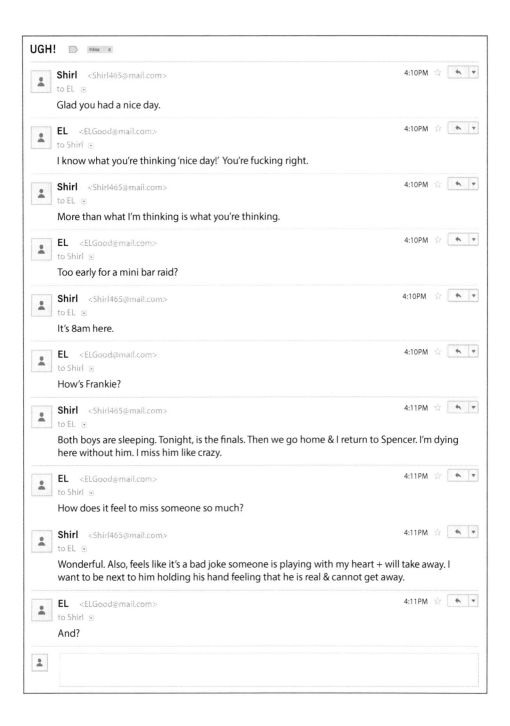

UGH! Inbox x

Shirl <Shirl465@mail.com>   4:10PM
to EL

Glad you had a nice day.

EL <ELGood@mail.com>   4:10PM
to Shirl

I know what you're thinking 'nice day!' You're fucking right.

Shirl <Shirl465@mail.com>   4:10PM
to EL

More than what I'm thinking is what you're thinking.

EL <ELGood@mail.com>   4:10PM
to Shirl

Too early for a mini bar raid?

Shirl <Shirl465@mail.com>   4:10PM
to EL

It's 8am here.

EL <ELGood@mail.com>   4:10PM
to Shirl

How's Frankie?

Shirl <Shirl465@mail.com>   4:11PM
to EL

Both boys are sleeping. Tonight, is the finals. Then we go home & I return to Spencer. I'm dying here without him. I miss him like crazy.

EL <ELGood@mail.com>   4:11PM
to Shirl

How does it feel to miss someone so much?

Shirl <Shirl465@mail.com>   4:11PM
to EL

Wonderful. Also, feels like it's a bad joke someone is playing with my heart + will take away. I want to be next to him holding his hand feeling that he is real & cannot get away.

EL <ELGood@mail.com>   4:11PM
to Shirl

And?

UGH! 📧 Inbox x

👤	**Shirl** <Shirl465@mail.com> to EL	4:10PM ☆

Feel his cheek gently rub against mine.

👤	**EL** <ELGood@mail.com> to Shirl	4:11PM ☆

Ok. Stop. Ugh!

👤

MYJOURNAL.COM

Grandma Rose
Teddy Goodman

I do not know Grandma Rose very well. She and Benj have been estranged for years. When I was little she would visit us in New York and bring delicious chocolate chip cupcakes sprinkled with powdered sugar. This is all I remember about her. It is fucked up but I think Benj blames Grama Rose for his father's death. He left for school one morning and came home to learn that his father had died that day from a heart attack. The night before, Benj and his father had a huge fight and he died before they resolved it. They never said 'sorry'. He has been angry ever since. That was over thirty years ago. Makes me feel sad for Benj and for Grandma Rose. I'm not one to talk. I have spent a few years hiding and being fucking mad at the world, but cannot imagine keeping it going for another thirty years. It's a pretty lonely and tiring charade. I like Grandma Rose. She has great stories and she is very easy to talk to: She is on her 4th husband Theo. She says he is the love of her life - her soulmate. All the other husbands were warm up for Theo. I have watched her text with him over the last few days and she is always smiling. I'd say she is the happiest person on this trip and not a typically judgemental adult. Dad may never take her back, but I'm happy that she is in my life.

Aliza Goodman's Daily Motivational Quote #4:   now

"Know what sparks the light in you. Then use that light to illuminate the world."
Oprah Winfrey

MotiQuote.com

YM
Yasmin M.

AG
Aliza Goodman

ⓘ

4:10 PM

Just took a walk with Asher...alone! ☺   AG

YM   Is he still cute?

Yesssss even cuter than before! Hes so funny and smart i'm rly not sure why he likes me but I think he does   AG

YM   Did u guys kiss???

Yessssss we were on this really pretty cliff above the beach ♡   AG

and out to the sea & he said can I kiss u   AG

YAZ I must have sounded so fucking stupid   AG

I said I guess so & he kissed me quickly on the lips   AG

it was sooo nice I rly hope it happens again   AG

YM   Ur first official kiss & ur sooo calm

YM   That's sick im so jealous

YM   now you have to send me a selfie with him

YM   Forget the bat mitzvah now you're a woman!

I will soon   AG

Now hes coming with me back to J he wants to meet Lady Gaga cuz hes never met one   AG

This is crazy and when he texted his dad to say he wanted to go to J his dad was so chill w it   AG

He lives on a kibbutz an hour from here & another hour from J   AG

YM   OMG

YM   This means he really likes youuuuu!!!

Idk   AG

kids here are so independent   AG

Delivered

iMessage

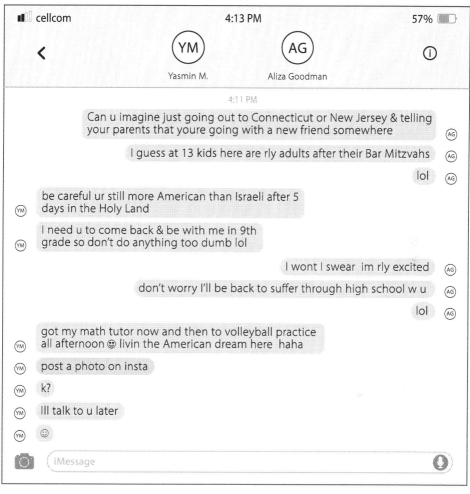

YM
Yasmin M.

AG
Aliza Goodman

4:11 PM

Can u imagine just going out to Connecticut or New Jersey & telling your parents that youre going with a new friend somewhere

I guess at 13 kids here are rly adults after their Bar Mitzvahs

lol

be careful ur still more American than Israeli after 5 days in the Holy Land

I need u to come back & be with me in 9th grade so don't do anything too dumb lol

I wont I swear im rly excited

don't worry I'll be back to suffer through high school w u

lol

got my math tutor now and then to volleyball practice all afternoon ☺ livin the American dream here haha

post a photo on insta

k?

Ill talk to u later

☺

iMessage

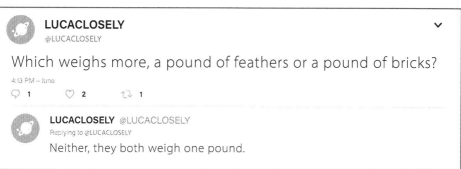

LUCACLOSELY
@LUCACLOSELY

Which weighs more, a pound of feathers or a pound of bricks?

4:13 PM – June

1   2   1

LUCACLOSELY @LUCACLOSELY
Replying to @LUCACLOSELY

Neither, they both weigh one pound.

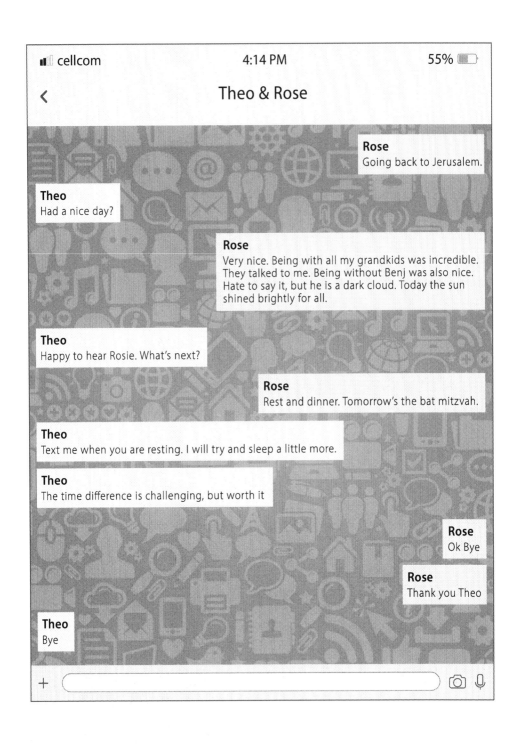

cellcom 4:14 PM 55%

< **Theo & Rose**

Rose
Going back to Jerusalem.

Theo
Had a nice day?

Rose
Very nice. Being with all my grandkids was incredible. They talked to me. Being without Benj was also nice. Hate to say it, but he is a dark cloud. Today the sun shined brightly for all.

Theo
Happy to hear Rosie. What's next?

Rose
Rest and dinner. Tomorrow's the bat mitzvah.

Theo
Text me when you are resting. I will try and sleep a little more.

Theo
The time difference is challenging, but worth it

Rose
Ok Bye

Rose
Thank you Theo

Theo
Bye

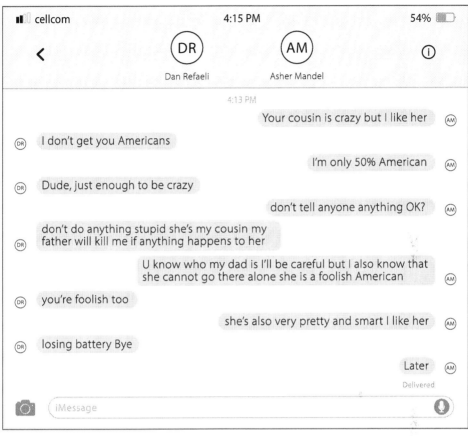

cellcom   4:17 PM   54%

(HM)   **(AM)**   ⓘ

Hezzi Mandel   Asher Mandel

4:15 PM

I'm on their bus back to J they're all asleep strange to see Israel like a tourist

Have fun be a good Israeli son

mom says there's no such thing as a good Israeli

Not sure your mom is always right

I will be sure to tell her U said so when she comes back

You do that now, keep your eyes open J is not the Kibbutz.

Good I need a break from the boring kibbutz

I know be smart and safe

Of course

K

And be polite to her parents OK?

I will they're not on the bus they did not come to beach

Are they ok?

I think so

Stay in touch son

K

I will

Bye

iMessage

JN24:   now

A suspicious piece of luggage was found at Ben Gurion Airport this afternoon causing the terminal to shut down and delay flights.

Jewish News You Can Use

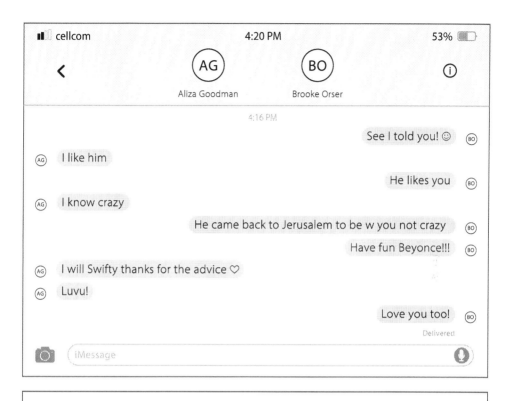

AG
Aliza Goodman

BO
Brooke Orser

4:16 PM

See I told you! ☺ (BO)

(AG) I like him

He likes you (BO)

(AG) I know crazy

He came back to Jerusalem to be w you not crazy (BO)

Have fun Beyonce!!! (BO)

(AG) I will Swifty thanks for the advice ♡

(AG) Luvu!

Love you too! (BO)

Delivered

iMessage

MYPOETRY.COM

A First Kiss

Brooke G.O.

★ ★ ★

A first kiss
Soft and salty
Unexpected
Tender and fresh
Changes
Light and crisp
Empowers
Gentle and warm
Renews
Sunny and forever

♡ 180

219 👁

Dear Mom,

I went out with my friend Asher to take photos of Jerusalem. Told Lucas I was leaving, but he is very busy winning a basketball game on his iPad. I think you should seriously consider the amount of time he spends on the ipad & the effects it is having on his brain's development. All those EMFs are very dangerous. He does not even have a book here to read. I may not be his parent, but you are & I think this is a real problem. I'm just saying....

I'll be back soon.

Love, Aliza

Ps — Had a great time at the beach. Hope you had a great day in J!

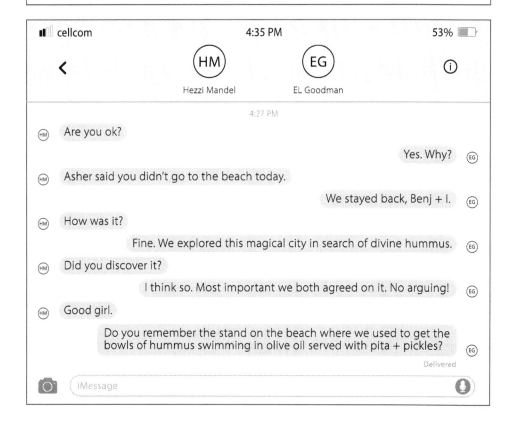

                                4:33 PM

(HM) EL I can still taste your lips doused in hummus. I
     remember it like it was yesterday.

                              It was almost 30 years ago. (EG)

                    I think I was salty + sandy that whole summer as
                    you worked as a lifeguard. (EG)

(HM) One of my best jobs ever.

                    And your girlfriend sat around reading by your side
                    all summer. You had a good gig. (EG)

(HM) I know I did. You did not suffer much either.

                              Probably the happiest I ever was. (EG)

(HM) We were both so happy. And so great together.

                    When I was younger, I used to wish my parents sent me to the
                    luxury sleep away camps with my school friends by lakes where
                    they dressed like Indians + sang kumbaya songs. Each year they
                    came back to school with epic stories + I was so jealous. I loved
                    the kibbutz, but my stories were not as romantic as theirs until
                    the summer we spent on the beach. I never once thought about
                    what I was missing. I did not want to go home. Remember? (EG)

(HM) Yes.

                    I could not abandon my parents, but I wonder what would
                    have happened if I stayed + finished school in Israel? (EG)

(HM) Will never know.

                              No, we won't. (EG)

(HM) Still feels so real.

                              It does. (EG)

(HM) No going back huh?

                    No. I'm glad you are back in my life. (EG)

                              Delivered

📷 (iMessage   🎤)

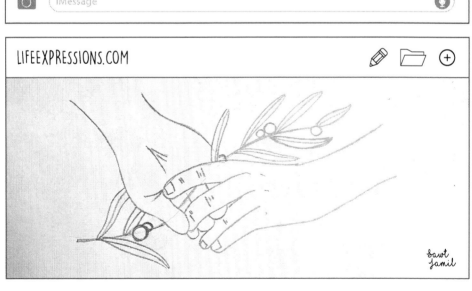

Dear Lucas Goodman, Astronaut in Training –

@JUNIORNASAUSA

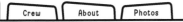

| Crew | About | Photos |

TODAY ON THE INTERNATIONAL SPACE STATION:

Most of the photos we take from the International Space Station (@ISS) are from the Cupola, Italian for "dome," which is a seven-window observatory. Today, we are traveling over the amazing islands, islets and coral reefs of the Florida Keys and the beautiful Bahama Islands. We captured these warm water images of the gorgeous pink and orange reefs and the turquoise, aquamarine, blue waters all the way down to the Central American countries of Honduras and Nicaragua.

Aliza Goodman's Daily Motivational Quote #5:   now

"Kindness in words creates confidence. Kindness in thinking creates profoundness. Kindness in giving creates love."   Lao Tzu

MotiQuote.com

Jack Billings' Notes

I have arrived in Israel. The flight was long and turbulent, but after a day of travel I made it to the Holy Land. Finally, I will cover the kind of story I have dreamed about - Jews and Palestinians who happily and successfully coexist living in a commune in the middle of a tumultuous region. I am excited to stay with them after a few days to overcome jetlag and explore this holy city. This evening, I am content with a glass of wine in hand and a small plate of almonds and cashews people watching in the hectic and very noisy hotel lobby. Next to me sits a woman who nervously drinks a glass of wine and stares out into space. After a few minutes, she is joined by a man who reaches over to kiss her but stares forward. Obviously unwelcome, he sits down next to her. I am intrigued. They are not lovers. Not old friends. I listen as they speak quietly. He orders a glass of wine.

Man - Remember when we used to sit at the kitchen table after school and drink ice cold milk and eat sugar cookies from the local bakery?
Woman - Another lifetime. When we were sister and brother.
Man - We are still brother and sister.
Woman (cries) - We are nothing. We are two distant people Ethan.
(Silence)
Man - I am sorry EL. I have regretted leaving you for all these years. I was selfish. I am sorry.
(Silence)
Man - I will do whatever it takes for you to let me back into your life. I dearly want to be back in your life EL.
EL - Why now Ethan?
Ethan - I have tried over the years and I know you did not want me. Our parents are dead. Now I am here to celebrate my niece's bat mitzvah and in that spirit, please talk to me and allow me to begin repairing our relationship. I take full responsibility for fracturing us many years ago. I want this more than anything in my life.
EL - You should have thought about this before you left.
Ethan - I was a confused, angry 18-year-old and escape was the only option I saw for myself.
EL - Why did you leave?
Ethan - Truth?
EL - At this point if it is not the truth, do not bother.
(Pause)
Ethan - Dad hated me. He was charming at work and with

his friends. He was kind to mom and to you. But he was unbearably hard on me. He was so cold; he rarely spoke to me when we were alone. At dinner, he only spoke to you and mom. You were too young to notice and you also basked in his love. He never did anything alone with me. My grades were never good enough. My thoughts were ridiculed. My actions were always wrong. When I played the piano and you sang, he only complimented you and after would get me alone and criticize my playing. He bullied me and my self-confidence was decaying. I thought about this over the years as I recovered and discovered that I was not a bad person at all. I always thought you would survive just fine. Mom took great care and Dad loved you - you were his sunshine. He would smile when you walked into a room. After graduating high school, I knew I had to get out. Or I would kill myself. I don't say this lightly. I spent many years planning my own death. I could not do it to you or mom and I could not do it to dad. Even though I knew he hated who I was, I also knew his history and could not have him witness another death in his family. I know that the holocaust ruined him. But I was 18 and there was still a little flame burning in me that gave me hope for myself. But my hope was dependent on getting out and going away. There was no Internet. I did call mom and each time, she said you did not want to talk to me.

EL - She never told me you called.

Ethan - I called. I also called every year on your birthday and she said you could not come to the phone but that she would tell you I called.

EL (crying) - She did not. When you left, it was as if you were dead to them.

Ethan - But I was not buried in a grave and this made my 'death' liveable for both especially Dad. I have a very comfortable life with Bruno; he is a loving and good man. I am lucky to have him share my life. But I need you back. I want you in my life. I will not run away ever again. Quite the opposite, I will be here for you unconditionally and always. Please make room for me and let me back in.

(Ethan crying.)

(EL crying.)

EL - It will take me time.

Ethan - I am a patient man. Hell, I have waited over thirty years. (laugh) I know I am asking a lot but all I want now in my life is to get back into your life.

EL - My traitor children have already taken you in. (EL laughs)

Ethan - Your children are amazing. You have done a wonderful job raising them.

EL - Do not even go there.

Ethan - I am just reporting objectively. I have no ulterior motives. You are a great mom EL. I know you have other issues, but being a wonderful mother needs to be celebrated fully every moment. I am a reporter and a damn good one. I do not make up stories and I do not fabricate, I report the facts (laugh) This may be the reason my articles do not end up on the cover of the newspaper, but this is not why I write. (Ethan takes EL's hands in his own) I am sincerely sorry. I will make it up to you every day. This I promise. Please let me back in EL.

(Silence)

EL - Okay. I will try. Do you still play the piano?

Ethan - Yes. Do you still sing?

EL - Yes. Mostly in the shower. (EL laughs)

Ethan - We must do something about that.

EL - Ok.

(Ethan and EL hug.)

Report Update 📎 Inbox ✕

Laura ‹ L.Friedman@SHH.com› 5:30PM ☆ ↰ ▾
to Benj ▾

I have confirmed your meeting at Hopper for 10am next Wednesday. Who else do you want at the meeting? What did you think of the documents I sent to you? Are they ok?

Benj ‹B.Goodman@SHH.com› 5:30PM ☆ ↰ ▾
to Laura ▾

They are great. Tell Ricardo he is fired.

Laura ‹ L.Friedman@SHH.com› 5:31PM ☆ ↰ ▾
to Benj ▾

Very funny.

Benj ‹B.Goodman@SHH.com› 5:31PM ☆ ↰ ▾
to Laura ▾

It's not a fucking joke. That asshole is out to lunch. If you didn't do clean up, we would be fucked.

Laura ‹ L.Friedman@SHH.com› 5:31PM ☆ ↰ ▾
to Benj ▾

I'll let you deal with it when you are back. Anything else?

Benj ‹B.Goodman@SHH.com› 5:32PM ☆ ↰ ▾
to Laura ▾

Ask Andrea and Roy to prepare the presentation to send to me by tomorrow. As well, tell them if it's too challenging that you'll do it for them.

Laura ‹ L.Friedman@SHH.com› 5:32PM ☆ ↰ ▾
to Benj ▾

Are you trying to get me killed?

Benj ‹B.Goodman@SHH.com› 5:33PM ☆ ↰ ▾
to Laura ▾

What? This is the real-world Laura and if people cannot keep up, then they are out. Too much riding on this for me to be a fucking boy scout. It is our survival of the fittest in a world that will eat us alive if we're not strong and out in front with everything we do. Look around at all the other suits in the elevators, the lobby and on the street. They're hungry for our territory and will do whatever it takes to get it if they see an opening. If we are weak or vulnerable, this will only kill us and wont look back. This is the real world.

Laura ‹ L.Friedman@SHH.com› 5:33PM ☆ ↰ ▾
to Benj ▾

Ok Mufasa.

Andy Orser
Now · Israel

GOY IN THE HOLY LAND PART 27

We went back to the Old City to buy t-shirts and souvenirs before dinner. We walked along the charming Old City cobblestone streets in the late afternoon crowded with French, Spanish, Russian, German and even Japanese tourists. The textured, ancient city and the diverse tourists coming together made me feel very small and at the same empowered - a strange confluence of growing emotions whirling inside of me. I bought three wooden backgammon boards from a large, dark eyed Arab vendor named Ahmed. The jovial proprietor missing two front teeth then brought me to his cousin to buy t-shirts and then to his brother for a glass of fresh pomegranate juice. Ahmed explained to me that his family had been in Jerusalem for more then six generations and they owned a dozen shops in the Arab Quarter of the Old City. His wife, Suham, came from Ramallah, and they were an arranged marriage and have five kids who are all in school and studying very hard. Like all parents I know, he talked about how important it was for the kids to study and stay out of trouble. I told him that I understood, but did I? This was unclear. He told me how difficult it was for Suham to visit her families in Ramallah with check points and that their children rarely see their grandparents in person but meet by Facetime. The distance between Jerusalem and Ramallah by land is eight miles, yet politically worlds apart. Ahmed invited me to his house in East Jerusalem for dinner tomorrow night. I explained we had our niece's bat mitzvah and he said "Mazel Tov! Nothing better than a family celebration!"

Dear Friends, the world is both large and very small. We all want to connect and be connected. We all value our families. #Mynewfriendahmed #shuk #Jerusalem

 Like   Comment   ⤳ Share

MYJOURNAL.COM

A Detente
Roaming Roman

EL & I have agreed to a detente. While we have time to work out all our peace efforts going forward, I am relieved to reach this understanding as the bat mitzvah is tomorrow & it needs to be a happy & joyful celebration. I have wasted so much time. Looking back I should have done this trip very differently. But now I have the opportunity to move forward with my sister in her life. I am full of happiness and hope in the Holy Land where miracles have occured for thousands of years.

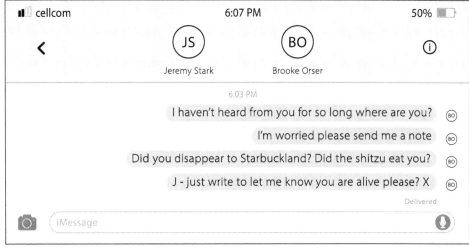

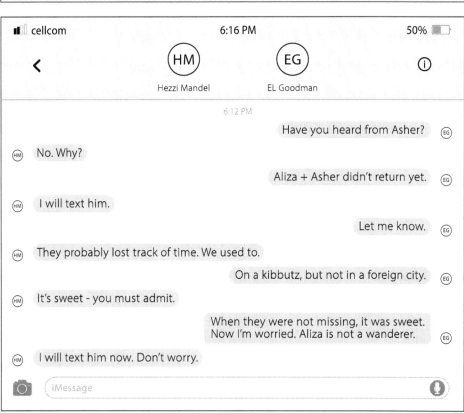

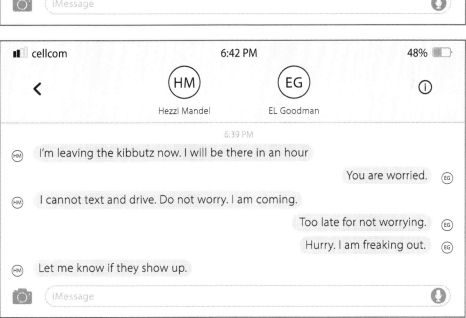

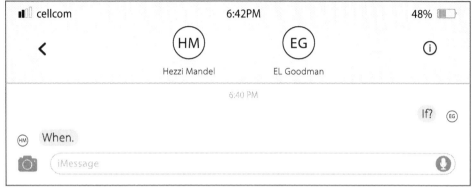

HM
Hezzi Mandel

EG
EL Goodman

6:40 PM

If? (EG)

(HM) When.

iMessage

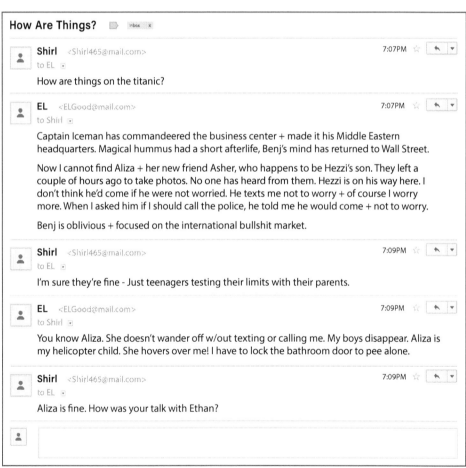

How Are Things?   Inbox   x

Shirl <Shirl465@mail.com>   7:07PM
to EL

How are things on the titanic?

EL <ELGood@mail.com>   7:07PM
to Shirl

Captain Iceman has commandeered the business center + made it his Middle Eastern headquarters. Magical hummus had a short afterlife, Benj's mind has returned to Wall Street.

Now I cannot find Aliza + her new friend Asher, who happens to be Hezzi's son. They left a couple of hours ago to take photos. No one has heard from them. Hezzi is on his way here. I don't think he'd come if he were not worried. He texts me not to worry + of course I worry more. When I asked him if I should call the police, he told me he would come + not to worry.

Benj is oblivious + focused on the international bullshit market.

Shirl <Shirl465@mail.com>   7:09PM
to EL

I'm sure they're fine - Just teenagers testing their limits with their parents.

EL <ELGood@mail.com>   7:09PM
to Shirl

You know Aliza. She doesn't wander off w/out texting or calling me. My boys disappear. Aliza is my helicopter child. She hovers over me! I have to lock the bathroom door to pee alone.

Shirl <Shirl465@mail.com>   7:09PM
to EL

Aliza is fine. How was your talk with Ethan?

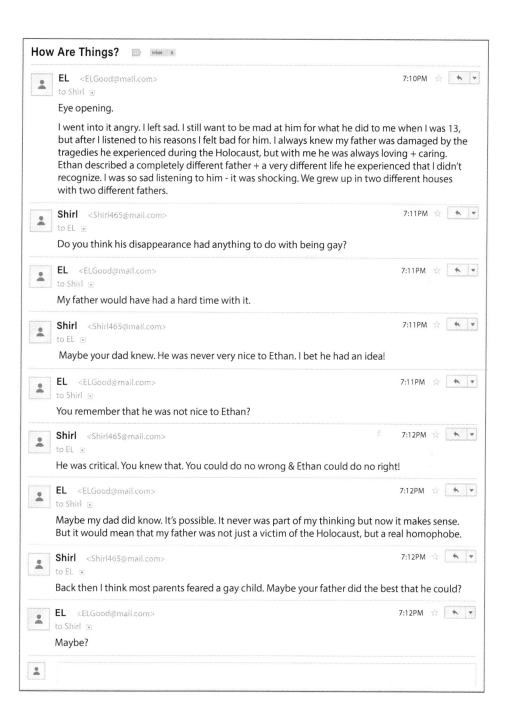

How Are Things? Inbox x

EL <ELGood@mail.com>   7:10PM
to Shirl

Eye opening.

I went into it angry. I left sad. I still want to be mad at him for what he did to me when I was 13, but after I listened to his reasons I felt bad for him. I always knew my father was damaged by the tragedies he experienced during the Holocaust, but with me he was always loving + caring. Ethan described a completely different father + a very different life he experienced that I didn't recognize. I was so sad listening to him - it was shocking. We grew up in two different houses with two different fathers.

Shirl <Shirl465@mail.com>   7:11PM
to EL

Do you think his disappearance had anything to do with being gay?

EL <ELGood@mail.com>   7:11PM
to Shirl

My father would have had a hard time with it.

Shirl <Shirl465@mail.com>   7:11PM
to EL

Maybe your dad knew. He was never very nice to Ethan. I bet he had an idea!

EL <ELGood@mail.com>   7:11PM
to Shirl

You remember that he was not nice to Ethan?

Shirl <Shirl465@mail.com>   7:12PM
to EL

He was critical. You knew that. You could do no wrong & Ethan could do no right!

EL <ELGood@mail.com>   7:12PM
to Shirl

Maybe my dad did know. It's possible. It never was part of my thinking but now it makes sense. But it would mean that my father was not just a victim of the Holocaust, but a real homophobe.

Shirl <Shirl465@mail.com>   7:12PM
to EL

Back then I think most parents feared a gay child. Maybe your father did the best that he could?

EL <ELGood@mail.com>   7:12PM
to Shirl

Maybe?

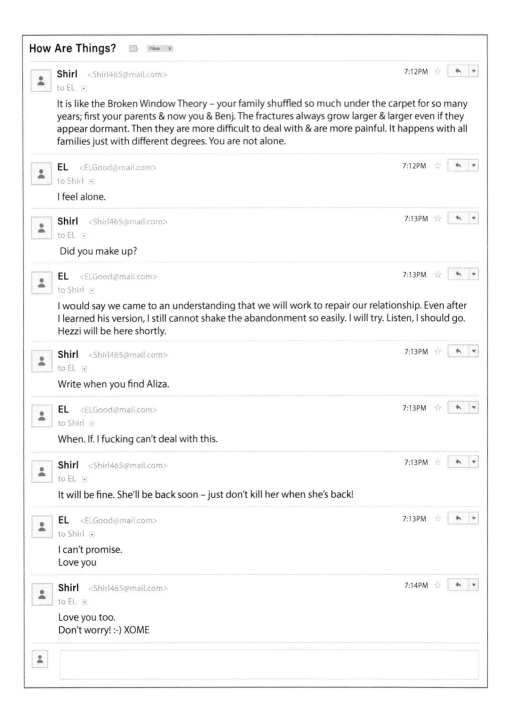

How Are Things? 📁 Inbox ✕

Shirl <Shirl465@mail.com>   7:12PM ☆ ↰ ▾
to EL ▾

It is like the Broken Window Theory – your family shuffled so much under the carpet for so many years; first your parents & now you & Benj. The fractures always grow larger & larger even if they appear dormant. Then they are more difficult to deal with & are more painful. It happens with all families just with different degrees. You are not alone.

EL <ELGood@mail.com>   7:12PM ☆ ↰ ▾
to Shirl ▾

I feel alone.

Shirl <Shirl465@mail.com>   7:13PM ☆ ↰ ▾
to EL ▾

 Did you make up?

EL <ELGood@mail.com>   7:13PM ☆ ↰ ▾
to Shirl ▾

I would say we came to an understanding that we will work to repair our relationship. Even after I learned his version, I still cannot shake the abandonment so easily. I will try. Listen, I should go. Hezzi will be here shortly.

Shirl <Shirl465@mail.com>   7:13PM ☆ ↰ ▾
to EL ▾

Write when you find Aliza.

EL <ELGood@mail.com>   7:13PM ☆ ↰ ▾
to Shirl ▾

When. If. I fucking can't deal with this.

Shirl <Shirl465@mail.com>   7:13PM ☆ ↰ ▾
to EL ▾

It will be fine. She'll be back soon – just don't kill her when she's back!

EL <ELGood@mail.com>   7:13PM ☆ ↰ ▾
to Shirl ▾

I can't promise.
Love you

Shirl <Shirl465@mail.com>   7:14PM ☆ ↰ ▾
to EL ▾

Love you too.
Don't worry! :-) XOME

Missing in Jerusalem

Roaming Roman

My 13-year-old niece & her Israeli friend are missing in Jerusalem. It is sunset & as the ancient city walls darken, Bruno & I look for them in every nook & cranny of this majestic religious enclave. We've shown hundreds of people Aliza's photo but no one remembers seeing her.

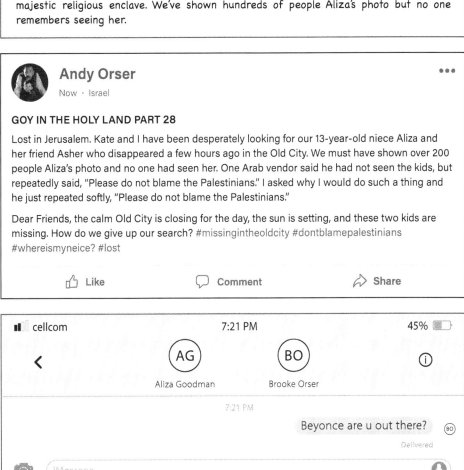

Andy Orser
Now · Israel

GOY IN THE HOLY LAND PART 28

Lost in Jerusalem. Kate and I have been desperately looking for our 13-year-old niece Aliza and her friend Asher who disappeared a few hours ago in the Old City. We must have shown over 200 people Aliza's photo and no one had seen her. One Arab vendor said he had not seen the kids, but repeatedly said, "Please do not blame the Palestinians." I asked why I would do such a thing and he just repeated softly, "Please do not blame the Palestinians."

Dear Friends, the calm Old City is closing for the day, the sun is setting, and these two kids are missing. How do we give up our search? #missingintheoldcity #dontblamepalestinians #whereismyneice? #lost

   👍 Like   💬 Comment   ↗ Share

📶 cellcom   7:21 PM   45% 🔋

<   **AG**   **BO**   ⓘ

Aliza Goodman   Brooke Orser

7:21 PM

Beyonce are u out there? 🅱

Delivered

📷 (iMessage) 🎤

Naked
Teddy Goodman

My sister is missing in Jerusalem. How ironic, the good kid in our family, who never gets into trouble, is causing problems. It should feel good to have the pressure off of myself, as I am usually the fucked-up problem child. Since we arrived in Israel, she has been acting strange. Everything about my family has been weird here: leaving our New York cocoon has accentuated so many of our problems. Reminds me of the story - The Emperor Has No Clothes - problems we ignore back home are now naked in my eyes in Israel. We have nowhere to hide - we are fully exposed: EL is the lefty-pleaser mother, Benj is the rightwing-workaholic narcissistic father, Aliza is the clever and sneaky teen daughter, Lucas is the sweet, adventurous brother, and I am the fucking asshole. The thing is that I may not want to be the asshole anymore. Need to figure out which character in this drama I want to play now.

Alone

Brooke G.O.

Alone
People vanish
Thoughts banish
Connection is lost
Accrue a heavy cost

An empty pail
Unimaginable tale
Voices echo
Feel so low

Run and hide
You lied
Friendship rested
Trust tested

♡ 191   307 ◉

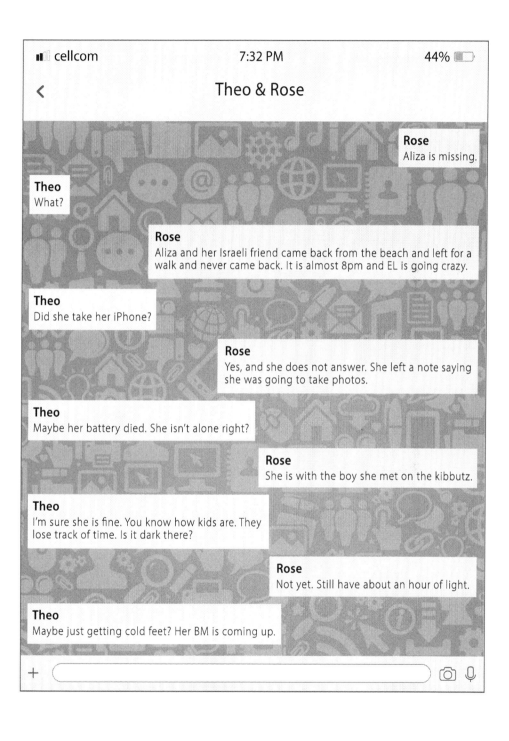

Rose
Aliza is missing.

Theo
What?

Rose
Aliza and her Israeli friend came back from the beach and left for a walk and never came back. It is almost 8pm and EL is going crazy.

Theo
Did she take her iPhone?

Rose
Yes, and she does not answer. She left a note saying she was going to take photos.

Theo
Maybe her battery died. She isn't alone right?

Rose
She is with the boy she met on the kibbutz.

Theo
I'm sure she is fine. You know how kids are. They lose track of time. Is it dark there?

Rose
Not yet. Still have about an hour of light.

Theo
Maybe just getting cold feet? Her BM is coming up.

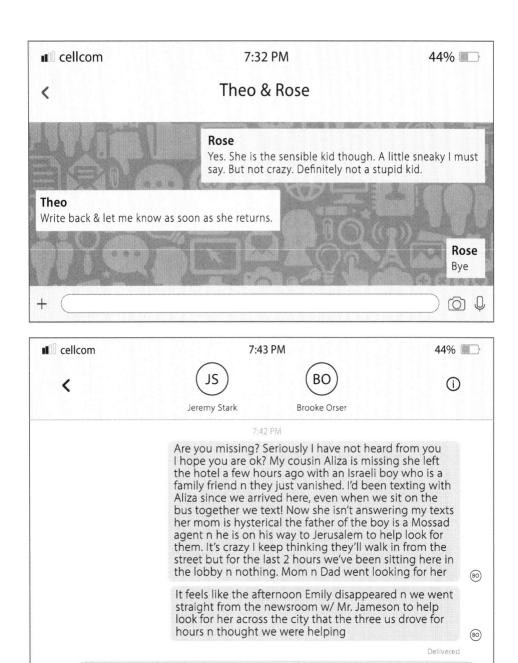

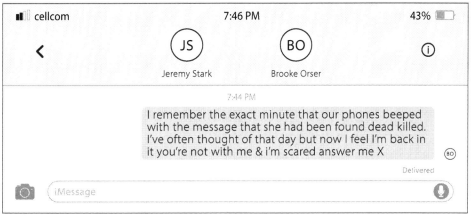

cellcom   7:46 PM   43%

JS Jeremy Stark   **BO** Brooke Orser

7:44 PM

I remember the exact minute that our phones beeped with the message that she had been found dead killed. I've often thought of that day but now I feel I'm back in it you're not with me & i'm scared answer me X

Delivered

iMessage

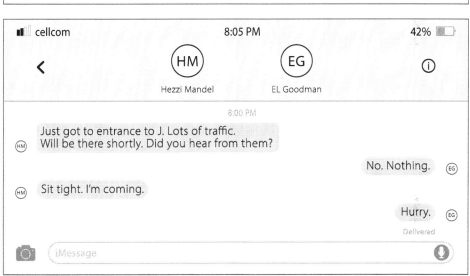

cellcom   8:05 PM   42%

HM Hezzi Mandel   **EG** EL Goodman

8:00 PM

Just got to entrance to J. Lots of traffic. Will be there shortly. Did you hear from them?

No. Nothing.

Sit tight. I'm coming.

Hurry.

Delivered

iMessage

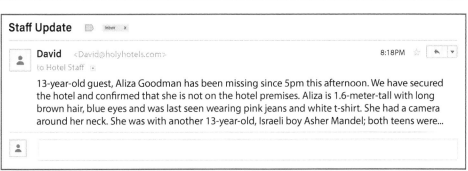

Staff Update   Inbox x

David <David@holyhotels.com>   8:18PM
to Hotel Staff

13-year-old guest, Aliza Goodman has been missing since 5pm this afternoon. We have secured the hotel and confirmed that she is not on the hotel premises. Aliza is 1.6-meter-tall with long brown hair, blue eyes and was last seen wearing pink jeans and white t-shirt. She had a camera around her neck. She was with another 13-year-old, Israeli boy Asher Mandel; both teens were...

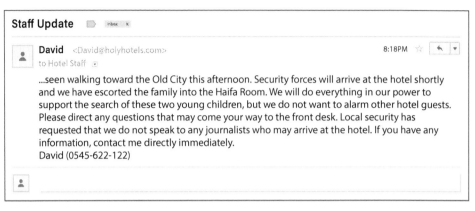

Staff Update 📬 inbox x

👤 **David** <David@holyhotels.com>   8:18PM ☆ ↰ ▾
to Hotel Staff ▾

...seen walking toward the Old City this afternoon. Security forces will arrive at the hotel shortly and we have escorted the family into the Haifa Room. We will do everything in our power to support the search of these two young children, but we do not want to alarm other hotel guests. Please direct any questions that may come your way to the front desk. Local security has requested that we do not speak to any journalists who may arrive at the hotel. If you have any information, contact me directly immediately.
David (0545-622-122)

MYJOURNAL.COM

Still Missing
Roaming Roman

Still no news on Aliza & Asher - two innocent 13-year-olds disappeared without a trace in Jerusalem. It is now dark outside & my sister, rightfully so, is freaking out. Asher's father just arrived & is organizing a search. The police have been called. Bruno & I looked for them for hours & now are sitting here feeling completely helpless.

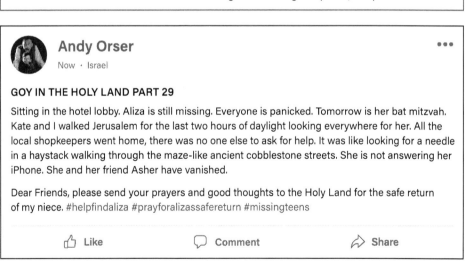

Andy Orser   •••
Now · Israel

GOY IN THE HOLY LAND PART 29

Sitting in the hotel lobby. Aliza is still missing. Everyone is panicked. Tomorrow is her bat mitzvah. Kate and I walked Jerusalem for the last two hours of daylight looking everywhere for her. All the local shopkeepers went home, there was no one else to ask for help. It was like looking for a needle in a haystack walking through the maze-like ancient cobblestone streets. She is not answering her iPhone. She and her friend Asher have vanished.

Dear Friends, please send your prayers and good thoughts to the Holy Land for the safe return of my niece. #helpfindaliza #prayforalizassafereturn #missingteens

👍 Like   💬 Comment   ↪ Share

Still Missing Cont.
Roaming Roman

Just met a reporter for the New York Times named Jack Billings. He came over & asked what was happening. I told him nothing. Do not want to blow this out of proportion until we have more information. Amazing how all of us journalists can smell blood from miles away. For now, I'm guarded and don't want to have him blow the story up. We know so little and personally feel so helpless and scared.

Jack Billings' Notes

Just met the fellow I eavesdropped on earlier (Ethan) speaking to his estranged sister. Seems his niece and another kid are missing in Jerusalem He is a reporter himself and did not divulge any information.

Jetlag has set in and my room is ready, but I think I will stay in the lobby and see what transpires. Missing teenagers in Jerusalem could turn into some story.

▪▫ cellcom	8:20 PM	41% 🔋

‹	(HM)	(AM)	ⓘ
	Hezzi Mandel	Asher Mandel	

8:20 PM

(HM) Son where are you?

(HM) Asher answer me.

📷 (iMessage) 🎤

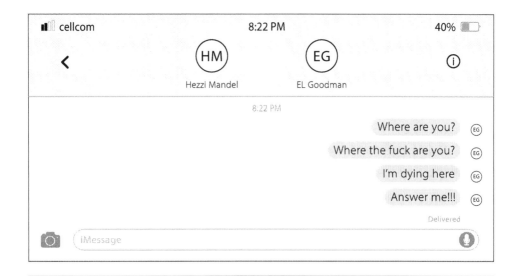

HM
Hezzi Mandel

EG
EL Goodman

8:22 PM

Where are you? EG

Where the fuck are you? EG

I'm dying here EG

Answer me!!! EG

Delivered

iMessage

Jack Billings' Notes

Family of missing teenager was just shuttled out of the hotel's lobby. Mother is hysterical. I spoke with the uncle who is a reporter for an Italian Newspaper. When I introduced myself as a Times reporter, he asked me to please wait as they did not want to involve the press. Will gather information until I can report. Two teenagers are missing in Jerusalem. Whereabouts are unknown. It is thought that they disappeared in the Arab section of the Old City. No one has seen them since the hotel security guard saw them leave the building around 5pm. The shops and the market place are closed now; there are no storeowners available for questioning. Aliza Goodman from New York City is in Jerusalem to celebrate her bat mitzvah tomorrow at the Davidson Center on the Southern Wall of the Temple Mount. Her extended family has traveled here from New York, California and Rome. She disappeared with a local Israeli boy, Asher Mandel.

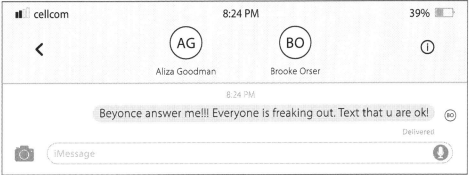

cellcom   8:24 PM   39%

<   (AG) Aliza Goodman   (BO) Brooke Orser   (i)

8:24 PM

Beyonce answer me!!! Everyone is freaking out. Text that u are ok! (BO)

Delivered

iMessage

cellcom   8:27 PM   39%

<   (AG) Aliza Goodman   (TG) Teddy Goodman   (i)

8:27 PM

Where the fuck are you? (TG)

Delivered

iMessage

MYJOURNAL.COM

Mossad Hezzi
Teddy Goodman

My mom's ex-boyfriend just arrived at the hotel to help look for Aliza and his son Asher who have been missing since this afternoon. This whole thing is very fucked up. My sister's missing in Jerusalem with the son of my mother's ex-boyfriend, Hezzi, a very muscular man with tanned and rough skin. He is wearing worn out jeans and an old tattered aqua polo shirt; quite the opposite of Benj who looks like a conservative middle-aged model for Brooks Brothers in a white shirt and khakis. Hezzi enters screaming into his cell phone in Hebrew. I understand most of what he is saying. It does not sound very good! He wonders where the fuck everyone is and why there aren't more people looking for the kids. Aliza's now officially fucked with our family; maybe I'm now freed from the asshole role that I've been playing?

JN24:

Missing American Teen vanished from Jerusalem while taking photos in the Old City with an Israeli friend from a local kibbutz. They were last seen walking toward the Jaffa Gate. Both kids dressed in jeans and tshirts. Any information on their whereabouts call 02-222-1212.

Jewish News You Can Use   now

Aliza's Missing 📭 inbox x

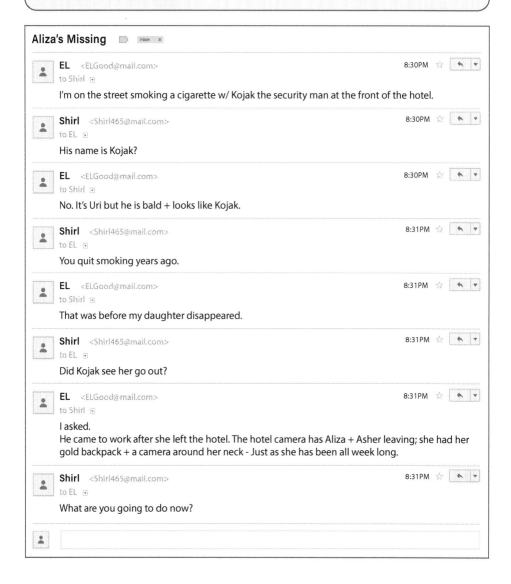

EL <ELGood@mail.com>	8:30PM ☆ ↩ ▾
to Shirl ▣	
I'm on the street smoking a cigarette w/ Kojak the security man at the front of the hotel.	

Shirl <Shirl465@mail.com>	8:30PM ☆ ↩ ▾
to EL ▣	
His name is Kojak?	

EL <ELGood@mail.com>	8:30PM ☆ ↩ ▾
to Shirl ▣	
No. It's Uri but he is bald + looks like Kojak.	

Shirl <Shirl465@mail.com>	8:31PM ☆ ↩ ▾
to EL ▣	
You quit smoking years ago.	

EL <ELGood@mail.com>	8:31PM ☆ ↩ ▾
to Shirl ▣	
That was before my daughter disappeared.	

Shirl <Shirl465@mail.com>	8:31PM ☆ ↩ ▾
to EL ▣	
Did Kojak see her go out?	

EL <ELGood@mail.com>	8:31PM ☆ ↩ ▾
to Shirl ▣	
I asked.	
He came to work after she left the hotel. The hotel camera has Aliza + Asher leaving; she had her gold backpack + a camera around her neck - Just as she has been all week long.	

Shirl <Shirl465@mail.com>	8:31PM ☆ ↩ ▾
to EL ▣	
What are you going to do now?	

Aliza's Missing   Inbox ✕

EL ‹ELGood@mail.com›　　　　　　　　　　　　　　　8:33PM
to Shirl

I don't know what to do. I couldn't sit in that room anymore. It was making me crazy. There has been no sight of Aliza for hours. It's dark here. Hezzi + his team have taken over the search. I went out to get some air. Saw Benj in the business lounge. He was fucking working! His 13-year-old daughter is missing in Jerusalem + the son of a bitch is working in the goddamn business lounge like he owns the place. I went in there + started to scream at him. He just listened. Shocked. Then I saw it, the Fucking New BB. I grabbed it + went to the street + threw it under cars speeding by. It felt good. Really good. For a brief moment, I had a great rush of adrenaline. Son of a bitch just waited for the cars to pass + then went to retrieve his damaged BB. He said nothing & walked back into the hotel. I bummed a cigarette from Kojak. I'm so fucking scared. I have no idea what I can do. I should have never let her go out alone. The child I trip over because she's always so close to me has disappeared. Vanished. Gone. What if something bad has happened to her? What if she is dead? I will never forgive myself. I should never have let her go out without an adult.

Shirl ‹Shirl465@mail.com›　　　　　　　　　　　　　8:34PM
to EL

She is not dead. Do not go there . Hezzi will find her.

EL ‹ELGood@mail.com›　　　　　　　　　　　　　　　8:34PM
to Shirl

Promise?

Shirl ‹Shirl465@mail.com›　　　　　　　　　　　　　8:34PM
to EL

Promise. Go back inside & see what's going on.

EL ‹ELGood@mail.com›　　　　　　　　　　　　　　　8:35PM
to Shirl

K.

Shirl ‹Shirl465@mail.com›　　　　　　　　　　　　　8:35PM
to EL

Love you. XOME

JN24:　　　　　　　　　　　　　　　　　　　　　　　now
American teen's final note to her parents, "Going out to take photos of Jerusalem." No other clues in the disappearance of two missing teenagers. Parents demand secret police investigation in East Jerusalem.
Jewish News You Can Use

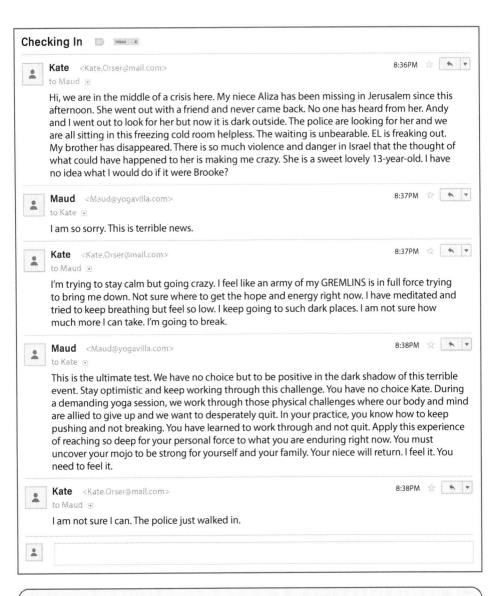

Checking In 📁 Inbox ✕

👤 **Kate** <Kate.Orser@mail.com>
to Maud ▾   8:36PM ☆ ↩ ▾

Hi, we are in the middle of a crisis here. My niece Aliza has been missing in Jerusalem since this afternoon. She went out with a friend and never came back. No one has heard from her. Andy and I went out to look for her but now it is dark outside. The police are looking for her and we are all sitting in this freezing cold room helpless. The waiting is unbearable. EL is freaking out. My brother has disappeared. There is so much violence and danger in Israel that the thought of what could have happened to her is making me crazy. She is a sweet lovely 13-year-old. I have no idea what I would do if it were Brooke?

👤 **Maud** <Maud@yogavilla.com>
to Kate ▾   8:37PM ☆ ↩ ▾

I am so sorry. This is terrible news.

👤 **Kate** <Kate.Orser@mail.com>
to Maud ▾   8:37PM ☆ ↩ ▾

I'm trying to stay calm but going crazy. I feel like an army of my GREMLINS is in full force trying to bring me down. Not sure where to get the hope and energy right now. I have meditated and tried to keep breathing but feel so low. I keep going to such dark places. I am not sure how much more I can take. I'm going to break.

👤 **Maud** <Maud@yogavilla.com>
to Kate ▾   8:38PM ☆ ↩ ▾

This is the ultimate test. We have no choice but to be positive in the dark shadow of this terrible event. Stay optimistic and keep working through this challenge. You have no choice Kate. During a demanding yoga session, we work through those physical challenges where our body and mind are allied to give up and we want to desperately quit. In your practice, you know how to keep pushing and not breaking. You have learned to work through and not quit. Apply this experience of reaching so deep for your personal force to what you are enduring right now. You must uncover your mojo to be strong for yourself and your family. Your niece will return. I feel it. You need to feel it.

👤 **Kate** <Kate.Orser@mail.com>
to Maud ▾   8:38PM ☆ ↩ ▾

I am not sure I can. The police just walked in.

📰 **JN24:**   now

Jerusalem police brought in to search for missing American teen Aliza Goodman and her Israeli boyfriend, Asher Mandel. Unknown if they fell in with a drug trafficking scheme or child pornography ring rumored to be run in the Old City.

Jewish News You Can Use

A group of loud Israeli security agents left the meeting room where the Goodmans have congregated to organize the search for the missing teenagers. I spoke with a few of these gentlemen who stood around screaming into their cell phones. No one would share information. I don't understand Hebrew. Security here is extremely tight. The tension is very thick.

MYJOURNAL.COM

The Triangle
Teddy Goodman

Hezzi's meeting with the security agents is over. Most of the men have left the room to continue looking for Aliza and Asher. Benj slipped in here a few minutes ago. He is pacing the room. EL just came back into the room and is now sobbing in Hezzi's arms. He is telling her that he will find the kids. Benj just pathetically watches. The embrace lasts for a long time until EL's body calms and Hezzi can let her go. Not sure if saving EL from fainting is part of his Mossad training, but shit the long, tight embrace is way fucking more than just safety. Hezzi was EL's boyfriend for a long time - not sure the feelings ever died watching them: I wonder if this hug is about their missing kids or more?

What's obvious is that Benj is a spectator at best. He shows no emotion towards anyone in the room: his wife, his kids, his sister, his mom or his missing daughter. He is a fucking piece of work. I hate him right now. Not like the hate I described to my therapist, but I despise the son of a bitch for not being present for us especially when we need him.

 JN24:

now

Father of missing teen, retired Mossad agent, has taken the lead in the investigation for the disappearance of two teenagers in Jerusalem this afternoon. One witness saw two teenagers enter a white truck headed toward Ramallah. IDF Security Forces are on high alert at all security checkpoints.

Jewish News You Can Use

Jack Billings' Notes

Just received a text that the press has picked up on the story. Many crazy conspiracy theories are spreading across the Internet and news. Wonder who leaked the story? Probably one of the hotel workers called the news. I returned to Ethan to tell him that the story is already out and spreading fast. I would be happy to report their story, but we need to get this out soon. He is a journalist. He knows the story needs to be controlled. He will get back to me shortly.

MYJOURNAL.COM

Operation Aliza
Teddy Goodman

I moved into the Business Center to get better Internet reception. No one in here at 10pm. Hezzi and his team are out looking for Aliza. Sitting around and waiting with my family is making me fucking crazy. I have spent more time with them in the last few days than I have in the last five years and now with Aliza missing, it is fucking unbearable. I am going to look for her on my own in my own way. I know that sneaky girl is up to something, but what the fuck is she doing? She is too clever to be kidnapped or caught up in some jihadist movement. She does not speak Hebrew. She does not know anyone in Israel but Hezzi's son Asher who is with her. He speaks Hebrew so she has that going for her. She is smart, but I'm smarter. I will start by hacking her phone calls. It is easy enough on our home server. I hope I can get to it from the hotel's shit computer.

 JN24:   now

Teenagers with no history of running away vanish into the Jerusalem night air. Parents fear they have been abducted by Hamas terrorist group of Izz Al Fasad. Jerusalem sercurity is heightened as fear spreads that there will be more abduction around the city.

Jewish News You Can Use

Still Missing Cont.
Roaming Roman

Sitting here holding Bruno's warm and secure hand. Scared beyond belief. No sign of my niece Aliza. Police & secret agents are going door to door in & around the Old City & East Jerusalem looking for her. I am completely helpless sitting in this very cold hotel meeting room. We are all motionless waiting for something to break the frozen silence and stir some life back into the room. I do not know Aliza well, but she seems like a smart girl. I have no idea what teenagers do. It has been so long and my teen years were so dark and challenging that I am not even a good example. I wonder what my life would be like had my path been easier and I had not had to hide myself from family. The pain of living a lie for so many years still pulsates through me and tonight as I let down my guard, I feel painfully exposed by Aliza's disappearance. Bruno's warmth is comforting but the anguish is far greater than the solace he can offer me. Covering wars did not prepare me for this experience. I'm lost.

▪ cellcom	9:09 PM	38% 🔋

‹ Theo & Rose

Rose
Still no news on Aliza and Asher.

Theo
Sorry Rosie.

Rose
It is strange. They just vanished. I have been sitting here playing games with Lucas. Unexpected bonding! It would be wonderful if it were not for the fact that his sister is missing. Keeping him busy is all I can do to help.

Theo
That's my girl. I wish I were there to be with you.

Rose
Thank you. I think he is very tired. We may retire from the backgammon marathon soon.

Theo
Who is winning?

Rose
The little bugger is - He is clever and strategic! Others are just sittingaround. EL keeps going in and out to smoke. I do not think she has had a cigarette in years. Her face is red from crying. Ethan keeps going out to keep her company. Benj is sitting staring into the air with his penetrating angry eyes. The same ones I remember after his father died. They still scare me. It's as though nothing has changed in 30 years.

Theo
Rosie. Go sit next to him. Take his hand & say nothing. If he speaks then you speak. If he says nothing, you say nothing. Just sit for as long as you can with his hand in yours.

Rose
I do not think I can do it. He hates me so much. He probably blames me for this too.

Theo
Holding his hand is for you Rosie. It may be for him at some point, but rightnow it is for you. Take care of yourself. Heal yourself. You cannot bring Aliza back yourself, but you can be strong & empathetic. You always said that before his father died he was sweet & a very thoughtful young man. Go hold that person's hand. He may still be there.

+ ⬭⬭⬭⬭⬭⬭⬭⬭⬭⬭⬭⬭⬭ ◎ 🎤

Theo & Rose

Rose
I don't know. Seems so foreign.

Theo
You can only find out one way. There is no downside to holding his hand.

Rose
Ok.

Theo
She will turn up soon. I have said prayers for her.

Rose
Pray harder.

Theo
I will. I love you.

MYJOURNAL.COM

Still Missing Cont.
Roaming Roman

Out with EL in front of the hotel. Traffic speeds by. Horns honk. EL, takes deep, long drags from a cigarette she bummed off the hotel security guard. She reminds me of the Roman teens gathered outside bars smoking. Not sure if she was a teen smoker? Missed so much of her life! Did she party in high school? What was she like? Now I just need to be here for her if she will let me?

Andy Orser
Now · Israel

···

GOY IN THE HOLY LAND PART 30

Still no sign of Aliza or Asher. The hotel lobby is packed with loud and boisterous tourists. This commotion, contradicted by the dead silence in the small room where we are waiting that is painfully, quiet and tense. The anticipation is cruel and endless. Early news reports involve kidnapping and blame Palestinian groups. I think about what the Arab vendor asked me earlier about not jumping to blame his people.

Dear Friends, Why does the quote, "I have met the enemy and he is us" keep playing in my mind? #whereisaliza? #Helpfindaliza!

👍 Like   💬 Comment   ↗ Share

 JN24:   now

Last year, two teenagers were kidnapped and robbed by Palestinian militants then released with no supplies to die in the Judean Desert; they wandered for three days before they were found dehydrated and exhausted by rescue crews. Police in Jerusalem are looking for any connection in kidnapping of American girl.

Jewish News You Can Use

MYJOURNAL.COM

Still Missing Cont.
Roaming Roman

Almost 10pm. Still no word. The pressure is killing us all. I keep thinking that Aliza will calmly walk in & wonder what all the commotion is about, but as each minute passes, this thought fades. I cannot help but think of my father whose soul was destroyed by the Nazis the day he returned home from work and learned that his mother and three younger siblings were all taken away. The pain and anguish he had to feel at that moment and each day as he realized he would likely never see them again. This tragedy is merciless and he never recovered. Tonight, the anguish of Aliza's disappearance evokes the cruel life my father was condemned to live and infected our whole family. I start to imagine the desperate nature of a man's soul struck by this existential reality of losing his family to brutal hate.

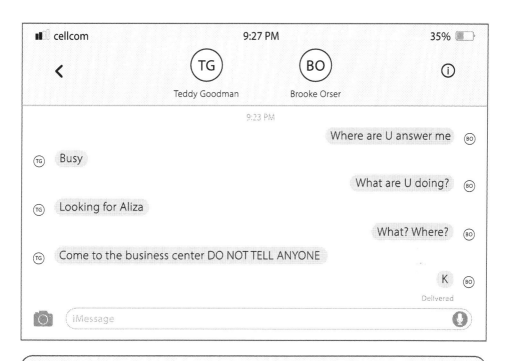

cellcom   9:27 PM   35%

TG — Teddy Goodman   BO — Brooke Orser

9:23 PM

> Where are U answer me (BO)

(TG) Busy

> What are U doing? (BO)

(TG) Looking for Aliza

> What? Where? (BO)

(TG) Come to the business center DO NOT TELL ANYONE

> K (BO)
> Delivered

iMessage

JN24:   now

US Embassy has been informed of the disappearance of U.S. Citizen Aliza Goodman, age thirteen who is traveling in Israel with her family to celebrate her bat mitzvah. Anyone with any detail that may lead to her discovery is asked to contact emergency desk at US Embassy - 03-999-1212.

Jewish News You Can Use

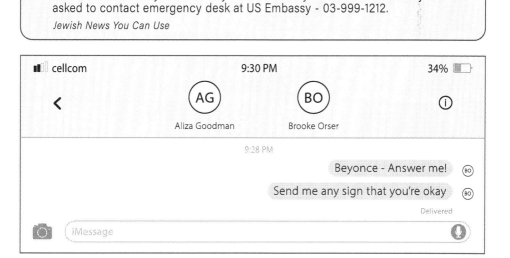

cellcom   9:30 PM   34%

AG — Aliza Goodman   BO — Brooke Orser

9:28 PM

> Beyonce - Answer me! (BO)

> Send me any sign that you're okay (BO)
> Delivered

iMessage

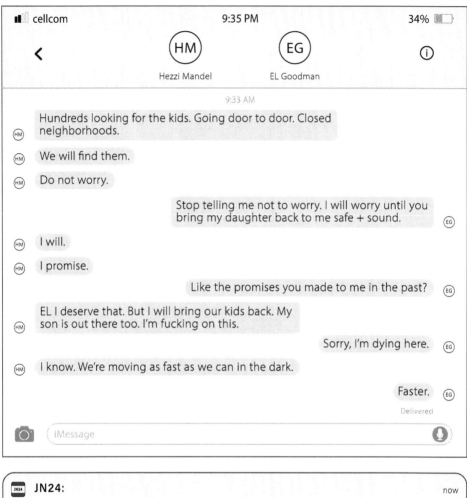

cellcom   9:35 PM   34% 🔋

HM Hezzi Mandel   **EG** EL Goodman

9:33 AM

HM: Hundreds looking for the kids. Going door to door. Closed neighborhoods.

HM: We will find them.

HM: Do not worry.

EG: Stop telling me not to worry. I will worry until you bring my daughter back to me safe + sound.

HM: I will.

HM: I promise.

EG: Like the promises you made to me in the past?

HM: EL I deserve that. But I will bring our kids back. My son is out there too. I'm fucking on this.

EG: Sorry, I'm dying here.

HM: I know. We're moving as fast as we can in the dark.

EG: Faster.

Delivered

iMessage

JN24:   now

A hotel room key found on the pavement outside El Rayouni Spice Bar in Arab Section of Jerusalem. Plastic room key could lead investigators to find the missing teenagers.
No other clues have surfaced.

Jewish News You Can Use

JN24:   now

Israel suffers a shortage of medical marijuana.

Jewish News You Can Use

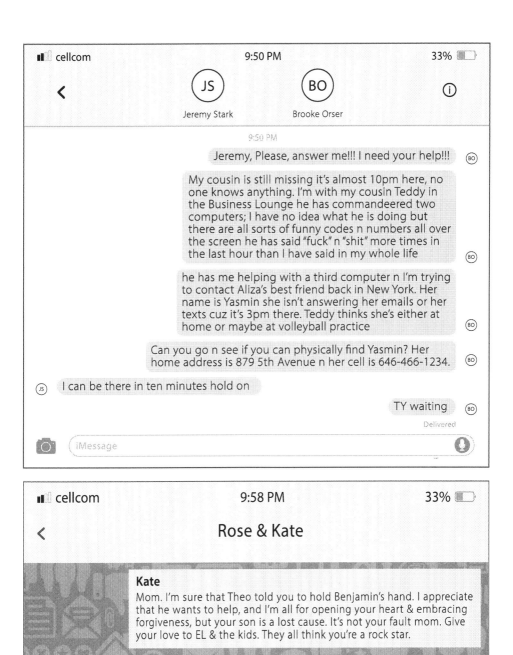

cellcom   9:50 PM   33%

(JS)   (BO)

Jeremy Stark   Brooke Orser

9:50 PM

Jeremy, Please, answer me!!! I need your help!!!

My cousin is still missing it's almost 10pm here, no one knows anything. I'm with my cousin Teddy in the Business Lounge he has commandeered two computers; I have no idea what he is doing but there are all sorts of funny codes n numbers all over the screen he has said "fuck" n "shit" more times in the last hour than I have said in my whole life

he has me helping with a third computer n I'm trying to contact Aliza's best friend back in New York. Her name is Yasmin she isn't answering her emails or her texts cuz it's 3pm there. Teddy thinks she's either at home or maybe at volleyball practice

Can you go n see if you can physically find Yasmin? Her home address is 879 5th Avenue n her cell is 646-466-1234.

I can be there in ten minutes hold on

TY waiting

Delivered

iMessage

---

cellcom   9:58 PM   33%

Rose & Kate

Kate
Mom. I'm sure that Theo told you to hold Benjamin's hand. I appreciate that he wants to help, and I'm all for opening your heart & embracing forgiveness, but your son is a lost cause. It's not your fault mom. Give your love to EL & the kids. They all think you're a rock star.

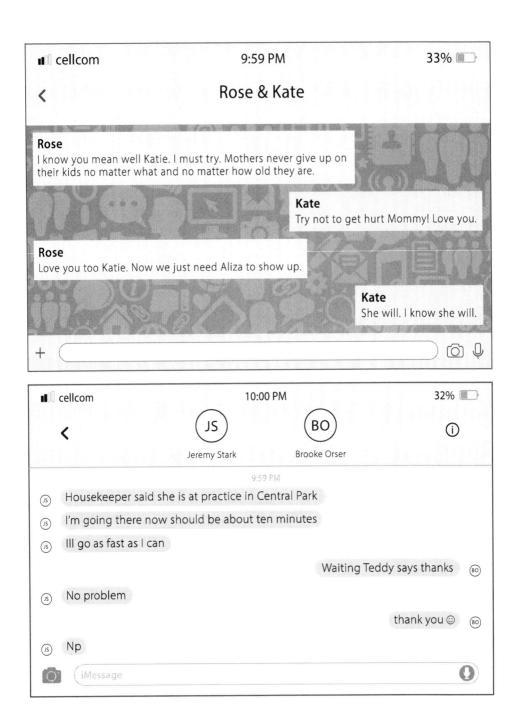

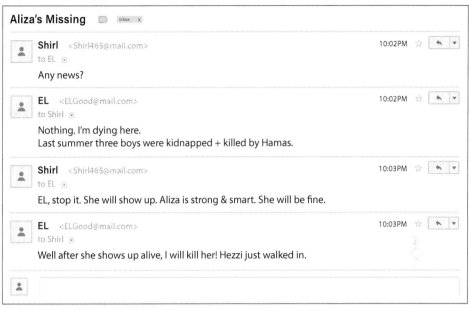

Aliza's Missing 📄 Inbox x

Shirl <Shirl465@mail.com>
to EL
10:02PM ☆ ↰ ▾

Any news?

EL <ELGood@mail.com>
to Shirl
10:02PM ☆ ↰ ▾

Nothing. I'm dying here.
Last summer three boys were kidnapped + killed by Hamas.

Shirl <Shirl465@mail.com>
to EL
10:03PM ☆ ↰ ▾

EL, stop it. She will show up. Aliza is strong & smart. She will be fine.

EL <ELGood@mail.com>
to Shirl
10:03PM ☆ ↰ ▾

Well after she shows up alive, I will kill her! Hezzi just walked in.

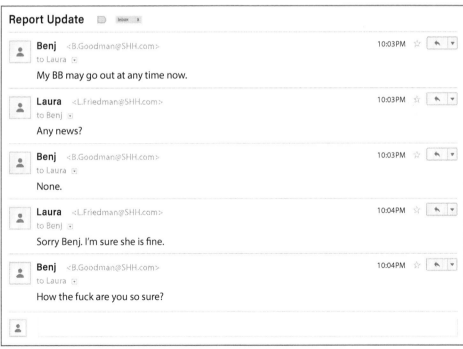

Report Update 📄 Inbox x

Benj <B.Goodman@SHH.com>
to Laura
10:03PM ☆ ↰ ▾

My BB may go out at any time now.

Laura <L.Friedman@SHH.com>
to Benj
10:03PM ☆ ↰ ▾

Any news?

Benj <B.Goodman@SHH.com>
to Laura
10:03PM ☆ ↰ ▾

None.

Laura <L.Friedman@SHH.com>
to Benj
10:04PM ☆ ↰ ▾

Sorry Benj. I'm sure she is fine.

Benj <B.Goodman@SHH.com>
to Laura
10:04PM ☆ ↰ ▾

How the fuck are you so sure?

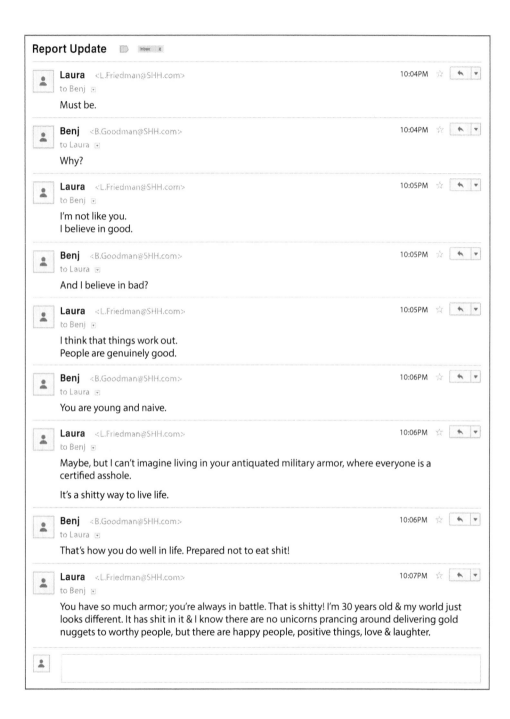

Report Update 📋 Inbox ✕

Laura <L.Friedman@SHH.com>   10:04PM ☆
to Benj

Must be.

Benj <B.Goodman@SHH.com>   10:04PM ☆
to Laura

Why?

Laura <L.Friedman@SHH.com>   10:05PM ☆
to Benj

I'm not like you.
I believe in good.

Benj <B.Goodman@SHH.com>   10:05PM ☆
to Laura

And I believe in bad?

Laura <L.Friedman@SHH.com>   10:05PM ☆
to Benj

I think that things work out.
People are genuinely good.

Benj <B.Goodman@SHH.com>   10:06PM ☆
to Laura

You are young and naive.

Laura <L.Friedman@SHH.com>   10:06PM ☆
to Benj

Maybe, but I can't imagine living in your antiquated military armor, where everyone is a certified asshole.

It's a shitty way to live life.

Benj <B.Goodman@SHH.com>   10:06PM ☆
to Laura

That's how you do well in life. Prepared not to eat shit!

Laura <L.Friedman@SHH.com>   10:07PM ☆
to Benj

You have so much armor; you're always in battle. That is shitty! I'm 30 years old & my world just looks different. It has shit in it & I know there are no unicorns prancing around delivering gold nuggets to worthy people, but there are happy people, positive things, love & laughter.

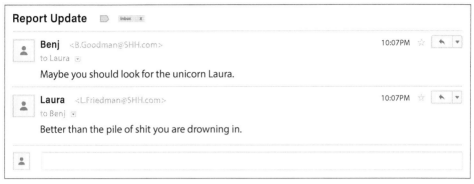

Report Update

Benj <B.Goodman@SHH.com>
to Laura

Maybe you should look for the unicorn Laura.

10:07PM

Laura <L.Friedman@SHH.com>
to Benj

Better than the pile of shit you are drowning in.

10:07PM

cellcom   10:10 PM   32%

(AG)   (BO)

Aliza Goodman   Brooke Orser

10:10 PM

Your brother just figured out that I'm Swifty he laughed at me n told me I was the biggest loser please answer me!

Delivered

iMessage

MYJOURNAL.COM

Still Missing Cont.
Roaming Roman

EL's ex-boyfriend, Mossad agent & father of missing boy came back. They found a woman who remembered seeing Aliza & Asher walking with a third teenager. All their heads were covered with scarves & she knew they were not locals, but does not know where they went. Security forces are focusing on a couple of specific neighborhoods in East Jerusalem. It appears that there is a black out in many parts of East Jerusalem as retribution for the Palestinians not paying their electric bill to the Israelis. This appears to slow down the search and cause confusion amongst the security agents.

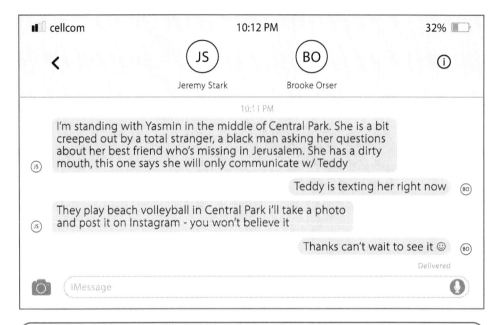

JS   **BO**   ⓘ

Jeremy Stark   Brooke Orser

10:11 PM

I'm standing with Yasmin in the middle of Central Park. She is a bit creeped out by a total stranger, a black man asking her questions about her best friend who's missing in Jerusalem. She has a dirty mouth, this one says she will only communicate w/ Teddy

Teddy is texting her right now

They play beach volleyball in Central Park i'll take a photo and post it on Instagram - you won't believe it

Thanks can't wait to see it ☺

Delivered

iMessage

JN24:   now

The missing teenagers, Aliza Goodman and Asher Mandel were photographed by security camera passing the Al Akhbar Hookah Bar in Arab Quarter wearing headdresses and large abayas.

Jewish News You Can Use

LIFEEXPRESSIONS.COM

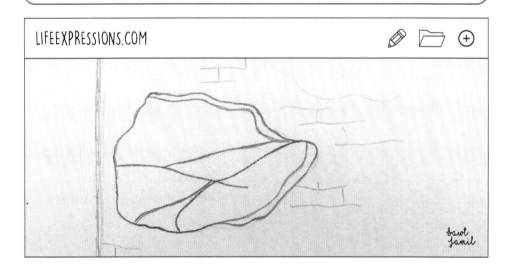

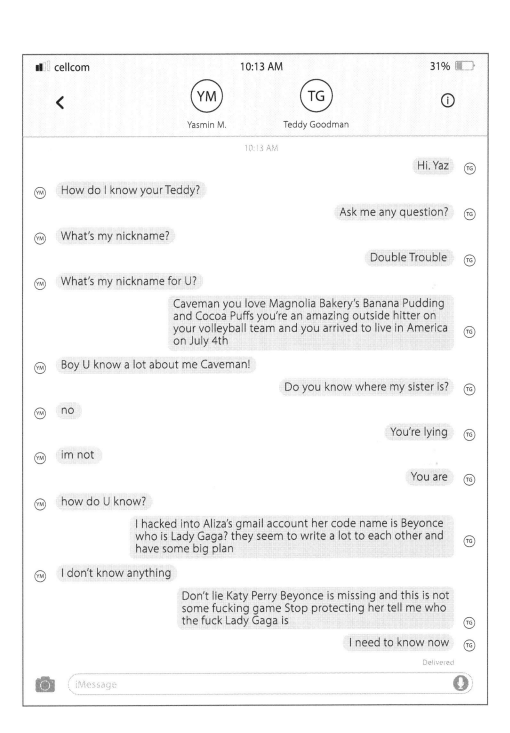

cellcom   10:13 AM   31%

YM — Yasmin M.   TG — Teddy Goodman

10:13 AM

TG: Hi. Yaz

YM: How do I know your Teddy?

TG: Ask me any question?

YM: What's my nickname?

TG: Double Trouble

YM: What's my nickname for U?

TG: Caveman you love Magnolia Bakery's Banana Pudding and Cocoa Puffs you're an amazing outside hitter on your volleyball team and you arrived to live in America on July 4th

YM: Boy U know a lot about me Caveman!

TG: Do you know where my sister is?

YM: no

TG: You're lying

YM: im not

TG: You are

YM: how do U know?

TG: I hacked into Aliza's gmail account her code name is Beyonce who is Lady Gaga? they seem to write a lot to each other and have some big plan

YM: I don't know anything

TG: Don't lie Katy Perry Beyonce is missing and this is not some fucking game Stop protecting her tell me who the fuck Lady Gaga is

TG: I need to know now

Delivered

iMessage

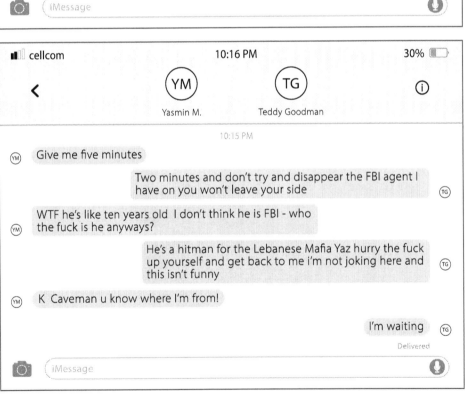

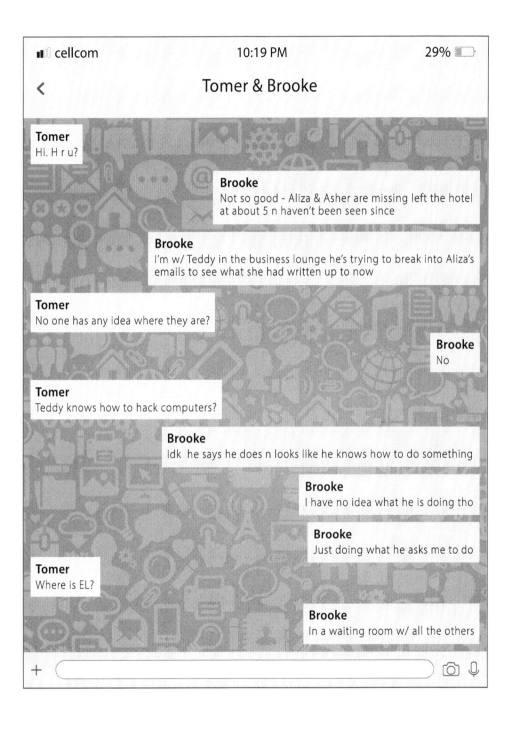

Tomer
Hi. H r u?

Brooke
Not so good - Aliza & Asher are missing left the hotel at about 5 n haven't been seen since

Brooke
I'm w/ Teddy in the business lounge he's trying to break into Aliza's emails to see what she had written up to now

Tomer
No one has any idea where they are?

Brooke
No

Tomer
Teddy knows how to hack computers?

Brooke
Idk he says he does n looks like he knows how to do something

Brooke
I have no idea what he is doing tho

Brooke
Just doing what he asks me to do

Tomer
Where is EL?

Brooke
In a waiting room w/ all the others

cellcom 10:21 PM 29%

Tomer & Brooke

Brooke
Asher's dad is leading the search but there's very little information

Brooke
A lot of waiting around it's terrible & so scary

Brooke
Maybe you are used to this being an Israeli?

Tomer
You never get used to it I wish I were there but stuck on guard duty at the base til 8am tomorrow

Brooke
I wish u were here too

Tomer
You know that Hezzi & EL almost got married when they were young?

Brooke
Aliza told me

Tomer
Weird how their kids are now missing together

Brooke
Yeah

Tomer
Text me if there is any news K?

Brooke
Of course bye

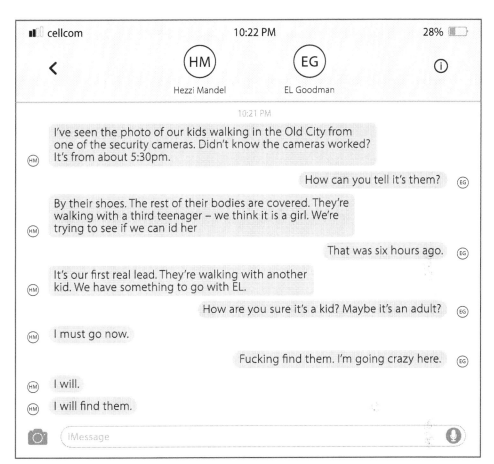

HM Hezzi Mandel   **EG** EL Goodman

10:21 PM

HM: I've seen the photo of our kids walking in the Old City from one of the security cameras. Didn't know the cameras worked? It's from about 5:30pm.

EG: How can you tell it's them?

HM: By their shoes. The rest of their bodies are covered. They're walking with a third teenager – we think it is a girl. We're trying to see if we can id her

EG: That was six hours ago.

HM: It's our first real lead. They're walking with another kid. We have something to go with EL.

EG: How are you sure it's a kid? Maybe it's an adult?

HM: I must go now.

EG: Fucking find them. I'm going crazy here.

HM: I will.

HM: I will find them.

MYJOURNAL.COM

Still Missing Cont.
Roaming Roman

Mossad Hezzi just texted EL. They have a photo of the kids walking in the Old City from earlier today. Looking to see who the 3rd teenager is? Just spoke to the writer for the Times again. Holding EL's hand as we wait. Bruno & Lucas are playing cards. No one is talking. The room is freezing cold & the only sound is the air conditioning blowing.

Andy Orser
Now · Israel

GOY IN THE HOLY LAND PART 31

Miracles do take place in the Holy Land. Kate's brother, Benj and his mother who have not been together for years are sitting here holding hands. My sister-in-law EL and her estranged brother who she has not seen in years are sitting next to each other holding hands. Kate is dozing with her head on my shoulder.

Dear Friends, thank you for sending your love and prayers for my niece's safe return. I know she will show up. She must. #miracleintheholyland

👍 Like   💬 Comment   ↗ Share

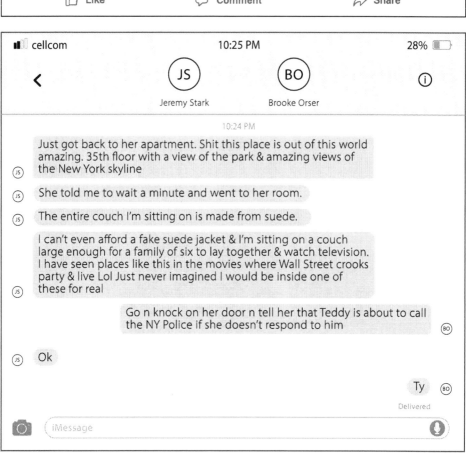

cellcom   10:25 PM   28% 🔋

JS   **BO**
Jeremy Stark   Brooke Orser

10:24 PM

Just got back to her apartment. Shit this place is out of this world amazing. 35th floor with a view of the park & amazing views of the New York skyline

She told me to wait a minute and went to her room.

The entire couch I'm sitting on is made from suede.

I can't even afford a fake suede jacket & I'm sitting on a couch large enough for a family of six to lay together & watch television. I have seen places like this in the movies where Wall Street crooks party & live Lol Just never imagined I would be inside one of these for real

Go n knock on her door n tell her that Teddy is about to call the NY Police if she doesn't respond to him

Ok

Ty

Delivered

iMessage

354

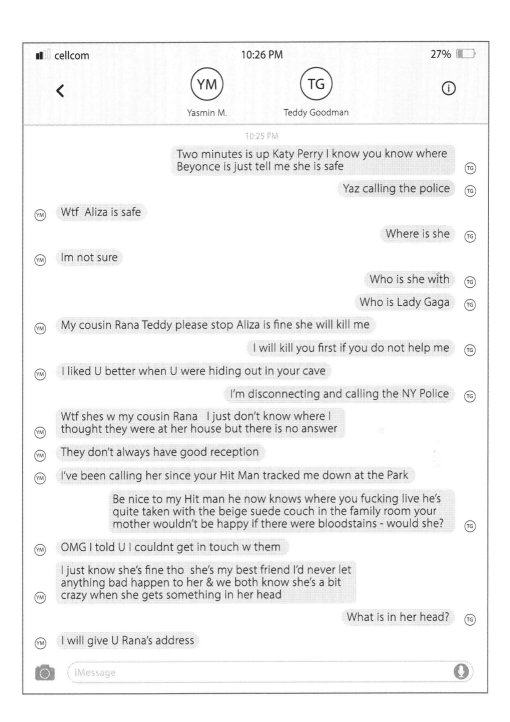

YM   TG

Yasmin M.   Teddy Goodman

10:25 PM

Two minutes is up Katy Perry I know you know where Beyonce is just tell me she is safe

Yaz calling the police

Wtf Aliza is safe

Where is she

Im not sure

Who is she with

Who is Lady Gaga

My cousin Rana Teddy please stop Aliza is fine she will kill me

I will kill you first if you do not help me

I liked U better when U were hiding out in your cave

I'm disconnecting and calling the NY Police

Wtf shes w my cousin Rana   I just don't know where I thought they were at her house but there is no answer

They don't always have good reception

I've been calling her since your Hit Man tracked me down at the Park

Be nice to my Hit man he now knows where you fucking live he's quite taken with the beige suede couch in the family room your mother wouldn't be happy if there were bloodstains - would she?

OMG I told U I couldnt get in touch w them

I just know she's fine tho she's my best friend I'd never let anything bad happen to her & we both know she's a bit crazy when she gets something in her head

What is in her head?

I will give U Rana's address

iMessage

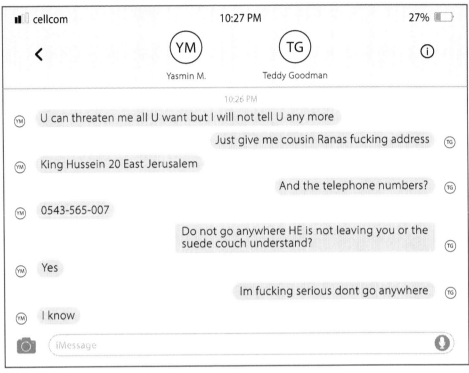

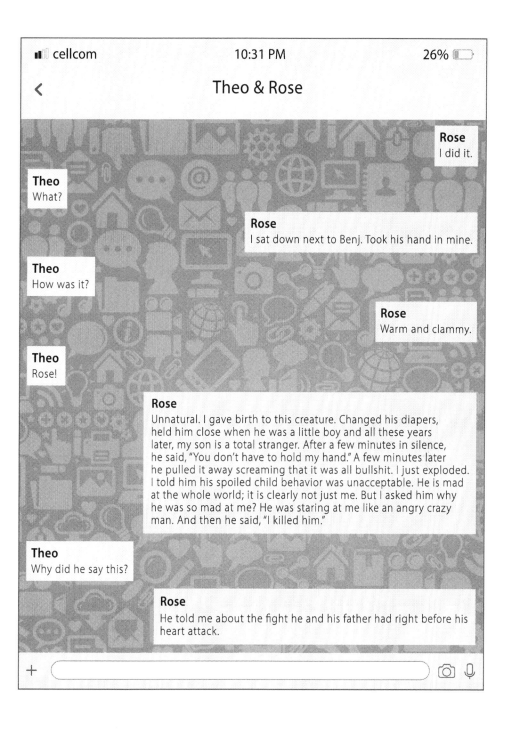

Theo & Rose

Rose
I did it.

Theo
What?

Rose
I sat down next to Benj. Took his hand in mine.

Theo
How was it?

Rose
Warm and clammy.

Theo
Rose!

Rose
Unnatural. I gave birth to this creature. Changed his diapers, held him close when he was a little boy and all these years later, my son is a total stranger. After a few minutes in silence, he said, "You don't have to hold my hand." A few minutes later he pulled it away screaming that it was all bullshit. I just exploded. I told him his spoiled child behavior was unacceptable. He is mad at the whole world; it is clearly not just me. But I asked him why he was so mad at me? He was staring at me like an angry crazy man. And then he said, "I killed him."

Theo
Why did he say this?

Rose
He told me about the fight he and his father had right before his heart attack.

357

Theo & Rose

Rose
He threatened Wayne to tell me the truth that he literally caught his father in bed with one of the actresses in the movie he was directing that summer. Wayne was furious. He forbade Benj from telling me anything. Benj held it for a couple of months; He went to his dad and said he could no longer keep the secret. Wayne and Benj had a huge blow out the day before the heart attack. My son has held this in for 30 years. I thought all this time the fight was over too much partying and bad grades. Regular teenage stuff – I could never have imagined. But he kept this secret all these years.

Theo
But you knew Wayne was unfaithful.

Rose
Yes. His nickname was Whip it out Wayne. I learned about his infidelity years earlier, but I had small children and decided to stay in the marriage. I always believed Wayne loved the kids and me. He took care of us; he just couldn't contain himself with pretty actresses. And they with him, the goodlooking Hollywood film director. It was all so cliché! I didn't see a reason to tell the kids after his death that their father was a cheater. They had him for so few years, I figured why spoil what they thought they had. He was dead, telling them would not have changed their father. He died of a heart attack like his father before him. At that time is was best to just move on.

Theo
Are you okay Rosie?

Rose
I guess. Did I make a mistake?

Theo
No, you did not.

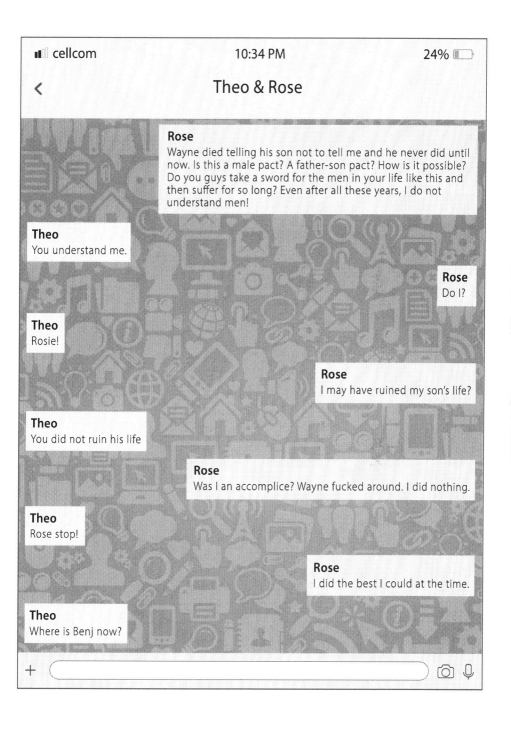

Theo & Rose

Rose
Wayne died telling his son not to tell me and he never did until now. Is this a male pact? A father-son pact? How is it possible? Do you guys take a sword for the men in your life like this and then suffer for so long? Even after all these years, I do not understand men!

Theo
You understand me.

Rose
Do I?

Theo
Rosie!

Rose
I may have ruined my son's life?

Theo
You did not ruin his life

Rose
Was I an accomplice? Wayne fucked around. I did nothing.

Theo
Rose stop!

Rose
I did the best I could at the time.

Theo
Where is Benj now?

Theo & Rose

Rose
He left the waiting room. It is terrible in here. So quiet and so tense. What if something bad happened to Aliza?

Theo
She will be fine. You must be positive.

Rose
I wish you were here next to me. I cannot be alone anymore. I need you with me always. Promise me!

Theo
I promise you

Theo
Who is there with you?

Rose
Kate and Andy are playing cards with Lucas. Bruno looks like he is praying. EL and Ethan are outside again

Theo
Go & sit with the others. Do not sit alone.

Rose
Ok. Don't go far. I will text again soon.

Theo
I love you Rosie.

Rose
I love you Theo.

> **JN24:**   now
>
> Two teenagers missing in West Bank feared to have fallen into the hands of
> Islamic terrorists. They have not been heard from in hours. Authorities have
> few clues in their disappearance. Anyone who has information on these
> teeangers is asked to call the local police immediately - 611.
>
> *Jewish News You Can Use*

Report Update ▶ inbox ×

👤	**Benj** <B.Goodman@SHH.com> to Laura ▾	10:58PM ☆ ↰ ▾

Still no sign of Aliza.

| 👤 | **Laura** <L.Friedman@SHH.com>
to Benj ▾ | 10:58PM ☆ ↰ ▾ |

I'm sorry.

| 👤 | **Benj** <B.Goodman@SHH.com>
to Laura ▾ | 10:59PM ☆ ↰ ▾ |

Thanks.

| 👤 | **Laura** <L.Friedman@SHH.com>
to Benj ▾ | 10:59PM ☆ ↰ ▾ |

Where are you?

| 👤 | **Benj** <B.Goodman@SHH.com>
to Laura ▾ | 10:59PM ☆ ↰ ▾ |

I'm at the hotel bar. Jus had a drink - well, two drinks. Jus had blow out with my mother. We
havnt talked in 30 years.

| 👤 | **Laura** <L.Friedman@SHH.com>
to Benj ▾ | 10:59PM ☆ ↰ ▾ |

Why?

| 👤 | **Benj** <B.Goodman@SHH.com>
to Laura ▾ | 10:59PM ☆ ↰ ▾ |

We have had the polite - Hi. Hi. How are yu? Fine. How are you - conversations? This it is. Nothing
important has been said cuz.

| 👤 | **Laura** <L.Friedman@SHH.com>
to Benj ▾ | 10:59PM ☆ ↰ ▾ |

Because?

| 👤 | | |

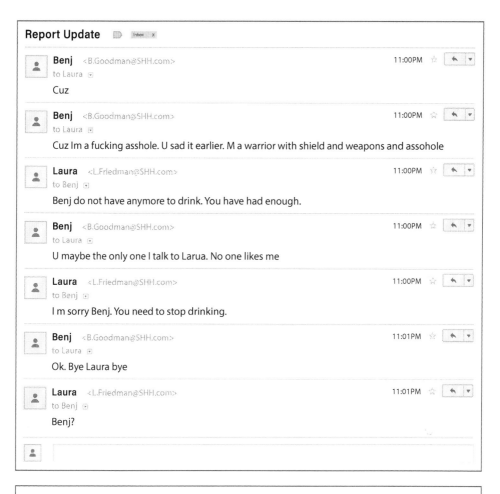

Report Update ✉ Inbox ×

Benj <B.Goodman@SHH.com>   11:00PM ☆ ↩ ▾
to Laura ▾

Cuz

Benj <B.Goodman@SHH.com>   11:00PM ☆ ↩ ▾
to Laura ▾

Cuz Im a fucking asshole. U sad it earlier. M a warrior with shield and weapons and assohole

Laura <L.Friedman@SHH.com>   11:00PM ☆ ↩ ▾
to Benj ▾

Benj do not have anymore to drink. You have had enough.

Benj <B.Goodman@SHH.com>   11:00PM ☆ ↩ ▾
to Laura ▾

U maybe the only one I talk to Larua. No one likes me

Laura <L.Friedman@SHH.com>   11:00PM ☆ ↩ ▾
to Benj ▾

I m sorry Benj. You need to stop drinking.

Benj <B.Goodman@SHH.com>   11:01PM ☆ ↩ ▾
to Laura ▾

Ok. Bye Laura bye

Laura <L.Friedman@SHH.com>   11:01PM ☆ ↩ ▾
to Benj ▾

Benj?

Jack Billings' Notes

Aliza Sophia Goodman disappeared in Jerusalem this evening
with a friend, Asher Mandel from a local kibbutz. These two
13-year-olds set out to take photos and visit the Jewish
section of the Old City and have not been heard from since.
There is an extensive manhunt taking place with police going
house to house in the neighborhood where they are believed
to have gone missing. The ground search has been complicated

Jack Billings' Notes Cont.

by a black out in East Jerusalem. Aliza Goodman comes from New York City and is in Israel to celebrate her bat mitzvah tomorrow at the Davidson Center with her family from New York, Los Angeles, and Rome, Italy. She is a smart, beautiful teenager who loves hip-hop dance; she is a straight A student who her family describes as outgoing and thoughtful. She went missing with Asher Mandel of Kibbutz Hatzor, whose father is a former Mossad agent. Asher loves soccer and is involved in the young Zionist Scouts. Both families are concerned as neither child has a history of running away or delinquency.

Aliza's Missing   inbox x

Shirl <Shirl465@mail.com>   11:21PM ☆ ↩ ▾
to EL ▾

Molly heard from the senator's chief of staff that the State Department is tracking Aliza's disappearance. It's too early for them to make a public statement on her disappearance.

Andy Orser   •••
Now · Israel

GOY IN THE HOLY LAND PART 32

We still have no news about my niece Aliza's whereabouts. Hundreds of police are looking for her in Jerusalem. There are very few clues. It is as if she vanished in thin air. News reports suspect foul play and report on possible Islamic terrorist cells that could be involved. I keep thinking about the kind Arab vendor in the market who a few hours ago asked me not to blame the Arabs. Did he know something or was just accustomed to the system of blame in this region?

Dear Friends, Everyone I have met here - Israeli Jews and Israeli Arabs - are so nice. The reality on the street is incongruent with the news report. For now, the focus is on getting Aliza back and everyone is looking together. #Helpusfindliza #JewsandArabs #peaceandcoexistence

👍 Like   💬 Comment   ↪ Share

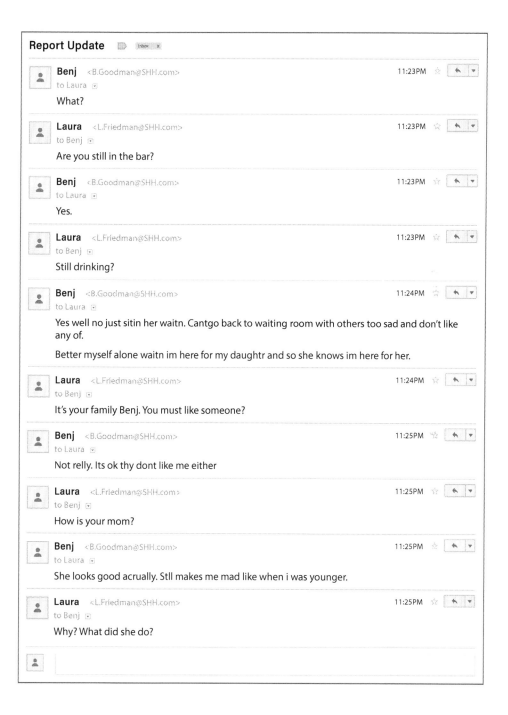

Report Update 📁 Inbox x

Benj <B.Goodman@SHH.com>   11:23PM ☆ ↰ ▾
to Laura ▾

What?

Laura <L.Friedman@SHH.com>   11:23PM ☆ ↰ ▾
to Benj ▾

Are you still in the bar?

Benj <B.Goodman@SHH.com>   11:23PM ☆ ↰ ▾
to Laura ▾

Yes.

Laura <L.Friedman@SHH.com>   11:23PM ☆ ↰ ▾
to Benj ▾

Still drinking?

Benj <B.Goodman@SHH.com>   11:24PM ☆ ↰ ▾
to Laura ▾

Yes well no just sitin her waitn. Cantgo back to waiting room with others too sad and don't like any of.

Better myself alone waitn im here for my daughtr and so she knows im here for her.

Laura <L.Friedman@SHH.com>   11:24PM ☆ ↰ ▾
to Benj ▾

It's your family Benj. You must like someone?

Benj <B.Goodman@SHH.com>   11:25PM ☆ ↰ ▾
to Laura ▾

Not relly. Its ok thy dont like me either

Laura <L.Friedman@SHH.com>   11:25PM ☆ ↰ ▾
to Benj ▾

How is your mom?

Benj <B.Goodman@SHH.com>   11:25PM ☆ ↰ ▾
to Laura ▾

She looks good acrually. Stll makes me mad like when i was younger.

Laura <L.Friedman@SHH.com>   11:25PM ☆ ↰ ▾
to Benj ▾

Why? What did she do?

👤

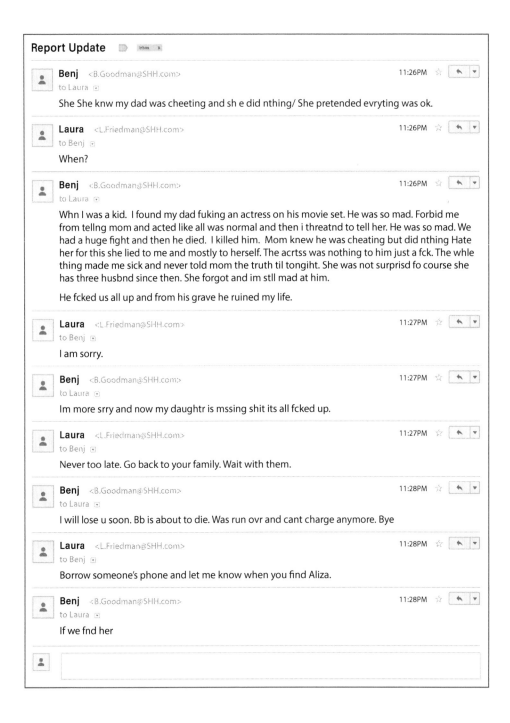

Report Update — Inbox x

Benj <B.Goodman@SHH.com>   11:26PM
to Laura
She She knw my dad was cheeting and sh e did nthing/ She pretended evryting was ok.

Laura <L.Friedman@SHH.com>   11:26PM
to Benj
When?

Benj <B.Goodman@SHH.com>   11:26PM
to Laura
Whn I was a kid. I found my dad fuking an actress on his movie set. He was so mad. Forbid me from tellng mom and acted like all was normal and then i threatnd to tell her. He was so mad. We had a huge fight and then he died. I killed him. Mom knew he was cheating but did nthing Hate her for this she lied to me and mostly to herself. The acrtss was nothing to him just a fck. The whle thing made me sick and never told mom the truth til tongiht. She was not surprisd fo course she has three husbnd since then. She forgot and im stll mad at him.

He fcked us all up and from his grave he ruined my life.

Laura <L.Friedman@SHH.com>   11:27PM
to Benj
I am sorry.

Benj <B.Goodman@SHH.com>   11:27PM
to Laura
Im more srry and now my daughtr is mssing shit its all fcked up.

Laura <L.Friedman@SHH.com>   11:27PM
to Benj
Never too late. Go back to your family. Wait with them.

Benj <B.Goodman@SHH.com>   11:28PM
to Laura
I will lose u soon. Bb is about to die. Was run ovr and cant charge anymore. Bye

Laura <L.Friedman@SHH.com>   11:28PM
to Benj
Borrow someone's phone and let me know when you find Aliza.

Benj <B.Goodman@SHH.com>   11:28PM
to Laura
If we fnd her

Report Update Inbox x

Laura <L.Friedman@SHH.com> 11:29PM
to Benj

I don't care how much you have had to drink or how sad you feel, don't say IF.

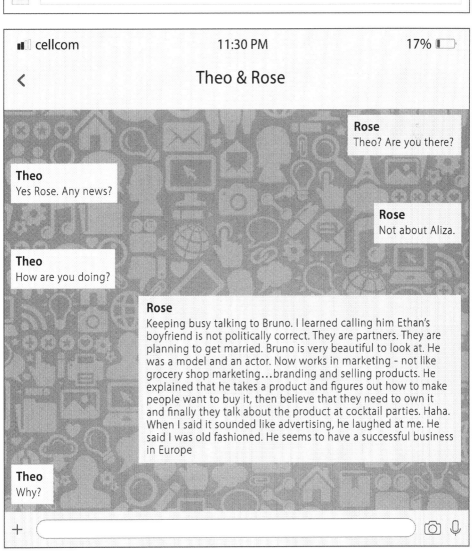

cellcom 11:30 PM 17%

Theo & Rose

Rose
Theo? Are you there?

Theo
Yes Rose. Any news?

Rose
Not about Aliza.

Theo
How are you doing?

Rose
Keeping busy talking to Bruno. I learned calling him Ethan's boyfriend is not politically correct. They are partners. They are planning to get married. Bruno is very beautiful to look at. He was a model and an actor. Now works in marketing - not like grocery shop marketing...branding and selling products. He explained that he takes a product and figures out how to make people want to buy it, then believe that they need to own it and finally they talk about the product at cocktail parties. Haha. When I said it sounded like advertising, he laughed at me. He said I was old fashioned. He seems to have a successful business in Europe

Theo
Why?

Rose
Marketing is much bigger and can sell things to more people like a whole country or the whole world at one time. His company sells products to all of Italy and all of Europe. Not on paper, but all on the computer. But this is not the most important thing I learned.

Theo
What?

Rose
He told me all about how Ethan and he met on a photo shoot in Rome. They were first friends for a long time and were both with other partners. Slowly they fell in love. It is very sweet. They are crazy in love. I may be old, but love is love and I do not care if it is two men or two women. I watch EL and Benj who are supposed to be a traditional couple and they hate each other. Ethan and Bruno are so kind to each other. Kate and Andy are also so caring for each other and I have you. I know it is possible. But there is more I learned.

Theo
More than how lovely real love is? You cannot live without me?

Rose
I learned why Ethan left home and disappeared.

Theo
How we are soulmates?

Rose
When Ethan was eighteen, his father found him with another boy and discovered that his son was gay. He demanded that he stop being with men or he would consider him dead. Ethan and his dad never got along, but this was the tipping point for his departure from their family. I am not sure that EL even knows this. Bruno swore it was the truth, as I could not believe that EL's father would do this.

‹   Theo & Rose

Rose
Ethan tried for years to get back in through his mom, but other than phone calls, he was never allowed to come home as a gay man. He attended both of his parents' funerals, but this is the first that Ethan has spent time with EL since he left home at eighteen.

Theo
Your family is complicated Rosie.

Rose
You will not run away?

Theo
I'm in love with you Rose. I am running to you not away from you. I love you more each day even when you are away from me.

Rose
Thank you. I needed to hear that.

Theo
I will be telling this to you for eternity.

Rose
I better go. I will write you later. I needed this break.

Rose
Thank you.

Theo
You're welcome.

Rose
Bye my love

+ ⟨   ⟩ 📷 🎤

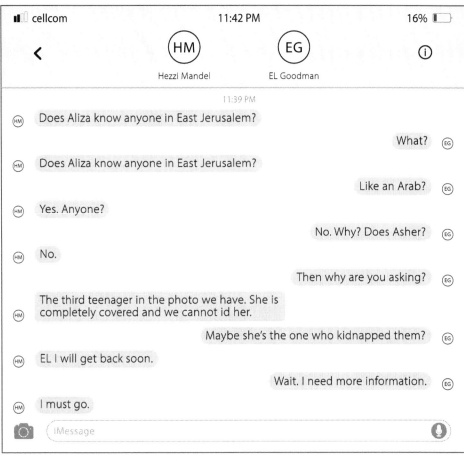

HM Hezzi Mandel **EG** EL Goodman

11:39 PM

HM Does Aliza know anyone in East Jerusalem?

What? **EG**

HM Does Aliza know anyone in East Jerusalem?

Like an Arab? **EG**

HM Yes. Anyone?

No. Why? Does Asher? **EG**

HM No.

Then why are you asking? **EG**

HM The third teenager in the photo we have. She is completely covered and we cannot id her.

Maybe she's the one who kidnapped them? **EG**

HM EL I will get back soon.

Wait. I need more information. **EG**

HM I must go.

iMessage

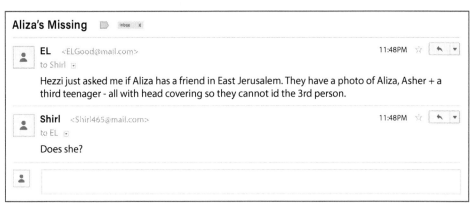

Aliza's Missing Inbox x

EL <ELGood@mail.com> 11:48PM
to Shirl

Hezzi just asked me if Aliza has a friend in East Jerusalem. They have a photo of Aliza, Asher + a third teenager - all with head covering so they cannot id the 3rd person.

Shirl <Shirl465@mail.com> 11:48PM
to EL

Does she?

Aliza's Missing 📨 Inbox ✕

EL <ELGood@mail.com>   11:49PM ☆ ↰ ▾
to Shirl ▾

Aliza has never been to East Jerusalem. The last time we were in Israel she was little.

Shirl <Shirl465@mail.com>   11:49PM ☆ ↰ ▾
to EL ▾

Maybe she met someone on-line? A predator who discovered that she was coming to Israel + has taken her?

EL <ELGood@mail.com>   11:50PM ☆ ↰ ▾
to Shirl ▾

Shit Shirl. She is not that stupid.

Shirl <Shirl465@mail.com>   11:50PM ☆ ↰ ▾
to EL ▾

Teenagers don't look at the Internet as a dangerous place where they can get in trouble. There are no boundaries & no rules. It is full of crazies.

EL <ELGood@mail.com>   11:51PM ☆ ↰ ▾
to Shirl ▾

You're freaking me out.

Shirl <Shirl465@mail.com>   11:51PM ☆ ↰ ▾
to EL ▾

Are you sure she hasn't been surfing the net & been enticed into some network that feeds on naive teenagers? There are many stories of ISIS doing this.

EL <ELGood@mail.com>   11:51PM ☆ ↰ ▾
to Shirl ▾

Stop.

I know you mean well, but don't keep going. I should go back inside.

Ethan is here with me outside hovering + making up for 30 years in 30 minutes. It's like speed dating. I should be grateful but he's freaking me out too. Everything is. Bye.

Shirl <Shirl465@mail.com>   11:51PM ☆ ↰ ▾
to EL ▾

Bye. Sorry if I freaked you out more. :-) XOME

EL <ELGood@mail.com>   11:51PM ☆ ↰ ▾
to Shirl ▾

xo

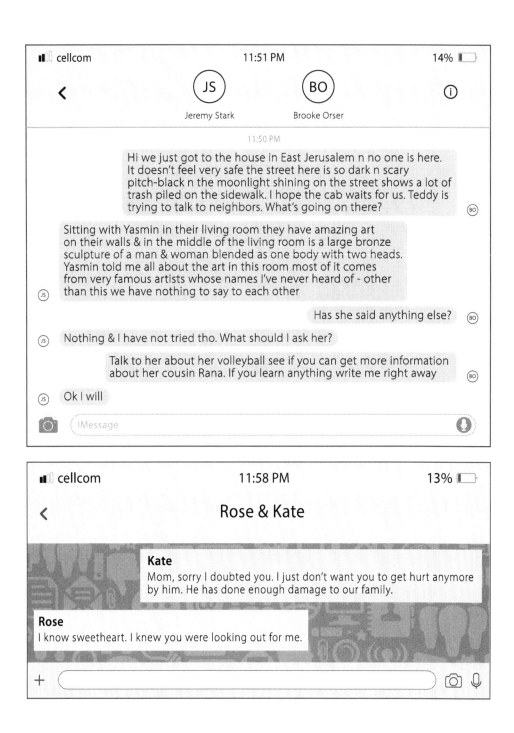

cellcom 11:51 PM 14%

JS — Jeremy Stark

BO — Brooke Orser

11:50 PM

Hi we just got to the house in East Jerusalem n no one is here. It doesn't feel very safe the street here is so dark n scary pitch-black n the moonlight shining on the street shows a lot of trash piled on the sidewalk. I hope the cab waits for us. Teddy is trying to talk to neighbors. What's going on there?

Sitting with Yasmin in their living room they have amazing art on their walls & in the middle of the living room is a large bronze sculpture of a man & woman blended as one body with two heads. Yasmin told me all about the art in this room most of it comes from very famous artists whose names I've never heard of - other than this we have nothing to say to each other

Has she said anything else?

Nothing & I have not tried tho. What should I ask her?

Talk to her about her volleyball see if you can get more information about her cousin Rana. If you learn anything write me right away

Ok I will

iMessage

---

cellcom 11:58 PM 13%

Rose & Kate

Kate
Mom, sorry I doubted you. I just don't want you to get hurt anymore by him. He has done enough damage to our family.

Rose
I know sweetheart. I knew you were looking out for me.

374

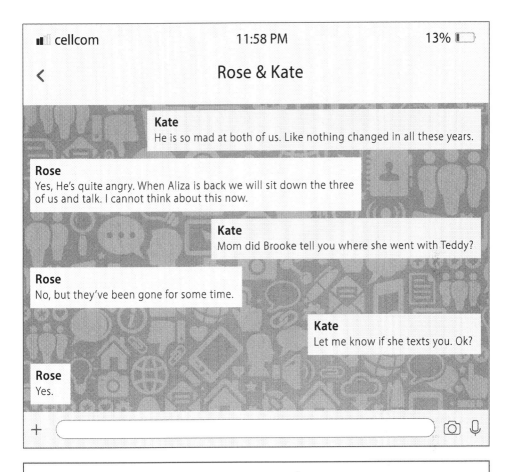

Kate
He is so mad at both of us. Like nothing changed in all these years.

Rose
Yes, He's quite angry. When Aliza is back we will sit down the three of us and talk. I cannot think about this now.

Kate
Mom did Brooke tell you where she went with Teddy?

Rose
No, but they've been gone for some time.

Kate
Let me know if she texts you. Ok?

Rose
Yes.

Jack Billings' Notes

This has been a relatively calm period in East Jerusalem over the last few months. Today's disappearance of Aliza Goodman + Asher Mandel is shocking. Police and security are going door to door looking for these two young people. The hotel lobby is full of tourists from all over the world coming and going out for the evening. I just received a text from the missing teenager Aliza Goodman's uncle to join their family in the waiting room.

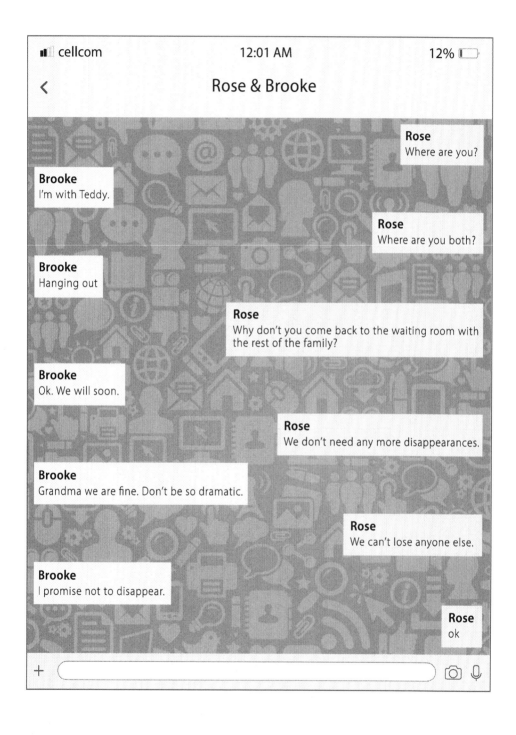

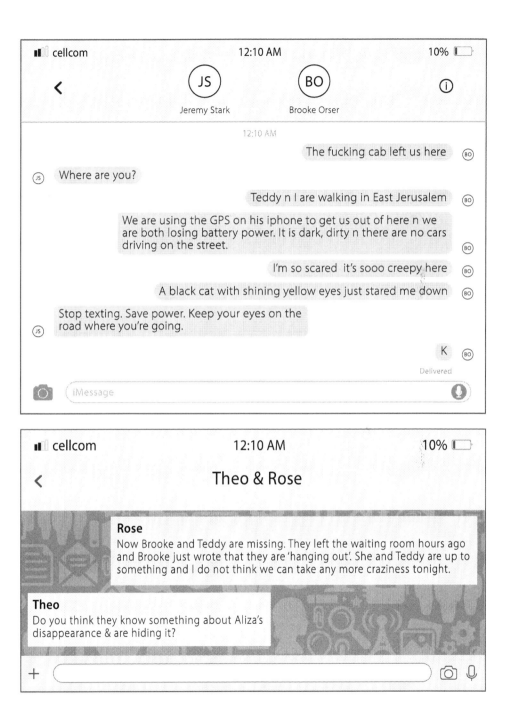

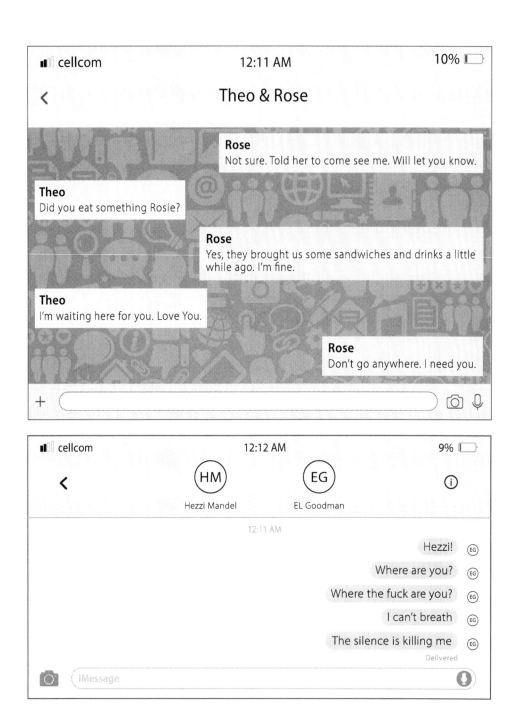

Aliza's Missing

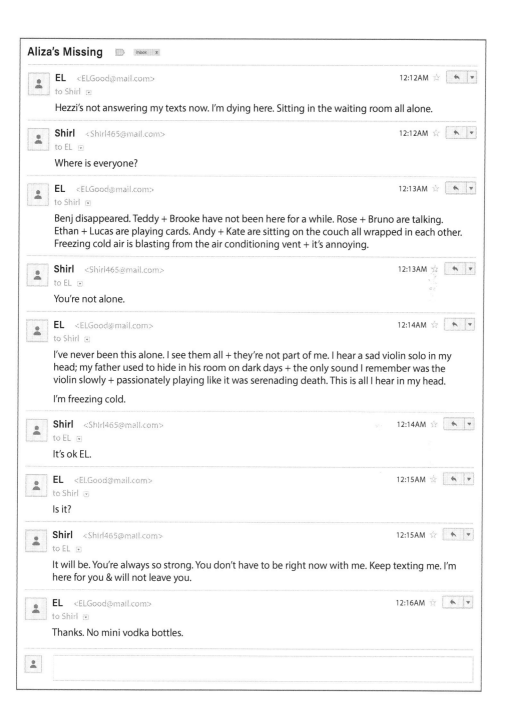

EL <ELGood@mail.com>
to Shirl
12:12AM

Hezzi's not answering my texts now. I'm dying here. Sitting in the waiting room all alone.

Shirl <Shirl465@mail.com>
to EL
12:12AM

Where is everyone?

EL <ELGood@mail.com>
to Shirl
12:13AM

Benj disappeared. Teddy + Brooke have not been here for a while. Rose + Bruno are talking. Ethan + Lucas are playing cards. Andy + Kate are sitting on the couch all wrapped in each other. Freezing cold air is blasting from the air conditioning vent + it's annoying.

Shirl <Shirl465@mail.com>
to EL
12:13AM

You're not alone.

EL <ELGood@mail.com>
to Shirl
12:14AM

I've never been this alone. I see them all + they're not part of me. I hear a sad violin solo in my head; my father used to hide in his room on dark days + the only sound I remember was the violin slowly + passionately playing like it was serenading death. This is all I hear in my head.

I'm freezing cold.

Shirl <Shirl465@mail.com>
to EL
12:14AM

It's ok EL.

EL <ELGood@mail.com>
to Shirl
12:15AM

Is it?

Shirl <Shirl465@mail.com>
to EL
12:15AM

It will be. You're always so strong. You don't have to be right now with me. Keep texting me. I'm here for you & will not leave you.

EL <ELGood@mail.com>
to Shirl
12:16AM

Thanks. No mini vodka bottles.

Aliza's Missing

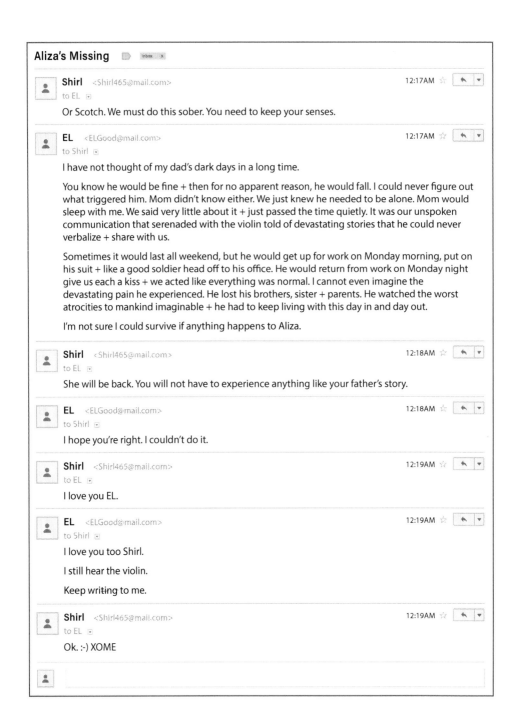

Shirl <Shirl465@mail.com>
to EL

12:17AM

Or Scotch. We must do this sober. You need to keep your senses.

EL <ELGood@mail.com>
to Shirl

12:17AM

I have not thought of my dad's dark days in a long time.

You know he would be fine + then for no apparent reason, he would fall. I could never figure out what triggered him. Mom didn't know either. We just knew he needed to be alone. Mom would sleep with me. We said very little about it + just passed the time quietly. It was our unspoken communication that serenaded with the violin told of devastating stories that he could never verbalize + share with us.

Sometimes it would last all weekend, but he would get up for work on Monday morning, put on his suit + like a good soldier head off to his office. He would return from work on Monday night give us each a kiss + we acted like everything was normal. I cannot even imagine the devastating pain he experienced. He lost his brothers, sister + parents. He watched the worst atrocities to mankind imaginable + he had to keep living with this day in and day out.

I'm not sure I could survive if anything happens to Aliza.

Shirl <Shirl465@mail.com>
to EL

12:18AM

She will be back. You will not have to experience anything like your father's story.

EL <ELGood@mail.com>
to Shirl

12:18AM

I hope you're right. I couldn't do it.

Shirl <Shirl465@mail.com>
to EL

12:19AM

I love you EL.

EL <ELGood@mail.com>
to Shirl

12:19AM

I love you too Shirl.

I still hear the violin.

Keep writing to me.

Shirl <Shirl465@mail.com>
to EL

12:19AM

Ok. :-) XOME

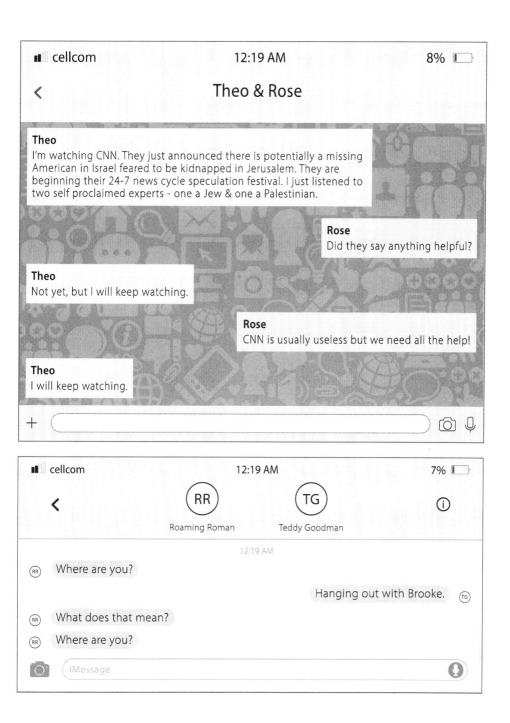

Theo
I'm watching CNN. They just announced there is potentially a missing American in Israel feared to be kidnapped in Jerusalem. They are beginning their 24-7 news cycle speculation festival. I just listened to two self proclaimed experts - one a Jew & one a Palestinian.

Rose
Did they say anything helpful?

Theo
Not yet, but I will keep watching.

Rose
CNN is usually useless but we need all the help!

Theo
I will keep watching.

Roaming Roman Teddy Goodman

12:19 AM

Where are you?

Hanging out with Brooke.

What does that mean?

Where are you?

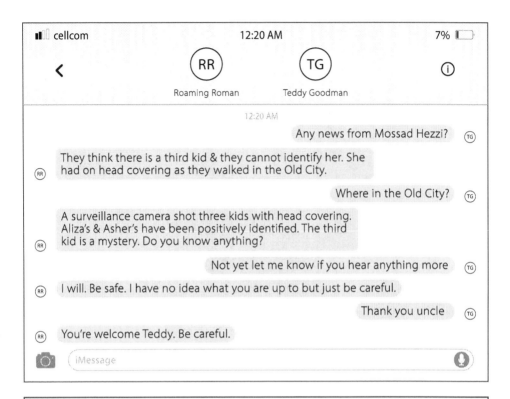

Jack Billings' Notes

I am sitting in the waiting room with Aliza Goodman's family: A strong and united family - three generations - all with great hope that Aliza will return shortly. Aliza has been missing for seven hours and they have not had any word from her or anyone related to her disappearance. The Goodman family is in Israel to celebrate Aliza's bat mitzvah tomorrow after a week of touring the Holy Land. Aliza's Grandfather Yacov Bernard arrived in Israel in 1948. Prior to his internment at Auschwitz-Birkenau during World War II, he was a resident of the Lodtz Getto. He survived by his nimble and wise character; his whole family perished in concentration camps. He came to Israel where he met his wife Shula Benjamin, an Iraqi immigrant. The Iraqi Jews departed in a mass exodus in 1950 and arrived in Israel first occupying immigrant camps and then assimilating into Israeli society. Aliza's grandfather an Ashkenazi Polish Jew and her grandmother a Sephardic Iraqi Jew were married on the kibbutz where they worked for a few years helping build the foundation of the young Jewish Nation until they immigrated to the United States in the late in 1950s. They settled in New York and raised their American children with strong ties to their Israeli family.

---

cellcom 12:21 AM 6%

JS Jeremy Stark   **BO** Brooke Orser   ⓘ

12:18 AM

JS Where are you?

> We just left East Jerusalem n are back in West Jerusalem. have 6% and Teddy has 5% battery. **BO**

> we are dying **BO**

JS Did you have to go through security?

> no we crossed a street lol **BO**

JS That's it? No guards?

> none! did Yasmin tell U anything? **BO**

JS She is from Beirut. She speaks Arabic French & takes Spanish in school. She came to New York in 4th grade & became friends with Aliza. She said Aliza was the only girl in the class to even say hi to her the day she arrived at school. Since then they are best friends & debate partners, she keeps saying she won't throw Aliza under the bus...She'll take a sword for her...She is obsessed with metaphors & dramatic quotes

iMessage

JS
Jeremy Stark

BO
Brooke Orser

12:21 AM

She's very clever but I think she isn't clear where Aliza is. She believed that they were at her cousin's home her eyes had a look of shock when I told her you went there & no one was home

Anything else?

All her family left Beirut in the last ten years. No one is left there so they haven't gone back. She has family in Geneva, London & New York. She and Aliza are debate partners & they were league champions last year at school. She plays volleyball on a traveling team like you, i'm sure she is good she's very intense!

Oh, one more thing, the cousin in East Jerusalem - Lady Gaga - is the daughter of Yasmin's dad's older sister who left Beirut when she was very young & married a Palestinian chef. They have two older boys then Lady Gaga. This family has a restaurant in Jerusalem & the whole family works there

What else?

I'm not a reporter like you Brooke. Doing the best I can here with this highly charged 13-year-old Lebanese American Volleyball Princess.

Are you saying I'm intense?

Well...

We'll deal w this later

Im sure we will

LOL

Yes...thanks for ur help

bye

Ty

Delivered

iMessage

Theo & Rose

Rose

Mossad Hezzi is on his way back to the hotel. This waiting is so painful. The room is freezing. Lucas is asleep on the floor in the corner of the room. They brought us some blankets so I covered him. He looks so peaceful and we are awake and anything but peaceful.

I am sitting on the small couch and EL came in with a red face and looked at me with such sadness. I smiled at her. She just came over, sat down next to me and layed her head on my shoulder. She just cried and cried. I held her so close and we both sat there and said nothing. Keeping warm and trying to feel secure under the circumstances. She just went to the bathroom with Kate.

Theo

CNN just reported that they have a lead in the disappearance. They said they have photo of three kids fully covered walking in the Old City. They believe them to be somewhere in the area & not having left as was earlier reported.

Rose

We saw the photo as well. They are trying to figure out who the third kid is? It is difficult as they are fully covered and only their shoes are showing!

Theo

Does Aliza know anyone else in Israel?

Rose

No. But maybe her friend did. Hezzi's son.

Theo

You told me that Aliza had shared that she had a streak for adventure & wanted to make a change in the world. Maybe she is up to something & is hiding to do a secret mission?

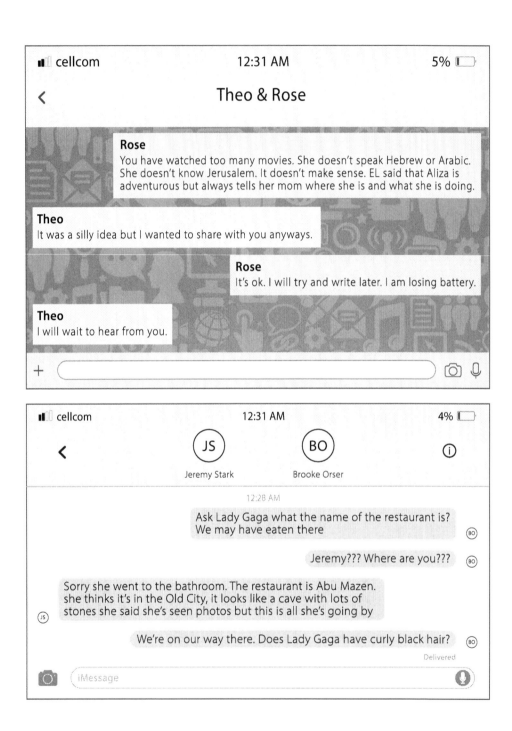

Rose
You have watched too many movies. She doesn't speak Hebrew or Arabic. She doesn't know Jerusalem. It doesn't make sense. EL said that Aliza is adventurous but always tells her mom where she is and what she is doing.

Theo
It was a silly idea but I wanted to share with you anyways.

Rose
It's ok. I will try and write later. I am losing battery.

Theo
I will wait to hear from you.

---

cellcom 12:31 AM 4%

JS — Jeremy Stark   BO — Brooke Orser

12:28 AM

Ask Lady Gaga what the name of the restaurant is? We may have eaten there

Jeremy??? Where are you???

Sorry she went to the bathroom. The restaurant is Abu Mazen. she thinks it's in the Old City, it looks like a cave with lots of stones she said she's seen photos but this is all she's going by

We're on our way there. Does Lady Gaga have curly black hair?

Delivered

iMessage

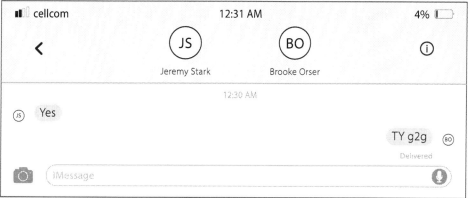

JS — Jeremy Stark   BO — Brooke Orser

12:30 AM

JS Yes

TY g2g BO

Delivered

iMessage

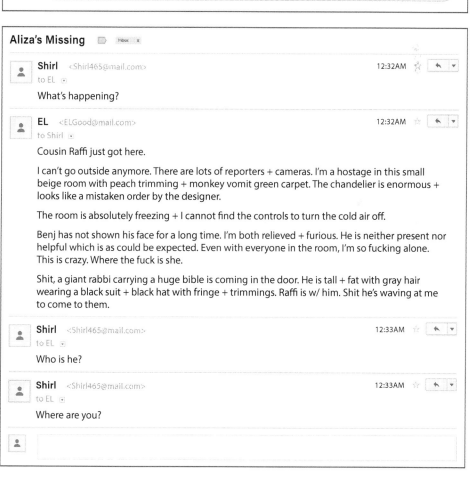

Aliza's Missing   Inbox x

Shirl <Shirl465@mail.com>   12:32AM
to EL

What's happening?

EL <ELGood@mail.com>   12:32AM
to Shirl

Cousin Raffi just got here.

I can't go outside anymore. There are lots of reporters + cameras. I'm a hostage in this small beige room with peach trimming + monkey vomit green carpet. The chandelier is enormous + looks like a mistaken order by the designer.

The room is absolutely freezing + I cannot find the controls to turn the cold air off.

Benj has not shown his face for a long time. I'm both relieved + furious. He is neither present nor helpful which is as could be expected. Even with everyone in the room, I'm so fucking alone. This is crazy. Where the fuck is she.

Shit, a giant rabbi carrying a huge bible is coming in the door. He is tall + fat with gray hair wearing a black suit + black hat with fringe + trimmings. Raffi is w/ him. Shit he's waving at me to come to them.

Shirl <Shirl465@mail.com>   12:33AM
to EL

Who is he?

Shirl <Shirl465@mail.com>   12:33AM
to EL

Where are you?

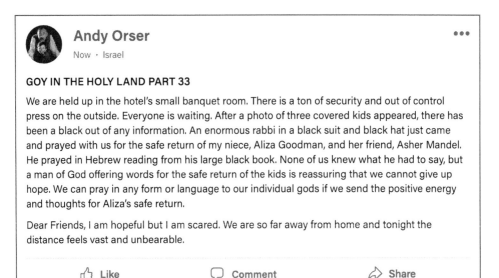

Andy Orser
Now · Israel

GOY IN THE HOLY LAND PART 33

We are held up in the hotel's small banquet room. There is a ton of security and out of control press on the outside. Everyone is waiting. After a photo of three covered kids appeared, there has been a black out of any information. An enormous rabbi in a black suit and black hat just came and prayed with us for the safe return of my niece, Aliza Goodman, and her friend, Asher Mandel. He prayed in Hebrew reading from his large black book. None of us knew what he had to say, but a man of God offering words for the safe return of the kids is reassuring that we cannot give up hope. We can pray in any form or language to our individual gods if we send the positive energy and thoughts for Aliza's safe return.

Dear Friends, I am hopeful but I am scared. We are so far away from home and tonight the distance feels vast and unbearable.

👍 Like   💬 Comment   ↪ Share

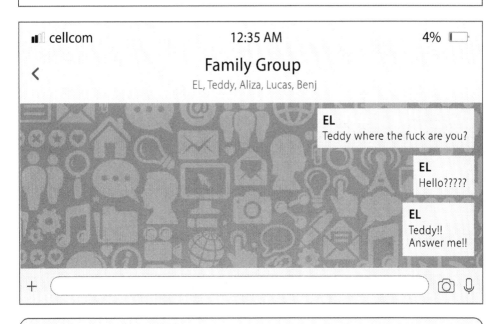

📶 cellcom   12:35 AM   4% 🔋

Family Group
EL, Teddy, Aliza, Lucas, Benj

EL
Teddy where the fuck are you?

EL
Hello?????

EL
Teddy!!
Answer me!!

 JN24:   now
France initiates a project to return artwork to Jewish families stolen by the Nazis.
Jewish News You Can Use

HM   **EG**

Hezzi Mandel   EL Goodman

12:35 AM

Where the fuck are you? I'm waiting to hear something even if you have nothing.

Teddy also disappeared. Raffi came + brought a religious rabbi in a black suit + hat to pray with us. He told me that this rabbi is famous for bringing about miracles. I didn't understand a fucking thing he said or did, but I was a believer. I'm now religious. Do I need a miracle? I have never prayed this hard. Am I going to get my daughter back? I need to hear from you. Call me. I'm nauseous. I'm not sure I can take much more.

Delivered

iMessage

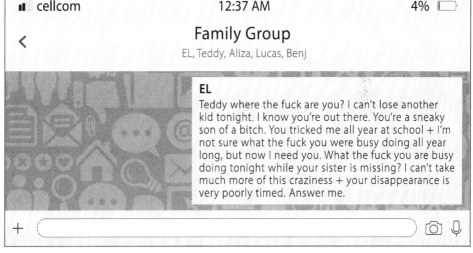

Family Group

EL, Teddy, Aliza, Lucas, Benj

EL

Teddy where the fuck are you? I can't lose another kid tonight. I know you're out there. You're a sneaky son of a bitch. You tricked me all year at school + I'm not sure what the fuck you were busy doing all year long, but now I need you. What the fuck you are busy doing tonight while your sister is missing? I can't take much more of this craziness + your disappearance is very poorly timed. Answer me.

 JN24:   now

Most Israelis do not want the Rabbinate deciding for them who is a Jew.

Jewish News You Can Use

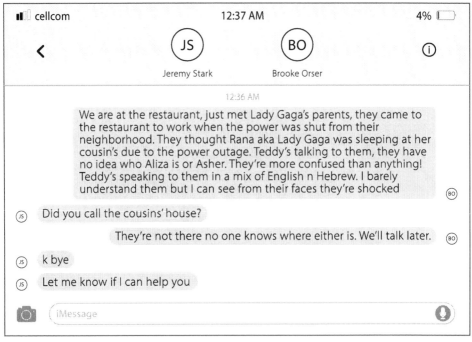

cellcom   12:37 AM   4% 🔋

(JS)   (BO)

Jeremy Stark   Brooke Orser

12:36 AM

We are at the restaurant, just met Lady Gaga's parents, they came to the restaurant to work when the power was shut from their neighborhood. They thought Rana aka Lady Gaga was sleeping at her cousin's due to the power outage. Teddy's talking to them, they have no idea who Aliza is or Asher. They're more confused than anything! Teddy's speaking to them in a mix of English n Hebrew. I barely understand them but I can see from their faces they're shocked

Did you call the cousins' house?

They're not there no one knows where either is. We'll talk later.

k bye

Let me know if I can help you

iMessage

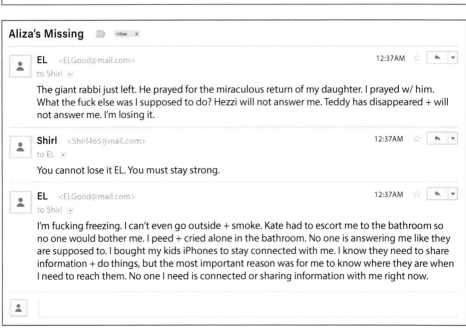

Aliza's Missing   Inbox ×

EL   <ELGood@mail.com>   12:37AM
to Shirl

The giant rabbi just left. He prayed for the miraculous return of my daughter. I prayed w/ him. What the fuck else was I supposed to do? Hezzi will not answer me. Teddy has disappeared + will not answer me. I'm losing it.

Shirl   <Shirl465@mail.com>   12:37AM
to EL

You cannot lose it EL. You must stay strong.

EL   <ELGood@mail.com>   12:37AM
to Shirl

I'm fucking freezing. I can't even go outside + smoke. Kate had to escort me to the bathroom so no one would bother me. I peed + cried alone in the bathroom. No one is answering me like they are supposed to. I bought my kids iPhones to stay connected with me. I know they need to share information + do things, but the most important reason was for me to know where they are when I need to reach them. No one I need is connected or sharing information with me right now.

Aliza's Missing 📩 Inbox ✕

Shirl <Shirl465@mail.com>	12:38AM ☆ ↩ ▾
to EL ▾	

Where is Ethan?

EL <ELGood@mail.com>	12:38AM ☆ ↩ ▾
to Shirl ▾	

What's he supposed to do? He knows hardly anything about anyone + now is one of the only people I have by my side. I don't feel very confident! He left me to survive on my own so long ago; I cannot depend on him over night just because we were born to the same parents. He is trying + I know he is freaked out, but I just don't feel the same closeness to him. This is fucking brutal.

MYPOETRY.COM

God

Brooke G.O.

★ ★ ★

Spark my mind to feel her presence
Embraced by unidentified love and comfort
I'm alone
Trash piled high where old cars park
Streets are blinding dark

★ ★ ★

Everyone tells me she exists
Appearing when least expected
I gave up hope
Help never came to play
This long torturous day

★ ★ ★

Then I closed my eyes
Looked deep within
Comforted by the familiar fear of being alone
Still waiting for that place
Her promised warm embrace

♡ 200   312 👁

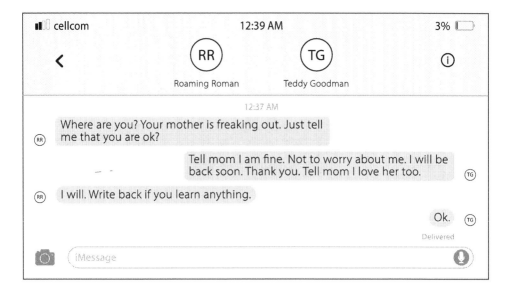

RR

Roaming Roman

TG

Teddy Goodman

12:37 AM

Where are you? Your mother is freaking out. Just tell me that you are ok?

Tell mom I am fine. Not to worry about me. I will be back soon. Thank you. Tell mom I love her too.

I will. Write back if you learn anything.

Ok.

Delivered

iMessage

JN24:   now

BREAKING NEWS. Two teenagers disappeared without a trace. Israeli and Palestinian police coordinating search efforts in Jerusalem. This event takes place following a week of violence. Three Katusha rockets landed in Northern Israeli town of Nahariya injuring five young boys playing in a field; 12 rockets hit southern city of Sderote hitting a supermarket and injuring 22; Settlers shot and injured 3 boys stealing fruit from West Bank orchard; and all amidst tension with trash collectors threatening to go on strike and a record heat wave across the nation.

Jewish News You Can Use

 Aliza's Missing   Inbox x

EL   <ELGood@mail.com>   12:40AM
to Shirl

Ethan just showed me a text from Teddy that he is fine. He told him to tell me that he loved me. He hasn't spoken to me in forever + now he's off playing James Bond + sending me love notes through my recently returned brother.

Shirl   <Shirl465@mail.com>   12:40AM
to EL

Well he's staying connected as you asked for.

Aliza's Missing 📬 Inbox ✕

EL `<ELGood@mail.com>`   12:40AM ☆ ↰ ▾
to Shirl

Yes. But where the fuck is he?

Shirl `<Shirl465@mail.com>`   12:40AM ☆ ↰ ▾
to EL

Looking for his sister.

EL `<ELGood@mail.com>`   12:41AM ☆ ↰ ▾
to Shirl

Yes, but it's dangerous.

Shirl `<Shirl465@mail.com>`   12:41AM ☆ ↰ ▾
to EL

Teddy is clever. He lives in Manhattan. He just received the Leonardo Da Vinci Award.

EL `<ELGood@mail.com>`   12:42AM ☆ ↰ ▾
to Shirl

I only have 1 child left. Lucas is fast asleep on the small couch + still looks angelic. I made a decision.

Shirl `<Shirl465@mail.com>`   12:42AM ☆ ↰ ▾
to EL

What?

EL `<ELGood@mail.com>`   12:42AM ☆ ↰ ▾
to Shirl

If I get through this whole disaster, I must change my life. I cannot go on like this. I'm not sure what but I will never take another day for granted. Not another wasted moment feeling bad about my life or myself. I can't think now but I just know I'm done living in the fucking past + planning for the future. I need to live in the present. I'm all fucking alone. Benj is not even here during this whole thing. I'm all fucking alone.

Shirl `<Shirl465@mail.com>`   12:43AM ☆ ↰ ▾
to EL

Yes. You are. Your kids will all come back to you but life will never be the same. I'm here for you EL. You are the only one who can make the changes!

EL `<ELGood@mail.com>`   12:43AM ☆ ↰ ▾
to Shirl

I'm fucking dying here. The only good news is that I bought the mophie from the Nigerian street-corner vendor before I left New York + I still have battery power. Maybe I need to go out + look for the kids myself? It is better than sitting here + waiting for others to help me.

393

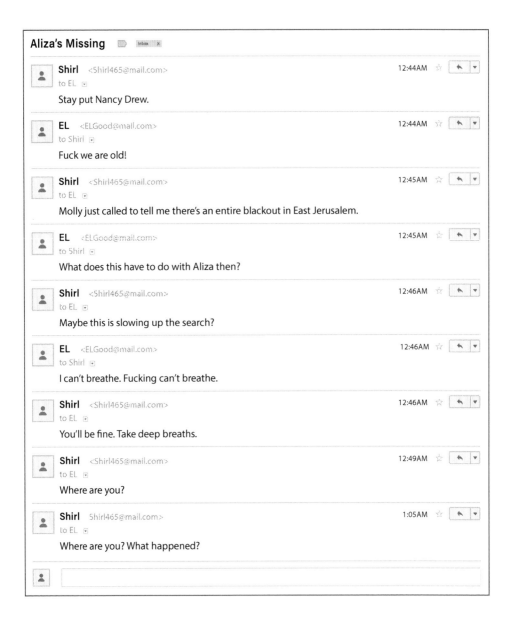

Aliza's Missing 📨 Inbox ×

Shirl <Shirl465@mail.com>   12:44AM
to EL
Stay put Nancy Drew.

EL <ELGood@mail.com>   12:44AM
to Shirl
Fuck we are old!

Shirl <Shirl465@mail.com>   12:45AM
to EL
Molly just called to tell me there's an entire blackout in East Jerusalem.

EL <ELGood@mail.com>   12:45AM
to Shirl
What does this have to do with Aliza then?

Shirl <Shirl465@mail.com>   12:46AM
to EL
Maybe this is slowing up the search?

EL <ELGood@mail.com>   12:46AM
to Shirl
I can't breathe. Fucking can't breathe.

Shirl <Shirl465@mail.com>   12:46AM
to EL
You'll be fine. Take deep breaths.

Shirl <Shirl465@mail.com>   12:49AM
to EL
Where are you?

Shirl Shirl465@mail.com>   1:05AM
to EL
Where are you? What happened?

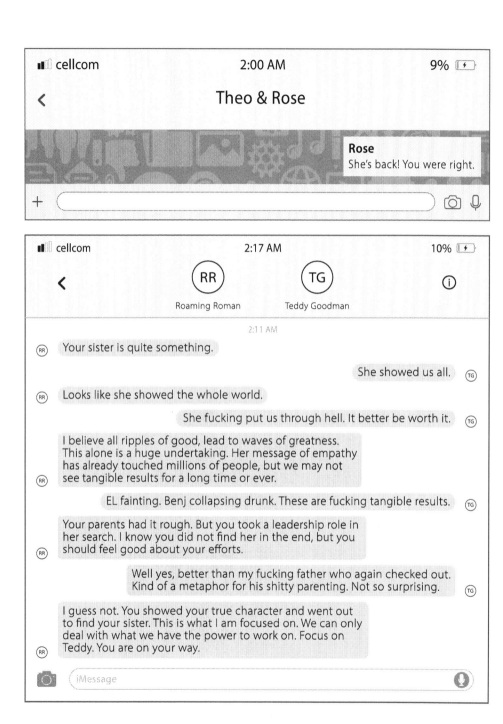

cellcom   2:00 AM   9% 🔋

Theo & Rose

Rose
She's back! You were right.

---

cellcom   2:17 AM   10% 🔋

RR   **TG**   ⓘ
Roaming Roman   Teddy Goodman

2:11 AM

(RR) Your sister is quite something.

She showed us all. (TG)

(RR) Looks like she showed the whole world.

She fucking put us through hell. It better be worth it. (TG)

(RR) I believe all ripples of good, lead to waves of greatness. This alone is a huge undertaking. Her message of empathy has already touched millions of people, but we may not see tangible results for a long time or ever.

EL fainting. Benj collapsing drunk. These are fucking tangible results. (TG)

(RR) Your parents had it rough. But you took a leadership role in her search. I know you did not find her in the end, but you should feel good about your efforts.

Well yes, better than my fucking father who again checked out. Kind of a metaphor for his shitty parenting. Not so surprising. (TG)

(RR) I guess not. You showed your true character and went out to find your sister. This is what I am focused on. We can only deal with what we have the power to work on. Focus on Teddy. You are on your way.

iMessage 🎤

398

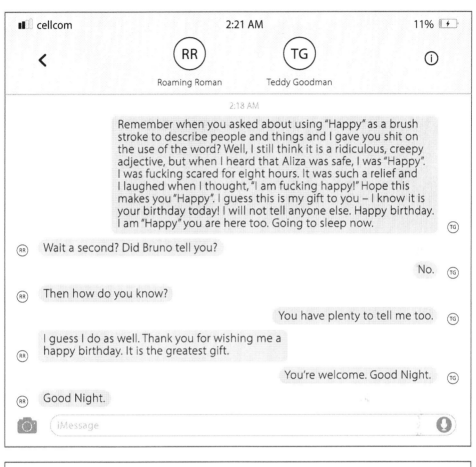

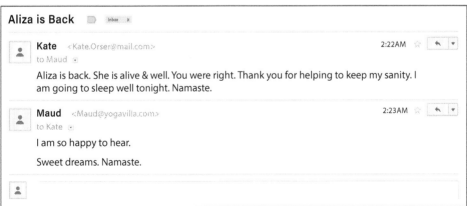

Andy Orser
Now · Israel

•••

GOY IN THE HOLY LAND PART 34

Aliza is back!! She is safe and sound! If you haven't already seen her video, check out this link – 60SecondsOfLight.com. Aliza's disappearance was a series of delays in trying to send out a magical video that she made in partnership with her Palestinian friend. 60SecondsOfLight brilliantly inspires millions of youth around the world to unite metaphorically shining attention on the problems their generation face; war, gender injustice, poverty, clean drinking water, pollution, global warming, to name a few. Tomorrow, well, tonight, at 10pm the world's youth wherever in the world they might be are invited to go outside and join others with an iPhone, candle, flashlight, or any instrument to make light and shine into the sky. As the world turns and the clock strikes 10pm, the future generations will come together to shine light and say we all are united – we are not alone.

Dear Friends, Thank you for your love and support in the last ten hours. I feel the warmth of our connection and will be forever grateful for our partnership in this world. Please pass this message on to your friends and family on Facebook, Instagram, Twitter, and Snap Chat; go out and shine a light at 10pm Thursday night wherever you are to join Aliza in 60SecondsOfLight. This is an incredible message that we are all connected and can be each other's greatest support - we are not alone in this big world. #60SecondsOfLight #thefuture #Alizaissafe

👍 Like   💬 Comment   ↗ Share

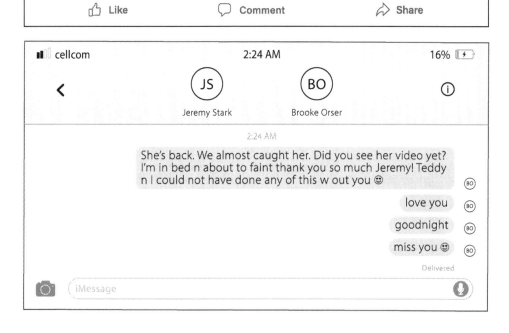

Report Update Inbox x

Laura <L.Friedman@SHH.com>   2:27AM
to Benj

Are you ok? I have been glued to the television in the office worried about Aliza. She scared us all. Hope you are doing ok. I cannot imagine what its been like but she is safe now. That's all that matters.

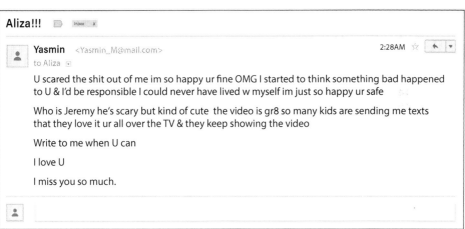

Aliza!!! Inbox x

Yasmin <Yasmin_M@mail.com>   2:28AM
to Aliza

U scared the shit out of me im so happy ur fine OMG I started to think something bad happened to U & I'd be responsible I could never have lived w myself im just so happy ur safe

Who is Jeremy he's scary but kind of cute the video is gr8 so many kids are sending me texts that they love it ur all over the TV & they keep showing the video

Write to me when U can

I love U

I miss you so much.

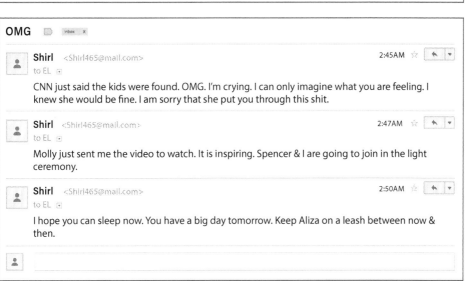

OMG Inbox x

Shirl <Shirl465@mail.com>   2:45AM
to EL

CNN just said the kids were found. OMG. I'm crying. I can only imagine what you are feeling. I knew she would be fine. I am sorry that she put you through this shit.

Shirl <Shirl465@mail.com>   2:47AM
to EL

Molly just sent me the video to watch. It is inspiring. Spencer & I are going to join in the light ceremony.

Shirl <Shirl465@mail.com>   2:50AM
to EL

I hope you can sleep now. You have a big day tomorrow. Keep Aliza on a leash between now & then.

Jack Billings' Notes

Aliza Sophia Goodman of New York City and Asher Mandel of Kibbutz Hatzor have been found. They are alive and well. They were discovered at 1:47am at The American Colony Hotel in East Jerusalem after having gone missing for nine hours.

These two teenagers disappeared in East Jerusalem last night causing great fear and speculation as to their safety in this turbulent city. Rumors circulated that Islamic Jihad had kidnapped them, but they were engaged in their own propaganda - sending a powerful video inspiring youth around the world to be united in a movement known as 60 Seconds of Light tonight at 10pm to shine a light to the sky that unites the youth of the world against injustice.

She powerfully brings this message together in twenty languages with the support of her friends in the international community beautifully and movingly accompanied by a hip-hop version of John Legend's song, Are You Out There? All the young people in the video encourage their peers to come together and tell the world's adults that they are united against the ills brought on by the older generations.

60SecondsOfLight can be viewed on YouTube. The simple and thoughtful message is heartwarming and portrays a profound brilliance that via the Internet, the world can be connected for good and change.

 JN24: now

Aliza Goodman and Asher Mandel have returned unharmed and with a message of peace and hope.

Jewish News You Can Use

Hell + Hope

<u>Brooke G.O.</u>

★ ★ ★

Hell is not a place to be
Hell is not a thing to see
Hell permeates the soul
Hell's journey has its toll

★ ★ ★

Hope is a place to be
Hope is a thing to see
Hope permeates the soul
Hope's journey is the goal

★ ★ ★

♡ 59   101 ◉

Words of Encouragement   Inbox x

Dahlia   <FreeDahlia@mail.com>   3:00AM ☆ ↩ ▾
to EL. ▾

What a terrible ordeal you have passed. Y'mama must be chucklin' about her granddaughter's Save the World Gene poppin' up in the Holy Land. I wish she were here to enjoy this precious moment sugah!

■■ cellcom   3:06 AM   21% 🔋

<   JS   BO   ⓘ
      Jeremy Stark   Brooke Orser

3:06 AM

Love you too. Happy it all worked out.
Sleep well.

📷 (iMessage   🎤)

BOKER TOV

Goodman Family!

Welcome to day seven of your Holy Land excursion!
Here is today's schedule:

The Mitzvah!

Boker Tov.

We will pick you up at 4:45pm for Aliza's bat mitzvah service and museum tour.

We will visit the spectacular Davidson Center located along the Southern Wall of the Temple Mount and walk the same street that 2000 years ago bustled with pilgrims, tourists, and prominent religious Jews and leaders making their way to the Temple to pray. Please wear comfortable shoes and bring a sweater, as the Jerusalem night will be chilly.

Aliza's service will begin at 6pm at the base of wall. After her mitzvah, we will walk to the beautiful apartment patio for a remarkable view and delicious dinner.

Today's Temperature:

 The weather today will be a warm 31˚c / 88˚f

Shalom,

Moshe
Rimon Tours

< 　　　　(YM)　　　　　　(AG)　　　　　ⓘ

Yasmin M.　　　　　Aliza Goodman

7:45 AM

Hiiii (AG)

(YM) Hii U did it

Yeah but omg I'm in so much trouble! (AG)

(YM) Why what happened? When u disappeared I started
freaking out thinking something bad happened to u.
I thought it was my fault!! Tell me what happened

I'm in the hotel under house arrest (AG)

(YM) Why?

May be grounded for the rest of my life lol im
not supposed to be on my phone (AG)

(YM) Yes, but you're famous…so sick!!! Tell me what happened!!

Asher & I met Rana and we covered our heads & bodies with
robes like the Arabs wear so that we didn't look like foreigners (AG)

It was really cool walking around & looking out & no one could
look in & see us! We made it to her house & no one stopped us (AG)

I made the video of Asher + Rana + started to do the final
edit but the electricity went out & there was no Internet. (AG)

At first we thought it was just her house so we waited and she
said black outs were normal for short periods. Then we covered
up again & went to her cousin Hana's house. There was no
electricity there either and I had no more battery or Internet (AG)

We had to hide in her small room cuz her parents
were home. They would've reported us (AG)

I was dying. All the planning & I couldnt finish the video or send
it out. We waited soooo fucking long my phone almost died
and I freaked cuz I couldnt get Internet and all the addresses &
info was on my phone so I had to turn it off just in case (AG)

(YM) What did you do to get it out?

📷 (iMessage 　　　　　　　　　　　　　　 🎤)

407

YM
Yasmin M.

AG
Aliza Goodman

7:45 AM

Rana's cousin Hana has a cousin whose husband works at The American Colony.

What's that?

A rly cool hotel in East Jerusalem they had a generator – the only power we could find everything else was pitch black. It was scary moving quickly in our robes hiding from the police we saw along the way. If we were caught the whole thing wouldn't have gone out. Four of us had to sneak in thru the back gate & wait behind a bush till the dinner service was over

It was cold & I had to pee soo badly lol

Why didn't u just pee in the bush?

Asher was there!!

U like him?

Yes but that's a whole other story

So what happened then?

We snuck inside the hotel's kitchen & hooked up to their wifi it didn't take long to finish the video and post it

it's crazy how fast it spread Everyone I know loves it! u did it!!!!!

Now we just have to see if it works tonight

Tonight'll be great.

The message is out!! ☺

Thank you! Couldn't have done it ☺ without u Gtg now wish me luck

Have fun & text me later

Send pics!! I wish I was there

Me too love you ♡

Delivered

iMessage

Aliza Goodman's Daily Motivational Quote #1: now

"Peace is a daily, a weekly, a monthly process, gradually changing opinions, slowly eroding old barriers, quietly building new structures." John F. Kennedy

MotiQuote.com

 JN24: now

Missing teenagers, Aliza Goodman and Asher Mandel, are back at home after an exhaustive nationwide search. These adventurous teenagers with an unidentified Palestinian youth turned a nation around in their quest to send a message of peace and hope to the world. Their world-shattering video is rapidly spreading virally around the globe and will culminate this evening at 10pm with a demonstration of the world's youth united and shining a light on humankind's problems. 60SecondsOfLight.com

Jewish News You Can Use

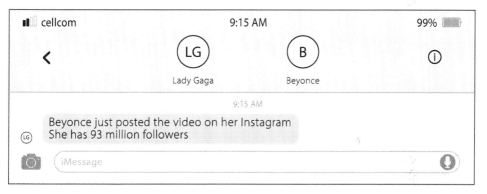

Aliza
Teddy Goodman

My sister is fucking crazy. Today I am her biggest fan. She managed to pull one over on me, the family, the country and maybe the whole fucking world. She is smart, she is determined and she is fucking lucky. I spent the greater part of last night looking for her in Jerusalem. Two sides of a divided city - the Jewish side and the Palestinian side. They share many similar qualities and are distinctly different at the same time. On the Palestinian side, all the signage is in Arabic, which I could not read. We also had to make our way through very dark streets with moonlight as our only guide. Looking for a few teenagers who didn't fucking want to be discovered was challenging for me and even for the police. None of us found them, they found us. I am still unsure of all their trickery and believe that I was only one step behind them most of the night. My phone battery died around midnight and Brooke's a short while later. We were without connection. We only had our intuition and each other. Two cousins who had spent very few hours together growing up, separated by 3000 miles and lots of resentment and confusion between their parents for many years. Last night solidified that our generation would not adopt the hate and the distrust of our parents. Alone and frightened for Aliza and I think for ourselves at some points, we realized all we had was each other. It was pitch black and the streets were a maze of dark, dingy roads with lots of trash piled up, black cats with yellow eyes darting around and a strong, disgusting stench floating through the air; we had to keep moving forward to find my crazy little sister. We fucking depended on each other and we liked each other. At one point, we sat silently in a small, dark alcove shoulder to shoulder with a tinge of moonlight and waited. The silence was unbearable and yet neither of us dared to break it until we had the right words to interject. My backpack started to vibrate. My phone was dead. I reached in and discovered my little brother Lucas' phone was vibrating. The locked screen had a message from Aliza. I put in his code 'spongebob' and there was the 60 Seconds of Light video. Brooke and I watched and laughed. She got us!

 JN24:   now

Teenager's 60SecondsOfLight video is the fastest spreading video internationally. Millions of youth around the world are expected to go outside tonight at 10pm and shine a light to the sky in an act of solidarity.
Jewish News You Can Use

FOOD AFFAIR WITH KATE

DIVINE, DELICIOUS, AND DELIGHTFUL   ABOUT   RECIPES   CONTACT

I Had A Dream

★ ★ ★ ★ ★

Cheese bourekas, a basic comfort food with light, flakey phyllo crust, soft moist inner dough and tangy cheese filling calls me out of bed after a tumultuous sleep. Last night, my niece disappeared into the Jerusalem night air, we spent nine hours searching, fearing for her life. Her miraculous return marked the release of her social justice video - 60SecondsOfLight - asking young and old across the world to unite against Hate. In the early morning light, I find myself retracing last night's murky steps searching for my niece on the blackening Jerusalem streets. A small corner bourekas bar had caught my eye, and I promised myself upon her reappearance, I would return to this hole in the wall to celebrate with freshly baked bourekas.

An ancient, dark skinned woman with thick, deep lines around her eyes and mouth welcomes me. Tova smiles with pride and pleasure, as she describes in Hebrew with a few English words thrown in, lots of pointing, the diverse bourekas filling her counter. Tova serves me different shaped and filled bourekas on her small side table specked with crumbs from prior customers: one mushroom, one potato, one spinach, one with a slow-cooked brown hard boiled egg and one with cheese. She also serves me a small glass of piping hot mint tea with leaves floating. Dutifully I eat the five different bourekas, Tova's cobalt blue eyes intensely watch me. "Ta-yeem, Ta-yeem, Ta-yeem", she chants, which means, "Tasty, tasty, tasty." Her workspace dusted with flour, rolling pins and a sharp knife all right next to where I sit, wedged between a refrigerator and oven.

Filled with burning questions I know will go unanswered with few shared words, I imagine exact spices and ingredients, her recipes passed down for generations, alive in her head and rolled out with her well-seasoned hands. Nothing more delicious and memorable than eating fresh, warm bourekas straight from the chef's hands on a tiny, wobbly chair at a crumby table on a cool Jerusalem Old City morning. See the photos below and check out Food Affair with Kate on Instagram and Facebook. #Bourekas #Jerusalem #Tayeem

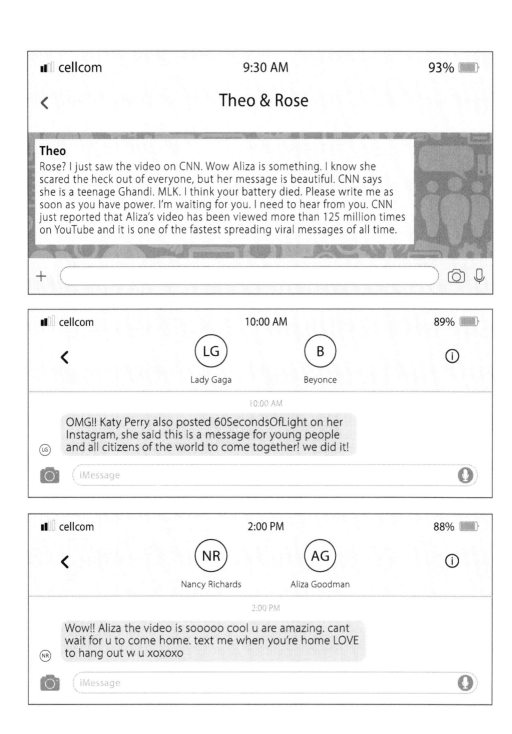

cellcom   9:30 AM   93%

< Theo & Rose

Theo
Rose? I just saw the video on CNN. Wow Aliza is something. I know she scared the heck out of everyone, but her message is beautiful. CNN says she is a teenage Ghandi. MLK. I think your battery died. Please write me as soon as you have power. I'm waiting for you. I need to hear from you. CNN just reported that Aliza's video has been viewed more than 125 million times on YouTube and it is one of the fastest spreading viral messages of all time.

---

cellcom   10:00 AM   89%

<   (LG) Lady Gaga   (B) Beyonce   ⓘ

10:00 AM

OMG!! Katy Perry also posted 60SecondsOfLight on her Instagram, she said this is a message for young people and all citizens of the world to come together! we did it!

iMessage

---

cellcom   2:00 PM   88%

<   (NR) Nancy Richards   (AG) Aliza Goodman   ⓘ

2:00 PM

Wow!! Aliza the video is sooooo cool u are amazing. cant wait for u to come home. text me when you're home LOVE to hang out w u xoxoxo

iMessage

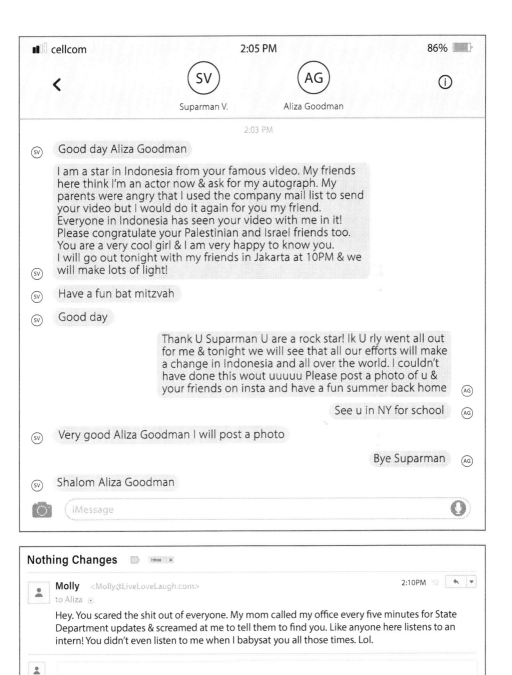

Suparman V.   Aliza Goodman

2:03 PM

(SV) Good day Aliza Goodman

I am a star in Indonesia from your famous video. My friends here think I'm an actor now & ask for my autograph. My parents were angry that I used the company mail list to send your video but I would do it again for you my friend.
Everyone in Indonesia has seen your video with me in it!
Please congratulate your Palestinian and Israel friends too.
You are a very cool girl & I am very happy to know you.
I will go out tonight with my friends in Jakarta at 10PM & we will make lots of light!

(SV) Have a fun bat mitzvah

(SV) Good day

Thank U Suparman U are a rock star! Ik U rly went all out for me & tonight we will see that all our efforts will make a change in Indonesia and all over the world. I couldn't have done this wout uuuuu Please post a photo of u & your friends on insta and have a fun summer back home **(AG)**

See u in NY for school **(AG)**

(SV) Very good Aliza Goodman I will post a photo

Bye Suparman **(AG)**

(SV) Shalom Aliza Goodman

iMessage

Nothing Changes Inbox x

Molly <Molly@LiveLoveLaugh.com>
to Aliza   2:10PM

Hey. You scared the shit out of everyone. My mom called my office every five minutes for State Department updates & screamed at me to tell them to find you. Like anyone here listens to an intern! You didn't even listen to me when I babysat you all those times. Lol.

my grandmother in Seattle just texted me that she watched the video at her retirement home! its crazy, she and her friends will go out tonight too! lol grandparents are the new youth!

Safe + Sound   Inbox x

Shirl <Shirl465@gmail.com>
to EL

Hi. How are you doing?

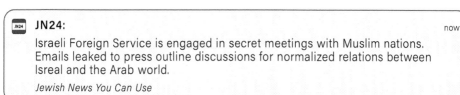

JN24:   now

Israeli Foreign Service is engaged in secret meetings with Muslim nations. Emails leaked to press outline discussions for normalized relations between Isreal and the Arab world.

Jewish News You Can Use

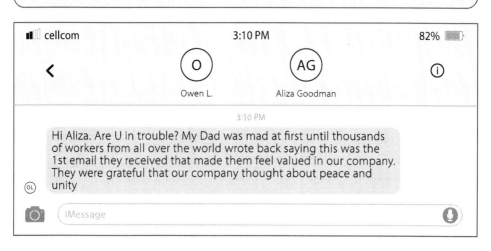

Hi Aliza. Are U in trouble? My Dad was mad at first until thousands of workers from all over the world wrote back saying this was the 1st email they received that made them feel valued in our company. They were grateful that our company thought about peace and unity

OL — Owen L

AG — Aliza Goodman

3:11 PM

OL: mom told him that he should give me all the credit and he said he would! nfw this is going to ever happen but I dont care, Im just happy I could help u get this done

OL: tonight Im going w some friends to the Park

OL: I hope that NASA's snapping spy photos will see our lights from millions of miles away. should be cool photos!!

OL: let me know when youre back and we will go and celebrate! mom and dad want u and your parents to come for Shabbat dinner

AG: Thanks! Will call when I'm back! if I'm not grounded forever then we can hang out

AG: My bat mitzvah is in a few hours... still no sign of God! making me crazy! I know the Rabbi Harvey told us we dont need to believe in God but wish I did or even knew what to believe in

OL: youre the most optimistic person I know. most teenagers are negative and mad but u are positive and happy

OL: im the biggest jerk and u are still nice to me this is proof of something superhuman in u Haha

OL: im a lousy student and still have not been kicked out of school! I know my parents cannot pay for the school to keep me there so I believe there is some other power out there keeping me from failing and completely fucking up a God who gave me a friend like u who puts up w me. I don't know why knowing or understanding God is so important for u but there are some things we cannot explain and just must accept

OL: the video u made and we all helped u to send out is proof that your cool w or w/out God

OL: Mazel Tov on your bat mitzvah haha! I speak Hebrew! have fun reading from the Torah Haha I know u will be great because u are the best in our Hebrew class & the nicest person I know

OL: thank u for putting up w me God knows I dont always deserve it lol

iMessage

No to Hate, Yes to Love
Roaming Roman

I have been a reporter for thirty years traveling vast distances and observing the greatest adversity on this planet. I have written extensively on endless man made wars and observed human tragedy that man inflicts on his fellow man. The motto of news especially in the 24-hour news cycle that predominates our world, "If it bleeds, it leads," is the key component selling the world stories that are rarely positive and generally heartbreaking.

I write now with tears streaming down my face, blown away by the positive impact created by one gutsy teenager from New York who happens to be my niece. She is the brainchild behind this simple and yet influential video, 60SecondsOfLight. Aliza Goodman's video has one straightforward message portrayed by each young person's smile and the words spoken in their native tongue; "I am a Jew, a Muslim, an Atheist, an African, a German, a Brazilian, a Korean, a Cuban, an Armenian, an Indian, a Budhist, a Kurd, a Christian, a Methodist, an Italian" each holding a poster with the words, "We are united against hate for a brighter future, Join us!...Show your power in 60SecondsOfLight" in their native script. All of this with the divine words of John Legend's song, If You Are Out There? "No more broken promises, no more calls to war, unless it's love and peace that we're really fighting for. We can destroy hunger, we can conquer hate, put down the arms and raise your voice, we're joining hands today." We are all joining hands with Aliza and her peers on this very special day declaring in beautiful and unified voices, "No to hate and Yes to love."

If you have not already seen the video - check it out 60SecondsOfLight.com

Safe + Sound ▷ Inbox ×

Shirl <Shirl465@mail.com> 3:15PM
to EL

CNN just interviewed John Legend & asked him for a comment on Aliza's video using his song. He was proud that she used his words. They share the message of uniting & bringing positive change to the world. He said he wants to meet her. Can I come too? I love John Legend.

< **Theo & Rose**

Rose
It's the middle of the night for you. Aliza is safe. I just slept for a few hours and soon we will get ready for the bat mitzvah. My granddaughter is a crazy girl. You were correct. She disappeared to send a video to the world with her secret Palestinian friend. A peaceful, social demonstration she calls it. EL has a black eye from when she fainted and fell on her face. The paramedics thought she might have a concussion but she insists she is fine. Hezzi brought the kids back to the hotel at 2:00am. They were tired, but fine. EL just wrapped her arms around Aliza and cried. Aliza repeatedly said she was sorry and cried too. Everyone was exhausted. I do not think she had any idea of what she put her family through. She got on a teenage mission and quickly forgot about those around her. Do you remember when Brooke was mad at her parents and disappeared from her house? She ended up hiding in my home while I was on vacation. We were all so worried and she was happily enjoying her freedom. I do not understand how these kids do this? I never would've scared my parents. Would you have?

 +

⟨   (HM)   (EG)   ⓘ

Hezzi Mandel   EL Goodman

3:25 PM

(HM) **Are you speaking with me yet?**

Yes. Thank you. I know you did everything to find the kids last night. (EG)

(HM) **In the end, they found us. Your daughter is quite sneaky.**

Your son is too! (EG)

(HM) **I'm sorry that you had to go through this last night.**

The worst nightmare a parent can experience. I imagined that my daughter was dead. I lost hope. It was so dark. I had no information + being stuck in the hotel was torture. I would've been better out looking for her myself like you or Teddy not stuck in the freezing room (EG)

(HM) **She's safe. Have you seen the video?**

Yes! I know. It's very special, but she worried me to death. I have a black eye + feel like a camel ran over me. (EG)

(HM) **Nice use of the camel.**

When in Jerusalem. (EG)

(HM) **Asher & I are leaving soon for the bat mitzvah. Do you still want me there?**

Yes. Do you still want to come? (EG)

(HM) **Yes.**

Good. (EG)

(HM) **See you soon then.**

Good. (EG)

(HM) **I love you EL.**

I love you too. (EG)

Delivered

📷 (iMessage) 🎤

DF Dana Feldman   **AG** Aliza Goodman

3:30 PM

moms assistant Monte at the office who helps us w our home server was so happy to send your video out. he said over & over again how much he loves the tech revolution helping the world. he called U a tech peace activist. he knows like a million peeps!!

omg & my moms both love John Legend and have watched the video for the last hour. they are walking around the apartment harmonizing, "If you hear this message wherever you stand I'm calling every woman calling everyman we're the generation we cant afford to wait the future started yesterday & we're already late if youre out there if youre out there"

I will hear it in my head for a long time but they sound pretty good harmonizing lol see u in the sky at 10pm tonight!!

have a great bat mitzvah Mazel Tov Aliza!

iMessage

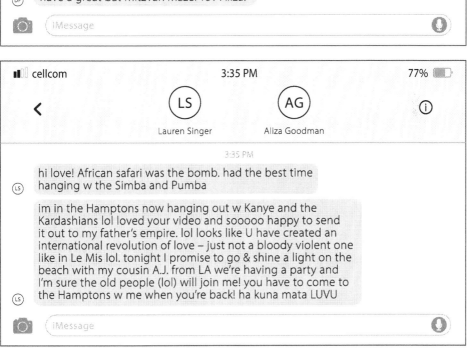

LS Lauren Singer   **AG** Aliza Goodman

3:35 PM

hi love! African safari was the bomb. had the best time hanging w the Simba and Pumba

im in the Hamptons now hanging out w Kanye and the Kardashians lol loved your video and sooooo happy to send it out to my father's empire. lol looks like U have created an international revolution of love – just not a bloody violent one like in Le Mis lol. tonight I promise to go & shine a light on the beach with my cousin A.J. from LA we're having a party and I'm sure the old people (lol) will join me! you have to come to the Hamptons w me when you're back! ha kuna mata LUVU

iMessage

GOY IN THE HOLY LAND PART 35

Aliza's bat mitzvah will start shortly. Her Palestinian friend will not join for fear of endangering her family and herself. She cannot appear to be on the side of the occupier, the Zionists, the Westerners – those deemed the enemy by certain Palestinian factions. This beautiful and daring teenage girl is nameless in the media. She is also faceless in the 60SecondondsOfLight Video, her head and face completely covered by a traditional Muslim hijab. I think back to Mohammad and Hussein, the two men I met on the beach, who shared their painful, personal thoughts on the dissonance of being an Arab living in a Jewish state. I remember the affable and thoughtful Ahmed who shared bits of his family's struggle but his zest for life and symbiotic nature prevailed. Sadly, the dominant image of the old, cautious Arab I met last night as darkness enveloped the Old City and who calmly repeated, "Please do not blame the Palestinians," repeatedly, remains the dominant image for me. Last night as we searched desperately for Aliza, we arrived at the terrible conclusions that the old Arab predicted we would. I was disappointed in myself and painfully recognized this cruel reality. I hope to take away from this experience an enlightenment that I can share personally and portray in my future documentary work for others to understand. Aliza's short motivational video 60SecondsOfLight incorporates this understanding and gives hope that future generations will not be weighed down by prejudice and will be more tolerant and cooperative.

Dear Friends, there is always time to change, to grow and to be more thoughtful. We all struggle with these challenges and for some, these demons. Traveling the Holy Land continues to inspire me and I hope my posts inspire you to expand your hearts and lower the shields around you. Shalom. Namaste. Peace.

    👍 Like   💬 Comment   ↪ Share

LIFEEXPRESSIONS.COM   ✏️ 📁 ⊕

Sawt
Jamil

MYPOETRY.COM

Woman

Brooke G.O.

Time closes in
Today a woman
Yesterday a child
Small n' wild

Her heart races with speed
Powerful minds lead
She sees beyond her reflection
Thoughtul inflection

Covered by innocent lies
Her secrets rise
She is bolder
I am older

Greater hunger
Far younger
Cannot wait
Won't be late

She stands proud
Words ring loud
Empathy calls
Hate falls

Follow with heart
Take part
Joining across the land
Hand in hand

A girl she was
A woman she is
Watching her breeze
A moment to seize

A moment of light
Makes everything right
Hope not hate
It's never too late

♡ 300 650 👁

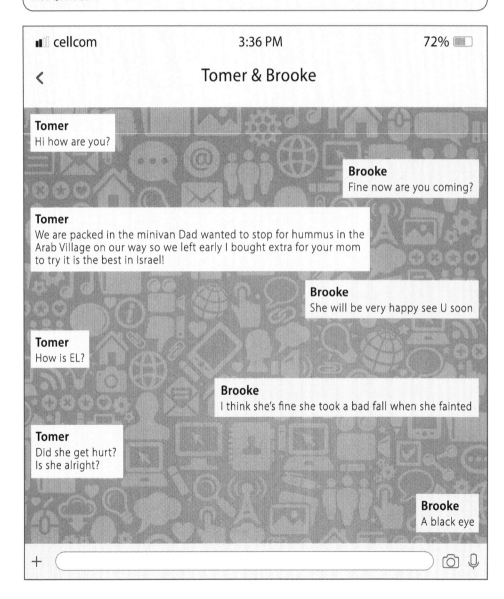

▮ cellcom	3:36 PM	72% ▭

⟨   **Tomer & Brooke**

Tomer
Hi how are you?

> **Brooke**
> Fine now are you coming?

Tomer
We are packed in the minivan Dad wanted to stop for hummus in the Arab Village on our way so we left early I bought extra for your mom to try it is the best in Israel!

> **Brooke**
> She will be very happy see U soon

Tomer
How is EL?

> **Brooke**
> I think she's fine she took a bad fall when she fainted

Tomer
Did she get hurt?
Is she alright?

> **Brooke**
> A black eye

+   ⬭   ◎ ⬚

Tomer & Brooke

Tomer
How is Aliza?

Brooke
She's fine she didn't realize that her disappearance was causing such national or international attention she was stupid

Tomer
We have an expression in Hebrew 'Tipeshesray' - a stupid teenager I was one too before I joined the army after I enlisted, I could not think only about myself anymore I had the other officers and the whole country to think about not sure what all the army teaches me but this is one of the things that I have had to learn or I would never have made it through basic training

Brooke
We all must grow up at some point she's just a more dramatic kid n had only good intentions when she went missing she thought her cause had great value or she would never have put her mom through this experience

Tomer
I got a notification a few minutes ago that 300 million people have seen the video I think everyone in Israel has seen the video it is very good I like how she said the same thing in so many languages & the kids' design work was very bright & fun I have had it sent to me 100 times! My parents like it too It is not just for kids I think people will go out at 10 tonight & make light it is very simple & brings people together Aliza is now one of the most famous people in Israel

Brooke
I think in the world It is crazy! We will go out n shine lights together tonight during the dinner party!

\+ ⟨_____⟩ ◎ ⌄

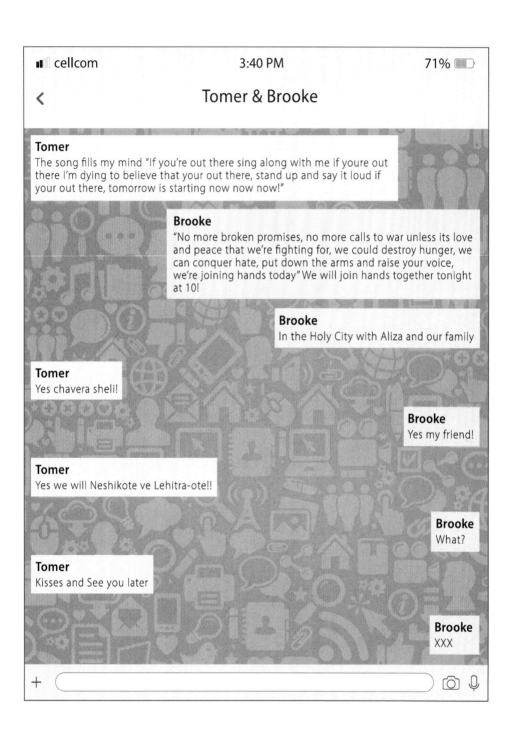

Tomer
The song fills my mind "If you're out there sing along with me if youre out there I'm dying to believe that your out there, stand up and say it loud if your out there, tomorrow is starting now now now!"

Brooke
"No more broken promises, no more calls to war unless its love and peace that we're fighting for, we could destroy hunger, we can conquer hate, put down the arms and raise your voice, we're joining hands today" We will join hands together tonight at 10!

Brooke
In the Holy City with Aliza and our family

Tomer
Yes chavera sheli!

Brooke
Yes my friend!

Tomer
Yes we will Neshikote ve Lehitra-ote!!

Brooke
What?

Tomer
Kisses and See you later

Brooke
XXX

Checking Up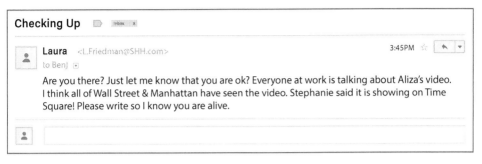

Laura <L.Friedman@SHH.com>   3:45PM
to Benj

Are you there? Just let me know that you are ok? Everyone at work is talking about Aliza's video. I think all of Wall Street & Manhattan have seen the video. Stephanie said it is showing on Time Square! Please write so I know you are alive.

Safe + Sound

EL <ELGood@mail.com>   3:50PM
to Shirl

Aliza is fine, as you have seen on CNN. But last night before she showed up, I fainted + got a black eye. After I woke, Hezzi called + I heard Aliza's voice on the phone. I screamed + cried. Then Hezzi brought her to me + I cried for an hour holding her. I was so relieved + so angry. I only slept after Rose gave me one of her horse tranquilizers. I'm sitting here having my hair blown dry by a very nice Israeli woman named Maya. She wants to talk to me because this morning I'm a celebrity - the mother of the amazing teenager Aliza Goodman. Lol. I can't look up. I have a black eye from when I fainted; I have large bags under both eyes from so much crying + I seriously feel like an out of control cement truck hit me head on. I have tried to write you a few times earlier, but no words came out + I just cried. I know that Aliza is safe, but I still can't get out of my head what I did wrong + what could have happened to her. It all feels too random + I feel so helpless. I had no way to find her last night. She could've disappeared + I wouldn't have been able to save my daughter. Shit Shirl. I did nothing but freak out + faint. I gave up on my daughter.

Hezzi, all the police, Teddy + Brooke - no one could find her. I can only tell you that I started to think I would have to come back to New York without one kid. I can't believe I went to such a ...dark place but I didn't see any light. I had no faith. There was no God.

Today I must smile + celebrate her bat mitzvah + all I want to do is crawl under the covers + hide. But I can't. I must go out + pretend to be fine. Pretend to be happy. Pretend I like my life. Pretend there is a God. Pretend I love my husband. Pretend I'm proud of my daughter when I'm so fucking angry with her for what she did to me. What she put me through. She's fucking saving the world + throwing me under the bus.

She's like my mom but in a 21 C way. Mom would go out + take care of all the poor + sick people in Manhattan + I would be home alone each afternoon. Fucking alone. Eating cupcakes, drinking Tab + watching Dinah Shore + Mike Douglas's talk shows. When Ethan would come home from band we would hang out in his room + listen to music together. Singing "Let's Get Physical" wishing I were a skinny, blue eyed blond Austalian Olivia Newton John or "I Love Rockn Roll", or "Another Brick in the Wall."

Then Ethan abandoned me too. I'm a survivor I know, but am at the edge of what I can deal with right now. Shit, I have not thought about any of this in such a long time.

JS
Jeremy Stark

BO
Brooke Orser

4:00 PM

The housekeeper was not happy I passed out on the swede sofa last night she screamed when she found me sleeping there this morning happy she woke me up so I could get to work on time

iMessage

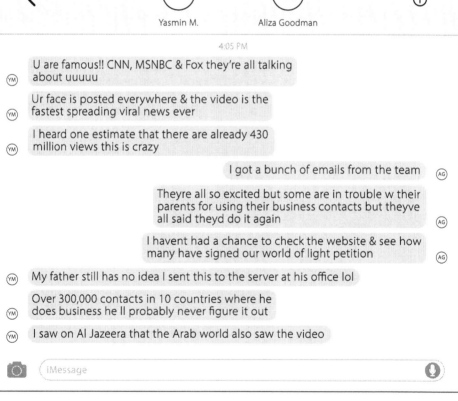

YM
Yasmin M.

AG
Aliza Goodman

4:05 PM

U are famous!! CNN, MSNBC & Fox they're all talking about uuuuu

Ur face is posted everywhere & the video is the fastest spreading viral news ever

I heard one estimate that there are already 430 million views this is crazy

I got a bunch of emails from the team

Theyre all so excited but some are in trouble w their parents for using their business contacts but theyve all said theyd do it again

I havent had a chance to check the website & see how many have signed our world of light petition

My father still has no idea I sent this to the server at his office lol

Over 300,000 contacts in 10 countries where he does business he ll probably never figure it out

I saw on Al Jazeera that the Arab world also saw the video

iMessage

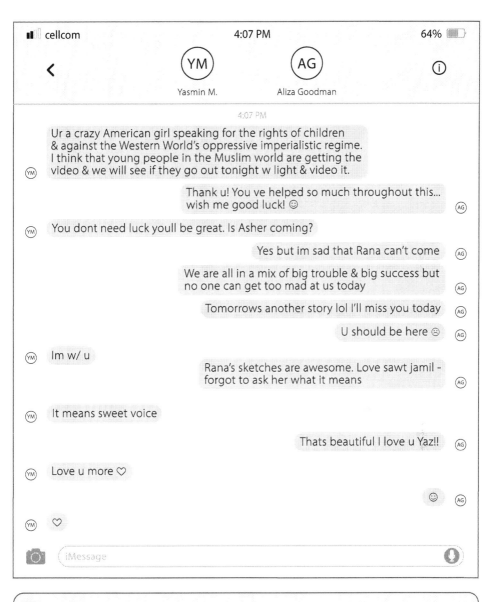

YM Yasmin M.   **AG** Aliza Goodman

4:07 PM

Ur a crazy American girl speaking for the rights of children & against the Western World's oppressive imperialistic regime. I think that young people in the Muslim world are getting the video & we will see if they go out tonight w light & video it.

Thank u! You ve helped so much throughout this... wish me good luck! ☺

You dont need luck youll be great. Is Asher coming?

Yes but im sad that Rana can't come

We are all in a mix of big trouble & big success but no one can get too mad at us today

Tomorrows another story lol I'll miss you today

U should be here ☹

Im w/ u

Rana's sketches are awesome. Love sawt jamil - forgot to ask her what it means

It means sweet voice

Thats beautiful I love u Yaz!!

Love u more ♡

☺

♡

 iMessage

JN24:   now

Israeli beaches are covered with jellyfish making bathing a challenge in the hot summer.

Jewish News You Can Use

427

Forgiveness

Molly <Molly@LiveLoveLaugh.com>   4:10PM
to Aliza

Remember when our families were at the beach & I was supposed to watch you? You disappeared while I changed out of my wet bathing suit & I was convinced you went back to swim & drowned. I had lifeguards searching the beach & the water. You had walked into town to buy chocolate chip cookies & came back an hour later with a stomachache. Both our moms blamed me & the lifeguards hated me the rest of the vacation. I was so fucking mad at you. When I thought you might be dead last night, I finally forgave you. LOL! Have a great bat mitzvah & I hope as a woman, you will make better decisions & not drive everyone around you crazy. I've been on the receiving end. It isn't fun. Mazel Tov on the bat mitzvah – welcome to womanhood. Mazel Tov on the video – it is really cool & it's all everyone in the Senator's office & all of DC is talking about today. Xxooxx

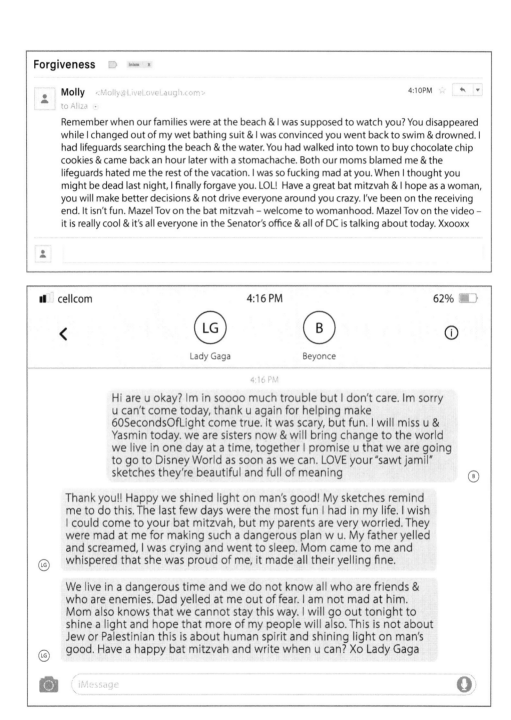

cellcom   4:16 PM   62%

<   **LG**   **B**   ⓘ

Lady Gaga   Beyonce

4:16 PM

Hi are u okay? Im in soooo much trouble but I don't care. Im sorry u can't come today, thank u again for helping make 60SecondsOfLight come true. it was scary, but fun. I will miss u & Yasmin today. we are sisters now & will bring change to the world we live in one day at a time, together I promise u that we are going to go to Disney World as soon as we can. LOVE your "sawt jamil" sketches they're beautiful and full of meaning

Thank you!! Happy we shined light on man's good! My sketches remind me to do this. The last few days were the most fun I had in my life. I wish I could come to your bat mitzvah, but my parents are very worried. They were mad at me for making such a dangerous plan w u. My father yelled and screamed, I was crying and went to sleep. Mom came to me and whispered that she was proud of me, it made all their yelling fine.

We live in a dangerous time and we do not know all who are friends & who are enemies. Dad yelled at me out of fear. I am not mad at him. Mom also knows that we cannot stay this way. I will go out tonight to shine a light and hope that more of my people will also. This is not about Jew or Palestinian this is about human spirit and shining light on man's good. Have a happy bat mitzvah and write when u can? Xo Lady Gaga

iMessage

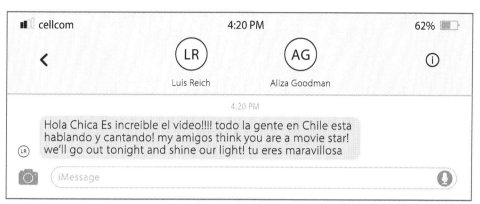

LR
Luis Reich

AG
Aliza Goodman

4:20 PM

Hola Chica Es increible el video!!!! todo la gente en Chile esta hablando y cantando! my amigos think you are a movie star! we'll go out tonight and shine our light! tu eres maravillosa

iMessage

MYJOURNAL.COM

Let There Be Light
Roaming Roman

Aliza's bat mitzvah will start shortly. Last night she was missing and today she is an international celebrity. Her video message is one of hope brilliantly shared by other youth across the globe. She was clever enough to send it right off to me and ask me to share it with Bruno. His company has over 5 million followers in Europe and of course, he was happy to send it out immediately. I look forward to the world's response tonight at 10pm – How will they demonstrate their objection to injustice and abuse? Will they come out and shine a light in solidarity? It is brilliant to imagine the potential of one small person in our world doing something so positive.

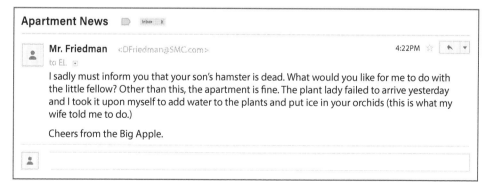

Apartment News   Inbox x

Mr. Friedman <DFriedman@SMC.com>   4:22PM
to EL

I sadly must inform you that your son's hamster is dead. What would you like for me to do with the little fellow? Other than this, the apartment is fine. The plant lady failed to arrive yesterday and I took it upon myself to add water to the plants and put ice in your orchids (this is what my wife told me to do.)

Cheers from the Big Apple.

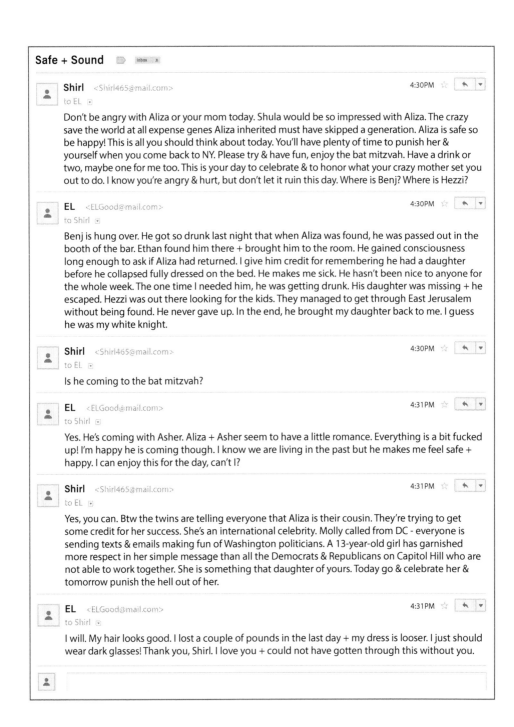

Safe + Sound 〉 Inbox x

Shirl <Shirl465@mail.com>   4:30PM
to EL

Don't be angry with Aliza or your mom today. Shula would be so impressed with Aliza. The crazy save the world at all expense genes Aliza inherited must have skipped a generation. Aliza is safe so be happy! This is all you should think about today. You'll have plenty of time to punish her & yourself when you come back to NY. Please try & have fun, enjoy the bat mitzvah. Have a drink or two, maybe one for me too. This is your day to celebrate & to honor what your crazy mother set you out to do. I know you're angry & hurt, but don't let it ruin this day. Where is Benj? Where is Hezzi?

EL <ELGood@mail.com>   4:30PM
to Shirl

Benj is hung over. He got so drunk last night that when Aliza was found, he was passed out in the booth of the bar. Ethan found him there + brought him to the room. He gained consciousness long enough to ask if Aliza had returned. I give him credit for remembering he had a daughter before he collapsed fully dressed on the bed. He makes me sick. He hasn't been nice to anyone for the whole week. The one time I needed him, he was getting drunk. His daughter was missing + he escaped. Hezzi was out there looking for the kids. They managed to get through East Jerusalem without being found. He never gave up. In the end, he brought my daughter back to me. I guess he was my white knight.

Shirl <Shirl465@mail.com>   4:30PM
to EL

Is he coming to the bat mitzvah?

EL <ELGood@mail.com>   4:31PM
to Shirl

Yes. He's coming with Asher. Aliza + Asher seem to have a little romance. Everything is a bit fucked up! I'm happy he is coming though. I know we are living in the past but he makes me feel safe + happy. I can enjoy this for the day, can't I?

Shirl <Shirl465@mail.com>   4:31PM
to EL

Yes, you can. Btw the twins are telling everyone that Aliza is their cousin. They're trying to get some credit for her success. She's an international celebrity. Molly called from DC - everyone is sending texts & emails making fun of Washington politicians. A 13-year-old girl has garnished more respect in her simple message than all the Democrats & Republicans on Capitol Hill who are not able to work together. She is something that daughter of yours. Today go & celebrate her & tomorrow punish the hell out of her.

EL <ELGood@mail.com>   4:31PM
to Shirl

I will. My hair looks good. I lost a couple of pounds in the last day + my dress is looser. I just should wear dark glasses! Thank you, Shirl. I love you + could not have gotten through this without you.

Safe + Sound   📥 Inbox ✕

Shirl <Shirl465@mail.com>   4:31PM ☆ ↩ ▾
to Laura ▾
I love you. :-) XOME

EL <ELGood@mail.com>   4:31PM ☆ ↩ ▾
to Laura ▾
Luv you too.

Aliza Goodman's Daily Motivational Quote #4:   now

"Our diversity is our strength, our unity is our power."
Speaker Nancy Pelosi

MotiQuote.com

Time for Change   📥 Inbox ✕

Laura <L.Friedman@SHH.com>   4:56PM ☆ ↩ ▾
to Benj ▾

Hi Benj.

I am not sure if you are getting emails? I just wanted to say Mazel Tov on your daughter's bat mitzvah. Today is your opportunity to celebrate your beautiful daughter, as she becomes a woman, marking her Jewish education and bringing down the walls of hurt that all families create. You are her father; your daughter needs you to be there for her. I understand the hurt you experienced with your father, but please I urge you to make peace with your mother, your sister, and yourself. A Jewish family's celebration is the ideal opportunity to mend fences and build futures.

I know I overstep my bounds as your assistant, but I'm also your friend and ghost writer. You told me a lot about Aliza. Today share with her your personal thoughts. Your speech is very good and meaningful. Now you can fire me, but I could not live with myself if I did not step back and take a breath to tell you what I believe. We spend many hours working together and I know you Benj. Under the asshole shield you have created, there is a good man who wants to be free.

Your daughter's video asks the world to shine a light for change. Perhaps this is your opportunity to shine a light on what you need to do for change. Shine a light on what is important. Your business deals will keep happening and you will keep getting richer and richer, but the great opportunities to enrich your family and your relationships will be harder and harder to find.

This is your time to shine. This is something money cannot buy.

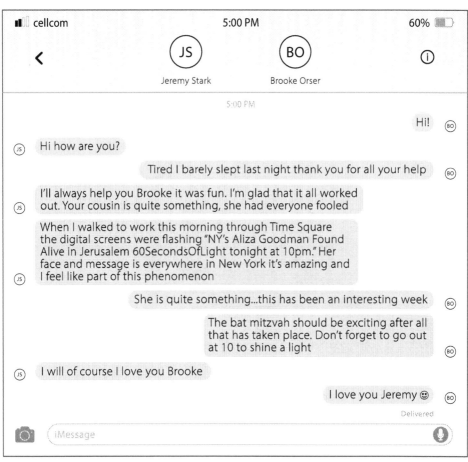

JS　　　　　　BO

Jeremy Stark　　Brooke Orser

5:00 PM

Hi!

Hi how are you?

Tired I barely slept last night thank you for all your help

I'll always help you Brooke it was fun. I'm glad that it all worked out. Your cousin is quite something, she had everyone fooled

When I walked to work this morning through Time Square the digital screens were flashing "NY's Aliza Goodman Found Alive in Jerusalem 60SecondsOfLight tonight at 10pm." Her face and message is everywhere in New York it's amazing and I feel like part of this phenomenon

She is quite something...this has been an interesting week

The bat mitzvah should be exciting after all that has taken place. Don't forget to go out at 10 to shine a light

I will of course I love you Brooke

I love you Jeremy ☺

Delivered

iMessage

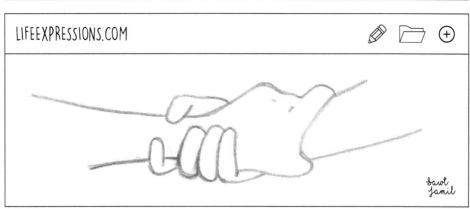

LIFEEXPRESSIONS.COM

< 　　　　　　**Theo & Rose**

Theo
I fell asleep on the couch. I am sorry I was not there for you. You are at the bat mitzvah now. This will be quite a celebration after the whole week together and the very long night you spent worrying to death. She is quite an interesting young woman. Her stunt garnished the world's attention. The CNN panel was divided on what she did. They all agreed that her message is a very good one but had she not caused a massive manhunt, the reaction to her video would have been much less. I think this is correct but it is not relevant. She is an international hero. They reported that almost a billion people could see her video by 10pm tonight. I think she will have great success in bringing the world together – not just the young people. I am going to walk down to the beach with Pam and Steve and join the folks there sending 60SecondsOfLight to the heavens. I miss you so Rose. Mazel Tov. Enjoy your family.

　　　　　　　　Rose
　　　　　　　　Thank you. I will my love. I will. Need to turn off the phone now.

+ 　(　　　　　　　　　　　　　　　)　

Aliza Goodman's Daily Motivational Quote #5:　　　　　　now
"Empathy is communicating that incredibly healing message of 'You're not alone.'"
Brene Brown

MotiQuote.com

Jack Billings' Notes

Aliza Sophia Goodman of New York City will shortly celebrate her bat mitzvah at the Southern Wall of the Temple Mount. Her American and Israeli family join her in this rite of passage, as she becomes a woman in the Jewish religion.

Tonight, as the sun sets on the vast stone walls and she chants her Torah, she will share her message that the youth of the world must come together to shine lights on the world's problems and challenges, showing solidarity across borders, religions, ethnicity, and beliefs. The future can be different and the patterns of their parents' generations do not need to continue.

Through Aliza's video 60SecondsofLight, she has asked the world to come together tonight wherever they live, go outside and shine lights to the sky in unison. Across the globe, the light will mark a new beginning - young and old realize they are all connected and in this world, together.

Almost 1 billion people have viewed 60SecondsOfLight internationally. This short video in over twentyfive languages shares a simple and powerful message of Love and Hope that all humans can appreciate. While the video addresses the youth of the world, social media indicates there will be a turn out from all ages empowered by this message of inclusion.

See you at 10pm tonight.

LIFEEXPRESSIONS.COM

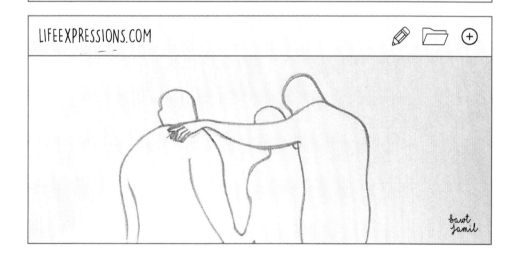

Dear Lucas Goodman, Astronaut in Training –

@JUNIORNASAUSA

| Crew | About | Photos |

TODAY ON THE INTERNATIONAL SPACE STATION:

Looking down on Earth from the International Space Station (@ISS) astronauts are accustomed to take breathtaking pictures of earth. Tonight, as the clock struck 10pm in the Northern and Southern Hempisheres, the Space Station raced around the globe capturing once in a lifetime, incredible photos of powerful light radiating from the earth's surface that we have never witnessed so intensely all at once. Aliza Goodman's 60SecondsOfLight Campaign sent the universe and those of us in outer space a clear message that the strength of the world's youth united goes beyond human imagination and there are no limits or boundaries. We observed substantial lights from lightly populated regions that usually appear pitch black at night; we viewed countries across the globe flickering with brighter lights with an unusually greater abundance of energy; and we were stunned to enjoy brilliant city centers illuminating exponentially grander than we have yet experienced from the Cupola's windows in the International Space Station.

As we circled the globe and passed through regions at 10pm local time, the positive energy emanating from the earth's surface was contagious and uplifting for all of us out here in space. This revolution is a testament to Aliza Goodman, a powerful young woman who encouraged the youth of the world to shine a light on the darkness of mankind and envisioned uniting the world simply with love and cooperation.

We are in space conducting experiments to help humans across the globe and proudly share in Aliza's emotional and thoughtful message of unity and hope.

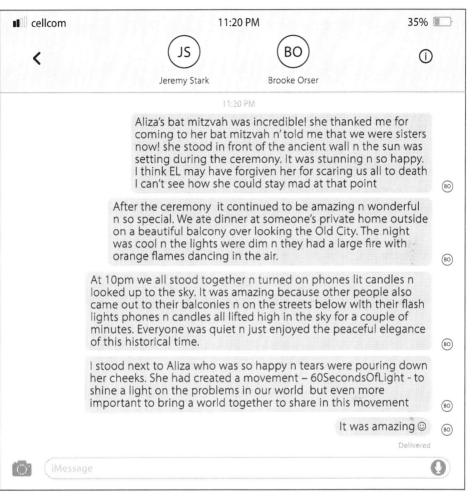

JS — Jeremy Stark
BO — Brooke Orser

11:20 PM

Aliza's bat mitzvah was incredible! she thanked me for coming to her bat mitzvah n' told me that we were sisters now! she stood in front of the ancient wall n the sun was setting during the ceremony. It was stunning n so happy. I think EL may have forgiven her for scaring us all to death I can't see how she could stay mad at that point

After the ceremony it continued to be amazing n wonderful n so special. We ate dinner at someone's private home outside on a beautiful balcony over looking the Old City. The night was cool n the lights were dim n they had a large fire with orange flames dancing in the air.

At 10pm we all stood together n turned on phones lit candles n looked up to the sky. It was amazing because other people also came out to their balconies n on the streets below with their flash lights phones n candles all lifted high in the sky for a couple of minutes. Everyone was quiet n just enjoyed the peaceful elegance of this historical time.

I stood next to Aliza who was so happy n tears were pouring down her cheeks. She had created a movement – 60SecondsOfLight - to shine a light on the problems in our world but even more important to bring a world together to share in this movement

It was amazing ☺

Delivered

iMessage

LIFEEXPRESSIONS.COM

60 Seconds of Light
Roaming Roman

Aliza's bat mitzvah was spectacular as the sun descended against the raw, ancient temple's southern wall. My niece performed her bat mitzvah service fluently and with amazing grace. Her Hebrew sounded natural and her speech about 'disputes and miracles', a topic close to my heart, was uplifting and extremely profound coming from a 13-year-old. She was divine, poised and smart; she made everyone feel so fortunate to be part of her life and her celebration. Aliza's frightful disappearance brought us all so close and her bat mitzvah engrained us all in her life forever. She may have stepped on to the bima a child, but she stepped down as a woman. While her service was remarkable, I was not prepared for the emotional impact of her 60SecondsOfLight phenomenon. At 10pm, we stood on the balcony in the Old City of Jerusalam where we feasted on a divine Israeli banquet and excitedly shined our lights to the skies with local Jerusalem residents. Everywhere I looked it was magical, people poured onto the streets and filled the Old City's balconies... passionately... participating in Aliza's request to shine a light of unity into the sky. Tears poured from all our eyes. I cannot remember experiencing this connection in such a vast setting in all my life. I have protested and marched with hundreds of thousands in vital movements, but this was even more remarkable and moving. 60SecondsOfLight brought the world together as a movement of collective empathy.

LIFEEXPRESSIONS.COM

Night Sky

Brooke G.O.

Bright lights shine
Love wins
Dark heavens illuminate
Abolish hate.

Currents change
Working together
Tides turn
People learn.

Showed up
Hope alive
People play
Fresh day.

Happy Birthday Inbox ✕

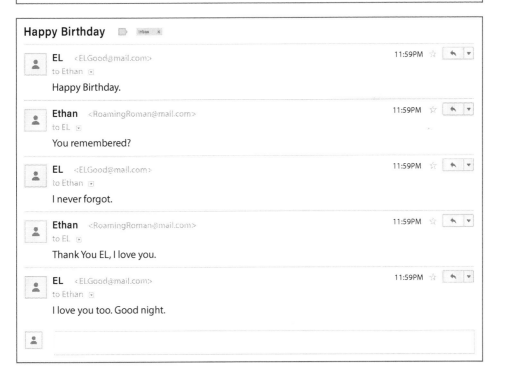

👤	**EL** <ELGood@mail.com> to Ethan ▾	11:59PM ☆ ↰ ▾
	Happy Birthday.	

👤	**Ethan** <RoamingRoman@mail.com> to EL ▾	11:59PM ☆ ↰ ▾
	You remembered?	

👤	**EL** <ELGood@mail.com> to Ethan ▾	11:59PM ☆ ↰ ▾
	I never forgot.	

👤	**Ethan** <RoamingRoman@mail.com> to EL ▾	11:59PM ☆ ↰ ▾
	Thank You EL, I love you.	

👤	**EL** <ELGood@mail.com> to Ethan ▾	11:59PM ☆ ↰ ▾
	I love you too. Good night.	

👤

FOOD AFFAIR WITH KATE

DIVINE, DELICIOUS, AND DELIGHTFUL   ABOUT   RECIPES   CONTACT

The Last Supper

★ ★ ★ ★ ★

Walking distance from where we dined, Jesus ate his final meal. I only hope his food was half as good as my final Jerusalem dinner lounging on an antique balcony under an open, star freckled dark sky in the holiest city celebrating my niece's bat mitzvah.

Tonight, we feasted on T'Beet, the Queen of Middle Eastern cuisine, a rice and chicken extravaganza sauted with a tomato and onion, over powered by spice, Baharat's pungent spice mix of cardamom, cassia, cinnamon, all spice, black pepper, nutmeg and cloves. T'Beet, traditionally a Sabbath meal, slowly cooks over a fire. After many hours over a low flame, the chicken and rice absorb a rich Baharat flavor, and remain tender while a thick crust develops along the large pot's bottom. T'Beet then serves upside down with the thick bottom crust becoming the dome shaped top. Eating this Iraqi treasure is a culinary adventure. Dark brown rice crust, rich and crunchy, sweet like a candy; perfectly moist and flavorful rice filled with chicken pieces. Each bite varied and divine invites another to passionately follow. This meal literally melts in your mouth and leaves a majestic understanding of history and tradition on your tongue. T'Beet will be one of those meals that stands out as perhaps the finest confluence of flavors, textures and enjoyment on this Israeli journey. Spices for T'Beet can be purchased at many Middle Eastern markets in the States.

See the photos below and check out Food Affair With Kate on Instagram and Facebook. #Israelcuisine #rice #iraqicuisine #lastsupper #divinedinner

Jack Billings' Notes

At 10pm this evening, the world was brighter as millions of youth across the globe shined a light of hope and empathy to the sky. This was part of New York teenager, Aliza Goodman's 60SecondsOfLight campaign. Barely 24 hours before, Aliza went missing in East Jerusalem and was the cause of a national search party. Her disappearance and then her campaign to shine light on the world's problems that the youth will inherit have brought people together around the globe. Tonight proved that when people of all religions and races want to come together for the good of humanity, anything is possible. The breathtaking photos from the International Space Station powerfully illuminate the increase in light viewed this evening in comparison to typical June nights from outer space. The miracle of one young woman with a vision is a lesson for citizens of the world and their leaders.

.ıl cellcom	12:59 AM	30% 🔋

‹   (YM)   (AG)   ⓘ

Yasmin M.   Aliza Goodman

12:59 AM

> We did it!!! tonight was a huge success from what I heard on the news & what I saw around me in Jerusalem (AG)

> At 10 we all stood on this balcony & shined our phones into the sky (AG)

> I was crying & smiling so much it was sick (AG)

> I felt happy & scared at the same time but I honestly cant explain why! Everywhere I looked people were on their balconies & on the streets below shining their lights too (AG)

Delivered

iMessage 🎤

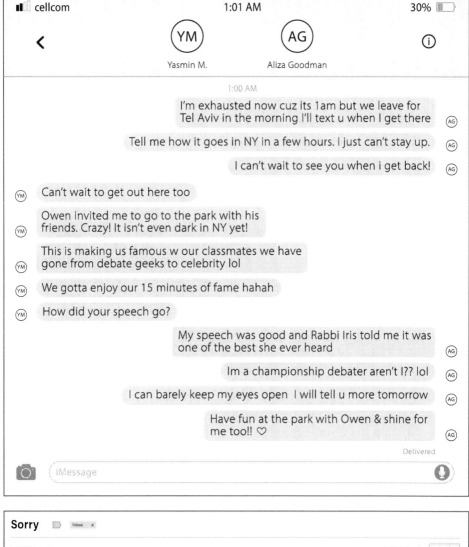

YM
Yasmin M.

AG
Aliza Goodman

1:00 AM

I'm exhausted now cuz its 1am but we leave for Tel Aviv in the morning I'll text u when I get there

Tell me how it goes in NY in a few hours. I just can't stay up.

I can't wait to see you when i get back!

Can't wait to get out here too

Owen invited me to go to the park with his friends. Crazy! It isn't even dark in NY yet!

This is making us famous w our classmates we have gone from debate geeks to celebrity lol

We gotta enjoy our 15 minutes of fame hahah

How did your speech go?

My speech was good and Rabbi Iris told me it was one of the best she ever heard

Im a championship debater aren't I?? lol

I can barely keep my eyes open I will tell u more tomorrow

Have fun at the park with Owen & shine for me too!! ♡

Delivered

iMessage

Sorry   Inbox x

Aliza   <AlizaGood@mail.com>   1:04AM
to Molly

Thank you for forgiving me Molly.

Im sorry but like it was for chocolate chip cookies.

Andy Orser
Now · Israel

•••

GOY IN THE HOLY LAND PART 36

Aliza's bat mitzvah was a life changing experience. If I had written and produced the most perfectly moving and meaningful movie, I could not have achieved the excellence in light, texture, context and story of this ceremony. Aliza's fearful disappearance one night earlier juxtaposed to her glorious bat mitzvah at the foot of the Ancient Temple wall was followed by the tremendous experience of standing in the Jerusalem dark night side by side with family and Israelis shining light in unison to the heavens for Peace and Hope, told an impactful story I am not sure could be captured by film. I am not convinced that one experiences this authentic breath of emotion once again in a life time. How do we get 60 Seconds of Lights to be just the beginning? We need to keep the energy alive and share it with everyone around the world to say no to hate, yes to love!

Clearly the strong message that we are all united in our efforts and at the end of the day, we all want the same things for our families and ourselves: Safety, Health, Love, Peace, Kindness, Respect and Connectivity. My niece at 13 years old made all of us stop and think, use technology for good and open our hearts to others around us and around the world. What a blessing. #peace #hope #60SecondsofLight

👍 Like   💬 Comment   ➤ Share

.ıl cellcom   1:12 AM   25% 🔋

< **Theo & Rose**

Rose
The bat mitzvah was special. I wish you had been there to see the magical evening. Little Aliza stood powerfully in front of the great big Southern Wall of the Temple Mount and performed her bat mitzvah with a lovely female rabbi by her side. Aliza gave a great speech in English and Hebrew. She spoke a little fast for me but I heard her clearly thank me for coming on her trip and how happy she was to have me in her life. I have three more grandchildren now, which is a Holy Land miracle. EL brought us all to tears. She said she would give her speech to Aliza later. After the events of the last 24 hours, she just could not read it.

+ (   ) 📷 🎤

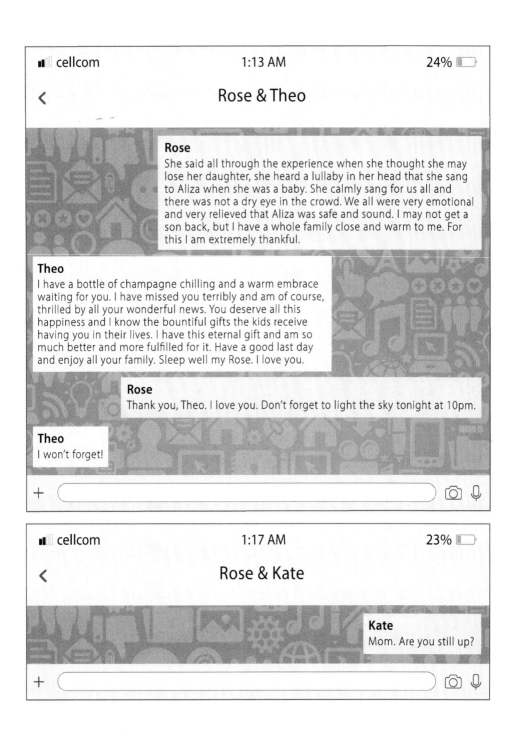

Rose & Theo

Rose
She said all through the experience when she thought she may lose her daughter, she heard a lullaby in her head that she sang to Aliza when she was a baby. She calmly sang for us all and there was not a dry eye in the crowd. We all were very emotional and very relieved that Aliza was safe and sound. I may not get a son back, but I have a whole family close and warm to me. For this I am extremely thankful.

Theo
I have a bottle of champagne chilling and a warm embrace waiting for you. I have missed you terribly and am of course, thrilled by all your wonderful news. You deserve all this happiness and I know the bountiful gifts the kids receive having you in their lives. I have this eternal gift and am so much better and more fulfilled for it. Have a good last day and enjoy all your family. Sleep well my Rose. I love you.

Rose
Thank you, Theo. I love you. Don't forget to light the sky tonight at 10pm.

Theo
I won't forget!

+ ⟨　　　　　　　　　　　　　　　　　⟩ ◎ ◉

Rose & Kate

Kate
Mom. Are you still up?

+ ⟨　　　　　　　　　　　　　　　　　⟩ ◎ ◉

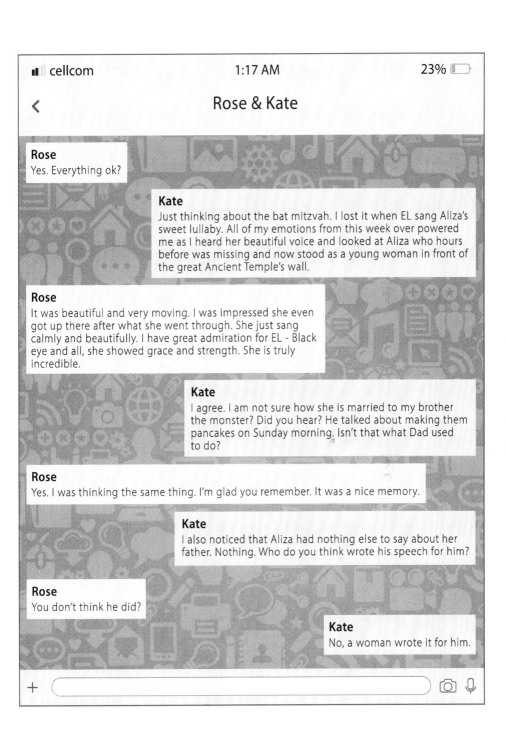

Rose
Yes. Everything ok?

Kate
Just thinking about the bat mitzvah. I lost it when EL sang Aliza's sweet lullaby. All of my emotions from this week over powered me as I heard her beautiful voice and looked at Aliza who hours before was missing and now stood as a young woman in front of the great Ancient Temple's wall.

Rose
It was beautiful and very moving. I was impressed she even got up there after what she went through. She just sang calmly and beautifully. I have great admiration for EL - Black eye and all, she showed grace and strength. She is truly incredible.

Kate
I agree. I am not sure how she is married to my brother the monster? Did you hear? He talked about making them pancakes on Sunday morning. Isn't that what Dad used to do?

Rose
Yes. I was thinking the same thing. I'm glad you remember. It was a nice memory.

Kate
I also noticed that Aliza had nothing else to say about her father. Nothing. Who do you think wrote his speech for him?

Rose
You don't think he did?

Kate
No, a woman wrote it for him.

\+   〇   🔲 📷 🎤

<   **Rose & Kate**

Rose
I did think it was awfully warm and friendly for him.

Kate
Aliza said wonderful things about you Mommy. All true of course!

Rose
Thank you. I did feel very special when she said how happy she was to have me in her life and to be at her bat mitzvah.

Kate
You are very special. I love you Mommy.

Rose
I love you Katie. Sweet dreams.

Kate
Xo

<   (LR)   (AG)   ⓘ

Luis Reich   Aliza Goodman

6:00 AM

Hola Chica. Fue increible! The whole city was out shining light to the skies! it was like a Santiago New Year's Eve Party! you made my friends a party! I think the whole country, maybe the whole world was out tonight. gracias chica... see you at school in a few months

iMessage

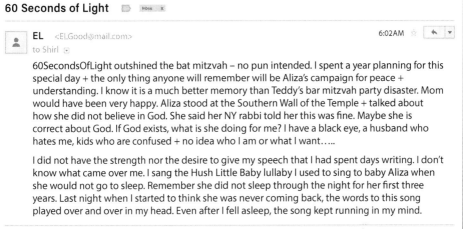

60 Seconds of Light 📥 Inbox ✕

EL <ELGood@mail.com>   6:02AM ☆ ↩ ▾
to Shirl ▾

60SecondsOfLight outshined the bat mitzvah – no pun intended. I spent a year planning for this special day + the only thing anyone will remember will be Aliza's campaign for peace + understanding. I know it is a much better memory than Teddy's bar mitzvah party disaster. Mom would have been very happy. Aliza stood at the Southern Wall of the Temple + talked about how she did not believe in God. She said her NY rabbi told her this was fine. Maybe she is correct about God. If God exists, what is she doing for me? I have a black eye, a husband who hates me, kids who are confused + no idea who I am or what I want…..

I did not have the strength nor the desire to give my speech that I had spent days writing. I don't know what came over me. I sang the Hush Little Baby lullaby I used to sing to baby Aliza when she would not go to sleep. Remember she did not sleep through the night for her first three years. Last night when I started to think she was never coming back, the words to this song played over and over in my head. Even after I fell asleep, the song kept running in my mind.

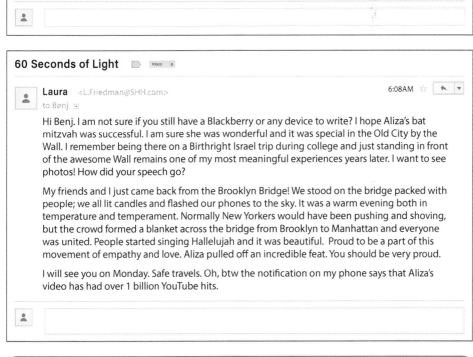

60 Seconds of Light 📥 Inbox ✕

Laura <L.Friedman@SHH.com>   6:08AM ☆ ↩ ▾
to Benj ▾

Hi Benj. I am not sure if you still have a Blackberry or any device to write? I hope Aliza's bat mitzvah was successful. I am sure she was wonderful and it was special in the Old City by the Wall. I remember being there on a Birthright Israel trip during college and just standing in front of the awesome Wall remains one of my most meaningful experiences years later. I want to see photos! How did your speech go?

My friends and I just came back from the Brooklyn Bridge! We stood on the bridge packed with people; we all lit candles and flashed our phones to the sky. It was a warm evening both in temperature and temperament. Normally New Yorkers would have been pushing and shoving, but the crowd formed a blanket across the bridge from Brooklyn to Manhattan and everyone was united. People started singing Hallelujah and it was beautiful. Proud to be a part of this movement of empathy and love. Aliza pulled off an incredible feat. You should be very proud.

I will see you on Monday. Safe travels. Oh, btw the notification on my phone says that Aliza's video has had over 1 billion YouTube hits.

JN24:   now

Jerusalem municipality removes anti-gay platforms of intolerance.

Jewish News You Can Use

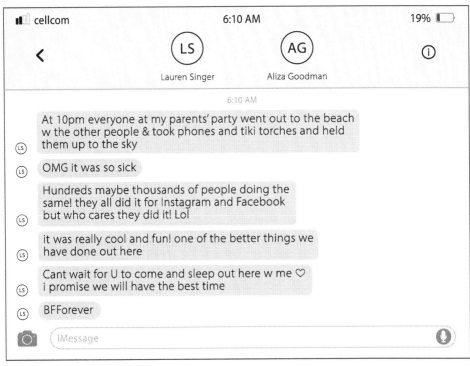

6:10 AM

At 10pm everyone at my parents' party went out to the beach w the other people & took phones and tiki torches and held them up to the sky

OMG it was so sick

Hundreds maybe thousands of people doing the same! they all did it for Instagram and Facebook but who cares they did it! Lol

it was really cool and fun! one of the better things we have done out here

Cant wait for U to come and sleep out here w me ♡ i promise we will have the best time

BFForever

iMessage

6:13 AM

My moms and I went up to our rooftop and shined all the lights we had up to the sky! it was so bright! Other neighbor's rooftops were full too. I think we made New York much brighter

My cousin Marci just texted me that she went out to Centennial Park in Tulsa Oklahoma where she lives and it was packed w people all shining light. They had John Legend blasting from the park's sound system and people were dancing and singing. u have made a revolution, it is awesome.

iMessage

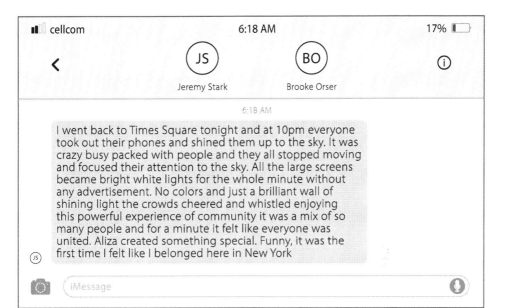

JS — Jeremy Stark

BO — Brooke Orser

6:18 AM

I went back to Times Square tonight and at 10pm everyone took out their phones and shined them up to the sky. It was crazy busy packed with people and they all stopped moving and focused their attention to the sky. All the large screens became bright white lights for the whole minute without any advertisement. No colors and just a brilliant wall of shining light the crowds cheered and whistled enjoying this powerful experience of community it was a mix of so many people and for a minute it felt like everyone was united. Aliza created something special. Funny, it was the first time I felt like I belonged here in New York

iMessage

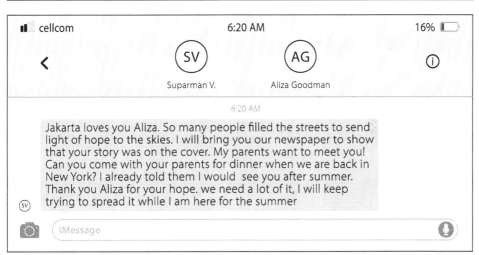

cellcom 6:20 AM 16%

SV — Suparman V.

AG — Aliza Goodman

6:20 AM

Jakarta loves you Aliza. So many people filled the streets to send light of hope to the skies. I will bring you our newspaper to show that your story was on the cover. My parents want to meet you! Can you come with your parents for dinner when we are back in New York? I already told them I would see you after summer. Thank you Aliza for your hope. we need a lot of it, I will keep trying to spread it while I am here for the summer

iMessage

 JN24: now

Shortly after residents of East Jerusalem filled the sky with their own lights at 10pm this evening, East Jerusalem power was restored after an extended and paralyzing black out.

Jewish News You Can Use

60 Seconds of Light

Aliza's video has been on the news all day. I went out to the beach with the neighbors here n we joined many others, well mostly young people havin' bon fires, drinkin' n singin' on a warm summer evenin'. At 10pm everyone stood up n shined his or her lights to the sky. It's been hazy but tonight the skies were unusually clear. Felt like they opened for Aliza's message. I think all of Florida was out tonight shinin' light to the sky. When I looked up, I swear I saw y' mama smilin' down. She would've been so proud n excited by her granddaughter. I'm sure she scared y'all to death but I hope y'can realize how amazin' her concept is n needed in this world! I'm plannin' to fly to New York on Tuesday n will stay at Marci's apartment. Y'remember Marci? She's the lovely woman who y'mama met when she studied to be a teacher. She also got pregnant n never worked as a teacher. Her husband was the famous cardiologist who had the talk show about healthy diets n exercise; remember one day in the middle of the show, he dropped dead from a heart attack? The talk around town was how he saved thousands of lives through diet n exercise, but couldn't save his own. Marci's on a cruise with her new boyfriend but her apartment has an extra room; she told me I could stay there whenever I came back to town. It is only a few blocks from y' place. We will have plenty of time to spend together talkin'. I'm also bringin' good walkin' shoes so we can take long walks in the park. We're long overdue. I have a lot to tell y'all.

I sure hope y' last day is a great one. Y' worked so hard to create a magical spectactular week for y' family n y' mama. Now y' take care of EL! I'll help y' but y' gotta start actin' like a big girl.

452

BOKER TOV

Goodman Family!

Welcome to day eight of your Holy Land excursion!
Here is today's schedule:

Inspiration and Independence

Shabbat Shalom. Aliza's bat mitzvah and 60SecondsOfLight were remarkable and inspiring events in our Holy City and across the world yesterday. This morning, we will travel to the City of Tel Aviv where even on Shabbat there is plenty to do and little time for rest. We say, "Haifa works, Jerusalem prays, and Tel Aviv plays."

We will make a brief stop at the Independence Hall Museum in Tel Aviv to see where the Declaration of the State of Israel took place on May 14, 1948. We will then visit Jaffa, South Tel Aviv, an ancient port city famous from biblical stories, battles and international trade; Jaffa served as the main port of entry for Jews to Israel in the 19th Century. Today, Jaffa is an incredible melting pot of Jews and Palestinian Christians and Muslims. Jaffa's narrow cobble stone streets are filled with incredible restaurants, artist galleries, flea markets, beautiful beaches and ports and stunning views of the Tel Aviv coast. We will check into the Intercontinental Hotel for the rest of the day. You will be free to walk the Tel Aviv Boardwalk, go to the beach or Dizengoff Street for last minute shopping. I have enjoyed this unique visit with your family and can honestly say, I have never had so many eye-opening experiences in my many years of touring as I did this week. You are an interesting, special family and I have greatly appreciated getting to know each of you and spending this week with you.

Todah EL!

Mazel Tov Aliza!

Shalom Chaverim.

Moshe
Rimon Tours

JN24:   now

Palestinian family sues Israeli government for destroying their family home after
their son died in a failed suicide bombing near an army outpost in the West Bank.
Jewish News You Can Use

Hi 📥 Inbox ✕

👤 **Shirl** <Shirl465@mail.com>   7:45AM ☆ ↩ ▾
   to EL ▾

   Where are you?

👤

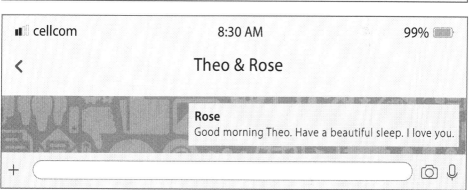

📶 cellcom   8:30 AM   99% 🔋

‹   **Theo & Rose**

> **Rose**
> Good morning Theo. Have a beautiful sleep. I love you.

＋ ⬭⬭⬭⬭⬭⬭⬭⬭⬭⬭⬭⬭⬭⬭⬭⬭⬭⬭ 📷 🎤

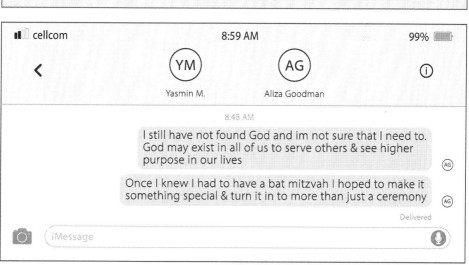

📶 cellcom   8:59 AM   99% 🔋

‹   (YM)   (AG)   ⓘ
           Yasmin M.   Aliza Goodman

                          8:48 AM

         I still have not found God and im not sure that I need to.
         God may exist in all of us to serve others & see higher
         purpose in our lives   (AG)

         Once I knew I had to have a bat mitzvah I hoped to make it
         something special & turn it in to more than just a ceremony (AG)

                                                    Delivered

📷 (iMessage   ) 🎤

<   (YM)   (AG)   ⓘ

Yasmin M.   Aliza Goodman

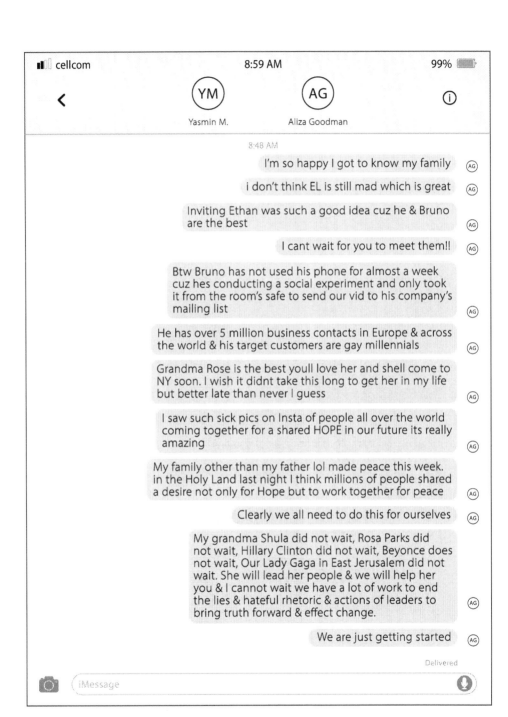

8:48 AM

I'm so happy I got to know my family (AG)

i don't think EL is still mad which is great (AG)

Inviting Ethan was such a good idea cuz he & Bruno are the best (AG)

I cant wait for you to meet them!! (AG)

Btw Bruno has not used his phone for almost a week cuz hes conducting a social experiment and only took it from the room's safe to send our vid to his company's mailing list (AG)

He has over 5 million business contacts in Europe & across the world & his target customers are gay millennials (AG)

Grandma Rose is the best youll love her and shell come to NY soon. I wish it didnt take this long to get her in my life but better late than never I guess (AG)

I saw such sick pics on Insta of people all over the world coming together for a shared HOPE in our future its really amazing (AG)

My family other than my father lol made peace this week. in the Holy Land last night I think millions of people shared a desire not only for Hope but to work together for peace (AG)

Clearly we all need to do this for ourselves (AG)

My grandma Shula did not wait, Rosa Parks did not wait, Hillary Clinton did not wait, Beyonce does not wait, Our Lady Gaga in East Jerusalem did not wait. She will lead her people & we will help her you & I cannot wait we have a lot of work to end the lies & hateful rhetoric & actions of leaders to bring truth forward & effect change. (AG)

We are just getting started (AG)

Delivered

📷 (iMessage   🎤)

We've Only Just Begun
Roaming Roman

I left home at eighteen determined to save my soul. A gay man pretending to be someone else for my parents was not sustainable for me. I have lived an honest life; my life partner and I love each other unconditionally, and yet while living truthfully, I never healed the wound of leaving and losing my family. More than thirty years later, painfully my parents have passed and I made peace only with my mother just before her death, I have reunited with my sister, who remains suspicious of my intent. I cannot blame her, as I have not shared my full story with her. We will both have to work backwards to fill in many chapters, verses and words of our shared story. I believe our childhood memories may be strong enough to weather the passage of time. I am grateful that my niece and nephew went out on a limb to invite me this week; they took a chance and it paid off. Many lessons have been learned in this Holy Land journey – I feel like some healing has started and I hope to continue. Hearing my sister sing even a sweet lullaby reminded me of our improvised shows as kids in our New York apartment where I played the piano and she sang. The two of us had great plans to take our act on the road, tour the world, perform for queens and kings, and be adored by thousands of screaming fans. Not bad dreams for the children of immigrants whose parents worked hard to give their kids the American Dream. It is too late to take our act on the road, but not too late to re-unite as sister and brother – as the Carpenters sang, "We've only just begun."

---

60 Seconds of Light ▢ Inbox x

Maud <Maud@yogavilla.com>   9:15AM ☆ ▢ ▾
to Kate ▢

Santa Monica Beach was ripe for a candle lighting ceremony. Adam and I sat on the sand with thousands of others shining our lights. Looking up the beach was a giant brush stroke of light all the way to the clearest point in Malibu that the naked eye could reach. Proof that humans can be motivated to think beyond themselves and come together to progress an inclusive and thoughtful agenda. Your niece and her passion for change inspired me. She is quite something. Earlier, I received a text from Kay and Bella in New Delhi; they're on their way to an Ashram for a month and wrote that they were in a large sea of people on the streets of Dehli shining lights to the heavens. They said it was incredible and very powerful. I look forward to seeing you next week. Travel with love and safety. Namaste.

"Peace is hard, but we know it is possible. So, together, let us be resolved to see that it is defined by our hopes and not by our fears. Together, let us make peace most importantly that will last."
Barack Obama

MotiQuote.com

LIFEEXPRESSIONS.COM

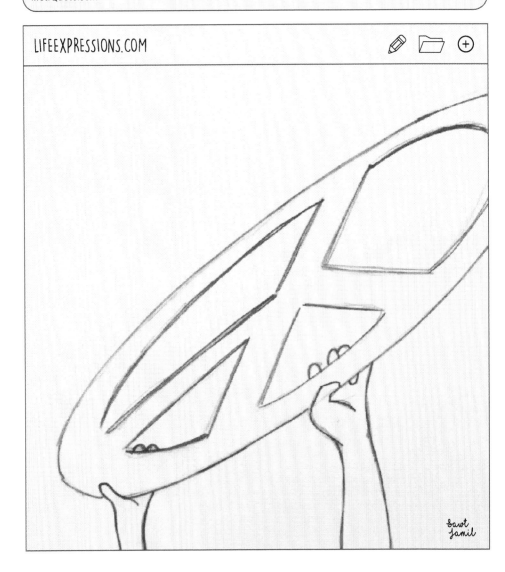

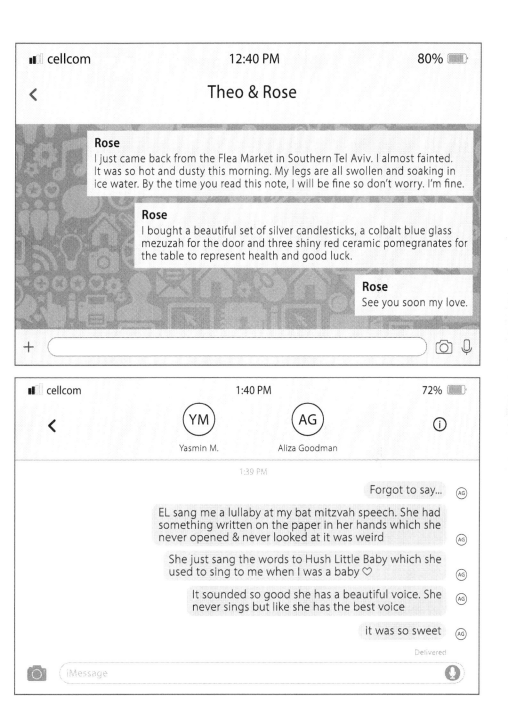

Theo & Rose

Rose
I just came back from the Flea Market in Southern Tel Aviv. I almost fainted. It was so hot and dusty this morning. My legs are all swollen and soaking in ice water. By the time you read this note, I will be fine so don't worry. I'm fine.

Rose
I bought a beautiful set of silver candlesticks, a colbalt blue glass mezuzah for the door and three shiny red ceramic pomegranates for the table to represent health and good luck.

Rose
See you soon my love.

cellcom 1:40 PM 72%

YM **AG**
Yasmin M. Aliza Goodman

1:39 PM

Forgot to say... (AG)

EL sang me a lullaby at my bat mitzvah speech. She had something written on the paper in her hands which she never opened & never looked at it was weird (AG)

She just sang the words to Hush Little Baby which she used to sing to me when I was a baby ♡ (AG)

It sounded so good she has a beautiful voice. She never sings but like she has the best voice (AG)

it was so sweet (AG)

Delivered

iMessage

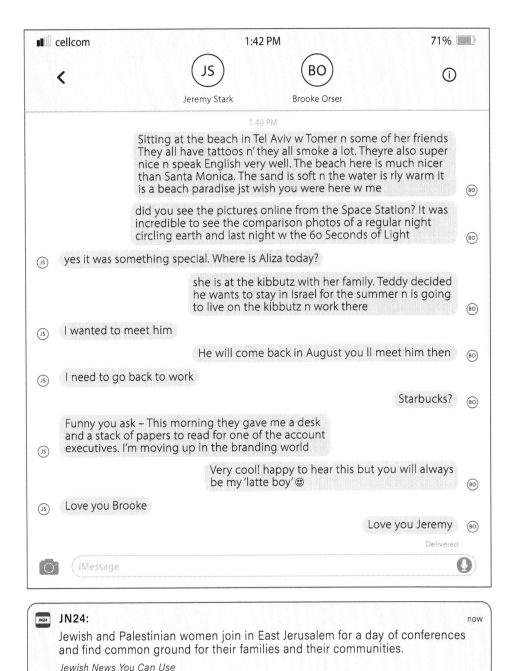

JS Jeremy Stark　　　**BO** Brooke Orser

1:40 PM

Sitting at the beach in Tel Aviv w Tomer n some of her friends They all have tattoos n' they all smoke a lot. Theyre also super nice n speak English very well. The beach here is much nicer than Santa Monica. The sand is soft n the water is rly warm it is a beach paradise jst wish you were here w me

did you see the pictures online from the Space Station? It was incredible to see the comparison photos of a regular night circling earth and last night w the 60 Seconds of Light

yes it was something special. Where is Aliza today?

she is at the kibbutz with her family. Teddy decided he wants to stay in Israel for the summer n is going to live on the kibbutz n work there

I wanted to meet him

He will come back in August you ll meet him then

I need to go back to work

Starbucks?

Funny you ask – This morning they gave me a desk and a stack of papers to read for one of the account executives. I'm moving up in the branding world

Very cool! happy to hear this but you will always be my 'latte boy' ☺

Love you Brooke

Love you Jeremy

Delivered

iMessage

JN24:　　　　　　　　　　　　　　　now
Jewish and Palestinian women join in East Jerusalem for a day of conferences and find common ground for their families and their communities.
Jewish News You Can Use

Andy Orser   •••
Now · Israel

GOY IN THE HOLY LAND PART 37

Aliza's Torah portion at her bat mitzvah told the story of three leaders from the Levi tribe wandering the wilderness, angry that God put Moses and Aaron in charge of the Israelites. These men lie to their followers and create a rebellion against Aaron and Moses. God's punishment is to burn the Israelites in a fire, open the earth for them to fall in and for good measure, God creates a plague and kills thousands more of the rebels intending to make them faithful believers.

God appears to have gone overboard, while teaching people a lesson about jealousy and hate. Ironically these same issues exist in the 21st Century between tribes and nations and many innocent people are victims. The battle between the Palestinians and the Jews in Israel is a ripe example.

Last night, my niece Aliza took this powerful theme and turned it 180 degrees in a different direction to show that people can protest and resist with an honest, non-violent approach and achieve much more positive results.

This morning we stopped at Independence Hall where Israel first announced her Independence back in 1948. Then we visited the stunning, antique Jaffa, in South Tel Aviv, where Jews, Muslims and Christians apparently live side by side in harmony. Jaffa's antique streets and shops, art galleries and flea markets, mosques and churches are full of Israelis wearing hijabs, kippahs and western dress. Diverse folks drink coffee and eat falafel sitting side by side along the beautiful Mediterranean with a stunning view of Tel Aviv City.

The greatest lesson I take from this week in the Holy Land is truly that we all have choices – we can choose love or hate. We need a new breed of leaders who reject war and crisis to keep power. My generation may be outdated and tired, but I have great hope that younger generations will live wiser, more thoughtfully and with greater inclusivity.

Last night felt like the kick off for this new movement! Aliza's role as a leader tells a new and very refreshing story. Coming to Israel has been revolutionary for me. I will miss so much but return to Los Angeles a bit wiser, more appreciative and energized to start my next film. Shalom Haver. Good Bye Friend.

 Like   Comment   Share

New Beginnings
Teddy Goodman

A week of travel with my astonishingly mysterious family wedged between familiar parental debates and disappearing siblings in this ancient land has changed me. I challenged myself to show up to an arena I have avoided for so fucking long, learning that I am ready to move on in bigger ways than I could have imagined when our plane took off from JFK Airport a week ago. The last 48 hours specifically catapulted me to a new dimension that prohibits me from returning to the old loser me. Curiously, I have no idea how the new and improved me will appear, but I am resigned to search for this new being without driving myself too crazy in the process.

Aliza's bat mitzvah is finally over. After her disappearance, I think the only way my non-God believing little sister could redeem herself was to ace her bat mitzvah. I had no doubt she would be great but on top of her newfound fame, she fucking nailed it. She was probably the most famous bat mitzvah in Jewish history after her 60SecondsOfLight Campaign that reached hundreds of millions of people here in Israel and all over the world. Security guards had to hold back the press at the Davidson Center where we had her ceremony. CNN managed to sneak a camera in and people all over the world's witnessed Aliza's service at the foot of the Southern Wall of the Temple Mount. It was pretty cool. She took the themes of her bat mitzvah Torah portion – Disputes + Miracles - and brought them to life in a meaningful manner before our eyes and the world's. She fucking motivated millions of people to protest peacefully together. Then at 10pm as she asked, we stood outside and flashed our phones' flashlights to the sky from the Jerusalem balcony where we ate dinner. All around us other people were also proudly shining their lights. The amount of lights emanating from our small area in the holy city was intense.

The Space Station passing over earth at 10 pm last night captured photos that showed an increased level of lights across the globe. Aliza and her propaganda were the subject of every news station on the hotel TV. She is fucking out there in the spotlight and I am proud of her gutsiness. She took a big chance.

My grandmother Shula must be smiling down from heaven. Her spirit is alive in my little sister. Shula always spoke about two things with great passion – taking care of those less fortunate and her second home in Israel. Mom likes to tell us how her best times were the summers spent on the kibbutz.

New Beginnings
Teddy Goodman

During Aliza's bat mitzvah dinner, I decided I had to also do something bold for myself and asked Uncle Raffi and Aunt Marcel if I could stay in Israel and get a job on the kibbutz. They were ridiculously excited by this notion and I almost regretted my idea as they exploded with enthusiasm. Despite their silly outbreak, I decided I did not care enough to change my mind.

EL and Benj could not say much and I think they may have been relieved to have me out of the apartment for a couple of months. I am sure EL wishes she could stay on the kibbutz too. I will keep writing from the kibbutz as I practice my Hebrew, learn about this interesting country and try to figure out who the fuck I am and what I want before I need to apply for colleges in the fall. I did not want to come on this family trip. I dreaded spending this much time with my family, but I can admit now that it was interesting and valuable.

My world has been shaken and I have a lot to figure out. I hope the kibbutz will be my vessel for self-evaluation and deep discovery – better than going back to my bedroom's four claustrophobic walls and telling my problems to a gray haired, wrinkled shrink.

Senior year will come soon enough. In the meantime, I am a kibbutznik.

Wish me good luck!

Or shall I say Mazel Tov!

Hello?   Inbox x

Laura <L.Friedman@SHH.com>   2:45PM
to Benj

Strange not to hear from you for almost 48 hours? I am quite sure you are not dead. Have a good weekend. Btw – the NYT had amazing photos from last night's 60 Seconds of Light. The aerial photo of the Brooklyn Bridge is beautiful. I will see you on Monday. Have a safe fight home.

Dayanu

The Day After

EL <ELGood@mail.com>
to Shirl

2:48PM

I'm at the kibbutz. A lot has happened. A lot keeps happening. Teddy decided to stay in Israel + will work on the kibbutz. He made these plans without me (what's new!) + everyone here is thrilled to have him. We are at Aunt Marcel's house + he is going to sleep in my old bedroom, look out the window at the fields, smell the fresh morning dew + eat Bamba + Tee-vol.

Shirl <Shirl465@mail.com>
to El

2:49PM

What is Bamba? Tee-vol?

EL <ELGood@mail.com>
to Shirl

2:49PM

Two of the best foods imaginable. Peanut butter puffs + corn shnitzel.

Shirl <Shirl465@mail.com>
to El

2:49PM

Sounds healthy! Are you jealous that he will get to see Hezzi? Maybe you are the one who should be staying?

EL <ELGood@mail.com>
to Shirl

2:49PM

Maybe!

Shirl <Shirl465@mail.com>
to El

2:49PM

What?

EL <ELGood@mail.com>
to Shirl

2:50PM

I am going to make a lot of changes. I am not sure what they are, but I cannot go back to where I was a week ago. I am so fucking predictable + none of it feels good anymore; it has not for a very long time. I am still furious with Aliza but I do give her credit for doing something completely crazy + now Teddy is putting himself out there to try something he could not have imagined doing a week ago. Lucas is always doing something unpredicatable.

Benj + I are stuck in a really bad place + I don't see any light. Not even 60 seconds of it! haha I am not doing anything drastic at this moment, but I know I must do something. I barely recognize my boring, miserable self.

Shirl <Shirl465@mail.com>
to El

2:50PM

Boring? You are on CNN singing Hush Little Baby at the Southern Wall.
You are famous. haha

The Day After 📨 Inbox ✕

EL <ELGood@mail.com> 2:50PM ☆ ↩ ▾
to Shirl ▾

Embarrassing!
I am still boring or shall I say bored with myself.
Seriously, I did make a sort of peace with Ethan.

Shirl <Shirl465@mail.com> 2:51PM ☆ ↩ ▾
to El ▾

Wow, a big step from just a few days ago.

EL <ELGood@mail.com> 2:51PM ☆ ↩ ▾
to Shirl ▾

He is practically the only person who wants to be with me. haha

Shirl <Shirl465@mail.com> 2:51PM ☆ ↩ ▾
to El ▾

I want to be with you.

EL <ELGood@mail.com> 2:51PM ☆ ↩ ▾
to Shirl ▾

I would not be here if it were not for you. Dahlia also has been trying to show me the silver lining.
I know I will survive. I better go now + say goodbye to Teddy.

Shirl <Shirl465@mail.com> 2:52PM ☆ ↩ ▾
to El ▾

What about Hezzi?

EL <ELGood@mail.com> 2:52PM ☆ ↩ ▾
to Shirl ▾

We said our good byes. I will tell you more when I am back home. Love You.

Shirl <Shirl465@mail.com> 2:52PM ☆ ↩ ▾
to El ▾

Travel safe. I love you too.

Aliza Goodman's Daily Motivational Quote #3: now

"There are still many causes worth sacrificing for, so much history yet to be made."
Michelle Obama

MotiQuote.com

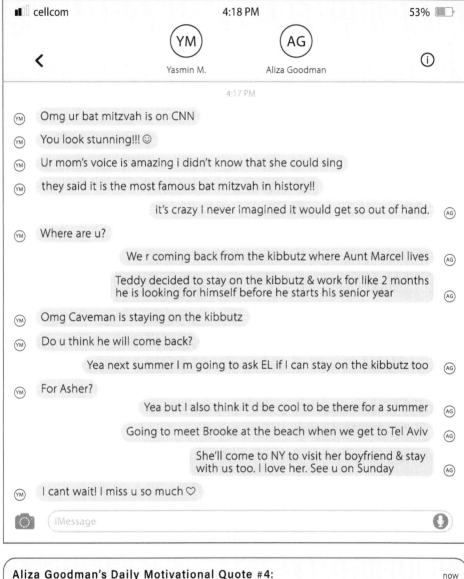

cellcom 4:18 PM 53%

YM Yasmin M. **AG** Aliza Goodman

4:17 PM

(YM) Omg ur bat mitzvah is on CNN

(YM) You look stunning!!! ☺

(YM) Ur mom's voice is amazing i didn't know that she could sing

(YM) they said it is the most famous bat mitzvah in history!!

it's crazy I never imagined it would get so out of hand. (AG)

(YM) Where are u?

We r coming back from the kibbutz where Aunt Marcel lives (AG)

Teddy decided to stay on the kibbutz & work for like 2 months he is looking for himself before he starts his senior year (AG)

(YM) Omg Caveman is staying on the kibbutz

(YM) Do u think he will come back?

Yea next summer I m going to ask EL if I can stay on the kibbutz too (AG)

(YM) For Asher?

Yea but I also think it d be cool to be there for a summer (AG)

Going to meet Brooke at the beach when we get to Tel Aviv (AG)

She'll come to NY to visit her boyfriend & stay with us too. I love her. See u on Sunday (AG)

(YM) I cant wait! I miss u so much ♡

iMessage

Aliza Goodman's Daily Motivational Quote #4:   now

"If you see something that is not right, not fair, not just, you have a moral obligation to do something about it."
Congressman John Lewis

MotiQuote.com

FOOD AFFAIR WITH KATE

DIVINE, DELICIOUS, AND DELIGHTFUL   ABOUT   RECIPES   CONTACT

Hummus, Health + Hope

★ ★ ★ ★ ★

Hummus is a divine creamy blend of garbanzo beans, olive oil, garlic and spices. Hummus is one of the most famous national Israeli foods and is adored and devoured all over the Middle East. Almost every meal we have eaten over the last week, including at the Palestinian Old City restaurant and the Bedouin Tent, we ate hummus. Chefs take great pride in their hummus and while it may appear to the naked eye the same, there are fine differences that make some hummus far more exciting than other. While there are many disagreement in the Middle East, with the outstanding qualities and tastes of hummus there is full accord. Hummus is also an inexepensive and solid source of protein. See the photos below and check out Food Affair with Kate on Instagram and Facebook. #hummus

LIFEEXPRESSIONS.COM

Sawt
Jamil

469

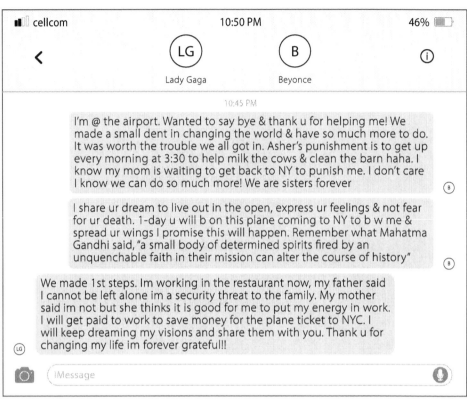

LG
Lady Gaga

B
Beyonce

10:45 PM

I'm @ the airport. Wanted to say bye & thank u for helping me! We made a small dent in changing the world & have so much more to do. It was worth the trouble we all got in. Asher's punishment is to get up every morning at 3:30 to help milk the cows & clean the barn haha. I know my mom is waiting to get back to NY to punish me. I don't care I know we can do so much more! We are sisters forever

I share ur dream to live out in the open, express ur feelings & not fear for ur death. 1-day u will b on this plane coming to NY to b w me & spread ur wings I promise this will happen. Remember what Mahatma Gandhi said, "a small body of determined spirits fired by an unquenchable faith in their mission can alter the course of history"

We made 1st steps. Im working in the restaurant now, my father said I cannot be left alone im a security threat to the family. My mother said im not but she thinks it is good for me to put my energy in work. I will get paid to work to save money for the plane ticket to NYC. I will keep dreaming my visions and share them with you. Thank u for changing my life im forever grateful!!

iMessage

LIFEEXPRESSIONS.COM

Disputes and Miracles
Roaming Roman

We are in Tel Aviv. Bruno and I are staying on in this dynamic coastal city for a few days and then driving through Nazareth. I keep returning to Aliza's Torah portion, 'disputes and miracles'. EL and I have had no relationship for many years and we now have miraculously reunited as brother and sister. I look at my little sister and see the thirteen-year-old who I left; and I feel terrible. I wish I could take back so much and change our history, but I know that it is not possible. I will keep working to earn her trust and respect. She is in a terrible marriage and cannot mask this with her painted-on "I'm fine!" smile. I am going to dedicate myself to helping her figure out the direction of her life. This is my role as her brother and there is no time better than the present to step up and do what I can. I do not think her husband will change and she is too young to give up and accept her unhappy life. I will travel to New York next month. I hope to offer the strength and love she will need. Aliza's bat mitzvah has produced many miracles. I know there are mulititudes more that will envelop us.

< Israel Family Group

EL, Kate, Andy, Teddy, Aliza, Brooke,...

Ethan

Travel safe dear family. Thank you EL for planning an incredible week for all of us to share. I will carry with me your sweet, beautiful voice singing Hush Little Baby at the foot of the Western Wall, as Aliza became a bat mitzvah. Aliza your words of Torah and actions with 60SecondsofLight are life changing for Bruno and me. I think I speak for millions of people across the globe who you empowered and changed with a simple message. You united the world and you gave everyone a moment to reflect and be accountable for his or her actions. I look forward to seeing the fruits of your movement and sharing in your life as you journey forward. I am honored and grateful for this week with all of you. Todah Rabah.

Brooke

I had no idea what I would discover on this trip. I could not have imagined that in one week I would change so dramatically. Thank you EL and Aliza for being the reason for this and for showing us all love and guidance. I am sorry I never knew Grama Shula but from all the stories you have shared, I think she is in each of you and must be very proud that her legacy lives on in both of you so vibrantly.

Rose

I did know Shula and Brooke my dear, you are right, she is beaming where ever she is watching the miracles that you both created this week for us individually, for the family and for the world. Her footprints are firmly engrained in each of your steps. We are all recipients of her love and thoughtfulness and that each of you carry and now share with us. Thank you.

+

 JN24:   now

The Palestinian teenager accomplice in the 60SecondsOfLight campaign remains unidentified for the security of her family.

Jewish News You Can Use

472

Dear Aliza,

Safta Shula's HOPE. Your grandfather and I were immigrants who arrived like so many after tragic lives in other countries. We came for the American Dream — if you worked hard, you could have a good life, raise a family, make money and feel connected to the country. Even in the safety of our adopted homeland, we did carry skeletons from our youth. I believe your grandfather still worried when he came home at night, turned the key that his family might not be there. He never erased the memory of returning home one day in Poland and discovering that his mother and three siblings had been taken away by the Nazis. He never heard their voices nor felt their breath again. A cruel existence I could never imagine nor console in him. We were partners, best friends, and lovers but this dark crevice was always present and I could never fill it. I gave up trying or thinking I could do this for the man I loved so deeply. Miraculously, the moment your grandfather held Teddy hours after he was born, I felt a change in him; Teddy's soft warm body breathed life long taken back in his being. He never lapsed back in to the same depression spells he experienced over the years. Then you and Lucas arrived to continue filling Yacov's heart and soul. He had never erased that part of his life but his future brought a freedom he thoroughly enjoyed. Every weekend we took Teddy and then you too. We said it was to give your mom a break, but I selfishly knew that his happiness was being with you kids. Your grandfather's survival was holding his grandchildren close. The happiest times I shared with Yacov were during his last thirteen years. We both loved being grandparents more than anything.

Aliza, I have watched you grow. We've sat side by side reading in bookstores, the park and the apartment; we've stood side by side in food pantries serving the homeless, at human rights demonstrations, and in the kitchen stirring tapioca pudding and then licking the pot and spoon; and we have layed side by side watching videos, eating oreos and relaxing to each other's breaths. Now as you become a bat mitzvah I am not physically with you, but I am shnuggling deep in your proud, beating heart. I know you have big plans, your bright eyes revealed this moments after you were born laying in my arms. Be a leader. Be a pioneer and please always be true to your heart and this will protect you no matter where you go or what you do. I am extremely proud of who you are and have loved every moment with you. I know there is lots to do and you will make differences as you blaze trails. You are my love. You are my hope.

Checking In 📩 Inbox ✕

Kate <Kate.Orser@mail.com>   11:02PM ☆ ↩ ▾
to Maud ▾

Thank you for all your love and support on this adventure. I learned once again that I have an inner strength to make it through challenges without numbing myself and shutting off. My brother and I did not repair our relationship, but I was present and appreciated all the rich experiences that this travel offered me. Andy and I are seriously considering going to Morocco next year after Brooke graduates; he has a project he has been dying to do and I will eat and write. Thank you for being with me each step of the way. I am grateful for this and for your love and friendship. I will see you on Monday morning. Shutting off the phone for flight. Bye.

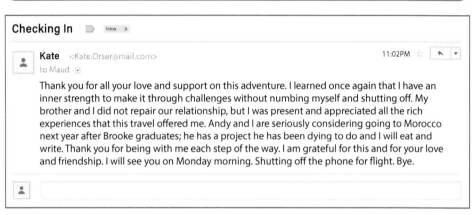

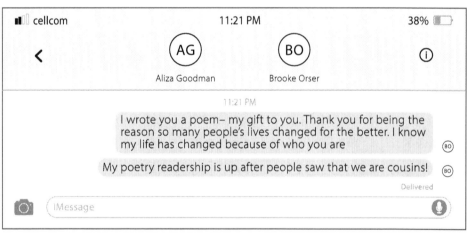

Dear Lucas Goodman, Astronaut in Training –
@JUNIORNASAUSA

| Crew | About | Photos |

TODAY ON THE INTERNATIONAL SPACE STATION:

Looking down on Earth from the International Space Station (@ISS) astronauts take beautiful pictures. One night after a brilliant tour around the globe where we witnessed the increased light from Aliza's 60SecondsofLight, we pass above the beautiful Italian boot with sparkling lights from the city centers and outlining the country's boot shape from the tip of the Sicilian toe to the Alps in the north of the country. Tonight, we all imagine sitting in a Tuscan trattoria eating a large cheese pizza, a bowl of spaghetti with fresh tomato sauce, and a glass of Chianti Wine. As there is no delivery in space, we eat freeze-dried foods heated and softened by hot water and fresh fruit, bread, and nuts. Even astronauts can dream...

| ▪ cellcom | 11:30 PM | 35% ▱ |

Israel Family Group
EL, Kate, Andy, Teddy, Aliza, Brooke,...

EL
I think mom was with us yesterday at Aliza's bat mitzvah. She definitely shared the love + light last night (: Thank you all for being a part of this wonderful journey. We certainly shared many remarkable adventures. I am so happy our family come together + may our paths keep crossing + joining all the years to come. At the end of the day, family is family. I love you all.

Kate
Thank you. We had the week of our lives.

A Woman

Brooke G.O.

Hope travelled across the world
Making up time long gone
Plant a new seed
Lightning speed

Trust earned with each step
Finding truth hidden away
Challenging pace
Discover grace

Belief searched in the dark
Questioning exposed elements
Arriving in haste
Little to waste

A little girl arrives
Changing lives
Taking others on her mission
Questioning tradition

Ancient desert sets the scene
A wild journey for this teen
Elements exposed and worn
Impediments thinned and shorn

Thousands of years on which to stand
Connecting the world hand in hand
Hope and heart lead the way
Hour by hour day by day

Questions search for answers
Hidden truth exposed by the elements
Fight through challenge n fears
Lost or hidden thousands of years

Desert winds blow a secret story
A woman's power n glory
Answers evolve and promise to grow
Future is ours to learn and know

An unknown child at sunrise
Hidden, sweet and wise
Heart to heart, head to toes
A woman at sunset the world now knows

♡ 350   500 ◉

Bat Mitzvah Speech for Aliza.....

Dear Aliza,

The moment you were born, my first instinct was to hold you very close and never let you go. I wanted to protect you and keep you safe. That first night of your life it was just you and me in the room and I held you so close and cried with pleasure as our hearts beat as one. In the days to come, your bright eyes began to tell a story, one that made it abundantly clear that you had arrived with serious life plans. I was enthusiastic to share your journey while feeling so vulnerable. My heart now roamed outside of me, eager to guide you as best as possible but knowing I could never fully protect you.

Before you turned one, you were literally off and dancing to the rhythms of whatever music you heard wherever you were.

By two years, we could not walk by a pet store as you cried for all the orphaned kittens and puppies.

At three, you asked if you could sit on the street corner and help people who begged for money.

When you were four, you refused to go on a school trip to the Central Park Zoo saddened that the animals were not free.

By the age of five, you begged me to take you with me to a women's rights march.

When you were six, you asked your friends to give you books for your birthday so you could donate them to the shelter for abused women and their children only after you read each book cover to cover.

At seven, your grandmother started to take you to the soup kitchens where you served the hungry with a warm smile.

On your eighth birthday, you sent letters to all hundred members of the US Senate, demanding Women get Equal Pay for Equal Work.

By nine, you became a vegetarian, refusing to eat meat.

When you were ten, you enrolled yourself in hip hop classes and never stopped dancing.

In 6th grade, you inspired your classmates to do a sit in after you discovered that school janitors were not getting the two-week Christmas holiday off.

In 7th grade, you and Yasmin created a Jewish-Muslim-Christian Youth Congress at school to share your feelings and ideas on religion, tolerance and peaceful relations.

8th grade has been the year of using debate to master your skills in persuasive speech and winning the state championship.

Sharing your first thirteen years has been breathtaking — you have inspired me and enriched my life beyond what I ever could have imagined. As your mother and biggest fan, I am excited for your journey forward. Clearly Safta Shula's Make a Difference in the World Gene you inherited is instrumental in leading your life's plans. Today's bat mitzvah ceremony in Jerusalem was your grandmother's dream. Israel welcomed Jewish refugees back home after persecution in the diaspora. Your grandmother arrived in Israel just after it became a nation and remained thankful for this acceptance after escaping religious persecution in Iraq; she carried the lessons with her to New York and lived tikun olam and tzadakah till her last breath.

Israel also welcomed your grandfather after the Nazis killed his family and left him an orphan; he arrived a broken man and Israel convalesced him and gave him back his life.

Sharing your bat mitzvah with American and Israeli family marks an incredible moment of healing and hope. You and your brothers bear a huge history on your shoulders and I know you will embrace this responsibility and carry it forward with grace and dignity.

My heart still roams outside my body knowing it cannot fully protect, but hopefully offering shade and comfort as you live your full life. I am proud and honored to be your mother. My love for you is more brilliant than a rainbow, greater than all the stars in the sky and larger than the entire universe — it is infinite.

***

Aliza, I wrote this speech for your bat mitzvah before your 60SecondsofLight debut. I am very proud of what you accomplished by bringing the world together to illuminate the world's problems. Your disappearance, however, sent me to the darkest place I have ever been as a mother — My heart abandoned me and I experienced my greatest fear of not being able to protect you. In honor of your bat mitzvah, I want to reconfirm my unconditional love and support for you always. I also must advise you that you are grounded indefinitely.

Love, EL

Acknowledgements

60 Seconds of Light is illuminated by all who helped and inspired me. I am in awe of the artistic talent of Amanda Jacob, a young graphic artist with a bright future. We worked together for a year online before we met in person. Amanda brought to life all that I asked of her and made each page stand out as authentic, artistic and inviting. Dhiya Sani made sure that the teenage texts were written in the real voice and words of teenagers and did not make fun of me for being clueless at the beginning on the specific language teens use for communicating online. Lydia Chavez, my assistant, edited the book many times and prepped the book for print. My friends who all took time to read and comment over the last couple of years not only helped me produce this unique book but encouraged me when insecurity showed its dark face. Thank you to Susan Berger, Marci Foster, Diane Levin, Shayne Lipsey, Kobe Hirsh Naftali, Talya Naftali, Nancy Remar, Susan Rovner, Kay Sides, Stephanie Daily Smith, and Jill Turner for their creative and thoughtful energy. I am grateful for the support and honesty of my life partner Silvio Eisenberg for his countless edits, comments and encouragement. Everyday I live inspired by my five children - Talya, Noa, Aaron, Eden and Kobe - who keep me humble and happy and remind me everyday that the most important things in life are FAMILY and LOVE.

Made in the USA
San Bernardino, CA
13 July 2020